The Albanian Adventure

Anthony Coles

A Smith Story

This is a work of fiction. Names, characters, places, and incidents either are the product of the author's imagination or are used fictitiously. Any resemblance to actual persons, living or dead, events, or locales is entirely coincidental.

Copyright © 2019 Anthony Coles

All rights reserved. No part of this book may be reproduced or used in any manner without written permission of the copyright owner except for the use of quotations in a book review. For more information, address: avcoles@gmail.com.

First paperback edition July 2020

"It is more shameful to distrust our friends than to be deceived by them." Confucius

"True friends stab you in the front. Oscar Wilde

Contents

Chapter 1: Prologue	1
Scene 1: Bologna Railway Station	
Scene 2: Hotel Orologio, Abano Therme	
Chapter 2: Venice and the Biennale	22
Scene 1: La Piazza San Marco	
Scene 2: La Traviata	
Chapter 3: A Sporting Interlude....................................	49
Scene 1: Tennis at Pau	
Scene 2: McDowell Disappeared	
Scene 3: McDowell Discovered	
Chapter 4: Opening Moves...	82
Scene 1: A Game of Chess	
Scene 2: Supper with Girondou	
Scene 3: Another Chance for Gentry	
Chapter 5: Keep Your Enemies Close.........................	115
Scene 1: The Enemy Identified	
Scene 2: The Enemy Closer	
Scene 3: Food for Thought	
Chapter 6: Casting the Net	175
Scene 1: Lunch and a Plan of Sorts	
Scene 2: Old School Tie and All That	
Scene 3: Ghosts from the Past	
Chapter 7: Engaging the Enemy	212
Scene 1: Problems and Solutions	
Scene 2: Score One for the Good Guys	
Scene 3: A Return Home	

    Scene 4: A De-briefing of Sorts
Chapter 8:   Interventions 267
    Scene 1:   Girondou
Chapter 9: Albania 1976 277
    Scene 1: Memories of a Betrayal
Chapter 10: Conversations 292
    Scene 1: Gentry's Turn for some Questions
Chapter 11: Burying the Dead 300
    Scene 1: McDowell
Chapter 12:   Conversation with Ruy Lopez 305
    Scene 1:   Gentry
Chapter 13:   Finale 313
    Scene 1: An Old Man's Secrets
    Scene 2: Changes in Perception

Chapter 1: Prologue

Scene 1: Bologna Railway Station, August 2nd 1980, 10:21am

Grantkov was unhappy. It wasn't because it was hot and humid. He didn't care about that. He had taught himself not to sweat and risk fogging the telescopic sight or making his grip on the gun slip at the crucial moment. He kept his body temperature low by staying in the shade and drinking water. In an extreme case he would use aluminium chloride powder but that wouldn't be necessary here. He had picked the location a couple of days before, scouted the escape, placed a locked bicycle in the rack in the hotel car park at the rear and made sure that the gates from it through the little garden to the Via Cesare Boldrini were never locked. There were no surveillance cameras to worry about. An emergency staircase ran down the back of the building and emerged directly into the car park, a few yards from the cycle rack. The doors were neither locked during the day, nor were they alarmed. Presumably the hotel guests found it too convenient. He timed his exact escape; less than forty seconds from firing position to the bike. All very simple. But he was still unhappy.

The problem was the distance. There just wasn't enough of it. The shot would over slightly fewer than ninety yards. He had looked in vain for a vantage point further away that still gave him a view of the second class waiting room on the left side of the railway station. The building he had to choose was immediately opposite the station entrance on the Viale Pietro Pietramellara. It was a seven stories high hotel; eight if he counted the double height ground floor. There were simply no higher buildings with direct line of sight situated further away. The hotel roof was the only suitable place and he didn't like it at all. The construction may have afforded good cover with lots of shadows at midday with the sun almost directly overhead. One advantage of the very short range was that he could hold the Dragunov SVD rifle in an arm cradle without having to use the front bipod legs. He could therefore locate himself well back from the edge in the shadow without any of the gun barrel overhanging the parapet. He also wouldn't need the telescopic sight at that range which meant the gun would breakdown into an innocuous collection of metal to be carried in a Spar supermarket shopping bag even more quickly than usual.

He actually felt very uncomfortable about being so near. He didn't care about seeing the damage the 7.62 mm round would do to the man's head. He'd seen it many times before through four times magnification of the usual PSO-1 optical sight. It was just that the very short range, so much shorter than he was accustomed to, made the whole thing much more personal. Usually it all felt rather detached - intellectual even - from a thousand yards away. Here he felt he could smell the man not just kill him and he didn't like that at all.

So now he stood, leaning against one of the concrete pillars in the dark shadow, looking down at the scene below him, the gun draped loosely in a webbing sling - just like the old days, he thought, when he was learning to shoot as a teenager. The station was busy; very busy. It was 10:15 on Saturday morning, August 2nd and the place was full of tourists arriving in the city for the day and locals leaving on their holidays. He had been told that the target would arrive with a companion to board a train to Rome at 10:45 and would be dressed in pale beige cotton trousers, a light cotton jacket and a straw hat. The hat would be distinctive as it would have an orange and yellow horizontally striped band around it.

It was indeed the hat that he saw first about ten minutes later as the two men arrived in a taxi, stepped towards the waiting room and stopped side-by-side to look up at the big departure board. With practiced ease he swung the rifle up and took its familiar weight in his arms rather like a father does with his child. He laid his cheek tenderly against the stock and took up the first part of the light trigger pressure.

They say that practice makes perfect and that is, of course, true. What in reality it means is that if you do something often enough in the same way, the procedure of doing what you want to do in the way you want to do it becomes more or less automatic. Not out of control, of course, but a completely natural sequence of events none of which individually needs a conscious decision. Playing the piano well doesn't require you to look at every little black dot printed on the paper in front of you, decide what stave line it is printed on and what actual note that line is supposed to correspond to. You do not then have to look and decide what is printed at the top of the stalk that comes out of the little black dot to see for how long the key that corresponds to this particular little dot should be played - given the speed with which you decided to start the whole thing off in the first place, of course. You don't have to look at or even remember what key you are in and therefore whether that particular black dot is to be sharpened or flattened by half a tone. You don't then decide which of the many little black or white ivory (nowadays plastic) keys below your fingers correspond to that particular little black printed dot and then press it with the correct finger for the correct period of time in, of course, the correct way. If all these little bits of work each required a series of conscious decisions then the dreaded chopsticks would never get played let alone a piece of Liszt that commonly requires you to make up to eight simultaneous sequences of such decisions at least once every twentieth of a second and to continue to do so for minutes on end. This also ignores the more personal and subjective problem of how hard to hit each key and how that should be in relations to the five or possibly fifty keystrokes that have preceded it that second and a similar number that follow it before that particular second has finished and the next one starts with its challenges all over again.

What saves pianists from being driven completely mad is, of course, practice. Not for nothing did the great violinist, Jascha Heifetz, supposedly lost en route to a concert ask a passing New Yorker: 'how do I get to Carnegie Hall?' The man apparently replied: ' You gotta practice!' Grantkov had fired countless rounds through his Dragunov over the years in the process of becoming one of the world's better assassins and long ago the whole process had become completely automatic. He was always amused to think that he had become one of the world's best killers without actually ever becoming one of the world's best marksmen. Shooting a gun correctly is actually very easy. Once everything was in place, he seemed completely to switch off and something else took over. The target was acquired, the gun aimed and fired without any conscious thought or effort. The sequence of events, once started, was unstoppable. Thus it was that when some considerable way through the sequence that would have led to his target's head being atomised into a bloody mist all over the wall of the Bologna railway station's second class waiting room wall, he was unable to stop the final millimetre of trigger travel that released the firing mechanism that sent the bullet on its way. However at that critical and uncontrolled split second something rather odd happened.

Looking over the open sights of his precisely aligned gun, Grantkov saw his target suddenly move violently move down out of view while almost instantaneously he was hit by a blast wave of enormous proportions with a simultaneous roar of sound. Looking back much later he thought grimly that had he been at his preferred range of more than a thousand yards he might have had time to do something. The blast wave might have taken half a second or so to reach him and that would have been enough to re-acquire the target and finish the job. But he had been too close and that chance never came.

The whole target area was engulfed in a thick cloud of black dust that billowed and curled out in all directions. Again practice took over. He had the gun broken down and into the plastic carrier bag in three seconds. He crossed to the open door at the head of the stairs and within a further twenty five seconds he was down the seven stories to ground level and riding the bike out of the car park. His car was half a kilometre away to the south and ten minutes later he had parked perfectly legally in the Palazzo Maggiore and joined the queue of tourists waiting to get into the Basilico di San Petronico. He left his shopping bag in the boot.

Scene 2: Grand Hotel Orologio, Abano Therme, August 2nd 1980 11:00am

The irony was that Smith hadn't really been involved at all. He was at a commercial trade show in Padua doing his usual day job of the moment; selling stuff to unsuspecting foreigners, as a friend once described his talents admiringly. This time it was a thoroughly prosaic exhibition of industrial laundry equipment for a week at the Padova Fiera. Always crushingly bored by trade shows, Smith was in surprisingly good humour considering his feet ached so much. It was not that he had suddenly learned to enjoy it. Famously disliking 'small talk' he particularly disliked trade shows put on 'by the industry for the industry' – whatever industry that happened to be at the time. It was the fact that he was in Padua, always a favourite place for him in August, and alone amongst his colleagues he felt completely happy in a heat that regularly rose about 80 Fahrenheit. He must have been one of the very few people who didn't mind that the air conditioning in the oldest of a fairly aged set of exhibition buildings that comprised the show site was operating at its most Italian; with much noise but very little effect. He loved the heat. For once the various bits of his body that had in varying degrees been damaged by a lifetime of violent sports and unfriendly personal encounters didn't actually hurt. He was also happy that his company's late decision to attend the show meant that they had been unable to get rooms on one of the local 'exhibition' hotels, all chromium plate, mirrors, teeth and prostitutes. His secretary, knowing him better that he did himself as all good secretaries do, had booked him into a rather luxurious small suite in the Grand Hotel Orologio at the famous old spa resort of Abano Terme a few miles outside the town. He had no time for the hot mud and water that smelt of sewage but being pampered by one of the better chefs in the area without being surrounded by the mindless babble of badly dressed business executives was a treat. He remembered the pleasure he felt on unpacking after arrival to discover that his secretary who usually did this sort of thing for him had packed his evening clothes. It was that sort of place.

Today was Saturday. Animal day. The show had started on the previous Monday and as is often the case, at the weekend the show was open to the public. Why anyone should want to spend their day off traipsing around exhibition stands full of huge industrial washing machines, dryers, ironers and a vast selection of the general paraphernalia that sits in the background to keep you supplied with clean sheets and towels whether you are in a hotel or a hospital, with table cloths and napkins when you go to a restaurant, Smith couldn't imagine. He knew that the day would be filled by the invasion of hoards of school children who would steal anything that was not either screwed down or weighed at least half a ton. Certainly industrial amounts of expensive brochures, flyers, give-away key rings, ball point pens, cigarettes lighters and other meaningless rubbish without which any trade show would be incomplete would vanish into thousands of brightly coloured polythene bags held tightly in an equivalent number of sweaty little hands. Locusts, he thought, just like the biblical plague.

He had decided therefore not to go into the show until after lunch when there would be a chance that the plague has passed on to the afternoon pleasures of the sports field or the sparse beaches of southern part of the Venetian lagoon. He had got up slowly, had his customary espresso and gone for a walk through the town before the heat really got up. He was now ensconced in a comfortable wicker armchair in the hotel lounge with the morning's newspaper while giving some thought to the treat of an early lunch before descending into the Padua. He looked at his watch. It had just turned 11:00 am; still too early for lunch so he decided to return to his room to collect his book and to spend the next hour consuming it and a cold prosecco with equal languor when he was conscious of a disturbance on the other side across the residents lounge at the entrance to the bar. He saw a rapidly increasing crowd of people looking at the bar television. Normally Smith would have assumed that the television was showing sport but it was too early in the day for that. Also, although the crowd got larger, the people were animated but almost completely silent. They were watching the TV intently. 'Odd,' though Smith. His curiosity got the better of him and, in any case, he had just decided to get his book ready to start on the next stage of his plan to avoid the school children.

What he saw across the heads of the crowd was no sporting event. There had been a large explosion at the railway station in Bologna. An hysterical TV commentator described the scene. Many people dead. Even more injured. A dreadful accident. Possible broken gas main. He was no expert in these things but it didn't look like an accident to him. He immediately thought of terrorism of some sort. Bologna and the north of Italy in general had form for that sort of thing from both the extreme left and the extreme right and, come to think of it, some less well-known group between. He went up to his room to follow the reports more privately. The commentary may have been somewhat overwrought but the pictures showed a scene of wide devastation. It was clearly nothing to do with him but Bologna was only a little more than an hour away by car. He thought he'd better check in.

He went to the small table that served as a desk in his bedroom and picked up the phone. The first group of six numbers got him through to what was known as a 'black' exchange. The hotel telephone logging system would show a call to the exhibition office in Padua, one of a number he had made during the last week as a routine precaution. The call actually went out onto a secure network somewhere, he knew not where, but when the automatic system in the black exchange answered he heard another dialling tone and then he started the second part of the call that would connect him with a number in central London. The call was answered instantly by the duty officer on the southern European desk at MI6. A couple of rather arcane exchanges told the officer that the line was not secure at the Italian end and that the man calling was one those odd, part time, operatives so beloved by the department. To an outsider listening it sounded like Smith was just calling his office. After a while he was connected with a woman.

'Hello there, how are you?'

The woman sounded not one iota like his much-valued secretary but anyone listening in would hardly know that.

'I'm fine, thanks. Just looking forward to getting home after the show finishes tomorrow. Have you seen the news about the explosion at Bologna station?'

No. How terrible. It'll probably be an hour or two before the news gets to England.'

'Yes, it doesn't look too good at all. Anyhow, I was just getting in touch to see if there are any last minute changes to my return travel arrangements.'

Smith had been due to fly back to the UK first thing on Sunday morning. The voice continued.

'I'm not sure. Perhaps you could call back later. About 7 your time this evening?'

'OK. You can always send me a fax to the hotel if something comes up.'

With that he put the phone down and frowned. With the commotion downstairs his plans for a quiet civilised lunch were clearly curtailed somewhat. With a sigh he changed into his lightweight summer suit and headed to the car park and his rented car. Half an hour later he entered the showground and went to work.

Immediately he realised that most of the exhibitors at the show had the same idea as he and had left for the day, even if they had bothered turning up in the first place, leaving their second teams to get run ragged by the children. Tomorrow, Smith thought, would have been a better day to do business had it not been for the tradition that most people, himself included, would be on their way home. For the life of him he couldn't imagine why the authorities always insisted that these events take in a weekend. Most of the exhibitors lobbied intensively against it but exhibition organisers the world over seemed not to agree. This Saturday, as the news from Bologna continued to come through, the show was increasingly a dead duck and the visitors and exhibitors alike, like the whole of Italy it should be said, were clustered around their television sets. Smith left. At least his room in the hotel was quiet.

The fax was a surprise. An important customer in Verona wanted to see him on Monday. Perhaps Smith might like to join him for lunch. His ever-efficient secretary had booked him into Verona's Due Torri Baglioni for Sunday night. He hated the place. Full of rich tourists going orgasmic over Juliet's mythical balcony. However that actually didn't matter much. It would have taken a very clever observer indeed to spot that the header on the fax was very slightly different from that usually topping faxes from his company. Smith also knew that he had no customers in Verona, important or not. Verona meant Venice and Venice meant business of a very different sort. Monday meant Sunday. Something was up and his presence was required. He saw that his hotel was still entirely too frenetic so he changed into slightly more casual clothes and took his book and strolled into the town to the restaurant Sotto Sotto where he installed himself at a small table at the back, near the kitchen door and settled into a long meal and chapter fourteen of Thomas Mann's Magic

Mountain not before noting, with a slightly ironic thought that, as things seemed to be turning out, a more suitable read would have been the same author's short story masterpiece, Death In Venice.

He started after a late breakfast the next day and arrived in Venice after a forty minute drive. He walked into the Piazza San Marco from the lagoon side having made a bit of a detour from a direct route from the huge but necessary excrescence that was the Tronchetto parking. The department actually had its main office somewhat prosaically in the commercial section of the British Consulate on the Piazzale Donatori de Sangue located not in Venice itself but in the more economic and deeply uninteresting Mestre on the nearby mainland. In high summer, even on a Sunday, there were enough distressed tourists seeking help to disguise the odd arrival of someone like Smith who, unlike most of the other visitors, had not actually lost anything - passport, money, credit cards, orientation, virginity, nor did he wish to apply for any form of official documentation. The routine this time was slightly different in that the bogus invitation to lunch mentioned in the fax was a signal for him to go directly to the department safe house in Venice itself and therefore to go through a slightly Byzantine contact procedure. Basically he had to wait to be contacted before going in. The routine changed from time to time but at the moment it was for him to take a leisurely coffee at the Café Quadri on the north side of the Piazza, spend about half and hour or so before calling for the bill. His change would include a one thousand lira note folded in half which was the signal that the rendezvous was on in a trattoria on the Rio Terà degli Assassini to the north of the opera house of La Fenice. The meeting had to happen within thirty minutes of the signal or it was cancelled. No thousand lire note meant no meeting. Come back tomorrow. The routines were slightly different in the winter when there were fewer tourists in the café but as none of his very occasional outings for the Service in Italy had ever happened during the Venetian winter, he had no idea what they were. All very James

Bond, Smith thought sourly but actually the arrangement was both necessary and efficient. How his presence was spotted by the relevant waiter was completely beyond him. Maybe it was the manager. He actually didn't want to know.

It was near midday. The sun was high but it wasn't the heat that drove him inside. Nor was it the dreaded piano quartet whose music perennially wallpapered the scene, although it might have been. Smith settled into the comfortable interior with the Sunday edition of Corriera della Sera which was inevitably filled with extensive coverage of the Bologna bombing. Predictably all the possible conspiracy theories were given full vent from the Red Brigade on one wing to any one of a number of neo-fascist groups on the far right with many in between. In common with most of the locals and a good proportion of the tourists who filled the café, Smith scanned his newspaper. Unlike most of his fellow readers he knew that there were a number of other possible culprits of a non-domestic nature as well.

In fact, his presence in Italy for purely commercial reasons furnished him with a cover story that was authentic and thus a meeting at the Consulate in insalubrious Mestre would have been the most natural thing in the world even on a Sunday. The summons to the Venice safe house, however, was somewhat unusual. Their contact, the passer of folded banknotes, was one of the senior café staff who have been working there for years and as a result merited a pitch of tables inside the air-conditioned splendour of the café. Smith glanced at his watch and called for his bill. He received a bank note folded into almost a perfect square.

Habit as well as training made Smith take an indirect route to the trattoria. Venice's little streets and alleyways can seem to be very difficult if you want to follow anyone, especially if there are crowds of window-shopping tourists. The downside is that the many canals and rive somewhat curtail the possibilities when choosing a route. However a good knowledge of what is essentially a relatively small number of street and canals can enable a skilled operator to follow someone else with relative ease often by anticipation rather than following. Smith had done it himself occasionally and had regularly been able to jump ahead of his quarry and watch the person he was following actually approaching and passing him. It is psychologically difficult to think of someone you are walking towards as someone who is actually following you. This time his route took him north towards San Salvador before cutting back west across towards the Calle Cavalli Castello. Arriving at the trattoria about five minutes before the deadline, holding the folded thousand lira note in his hand, he waited to be seated at a perpetually reserved table at the rear of the little restaurant. He had been here before and the table was both next to a rear door to the canal and virtually invisible to the rest of the room. Smith remembered sitting there on a number of occasions over the past years, not least on that occasion when Gentry was bleeding a couple of doors away. His host put a large glass of red wine in front of him unasked. Smith took a long pull and got up as if to find the toilet through a door also at the back of the restaurant. The door gave into a tiny lobby with both male and female facilities and a couple of another anonymous wooden doors. As he went though he heard a soft click as an electric bolt latched behind him.

His opening sentence was certainly should have been 'What the fuck...?' although he was undecided whether to continue with 'happened to you?' or 'are you doing here?' Gentry was sitting slumped in a small armchair naked from the waist up sporting an extensive network of bandages that criss-crossed his torso; some showing dark red splodges. Similar bandages covered much of the top of his head. For Smith who had only ever seen Gentry sitting tweedily in his little basement office in the old headquarters at Century House in Lambeth, surrounded by shelves of dusty books and piles of paper, it was a bit of a shock. Gentry was his control; the man who briefed him before he went out on a job and de-briefed him on his return. Both events were always low-key, detailed and completely stripped of any sense of excitement, romance or anything else that one might imagine associated with such activities. Gentry was utterly detailed in his planning and his operational control but no-one had ever seen him anywhere other than in the half-light of his windowless office. Secretly Smith thought he slept under his desk. However, here he was bleeding in a foreign country. Smith ultimately settled for:

'Well?'

Gentry smiled slightly.

'As you see, slightly out of my depth, I'm afraid.'

Smith decided on a third ending.

'What the fuck is going on?'

He looked angrily across at the anonymous medic demanding an explanation. Gentry raised a hand slightly and waved the man away. He left through another indistinct door in the darkened room. Gentry continued.

'Sit still Peter. This is a briefing – or sorts.'

Smith settled – if that's the right word for it – onto an uncomfortable upright Thonet-style chair with no arms of the sort you find in bad restaurants when they don't want you to stay too long.

'Yesterday I was accompanying someone – you don't need to know who at this point – from Bologna by train to Rome and we got caught up in the bomb. We were outside the waiting room when the bomb went off. I was knocked out by the blast and woke up in hospital about an hour later with a lot of others. My injuries were fortunately only superficial but when I enquired, I discovered that my, er, companion was also there in the hospital but in the morgue. The interesting thing is that he has a bit of bullet in him rather than just bits of railway station. I telephoned home, as it were, and by mid-afternoon our friends in the Italian service had got us both out of there and brought us to Venice.'

'Christ,' Smith interrupted, 'Not here for Chrissakes?'

The Venice safe house was a secret to most of the UK service let alone their Italian colleagues. Gentry was more than a little put out and replied crossly.

'Don't be ridiculous. They drove us from Bologna to the Consulate and Rogers bought us in last night by boat.'

Smith vaguely remembered the department liaison officer based in Mestre. He also knew that the fact he had been called so quickly to Venice meant that there was something going on and therefore he shouldn't spend a lot of time demanding explanations which wouldn't carry matters any further. He may be rather damaged and an unusually long way from home but Gentry was still his case officer.

'OK, Gentry, what do I need to know?'

Again a slightly crooked smile.

'Peter, you know, you aren't the maverick that many people at home think you are sometimes. You're right, of course. What you need to know is firstly that you have to escort me back to London by some method of your choosing. You are my bodyguard, if you like.'

Gentry sounded quite proud of himself. Smith grunted.

'Your nursemaid, more like.'

Gentry grimaced as he realised that he was right. Smith was still annoyed that his erstwhile desk-bound friend was here in the first place, let alone in pieces.

'Any idea where the bullet came from?'

'Our medic thinks high and behind.'

'A sniper, then.'

Gentry nodded painfully.

'My companion, being slightly more, er, portable, shall we say, will be returned by somewhat more undignified means by others. The second thing, which will undoubtedly answer the question that has already formed in your fertile mind, is that the aforesaid dead companion who was standing next to me in Bologna has a small addition to the various bits of flying masonry, glass, fabrics and other detritus that were embedded in both our bodies.'

Smith followed where he was obviously being led.

'And that was?'

Gentry paused for what he hoped was dramatic affect.

'A small amount of the business end of a 7.62 x 54r round was still lodged in his chest.'

Smith knew the round and also knew that it was a common amongst eastern European forces using the widely issued Dragunov service rifle. However he only knew of one man who used it for sniping.

'Grantkov'

Gentry nodded.

'Yes he's the only man I know who uses that particular gun.'

'Did you see anything?'

Gentry sighed.

'I'm really not sure, if truth be told. My companion was standing on my left as we both looked up to read the departure board. The train we were waiting for was late, of course. This was, after all Italy on a Saturday. I seem to remember him pitching forward at the same time as the explosion but I can't be sure.'

Smith became exasperated.

'Pitched forward? A 7.62 x 54r hollow point would have blown straight through him and deposited much of his body in sticky bits all over your precious departure board.'

He fell silent for a moment.

'Yet you found it still in his chest?'

Gentry nodded.

Smith drew a deep breath.

'The fact that you found bit of the round in him means that it had been doctored to achieve precisely the effect that we are now discussing. In its original form heavy ball form with a full 155 gram load it would have gone through your anonymous chum, the rest of the station and reached half way to Ferrara. In hollow form it would, as I mentioned, have vaporised much of your chum. An effect somewhere in the middle can mean a number of things depending on who he was actually after. If the shooter was after your companion then he did his job in spite of the explosion. If he was aiming at you, and God only knows why he would want to do that, then he missed which makes you both very lucky indeed and probably the first ever miss in the man's life it is was actually who we think it was. If it was a hit meant for you and then without the unexplained explosion you would be the one now also be on your way back to the UK in a rather smelly diplomatic bag out of the Aeroporto Marco Polo airport instead of sitting here talking to me. The doctored bullet would make accuracy hard. Maybe he was very near. That doesn't sound like Grantkov to me, though. As far as I remember he never does close-up work. These doctored bullets also tend to lose aerodynamic efficiency if they are not as per manufacturers recommendations. If it was a long shot, the man would have had to be good.'

Smith stopped. He still didn't know how well Gentry actually was. He looked over to his friend and as relieved to see that he was still being listened to attentively. Gentry asked quietly:

'And what conclusion do you want to draw from all this, old chap?'

Smith was silent while he gave his answer proper consideration.

'If it was Grantkov then he was obviously either after you or your anonymous chum or he may have just been told to send a message of some sort.'

Gentry nodded slowly. Valery Grantkov, a Romanian free-lance assassin was also the only one he too could think of who used the old Russian rifle.

'Who to?'

Again Smith paused to think.

'No idea. Could be you, although I can't for the life of me think why. You're not a field man – usually that is,'

Smith added a penetrating stare across the small room. Gentry ignored the implicit question. Smith continued:

'Maybe to your anonymous companion. Hardly to me. My visit to Padua wasn't exactly secret although I wasn't on Service business and there is no reason I can think of for me to be on anyone's radar at the moment. Perhaps I'll be in a better position to say after I see which of us gets back to London alive.'

Gentry nodded again. All of a sudden, Smith got fed up.

'Shit Gentry, unless you tell me what the hell you are doing here in the first place, I have no idea.'

Gentry made an unconvincing apologetic face.

'Sorry, old chap. Can't tell you this time.'

Smith had to let it go at that.

'It could have been a shot at you, then, as you seem to be coming blinking like an innocent into the big wide world of espionage. Whatever the reason you have a hit and a major terrorist explosion happening simultaneously. The big bang can't have improved Grantkov's aim which, as we both know, is usually pretty good. Maybe he just killed the wrong guy.'

It was an observation that Gentry refused to grace with a reply. He just continued to sit there looking glum. Instantly Smith was sympathetic. Gentry was a good friend as well as his Control and whatever was the cause of his breaking cover, he was still very inexperienced and was in all probability felling out of his depth as well as sore. He got up.

'OK. First things first. Now that you seem to have stopped leaking all over Giuseppe's nice clean trattoria, I'll make a few arrangements about getting you back home.'

'How do you intend to do that?' Gentry asked.

Smith couldn't resist it. He smiled and tapped the side of his nose conspiratorially.

'Need to know only, old chap. Need to know.'

Another thought struck Smith.

'How come they got you out of there so quickly? The place must have been swarming with carabinieri, rescue people and all sorts within minutes. How come you and your late lamented chum were spirited away without anyone getting in the way?'

Gentry just looked glum. Smith got the message very quickly.

'Shit, gentry, you had backup, a team even. Someone was expecting trouble and you were the patsy.'

Gentry looked even glummer.

'Gentry. You're an office badger. You live in the half light of your dusty old basement and never come out. You organise, plan, brief and de-brief. What the fuck are you doing playing decoy in an operation on foreign soil? I do this sort of shit and I am bloody good at it. If I had to name the person least well equipped in the entire world to be on active service in the field it would be you by a country mile.'

The embarrassed silence persisted.

'God, Gentry. You are just about my only friend. If I ever hear that you do anything like this again I will kill you myself and the people who send you. Do you understand?'

Gentry looked across at him.

'They didn't find my hat, did they by any chance?'

Smith was baffled and gulped.

'Your what?'

'My hat. My straw hat'

Smith was brusque.

'Of course they didn't. Why should they? The rescuers had more to do than saving miscellaneous bits of your clothing. They were, after all, somewhat preoccupied wading through the remains of nearly three hundred dead and dying.'

Gentry nodded in a distracted sort of way.

'Yes, I suppose your right. A bit sad though. It was rather a nice hat. It even had an nice ribbon around it.'

Smith snorted and left the room before he personally finished what someone at Bologna had so obviously started.

Chapter 2: Venice and the Biennale

Scene 1: La Piazza San Marco

He hated Venice. As far as he could remember, he always had. Even as a child. It was a completely personal thing. He loved the rest of Italy and most Italians; or, at least, liked them. Perhaps tolerated them in an amused and completely patronising way would be a better way of putting it. He certainly liked the food. He liked some of the buildings that occasionally decorated the city in the way a real diamond sparkles in a sea of paste. To the Piazza San Marco he afforded a grudging respect while still being uncertain about the magnificence of the regular and overstressed design. To him, the basilica's beauty was all internal; the infamous bronze horses looking as out of place as a wart on Sophia Loren. The ranks of Sansovino's building blocks stuck together to façade the Biblioteca Marciana and the Procurati Vecchi e Nuove always looked to him to be architecture by the yard – or was it metre? Even the figure of Peace, one of four Sansovino figures at the base of the Campanile, on whose iconography he had laboured so long and so uninterestingly for his master's thesis all those years ago, now seemed rather dull and droopy. The much more exciting Palazzo Ducale always seemed to be looking to escape from the strutting promenadism of the Piazza back around the corner, past the Ponte dei Sospiri and off east to the more countrified delights of the Arsenale. But sitting now in the plastic wicker chair outside Café Florian finally because he could afford to, able if not actually to enjoy the cold coffee at his elbow then at least to be able to pay for it without going without an evening meal, he realised why, over many years, he had failed to come to terms with the many and varied delights of the sinking city.

Nowhere on earth, he suddenly saw, so confronts you with your own inadequacies; at least when you're young for that is when he learned to hate this place. Money. Money, as always, was the key. Unless you can afford it, stay away from Venice. Europe is overbrimming with places where, with a certain amount of ingenuity, you can survive at whatever level your income requires. There are usually cheaper places to stay and eat, to drink and to see, although Smith would admit that they were getting increasingly difficult to find. Venice, for him at least, was the exception. Everything had always been expensive and quality really only did come at a price; a price that had invariably been too much for him. Whenever he had felt that his life finally progressed to providing the right level of income that would enable him to sample the delights of Café Florean, Harry's Bar or the Gritti Hotel someone upped the stakes and his budget became meagre again. Venice always had a way of telling him that he hadn't quite made it, and, to be honest, he resented that. Staying honest, he would have admitted that Venice had often been right but he had long transferred this particular dislike from himself to the town. By now he had become skilled at finding other reasons for disliking the place.

Thus he had received with a sinking heart the news from Martine that they were going to the Biennale. To say sinking was something of an understatement. Actually plummeting might have been a better description. But the obvious pleasure that lit her invariably beautiful face when she told him had prevented his actually refusing. A few days out of Provence was clearly something she relished and as usual he was touched and astonished that she regarded his participation in the adventure as so normal to be completely taken for granted. It was less than a year since he had bowed to the inevitable and acknowledged that the attraction they had felt for each other from the start had finally matured into love; much to his surprise and, it should be admitted, good-natured annoyance. He had valued his isolation as a curmudgeonly bachelor in his little house next to Arles's great Arena, sharing his baguettes and his life with Arthur, an equally retired ex-racing greyhound from the dark side of East London. However, two somewhat alarming perturbations to his hitherto tranquil retirement later, he had bowed with considerable pleasure to the inevitable and had admitted what she had known all along; that even this late in life he has indeed, at last, fallen in love. Thus when the dreaded prospect of rubbing minds – intellects would have been too substantial a word – with the jewelled glitterati of the Biennale became reality he was forced to admit that the prospect appalled him less than it might have in days before he had met Martine. Arthur would be pleased. It meant that he would take up residence at the Mas des Saintes near Le Sambuc in the Camargue that was home to Martine and her father. The dog and the old man doted on each other and days spent careering freely around the farm with the Émile Aubanet, chasing and being chased by his other great animal love, his herd of Camargue bulls would be enjoyed greatly even if the doggy mind was incapable of anticipation.

Martine unusually was happy to take a rare break from running the family's wide-spread and highly successful group of businesses so he felt it would have been churlish to refuse. The spirit that combined foreboding and displeasure even led him to decline the offer, made by a Martine who knew his feelings about La Serenissima, that he might just join her for a day or two towards the end of her ten day stay. No, he gritted his teeth and said yes to it all.

'So much for love,' he thought grimly. 'I must be mad'.

In the event, the rounds of vernissages, parties, cocktails and dinners had not turned out to be quite as bad as he imagined. He invariably anticipated such social events with a dark melancholy and, yet again, was a little irked to find that he actually enjoyed himself, and, once he got past the game of 'emperor's new clothes' that seemed to him to underpin much of the world's modern art world, he found a few people to talk to. Constant, however, was the pleasure he took in her company and her beauty and for the umpteenth time he found himself wondering how it had all happened. The September sun was warm but not, as he well knew, as hot as in his tiny garden in Arles, not as on the open scrubby meadows of the Camargue. His coffee on the twee little terrace table that litter the Piazza immediately outside Café Florian like expensive tin confetti had become cold and therefore tasteable which was not, he realised, necessarily a good thing. He sat idly thinking of their last two years together and watching the tourists pass back and forth.

As usual his heart leaped as he saw her walking towards him across the Piazza. This time he had dipped out. The occasion was a book launch. One of Martine's relations had spent a few years of his life and a considerable amount of the happily considerable Aubanet family fortune in tracing again the Homeric journeys around the Mediterranean after the Trojan Wars to compile yet another of those 'is this really where the Cyclopse lived?' grand tour books. Apart from finding book launches of any sort well beyond the pale, he couldn't understand why anyone would want to write on the subject yet again especially when the field was full of superior offerings, Wolfgang Geisthövel's Homer's Mediterranean being one of the latest and best.

She looked completely devastating in a rather old-fashioned full-skirted floral silk dress whose translucence flirted with transparency. She walked steadily and confidently towards him, hips swinging, dark hair streaming out from under a broad straw hat with that sort of relaxed pleasure in her face that graceful women can adopt when they know everyone is looking at them. No make-up, no jewellery except the small diamond Camargue croix des saintes that was always either round her neck or on a broach at her shoulder. She flung both arms around his neck and kissed him quite roughly and somewhat intimately on the mouth before slumping down in the chair next to him with a grace that would have decorated the Bolshoi.

'Campari soda, please before I die,' she cried as she swept the hat from her head and stretched her head back as if to loosen her neck muscles.

'God, Peter, not for the first time you were right.'

Resisting the rare opportunity to get one 'I told you so' ahead of her, he raised his hand and motioned to the waiter, leant over and kissed her exposed Adam's apple and returned to his seat all with a sort of grace and an economy of movement that might have surprised anyone watching this sixty something-year-old, slightly overweight Welshman. No one watched, of course. Most people were still watching Martine. However her arrival had at least ensured that the waiter appeared at their table within a few seconds, anxious to get a closer look.

'Due Campari Sodas, per favore,' said Smith in an accent that a lifetime of habit made a lot more foreign than it needed to be. He remembered that the same waiter had taken about fifteen minutes to notice him when he had arrived earlier alone.

'Why do you do that?' she asked smilingly. 'You speak Italian better that most of them.'

'Possibly because I do.' was his reply.

She knew what he meant. A lot of Smith's past had been to do with being someone else. The drinks arrived and Smith insisted on settling the account immediately. Another old habit. He wanted to be able to leave when he wanted and there was no certainty that the waiter wouldn't become blind again. Martine drained slightly more than half of her drink in a couple of restorative gulps and slumped in a serpentine manner lower in her seat. Smith looked across amusedly.

'That bad?'

'Worse.'

'Well, I did offer you the chance of doing something else.'

She grimaced: 'Don't remind me. And if you 'say I told you so' I'll scream.'

He did and she so did she. It was an old ritual but not one that usually startled so many pigeons. Having finished her drink, she stole his and, sitting with it firmly clenched in her hand to prevent repossession, she moved her chair so that they touched shoulders and they sat silently together looking at the passing throngs of tourists.

'OK,' he said, with a sigh, 'What next?'

He had long since given up trying to keep track of a list of appointments and rendezvous that seemed to get longer as the days went by.

'Ah, a big one, I'm afraid. Reception at the French Consulate at six and then to La Fenice at eight.'

Smith refrained from pointing out the obvious; that dinner seemed to have been left off the agenda. He sighed and looked at his watch. It was half past three only.

'And until then?' he asked with some concern.

She drained his glass with relish and got up. She stood in front of him, placed herself exactly between him and the sun, legs apart, hands on hips. The effect was, of course, exactly what she intended.

'Bed'.

Looking at her legs now perfectly outlined in detail in front of him he got up with a fake sigh on resignation.

'Oh. All right. If I must.'

She laughed, kissed him on the cheek and led him briskly off towards the little apartment near the Academia that they had rented for their stay.

Scene 2:   La Traviata

Fortunately it was Verdi. Smith had a passing respect of the old master who occasionally let his political leanings show - and occasionally had got into trouble for it. Smith whose taste in opera, passionate as it was, tended both to start and finish with Mozart, occasionally gave a nod to the great father of modern Italian opera. He seemed to go way beyond the superficial Italian composers who thought, as did most of their audiences, that to make art all they had to do was write tunes. Actually what they often made was just entertainment. A succession of intimidating German Jewish refugee academics had long ago drilled into him that it was not particularly important what things looked like. What they meant was important. A few years before, he had been invited to La Fenice to see Günther Krämer's spell-binding staging of Nabucco. Now that was art. His production of Va Pensiero, that magnificent moment that so commemorates Italy's profound and painful attempt to gain freedom from its rulers, when the Hebrew slaves, clothed in black and lying prone on the stage, each rose slowly holding a photograph of a concentration camp victim, was one of the most moving things he had ever seen at the opera and its memory still raised the odd tear when he let it.

This time it was Traviata and try as he might, even sitting in the same house where the opera was given its premier one hundred and sixty six years before, he tried hard to love it. He had last seen it in Paris, its original setting, where Dumas's story of the ultimately doomed, consumptive heroine made a lot more sense. Here in Italy the story, however pointed in an Italian context, seemed a little silly to him. He had said yes because Martine knew that Verdi was the only Italian opera composer he liked and it would have been churlish to refuse as even she didn't know how little he liked the play. It was yet another modern dress performance. He hated that. In spite of Krämer's Nabucco giving him a glance of how this travesty might work successfully, this time Robert Carsen had decided to pick a sort of cross between early twentieth century American Hollywood fantasy Paris and early twenty-first century exhibitionist soft porn. Thus the men wore leather trousers and goatee beards and the women, principals and chorus alike, were clothed, if that is the right word for it, in black g-strings, transparent negligees and patent stiletto pumps. Smith felt it said more about Robert Carsen's attitude towards women than about any radical new interpretation of Verdi's opera. The American also seemed to rely heavily on the services of chorus being able to act. Often a mistake as it clearly was this evening. Yet again an opera director mistook just walking around for acting.

He looked across at his beautiful companion with whom he was alone in their box on the side near the front and was for the umpteenth time that week was amazed he was at how or why this stunning Provençale beauty who was a rich, successful business woman, some fifteen years his junior could fall in love with him in spite of the dubious service that he had rendered her. It had been a night at the opera too when things had come to something of a head. She had asked him to accompany her to the Marseille opera where she was a patron and trustee. That night had been Madam Butterfly, probably his least favourite work in the entire opera repertoire. The tale of the moronic Pinkerton and the stupid, vacuous Cio-Cio-San was, to Smith at least, Puccini, always pretty bad, at his superficial worst. The grim satisfaction he felt about the story showing the Americans in a bad light hardly compensated. The evening also had other things going against it. It was a glad-handing evening when Martine had to meet and greet the Marseilles great and good who supported the opera. Not Smith's cup of champagne at all. The evening was all the more memorable for someone trying to kill them both on their drive home. It was an episode that left six local gangsters dead and Smith with an unexpected and, at the time, not altogether welcome relationship with this extraordinary woman. In time, he mused silently, at least that had changed.

She stared fixedly at the scene knowing that he was watching her. The ends of her mouth twitched. Without looking around she reached across the small gap between them, let her arm fall gently and buried her hand high up between his crossed legs and kept it there. He closed his eyes, grateful to have a reason not to continue to look fascinated at Violettas small but distinct fat rolls alternately cover and uncover her miniscule knickers as she breathed in and out to sing. He gently tightened his crutch muscles and she squeezed back almost making his eyes water.

He had survived the unaccountably long and slightly tedious second act and, suitably fortified by two hastily gulped interval proseccos, he sat to witness to Violetta's consumptive demise that monopolises the greatest last act in opera apart, he thought chauvinistically, from Don Giovanni's spectacular come-uppance in Mozart's eponymous masterpiece. The soprano was no Callas. The second team was on tonight. But having spent much of the first two acts singing ever-so-slightly sharp she had finally both warmed up and subsided to the correct pitch and was making a real fist of dying in act three. The Romanian singer had been given her European premier in Martine's beloved Marseilles opera house and their presence here was as much as gesture of support for her Venetian debut as anything else. Smith thought grimly that that meant one of those appalling after-show parties with much air kissing and bad bubbly.

The scene played out. Violetta died, surrounded in the tiny artist's apartment by the full, scantily clad, fifty strong chorus. The house stood and applauded enthusiastically for a performance that, with the best will in the world, was OK – just. The curtain calls started; principals, individually, in groups, all the cast together. The conductor, trying vainly to look happy with the performance, the orchestra who knew that they had to stay for one bow but immediately vanished for a much deserved drink at the local bar. The great olive green curtain descended and the calls outside the curtain began. Principals individually, then in pairs, trios, quads and so on. Finally – at last finally – they appeared in a line, Violetta flanked by the conductor and Alfredo, then alternatively arranged in order of their importance in the story if not their talent, Giorgio, Flora, Anmina and Gastone all bowed to a final time to take their last fix of temporary celebrity.

Old habits die hard, especially if those habits are ones that have kept you alive for time to time. A split second after a small black hole appeared in the precise centre of Violetta's consumptively pale forehead, Smith alone in a full house looked backwards. A thousand pairs of eyes stared immobile, transfixed, as the olive green velvet curtain turned glistening dark crimson specked with the grey white of fresh brain matter and the heroine again fell untidily to the floor in the space of five minutes but this time in the sort of inelegant heap that only completely dead people can really achieve.

Two seconds is a long time. A trained motor racing crew can change all four tires in that time and fill the car with fuel in four or five more while not looking hurried. Smith knew the entire audience at this undeniable if unconventional demise of Verdi's heroine, would be rendered immobile and insensible for at least ten. A lifetime. The killer would know this and could easily vanish in half that time. There was always a chance that he was complacent and that is what Smith relied on. He scanned the boxes that make up over half the great bejewelled interior of the Fenice. The killer wouldn't be in the stalls. It is hard to get a full-size sniper rifle up to the shoulder unnoticed if you are surrounded by large German hausfraus and badly dressed hamburger-fed Americans. The shot would have come from a box.

Pianists don't read every dot on a printed page of music, just as readers don't usually read every word of a sentence or every letter of a word. The eye scans and, subject to some pre-programmed criteria, the brain takes over, selects and interprets what is sees. Smith scanned for the eyes. You can change a lot with disguise and surgery but it is hard to change anything other than the colour the eyes. Even at a distance eyes tend to remain peculiarly visible. Character, setting, expression all tend to remain. The eye is the organ that grows least throughout life. You die with very nearly what you are born with. His brain filtered out the boxes with more than one person for the same reason that it ignored the stall seats. It looked at the boxes with a single occupant and then those that had no light. The house had been lit up fully long before the final curtain calls. A split second before they disappeared below the balcony rail he saw the eyes. He also saw an unfashionably thick silencer muzzle sliding from view.

He turned back to see that he was not the only person looking in the wrong direction. Martine was looking at him. She had an expression on her face that combined anger and inquisition; no fear, though.

'Well?' she asked.

He nodded.

'We'd better get out of here'.

He held out his hand and took hers. They got up, opened the tiny door at the back of the box and entered the curving corridor that connects all the boxes on that level. The fire exit was directly in front of them. Old habits, Smith thought, as he kicked the door open, ignored the alarm, and they joined the throng of tourists in the Calle Cao Torta and walked with them away from the opera house. They were out into the clammy Venetian night less than twenty seconds after the shot that had so casually re-written Verdi's ending.

She knew they were headed at considerable speed directly away from their rented apartment near the Academia which was south of the opera house. In a few short moments the whole Venice adventure had moved from her domain to his and she knew it. His hold on her hand was firm but not tight. They needed a certain fluidity as they threaded their way north through the crowds, up the Calle towards the Palazzo Fortuni, took a couple of cut-throughs until they got to the cul-de-sac that was the Rio Tera degli Assassini. In reality, it was no dead end at all as any Venetian knows. Water is as natural as land there and the end of the Rio gave onto a canal and offered a variety of escapes. A few short steps later on his urging they ducked into the trattoria and stood just inside the entrance.

A large, extravagantly moustachioed man greeted them. But as Martine saw clearly it was neither the greeting of a trattoria owner seeing yet another well-heeled tourist to charge the most while giving the least. Nor was it the casual indifference of a trattoria owner who sees a late tourist wanting feeding at precisely the moment he wanted to shut up shop and go home to the bambini. No, this man simply led then quickly and silently to a small booth at the back of the restaurant, waited until they sat down, then slid into the seat opposite. He reached across the small, slightly oily table and took the loose fold of Smith's cheek lightly between finger and thumb and squeezed it gently. His voice was barely audible.

'Good to see you Peter.'

'Also you, Giacomo,' was Smith's reply with a slight smile, 'may I present Signora Martine Aubanet?'

In a gesture that would have well graced the famous opera house they had just left, the Italian did not wait for the introduction but took Martine's hand and bent a kiss towards it, stopping the requisite half-inch short of actual contact.

'Signora Aubanet, I am honoured to meet you.'

Then with a frown that would have singed calamaris he added:

'She is much too beautiful for you, my old friend. She would do better with an Italian like me.'

Smith smiled with genuine pleasure while Martine had the grace to blush.

'I know, Giacomo. You may be right. But any more of that and I will tell Francesca.'

The restaurateur's magnificent moustache dropped at the prospect and the mention of the equally beautiful mother of his five children.

'Ah,' he murmured with an expression of deepest regret. At last he relinquished Martine's hand and his attitude changed. The generous and somewhat expansive host turned into a very un-Italian, flinty-eyed salamander.

'I wasn't expecting you, Peter. What' happened.'

While Smith told him, Martine looked around. The famous little restaurant was still very busy with people of all sorts eating although she noticed that in anticipation of the audience leaving the opera a good number of tables were reserved and laid up for new customers. She also noticed that their little table was a few feet from an open door that gave out onto the canal and a tiny quay. Tied up outside was the usual polished brown wooden motor launch ubiquitous in Venice for private and taxi use alike. It was only a very sharp attention to detail and a certain experience in the fleshpots of the French Riviera that enabled her to recognise this little boat as a little Riva Tritone; old certainly, legendary even, but still very, very fast if asked. She turned back to the conversation just as the briefing, for that is what it was, was ending. A unlabelled bottle of red wine had magically appeared and their glasses were full. Smith took her hand and a deep pull from his glass and waited as their host asked.

'You saw him?'

'Yes, I saw his eyes.'

The Italian let the silence ask the question.

'Grantkov.'

There was a palpable silence before the Italian replied:

'Shit. I thought that bastard was dead'

'Quite,' replied Smith. 'Either he is very much alive and still taking work or my eyes are failing.'

'I think not, old friend. Grantkov alive and on the loose is bad news for a number of people. Including you, I think.'

The Italian looked genuinely concerned as a number of unpleasant possibilities occurred to him.

'What the hell is that shit doing here in Venice again after all these years.'

Smith's voice was unlike anything Martine had ever heard from him before. He first turned to her and looked directly into her eyes.

'Do you trust me?'

She did and she nodded.

'Then you must do so now.'

Again she nodded and she sat silently, enthralled and concerned in equal measure as Smith turned to address his friend.

'Giacomo. Grantkov must have been contracted. That is what, after all said and done, he does for a living. He is Romanian as was the singer. Possibly a coincidence, possibly not. However, I have a feeling that the rest of all this may not actually be some dreadful coincidence. On a balance of probabilities he might not have seen me. You only see people in a situation like that if you are looking for them and there is no reason to think he knew I would at La Fenice tonight. But I need information. Instead of sitting there trying to seduce my girlfriend and look concerned at the same time, I suggest you have a quick scout around.'

The Italian nodded and left the table while Smith took his mobile phone from his pocket. It took some time before a sleepy voice answered in a tone of voice that was less than happy.

'Do you have any idea what time this is?

Gentry was obviously not impressed.

'Sorry, old friend but I thought you might to help me throw a little light on tonight's production of Traviata at La Fenice.'

Nor was Gentry in any mood for guessing games.

'Jesus, Peter. Have you had a lot to drink?'

He knew Smith well enough not to suggest that he had too much. Gentry doubted that such an amount actually existed in his case. Smith went on regardless of the disgruntlement of his friend in Arles.

'The heroine died.'

Gentry's exasperation showed. Being a man who knew more words than most, he was not someone who saw the need to use obscenities very often.

'Jesus, Peter, of course she dies. Consumption isn't it?'

'Usually, yes. But on this occasion it was a 134 50R in the cranium.'

Gentry woke up in a hurry. There was a short silence while he put two and two together. It didn't take long.

'Oh shit. Grantkov.'

'Unfortunately yes. Perhaps you might be good enough to find out why the bastard has seemingly risen from the dead and come back to cut short the career of a budding Romanian soprano in the most public manner possible. I doubt whether he had just taken up one of the more extreme versions of theatre criticism.'

Gentry's voice had dropped an octave and fifty decibels.

'You saw him?'

'Yes.'

'He saw you?'

'Er, no.'

'What do you mean, Er?'

'I'm not completely sure.'

'I'll call you back. Watch your back, old friend.'

And with that he rang off. Martine had sat silently, occasionally sipping her wine and looking at Smith with a level, almost analytical stare. She had seen this side of the man she had come to love very occasionally before and she didn't like it very much. But she also knew that it was precisely Smith in this mode that was the reason she was still alive. Their silence was broken by the return of the restaurateur.

'Nothing. Absolutely nothing. No word on the street, nothing from the police. A friend saw a boat heading very fast past San Michele and out towards the Baccan di Sant'Erasmo. Presumably it went east but apart from that, nothing.'

Smith shook his head slightly.

'OK Giacomo. There's nothing more we can do here. We'd better go home. Let me know if you hear anything more. There's no way that Grantkov could have anticipated my being there tonight. In all likelihood it was a coincidence. Our apartment should be safe, but I would appreciate someone to watch our backs.'

The Italian nodded.

'Already done, my friend. Take the boat and keep it for a while. Water is safer than land in Venice. Alfredo will take you and do the first stint of back-watching. I have also put a small evening picnic in the boat. If you can't eat with me you must, at least, eat something.'

Smith smiled his thanks. Some priorities never change whatever the circumstances.

The first thing that Smith noted was that the pretty little Tritone was very quiet. Its twin Chris Craft 175 Horse power engines may well have been able to propel the elegant old craft at well over forty knots but hardly burbled as it made its way down the Grand Canal towards the Academia and their apartment. In fact it was all but silent. The model had always been restrained, aimed, as it had been, at a 1960s market populated almost exclusively by European Royalty – that meant Monaco – and other distinguished old European nobilities, leavened by a sprinkling of the more respectable stars of film, opera and theatre. Built properly in mahogany and brass it was a jewel and worth a fortune. But by anyone's standards, the motor boat that proceeded down the Canale Grande hid well both visually and aurally in the throng of traffic that still covered the waterway in a haphazard sort of way. The competition for tips between the large numbers of loudly singing gondolieri jealously guarding their personal supine prey was well past the point where the murmur of the passing Tritone would make any sort of impression at all. Both Smith and Martine were lost in thought as they sat together low down on the white leather bench seat behind an equally silent Alfredo at the wheel. Smith held her very tightly. In fact the only sound she made was when they approached the little palazzo in which they had rented their apartment. This time the approach was from the canal side. A low wooden door on the water level set into a high brick wall that rose sheer above them more than twenty feet high swung open and they nosed gently into a dark indoor dock. As the door closed behind them with a quiet but emphatic click of an electric bolt running home she looked him straight in the eye with a look that combined annoyance with amusement.

'You remember, Peter, when we were planning this trip, you very kindly said that you would find somewhere nice to stay, I think was how you put it. How exactly did you find this place, my love.

Was it simple just a search on the Internet or am I missing something?'

Frantically trying to buy a little time before answering, Smith replied:

'Why don't we sit a little in the garden and have some of the Giacomo's supper and a nightcap? I have a feeling that I owe you a few explanations.'

That,' she replied in a dangerously gentle voice, 'is what you English call an understatement, I believe.'

It was well past midnight but it was still warm as they sat together in the tiny garden in the internal courtyard of the palazzo. They had changed into casual clothes, consumed Giacomo's excellent picnic and now each held a large glass of dilute whisky and soda in their hands.

'Right,' she said, 'I want to know what you think happened this evening, obviously, but first this apartment. Where exactly are we?'

Smith sighed. Another bit of his secret past was about to become public and he was never particularly happy about that even if the new custodian of the information was Martine Aubanet. He and others had spent much too long burying much of it.

'This little palazzo is owned by Her Britannic Majesties Government which sort of means the British taxpayer. It is run in a completely commercial way renting a number of apartments to holiday makers through an agency in the usual way. However, as you have just realised, this apartment on the ground floor with its little garden has, shall we say, a few additional facilities, like the boat dock, which are not usually available to visitors. If you examined the other apartments in the building you would see that insofar as they have windows facing this courtyard, they are small and don't open. They are mostly bathroom and toilet windows but made of armoured glass. The only door out of this garden onto the street, opens, as you know, with a key in the normal way but it also has electric locks and a steel core as does the front door onto the street.'

Martine frowned. 'It's a prison.'

'No, not exactly. It is a comfortable, elegantly appointed apartment that can be made very difficult to get into if required.'

'And out of,' his companion added slightly acidly.

'Quite so.' Smith hurried on, smiling slightly sheepishly.

'From time to time it is useful for the Service to have such a place for, shall we say, a variety of reasons.'

Martine remained un-mollified but wanted to move the conversation on as she was conscious that she was asking Smith about things that, in all probability, he did not really want to talk about or perhaps couldn't.

'And tonight?'

'Ah. Tonight. Yes.' Smith was not entirely sure how to proceed. 'I have no idea why your singer friend was a target for such a public assassination. No doubt we can find out if necessary or if you wish. What concerns me more is that I am pretty sure that I recognised the gunman; an old acquaintance called Valery Grantkov.'

'How could you possibly tell? You hardly saw him for more than a second or two. If that.'

'I caught enough of him to have a pretty good idea. I also saw the muzzle of the gun and it was a relatively old model of a widely used Russian service rifle. You note I say service rifle not sniper rifle. The Dragunov was not a specialist weapon. It was just a mass produced gun meant for wide use in eastern block countries. It was, however, designed to be very accurate. Our friend Grantkov is the only professional contract killer I have heard of using one. No one these days would even think of using one, but Grantkov was – or now I have to say – is, something of an eccentric.'

Smith took good pull at his whisky and continued, answering Martine's unasked question.

'Valery Maximovich Grantkov, born 4rd January 1947 in Bucharest to a middle ranking Romanian military family. Educated at a variety of schools in Romania and, as he showed promise, in Russia too. Did his military service there and learned how to shoot. The family moved to America when his father was appointed military attaché to the Romanian Embassy in Washington. Education continued in a number of American universities. Three years after his appointment, father returned home leaving the son to complete his studies. Little Valery ended up with a PhD in physics and a teaching job at Chicago University. Has spent much of his life teaching in America apart from taking time off occasionally for his small personal hobby, that is.'

Martine was ahead this time.

'Shooting people'.

Smith nodded. 'Yes. As far as we knew he was independent, completely non-political and very expensive. He operated on his own, worked for governments, businesses and private individuals. Anyone who would pay. He didn't miss. He never hit Americans, thus ensuring that he had a home to go to and even did some work for the CIA who, as we know, have difficulties with foreign languages let alone foreign cultures.'

'You seemed to think he was dead.'

'Yes.'

'Why?'

'Because I threw him off a train in 1980. As I recall the train was going rather fast at the time.'

'But you weren't sure.'

'No, but the fact that I had put two bullets in him moments before heaving him out of the door made the assumption reasonable. That and the fact that no-one seems to have heard from him in twenty years, although given the secrecy of his job he may have been working without us knowing. I don't know. Deveraux might know, though. Perhaps I should ask him.'

Martine was by now used to dealing with Smith's inability - or perhaps reluctance was a better word - to fill in the many blanks of an already unusual personal history. She knew he had alternated between the life of a scholarly art historian, patrolling the corridors of various universities on both sides of the Atlantic with that of some sort of businessman who was skilled at selling stuff to unsuspecting foreigners. She also knew that he had worked from time to time for the British Secret Intelligence Service, as it is correctly known, in a variety of operations some of which occasionally involved killing people. She had good reason to be grateful for some of his skills, she remembered. But it still came hard when the picture of the man she had grown to love remained so fragmented. As time went on she picked up more and more but the whole remained incomplete and probably always would. She reached over the small gap between their two chairs and took his hand.

'You do know, my dearest, that one day you are going to have to tell me everything?'

Smith squeezed her hand gently and shook his head.

'No, my love, that is precisely what I can't do. Not because of some ridiculous James Bond reason but because there are people out there who have reason to know me and they would assume that I wouldn't tell you. You already know more that they would guess. That is also the reason you might be safe if you ever got really caught up in some of this shit. If they genuinely believe that you know nothing they might not try to get it out of you.'

His voice dropped slightly.

'Ignorance is bliss as some say, I believe. Your safety means a lot to me.'

She answered quietly.

'Yes, I know. Peter. More than your own, I think.'

She understood but it was still a problem. He sensed the gap and immediately became business-like.

'In any case, I am pretty certain that tonight was just bad luck, for us at least, and for the moment we have nothing really to fear from Grantkov. If he is following his usual MO he would have been away within minutes and out of Italian territorial waters within forty minutes. Venice is a ridiculously easy place to escape from. That's why for centuries most of the great European powers have had intelligence offices here.'

'And that means we're safe?'

'For the moment, I think yes.'

Suddenly he stopped looking at it all just as an intriguing problem to be solved. He saw that yet again she was being drawn into something that was potentially dangerous, more dangerous than she probably knew. It was all to do with him and his past and although the circumstances of their meeting a couple of years before weren't exactly his fault – then, like now, he had been in the wrong place at the right time – their relationship had developed into a simple love affair in spite of his past regularly catching up with them in one form or another, often dangerously.

Martine got up and set her elegant wicker chair to face Smith but slightly parallel. Their seating became a detached version of a Victorian love seat. She transferred her whisky glass to her outside hand and took Smith's inside hand in hers.

'Now,' she said adopting a very business-like tone. Not for the first time Smith was reminded of the fact that, apart from occasionally adventuring with him, going off on cultural trips around Europe and generally leading the life of a rich, lady of independent means from the Camargue, she also ran a widely diverse group of companies whose annual turnover was in excess of a fifty million Euros.

'Let me see if I have got this right. As a result of my simple and thoroughly normal wish to visit the Venice Biennale we find ourselves staying in a British secret service safe house that can equally be a prison, attending a performance of La Traviata at which the leading star is shot dead in full gaze of her hitherto adoring audience by an American-based Romanian assassin using an antique rifle who those who know about these things assumed had been dead, thrown off an express train thirty years ago, made heavier by the weight of two bullets by the very man with whom I share my bed and who, in turn, might have been recognised by said American-based Romanian assassin and thus presumably remains retired from a hitherto over-adventurous life but potentially still in danger.'

Her tone dripped with heavy irony.

'Have I covered the essential points, Darling, or have I missed something important about our relaxing little cultural trip to the Veneto?'

Smith was faced with a dilemma. He really just wanted to leave the past behind. He also wanted to find a way to combine his yearning for personal freedom and solitude with his increasing love for the person who had become more and more his companion. It had occurred to him before that she was probably one of the very few people in his entire life to whom he had never lied.

He sighed.

'You have an admirable talent for précis, my dear. You've covered most of it, of course. But there are a few points that you might like to consider. From a practical point of view, there's probably very little danger to us personally. As I said, Grantkov was almost certainly paid for this specific job and has long since departed Venice. Had he been in a mind to avenge himself on me or others, he would have tried years ago. It wouldn't require a very chance sight of me witnessing him at work to kindle those sorts of long-dead fires into life. In any case we are well protected here as, incidentally, we have been since we arrived.'

After a long pause, Martine asked quietly: 'the others?'

'Gentry may not be especially pleased to hear that Grantkov is alive.'

Martine waited. Smith sighed and gave Martine an abbreviated account of the events following the Bologna bomb some thirty years before. They found out that Gentry had apparently been Grantkov's target only after Smith had got them both on the train back to England. Grantkov had boarded the train in Venice and it was only because Smith had put them into sleeping compartment that they weren't booked into that they had enough time to turn from being the target to being the hunters. Smith had dealt with the Romanian, or so he had always thought, while never knowing what Gentry was doing in Italy in the first place. He still didn't.

Again a long silence. Martine put two and two together very quickly.

'You think that if Grantkov saw you, he could think you might lead him back to your friend Gentry and there is unfinished business there.'

'Actually, my love, I don't. It's all too tenuous and coincidental. But I owe my continued existence to the fact that Gentry never leaves anything to chance; not even the smallest possible coincidental connection. That is his great strength.'

Chapter 3: A Sporting Interlude

Scene 1: Tennis at Pau

The court at Pau isn't really a proper Real Tennis court at all. In fact it's possible to say that there is no such a thing by modern standards, at least, Smith mused to himself as they sped along the autoroute west past Toulouse. Most of the fifty odd courts that remained playable around the world differ from each other in varying degrees. Some have bits others lack, some are markedly different sizes to others. All play differently from each other. Some have stone floors, some concrete. Walls differ similarly as do the hand-made balls one uses. It is, he mused, one of the enduring pleasures of playing the game that although one could play anywhere, to play well one had to learn the court as well as the game.

Pau's court in the very south west of France spends most of its time during the week being used for the game of Trinquet, a sort of indoor version of Pelota, that great and fast moving game so popular in the South of France and the Spanish Basque country Occasionally on Sundays the Real Tennis players are allowed to use it. The two short end penthouses of the original tennis court have long since disappeared to accommodate the Trinquet but the long side penthouse with its galleries arranged along the length of one of the main walls of the rectangular court still remains, allowing a modified game of Real Tennis the great and complex predecessor of lawn tennis to be played by a small group of enthusiasts.

Smith had come to Real Tennis too late to become any good at it. He hadn't gone to one of the very few UK schools that possessed a court or to one of the three universities that have one either. Given that England contains largest number of courts - twenty six at that time - it was hardly surprising that he had not stumbled across the game earlier. He had been too busy doing that nineteen sixties equivalent of going down to the gym workout - playing squash. He had been quite good but his stint in America doing postgradate work at the University of California and then teaching at the same institution meant that that too had become curtailed into being a hobby. He had had the talent to go further. Then after a number of years sitting on his arse behind a desk or in a library his doctor had looked him up and down in a tired sort of way and suggested that by still playing the occasional game of squash, he was only really hastening the inevitable heart attack. The same doctor had failed to diagnose high blood pressure which could engender the same result; a fact that accounted for Smith's low opinion of your average family doctor. A friend has introduced him to Real Tennis at a court at Holyport near Maidenhead and he had fallen in love with the game within minutes of completely missing the first dozen balls that were hit at him across the drooping net by the club professional. He was good at racquet and ball games - almost international level - and the fact that this ancient but beguiling game gave him a instant lesson in humility made him curious and an addiction had started. It is the medieval predecessor of lawn tennis; played in a rectangular, stone-faced building, back and forth across a curving net, using the walls and the roofs of a penthouse that ran around three sides of the rectangle rather in the manner of a medieval cloister on which, there is some opinion, the game is actually based.

In one form or another the game has been in existence for a thousand years or more and was once all the rage throughout Europe with Paris alone boasting more than one hundred courts. However it fell into obscurity soon after the British decided that they wanted to play the game outside on their immaculate grass lawns and in the eighteen seventies an English army officer, Walter Clopton Wingfield, used the newly invented vulcanised rubber to make the Real Tennis ball - hitherto handmade and very hard - bounce on grass. Real Tennis with its extensive courtesies and rituals as well as its scoring system of Byzantine complexity did, however survive albeit infinesimally.

Unless you have played the game it is impossible to understand the seduction that almost anyone who steps on that huge indoor space experiences. Once addicted, people usually spend the rest of their lives either playing or trying to play. In England this is less of a problem as slightly more than half of the world's courts are there. In France, once the centre of the game at the turn of the eighteenth century into the nineteenth, there remain but three, in Paris, Fontainebleau and Bordeaux. Smith had seldom lived within easy reach of a court. He had had a stint in Paris and played at the court on rue Lauriston which had been constructed in 1907 when the owners of the original pair of courts built end-to-end along the Rue de Rivoli on the north side of the Tulieries Garden were forced to sell up, making a lot of money in the process. The original beautiful building still exists as an art gallery, of course, as does the old game's French name. It is now the Galerie nationale du Jeu de Paume.

Real Tennis players rightly refer to their game as 'tennis' while the later versions played successively over the years on grass, then ashfalt, then clay then plastic are regarded as upstart newcomers being collectively and somewhat contemptuously referred to as 'lawn tennis' or 'lawners'. Tennis players are used to travelling long distances to indulge their passion. Thus the four hour drive from Arles to Pau to answer the challenge of an old friend living near Tarbes when the Pau court came back into use was no hardship; especially so because Martine had said in that particular manner that women often use when they disguise an instruction inside a suggestion that she wanted to come and watch. It was a day out and the prospect of a game and a good lunch at Auberge Labarth, just south of the town, a favourite restaurant in Pau for both of them but for very different reasons, gave them the prospect of an enjoyable day out.

They had started very early as dawn broke over the Camargue. Smith's game was scheduled for 11:00am. Much of the journey was spent at high speed with Madame driving her Range Rover with a carefree disregard for any speed restrictions or, indeed, radar detectors or cameras. There is, mused Smith wisely to himself only, a madness about the French when they drive on autoroutes that they should prove that Alain Prost, the great French Formula One world champion, was nothing special and that they, together with every other Frenchman, was perfectly capable of driving at equal speed and with an élan well in excess of prudence or even, for that matter, reality. Smith had a minor and unimportant amateur car racing youth buried deep in his past and could only see the consequence of such self-delusion. However, Madam was driving in stilettos which, while not vertiginous, were certainly high enough to keep him interested and additionally there was the considerable amount of extremely shapely thigh exposed by her short summer skirt – for comfort she claimed – for him temporarily to suspend his fears of imminent catastrophe.

He was looking forward to showing the game to her as much as he was to playing. Apart from her, his two daughters, the music of Mozart and chess, Real Tennis was one of the only great loves of his life. Looking back, as he was increasingly prone to do these days, much else seemed to be an unseemly struggle to achieve dubious ends. Now as he aged he remembered a piece of advice given to him during his student days by one his fierce uncompromising émigré German art history teachers that tried impatiently to educate him that wisdom lies, not from the never-ending quest for the new but in the gradual process of learning more and more about less and less.

Looking across at the beautiful woman he thought again how deep was his affection for her. Alone amongst everyone he had ever known, she made no judgments about him, required nothing from him that he didn't want to give. It was incomprehensible to him that she loved him but refused to make an issue out of it. He had known for some time that he would die for her, and almost had on occasions but nothing could match the contentment he felt as he sat there. Silently he leant across and kissed her very gently high up on her exposed thigh. She smiled, equally gently, and lightly touched the top of his head.

His game was with someone who had recently got in touch, almost out of the blue as they say. John McDowell was an old acquaintance, although they had not seen each other for a good few years. They had been at school together in the early nineteen sixties at Fettes College that underestimated but over-esteemed private school – or public school as the British perversely call them - in Edinburgh and had briefly and coincidentally come together while Smith was doing his doctoral research in the University of California, Berkeley in San Francisco. McDowell had become a nuclear physicist although, much to Smith's incomprehension, always claimed not to be a very good one. A bit like being almost a virgin, Smith had always thought. Their paths had crossed again a number of year later in Albania at a time when Albania was not exactly on the package holiday circuit. McDowell had been sent in to look at some very odd looking building works that looked suspiciously like new missile storage sites. Smith had been his minder. The brief and thoroughly unpleasant visit had required Smith's talents rather more than McDowell's. It was then that they discovered that they both worked part-time for the same employer, the British Secret Intelligence Service or SIS as it is more colloquially known. McDowell had got out well before Smith by virtue of some profitable if not strictly legal business side-lines in the old Balkans and had headed for retirement in the isolated countryside near Tarbes. The telephone call had come as a bit of surprise to Smith but as it had been Gentry who had supplied Smith's number he had only been mildly put out. Ultimately the prospect of a game of tennis was much too good to resist. Nearly three hundred and fifty miles and about four of hours after their departure they arrived with Smith feeling as fresh as Martine continued to look.

They were evenly matched in an ill-assorted sort of way. The sort of parity that Real Tennis seems to engender unlike most other games. Parity but not equality. Not because they were the same standard. Smith was infinitely the better tactician in a game where tactics are all - or almost all- while McDowell was fitter and, being slightly younger, had better ability to make his hand do what his brain instructed. This is a not inconsiderable advantage in the great game of Real Tennis. When they first come to the game most people think of the rules or the scoring as being the most difficult to master. These do indeed have their own peculiar complexities. However it is never too long before the beginner learns that simply hitting the ball has challenges all of its own. The racquet is made of wood, oddly shaped to allow for the fact that the hard ball hardly bounces on the stone floor. It is also heavy. Very. Difficult for those who have wrists of a delicate disposition. Equally the ball is solid and weighs significantly more than a modern tennis ball. Add to that the fact that a real tennis racquet is strung to the highest possible tension. This makes a certain modicum physical strength desirable. Unlike its more modern counterparts, the game also possesses a handicap system which allows the world's best to play on equal terms with the world's worst. In this the ancient game is also the most modern. Neither Smith nor McDowell played regularly enough to have a current handicap, so they agreed to play even and to see what happened.

What Smith treasured besides all this elaboration and complication is that the game is one of tradition and convention, of manners and courtesies. Dress is white and play is conducted within a complex ritual of honour and politeness, of traditions as to who proceeds who and when to do so, how the balls are managed and distributed in their hand-made baskets. This is a necessary arrangement as a traditional full "set" of balls to be on court at any one time numbers, of course, a gross or one hundred and forty four - obviously. Decisions made by umpires, or more correctly, markers, are never challenged. This is not done and can cause the perpetrator to find that he is no longer welcome at the court in the future. In any case such a discourtesy might result in the miscreant's tea, whisky or claret, kept at the net to refresh him as the players periodically change ends, not undergoing periodic refills - a matter of extreme gravity.

It turned out to be an enjoyable and competitive game in the manner of one where both players enjoy the competition rather than the victory. Both men laid enough good chases to be satisfied that they hadn't lost their long-remembered old skills. Both won and lost the resulting replays to settle the chases to know that these old skills and their old judgements were still there slightly dustily in the background. They still managed to retain enough to put the ball into the galleries they intended, more or less. Both remembered enough of the more than fifty named service variations that are in common use by the average player and hitting which particular bits of wall and penthouse roof each had to involve. The game even occasionally had a suggestion of elegance after they persuaded their knees to bend low to unaccustomed angles. It was always a game that rewarded intellect over brute force. Age also is no barrier. Smith recalled once watching a game of doubles at Queen's Club in London between four gentlemen of, shall be say, a certain age. The game had been played out with skill and elegance, with courtesy and competitiveness in equal measure. It was only in the bar afterwards over a post-game glass of scotch that Smith found out that the aggregate age of the four gentlemen on court was a few years short of three hundred and fifty years. It was that sort of a game. It was all light years away from the modern upstart played on plastic to the accompaniment of grunts and screams, tantrums and bad manners, sponsorship and vainglorious celebrity.

Martine was seated comfortably with a glass of wine in the *dedans*, the very small viewing areas behind the long gallery under the penthouse roof at the service end. She had been adopted by the good-looking young man who was the part-time professional at the club. It was his job to explain the game to people, and to give lessons when asked. He was earnestly explaining it all to Martine presumably in the hope of persuading her into a short white tennis skirt and onto court for her first lesson. His enthusiasm for his task caused him to get a little carried away and when his voice rose to a level that disturbed the two players it was restrained by a slight lifting of an eyebrow from McDowell when he gained the service end of the court and glanced through the netting that protected the spectators against 'forces for the dedans' - one of the few ways of wining a point outright - when the hard ball can reach speeds of well in excess of 100 mph.

After the first set which Smith had won by six games to four and they agreed that a slight handicap was in order to even thing up. Half fifteen was in order. Essentially that meant that Smith would start fifteen love down every other game. It obviously worked as McDowell won the next set six five. Their hour's play came to an end with the third set score at four all and there was a general consensus that this was an appropriate time to stop. Lunch was calling.

After showering unpredictably under a system that almost certainly dated from Ferdinand de Lesseps himself, they changed and emerged ready to eat to discover that the young professional had indeed persuaded Martine onto court and, having equipped her with a pair of gym shoes, was instructing her in the finer points of racquet grip; a process which, of course required much bodily contact.. They paid their fees and Martine's bar account and left, declining the offer of a post-game glass. The Auberge Labarth was beckoning.

The restaurant was almost full when they got there. It was one of those establishments that used to be widespread in France but now was increasingly rare. A good, almost traditional, restaurant where food was cooked with sensitivity and flair without the decorative excesses to which many Michelin starred establishments have descended over the years. The room was elegant but still a café. The food was from fresh produce correctly cooked without excesses or bizarre idiosyncrasy. No exotically shaped plates or infinite varieties of flavoured mousses surrounded by tiny decorations that looked like the leavings of a pigeon with a bowel problem. No exquisite little multi-coloured morsels that needed no teeth, pretending to be food created by overly self-important chefs who forgot that there was much more to cooking and eating than just taste.

The three sat in the restaurant. Martine, having taken one quick look at the menu announced brightly:

'Gentlemen, as you have provided the entertainment this morning, you are my guests for lunch. I will have the Merlu de ligne rôti, followed by the Râble de Lapereau farci.'

Smith smiled across gratefully at her. In a single, easy and graceful gesture she had remembered the bit of their conversation on the road an hour or two earlier when they had called the Auberge to reserve a table and he had remarked that in retirement McDowell was probably no longer particularly well off. She had set the bar very high by choosing one of the most expensive combinations on an already general expensive menu.

McDowell followed Martine while Smith started with Ravioles de Girolle then Filet de Veau and he added a white and a red from Jurançon and was pleased to see Madame nodding her head slightly in approval. Apart from running a group of family businesses that ranged from hotels and farming to real estate, she also helped her father produce some of the most extraordinary wine in the Camargue, although none of it ever seemed to reach the market. She also enabled a few of her family to run some small restaurants in and around Arles where the food was as startlingly good and it was cheap. The problem was never the price in these exclusive little restaurants. It was getting a table in the first place as they were usually taken up with locals rather than tourists – locals whose only budget seldom extended to more than a few Euros. That, however, was the point of her restaurants.

The conversation covered a wide variety of topics without ever really settling on anything in particular. McDowell, as Smith had anticipated, fell completely under the spell of the beautiful lady from the Camargue and, for the moment, at least, had forgotten that he had a perfectly charming wife of his own. Smith had noticed Martine having this affect on others as well in the past.

'I am sorry you wife couldn't join us,' Martine remarked, bringing, for a moment, at least, their guest back to a sort of reality with a wide and open smile as she went on. 'I would like to have met a fellow Frenchwoman who has decided to tame a curmudgeonly English bachelor. We could have compared notes and tactics.'

McDowell smiled in a comfortable sort of way that Smith had noticed before Martine managed to instil in even their most restrained friends and acquaintances.

'Unfortunately, Louise is visiting her mother and sister in Bayonne for a couple of days. Mother is ill and in her late eighties so it is a regular visit. Perhaps the next time?'

It was a relaxed and easy conversation, respectful of the fine food they were eating but not to the exclusion of companionship. They talked about a lot of things and much about the past but nevertheless managed to avoid any difficult bits. Smith could see that Martine was keen to find out more about him as this was the only person from that past she had ever met. He was amused to see that McDowell was as adept at avoiding some of her more leading questions as she was at posing them. It was a conversation not unlike their recent game, in fact, and that was a source of some satisfaction. Both thought they had learned a little more than they had given away. Perfect, he thought. It was the same sort of honourable draw that had concluded their tennis.

They arrived at coffee via some memorable desserts that would instantly have undone all the good that their recent hour's exercise might have done, had that been the point - which, of course, it hadn't been. Finally it was time to go home and they got up and left the restaurant. Both Smith and McDowell were a little intrigued to see that no bill was proffered - almost as intrigued as when a few moments later the chef himself came after them into the car park and effusively thanked her - not them Smith noted - for coming.

The trip back slightly slower but only slightly. Martine had again insisted on driving and Smith who was beginning a sort of creeping paralysis as the inevitable stiffness from the game began to seep into his body made little objection. The conversation was desultory with the memory of an excellent meal still fresh in their minds.

'Interesting man, your friend McDowell,' Martine murmured.

Smith wasn't sure if he was supposed to reply so contented himself with a quiet 'yes' and yet another shift of position in the leather seat.

She continued: 'I mean, I understand that you sorts of people don't talk much about some of the things you did but with both of you it seems to be more than just secrecy. It is almost that you have decided not to be interested in it anymore.'

Smith decided not to rise to the 'you sorts of people' remark but realised that with the move into psychoanalysis, he was expected to join in, however uninterested he was in doing so.

'I suppose it gets to be a bit of a habit after a while,' he sighed, 'Keeping secrets becomes easier if you just don't remember the stuff in the first place. Indifference is a useful way of achieving that.'

'So is cynicism, I suppose, although I know that you're neither deep down.'

'Neither what – or is it which?'

That didn't sound right either but he couldn't be bothered to explore his not inconsiderable well of syntax further.

'I don't think you are either cynical or indifferent. I know you care very deeply about things.'

'Only certain things, I think. I don't have a large repertoire of that sort of stuff.'

'Maybe, but you care more about some things than most people ever do about anything. I think that is why I love you.'

Smith started to feel uncomfortable about the way the conversation was going and decided to try to be clever, look for less difficult waters and to address her origin unspoken question.

'McDowell is certainly an interesting man. Very clever and very practical. The two don't always go together but in his case they do.'

Out of the corner of his eye he saw her smile and realised than he had fallen for it. If she had asked him outright about his friend, he would have found a way of avoiding it. Now he had started the conversation himself. He continued:

'All right, clever clogs. What do you want to know?'

She took her hand from the steering wheel momentarily to reach across and touch him on the knee by way of acknowledgement.

'Well, I only want to know a bit more about your past. I don't often get the chance of looking there.'

He drew a breath and sorted the memories into some sort of order.

'I was sent to ride shotgun on a particularly stupid CIA operation. About thirty five years ago, the Americans got it into their heads that the Chinese were building some sort of nuclear facility in Albania. God knows why they thought it or what it might be but once those idiots have got it into their heads that their land of hope and glory is in some sort of danger there is usually no stopping them.'

She glanced across to see whether her question would be a help or a hindrance to the story telling.

'How on earth could the United States feel threatened by something happening in a tiny country ten thousand miles away from them.'

'God knows,' Smith nodded, happy that he didn't have to hold a monologue.

'Albania is about the same distance from China too. However a small team was sent in to sniff around. The Americans didn't know the first thing about Albania in those days – they probably didn't even know where it was – so the UK was asked to join the fun. McDowell was put in because the yanks thought there might be something nuclear and the UK asked me to look after him. The whole thing was a complete balls-up. Nothing to see, of course, and they knew we were coming.'

'What happened?'

Smith debated for a moment about the length of his answer. Long or short were equal for him. They were still a couple of hours away from home, but he realised that her interest was in McDowell rather than the operation so he opted for short.

'Two dead Americans, a number of dead Albanians, McDowell brought back to the UK without a scratch by yours truly untouched except for a bullet in the arse.'

'I wondered what that little scar was,' she mused gently, 'I assumed you must have sat on something rather sharp.' She drew back to the story. 'I guess the Americans weren't too happy.'

Smith let a winterly smile cross his face as he remembered.

'You might say that. They weren't very happy with me either.'

'Why? Because they thought you let two of their people die?'

'No. Because I killed one of them.'

Smith didn't seem to want to continue and Martine knew better than to ask. As usual she trusted him to tell her if he could and if the knowledge wouldn't compromise her. With anyone else, it could have been a patronising attitude and thus to be disliked or scorned. However she knew now, as in fact, she had known ever since they met that this was very far from true. He wasn't that sort of person.

Another had fifty miles passed in companionly silence until she asked:

'Your place or mine?'

Smith realised that he was rather pleased with the assumption that they would stay together tonight. This was becoming, if not the rule, then certainly the default, as they say, now in spite of their still officially living apart. Martine divided her nights between the family mas and her own little *cabane* a mile or so distant. In spite of its humble origins as a bull herders cottage the rectangular, thatched, single story building had been turned into a very comfortable residence for one, or increasingly these days, for two. He then remembered Arthur who he had left in his little house on the Place de la Major next to the Roman amphitheatre in Arles. Actually the dog had the run of the house and the little garden through the door from the kitchen left open for him. He had no fears about leaving the house completely open. Apart from the fact that there was nothing in the house worth stealing, the little garden joined a number of others to form a little quadrangle completely enclosed by buildings primarily occupied by local families who observed the whole area with constant vigilance – more properly as nosiness. The final reason for Smith's lack of concern was that Arthur was a very large retired racing greyhound with very large teeth as the local cat population knew all to well. Any intruder would hardly know that Arthur's idea of the proper way to spend his retirement was to eat baguette, pate and camembert at least once a day and to look at television from a completely prone position on his own sofa. He looked fierce. Smith replied:

'It would be nice to go to the *cabane* if for no other reason that I will probably need your healing hands before too long. However, Arthur is at home.'

'Ah. I hope you'll forgive me but while you were playing I telephoned Jean-Marie and asked him to collect Arthur from Arles. I would think that for the last few hours he has been enjoying himself hunting over the farm.'

Smith was grateful to her and he also knew that she was completely right. It was unusual for a sight hound like Arthur to have unrestricted access to thousands of hectares of farmland and more than once Martine's father had been very happy indeed to mount his beloved Camargue horse and take Arthur off across his farm. It had become a new passion for the old man and Smith genuinely shared his pleasure. He also felt a slight frisson of anger that yet another small piece of his life had been chipped away without his knowing.

An hour or two later Smith had eased his increasingly painful body into a long reclining wicker chair on the veranda outside Martine's little cottage and was looking west out across the marsh and the Marais de Saint Siren which was covered with thousands of pink flamingos. It was still very warm and kingfishers darted about and the hot silence was punctuated with the occasional 'plop' of a diving water rat or an otter. Not for the first time Smith experienced the perfection of the place in spite of the creeping paralysis that was seeping up his body. The condition was, however, alleviated by the provision of a very large glass of sparkling rosé at his increasingly stiff elbow. He estimated that the glass held half a bottle. It was from the family vineyard on the opposite side of the huge Étang de Vaccarès that forms the centre of the Camargue and was definitely not a pink Crémant or pink type of champagne. Émile Aubanet was as almost as proud of his wine as he was of his bulls and that was a lot.

Her father had joined them at Martine's request. He only came to the cottage by invitation however frequently that was offered. The little building had been a personal gift from his late wife to her only daughter and he respected her privacy, a gesture that was as appreciated as it was unnecessary. A completely exhausted greyhound lay prone on the floor in the shade. Arthur had coursed and caught a hare and Émile was bursting with pride and had insisted that they come to eat the Provençale equivalent of jugged hare after the catch had been drained of blood and had the chance to hang for a few days. In reality the old man was much more interested in the exploits of his new four legged companion that he was of his daughter's trip to Pau.

Completely undeterred by the fact that she had driven for more than eight hours and consumed a large lunch, Martine set about preparing supper. A plate of salad that she still managed to make interesting while remembering Smiths antipathy to most things resembling salad leaves. The salad contained copious quantities of assorted seafood, tellines a tiny, clam-like mollusc found on the Camargue beaches, Also there were oysters from the famed beds in Bouzigues along the coast past Montpellier, mussels and a number of different varieties of crab, prawn and shrimp. Home-made mayonnaise and much crusty baguette completed the main dish. Smith noticed with a quiet smile that for him, notoriously lazy about working for his food, she had taken the morsels of sweet meat out of the Tellines. She and her father were obviously made of sterner stuff and the meal was punctuated with the sound of empty butterfly-shaped shells being regularly tossed into a large ceramic bowl in the middle of the table. She obviously thought that he was a big enough boy to handle the mussels and oysters himself.

They ate outside as the dusk settled gently across the marsh. The huge sun slipped down to the horizon as it always does and for a while the flat landscape was bathed in a light similar in colour to that of the flamingos. The simple meal was concluded by, cheese and fruit and not for the first time did Smith find himself counting the blessings of living in this enchanted place as a part of this extraordinary family. On impulse but without interrupting the animated conversation between Father and daughter about the prospects for their rice harvest, he reached across the small table and took Martine's hand, turned it over, placed a kiss in her palm and gently closed her fingers around it. He saw both of is companions smile gently without actually pausing in their impromptu business meeting. He was happy to listen in. Not only was he interested but it was a break from some other pressing concerns.

The meal over, Martine and Smith accompanied Émile back to the mas. All three were on horses and Smith, remembering some less than savoury moments in the past when his presence in their lives had brought them into not inconsiderable danger, was pleased to see that Jean-Marie, the family driver, body guard and general factotum, had appeared from nowhere as they came out of the cottage with their horses, tacked up and groomed. The hard little grey horse was the transport of choice on the farm and Jean-Marie who had never really thought that Smith was a true Camargue horseman allowed a smile to cross his face when he saw Smith hauling his increasingly rigid body into the saddle. Arthur also allowed his enthusiasm for the farm override his common sense trotted along beside them, unconscious of the fact that he was letting himself in for a three mile round trip.

By the time they got back to the *cabane* it was past midnight and dark. The light breeze was still warm and they both lay in the basketwork chaise longue in an embrace, loosely enough for them each to hold of glass of dilute whisky and water as a nightcap. Smith felt utterly content, especially as the alcohol he had consumed during the evening had deadened the pain from the assorted joints and muscles that were protesting their unaccustomed activity earlier in the day. That, Smith thought grimly, and half a dozen Ibuprofen gulped down hastily before supper. Even in the middle of the night the Camargue was alive with sound and light. Cicadas, frogs, even a few nightingales provided a musical backdrop while fireflies and glow-worms formed a carpet in front of them underneath a clear starry sky. Paradise.

Her voice was not exactly the most seductive as he could hear her chuckling.

'I think, my darling, that if you wish to have your evil way with me, you better have it tonight. I am not sure if you will be up to anything at all in the morning.'

Smith did not dignify the remark with an answer. He simple finished his whisky in one, stole hers and did the same, and led her swiftly off to bed. Nothing, he felt, should be left to chance on matters like these.

Scene 2: McDowell Disappeared

A late breakfast was in the walled garden of the mas; late for farmers, that is. About eight 'o clock. The sun was already up and beginning to warm the landscape. It was going to be hot again. As he anticipated, Smith was very stiff indeed and he sat uncomfortably at the table waiting for yet more secretly taken Ibuprofen to kick in. Both father and daughter were too polite to say anything but were clearly amused. However Smith saw that Émile was a little preoccupied but was prepared to wait while he consumed coffee and inappropriate amounts of baguette, salted butter and home-made apricot jam. Arthur was, as usual, under the old man's chair, enjoying his own very human breakfast. Finally the old man said what was on his mind.

'I received a phone call this morning.'

Smith's radar was not infallible. Quite the contrary. But he sensed something was up and waited.

'The call was from a French lady called Louise McDowell.'

A knot appeared in Smith's stomach. In a flash numerous bits of the last thirty years stuck themselves together in his mind and he feared the worst. He couldn't help himself. It was too great an effort he kept his silence any longer.

'He didn't arrive home.' His voice was a whisper.

Émile Aubanet nodded slowly.

'As usual, Peter, you're right. She apparently came home a day early from visiting her mother and found that her husband hadn't come home. She tried to telephone you but obviously you weren't at home. She remembered her husband talking about meeting you again and Martine. She knew her name and got in touch with me having found my number in the phone book.'

The three sat in silence while they digested the information very differently. Martine was the first to speak.

'Isn't it a little early to get worried. After all we saw him only a few hours ago and if he was expecting her not to be at home that evening he might simply have gone somewhere else rather than go home to an empty house.'

Smith shook his head. 'No, he would have told her.'

Looking at his host, 'Do you have a number?'

Émile Aubanet passed a piece of paper across the table, followed by a mobile phone. Knowing Smith's passionate hatred of anyone using phones while he was eating he said: 'please use it now. You don't have to leave the table.'

Smith dialled and waited.

'Louise, Peter.'

The voice that came back to him was steady but obviously worried.

'He's not back, Peter.'

It was unnecessary to ask any of the usual questions. She wouldn't have telephoned if there was an easy explanation.

'OK Louise. Just hold on. I will be with you in…'

He broke off both to made a mental calculation and to look across the table at his host. Aubanet nodded. He knew Smith didn't have a car at the mas.

'…. In three or four hours. I'll call you in half an hour with a mobile number.'

He rang off and sat still while he collected his thoughts. Turning to Martine.

'It's probably nothing but I think I should go and take a look.'

It was pretty obvious that there would be little actually to look at but all three around the table knew that Smith would have good reasons for going although they may well not have been able to guess many of them. It was also just the sort of thing that Smith would do for his friends. No explanation beyond that was necessary. Émile, sensitive as always to the practicalities of life, got up and went into the house. Smith, anticipating what Martine would want to say, leant over and took her hand.

'No, my love, I would prefer you to be here rather than gallivanting around southern France with me. Apart from the fact that you almost certainly have work to do here, I really don't think there is a problem. If there is, then it comes from way back before I knew you, and in any case I would prefer you to be here with your father and Jean-Marie.'

It was one of many reasons that Smith had allowed his retirement in Arles to be interrupted by both some unwelcome adventures and more welcome attentions of this most elegant of women; that she understood enough to know when to involve herself and when to leave well alone. She was born into a ancient Camargue family where loyalties and traditions bound people together infinitely more strongly than casual acquaintance or fashion. Blood ties were nothing new to her. Her family's history and heritage was based on such things. She understood more than most that blood also had to be spilt from time to time to maintain them. But she had never met a man like Smith who had no such ties, no history at all. No family, no roots, no past – at least little that was public knowledge. Smith only had a few friends. She knew that he would not only spill blood in their defence. He would unquestionably die for them. She also knew that he expected no less from them in return. They both rose from the table and stood together in a gentle embrace. Arthur, realising that the continuous supply from the table of pieces of baguette and jam had been replaced by this show of human affection, lay down in the shade deciding that a post-prandial nap was in order and closed his eyes.

'Take care,' she whispered kissing him on the lips.

He turned and walked briskly into the house and through into the courtyard. Émile Aubanet stood by the driver's door of the black Range Rover, holding it open to it. Smith got in while his host laid a hand on his shoulder.

'Take care, Peter. You won't be bothered by the police or the radars on the autoroute. I know you are in a hurry.'

Smith smiled his thanks as Émile continued:

'I have put a satellite phone in the glove compartment. Martine is on speed dial one, I am on two, Jean-Marie on three and Louise McDowell is on four. If you want to give her the number you will have to tell her as it won't come up on her phone. Oh, and we'll keep Arthur with us here. I just hope this isn't the beginning of another of your adventures, Peter.'

'Émile, I don't know how to thank you.'

The old man smiled.

'It reminds me of the old days, my son. The toys are different now, but I was doing this sort of thing before you were born. Good and bad memories. But just make sure you come back. Martine needs you.'

Smith covered his hand still resting on his shoulder with his own.

'I will, Émile, I know. I need her as well.'

Aubanet nodded and tightened his grip.

'Yes, I know. Bon Voyage. Keep us in touch with what you are up to and if you need anything.'

With that he stepped back and slammed the door shut. Smith turned the car and headed down the winding drive that led to the iron gates and on out into the Camargue. After a couple of miles he turned north up the Sambuc road towards the motorway. He leaned across and opened the glove compartment to take out the satellite phone and a hard smile came to his mouth. Not for the first time he wondered about the life in wartime occupied Arles and the exploits of the then teenage Émile Aubanet. Beside the telephone lay Smith's Glock 30 and two spare magazines. He didn't need to see if the gun was loaded or not.

Scene 3:   McDowell Discovered

Smith made the three hundred mile journey to the Lac de l'Arrêt Darré a few miles short of Tarbes in only very slightly more than three hours. Neither the odd motorway policeman, nor the electronic machinery that read the start and finish times on his passage through the télépéages on the road and can compute the average speed brought him to the notice of anyone. Smith knew that the overhead speed cameras on overhead gantries would also not deliver unwelcome news a week or two later. Émile Aubanet was clearly a man who could fix things.

As he sped along the motorway that changed from Le Languedocienne to The Autoroute des Deux Mers then finally to La Pyrénieénne all at the marketing man's behest, he wondered whether to involve Gentry in all this. In his heart he suspected that it could all revolve in some way around his old friend and he wasn't entirely happy with the suspicion. Gentry was more of a link between McDowell and him. One way to see how the land lay was to give the man something to do. So talking the satellite phone in hand somewhat recklessly give the speed he was going, he phoned Gentry. The number was obviously not one that Gentry's machinery recognised because all he got was an answering machine. Smith was far from amused. His tone of voice was only slightly modified by the fact that some idiot Spanish truck driver, half asleep from driving hours over his legal limit, travelling at seventy miles an hour chose that particular moment to pull out in front of him. Smith had to dial while undertaking the myopic moron. He was travelling at more than one hundred and thirty miles an hour at the time and had the satisfaction of seeing a completely astonished Spanish face waking up as quickly as it receded in his rear view mirror.

'Gentry for Christ's sake, answer the bloody phone.'

The answering voice was artificially cheery.

'Peter, dear chap. How are you?'

Smith definitely had no time for pleasantries. He précised the last twenty four hours in a few sentences. and then gave instructions.

'I need you to calculate McDowell's most likely route back from Pau to his home. There could be a million and one things that have happened to him. He may have chosen not to go home as he wasn't expecting Louise to be there or he make have a little bit of stuff on the side and decided to pay her a visit. But I have to start somewhere. Also find out if there have been any accident reports. He was driving a silver Peugeot 406. I'm afraid I didn't get the number but you could probably get that from Louise.'

Gentry clearly got both the message and the tone of urgency in Smith's voice so rang off without a further word.

Smith had never been to McDowell's home but his GPS brought him to a dusty halt in front of a small but pretty farm house buried deep in the Bois le Lansac that surrounds the lake. Smith noted that there were no neighbours to speak of. Louise stood in front of the door waiting anxiously and took his hands in hers as soon as he got out of the car. He recalled that he had met her only once a long time ago. It had been at McDowell's request. She looked younger than he remembered; a lot younger. She was the first to speak.

'Peter, thank you for coming so quickly. I'm sorry I telephoned. There was really no-one else I could think of to ask.'

Smith fixed a reassuring smile that he really didn't feel on his face and squeezed her hands gently. He couldn't bring himself to spout the usual platitudes.

'Louise. I have no idea what has happened but I'll see what I can do. I have to go out and do a bit of looking around. I'll be back within the hour.'

He drove off more or less towards the west and as soon as he was out of sight he pulled into the side of the road and called Gentry. His friend answered the phone immediately and started without preamble.

'Obviously this is complete guess work. McDowell was alone and his wife was away or so he thought. He presumably had only a moderate amount to drink with you at lunchtime but there is no reason at all to think that he would necessarily head straight home. I assume he gave you no indication at lunchtime as to what he was going to do as you haven't mentioned anything. He could have decided to anything that would have affected his route home. However we have to make some assumptions otherwise we will never get started and the only one we can usefully make is that if he went directly home he would go home by the route that was most familiar to him. The journey would have been about forty five miles so the first assumption is that he would take the autoroute for most of it as there are no convenient country roads. Using them would in any case more than double his journey time and he would probably not have wanted to drive for more than a couple of hours if he was feeling the effects of the game and lunch. So we assume he took the autoroute for most of the way. Once we get the car number we can probably check when and where he joined and left it. He either had an accident or he didn't and there have been no likely accident reports. If he didn't then he either wanted to vanish which we both think is unlikely at this stage, or someone got to him. If we are talking a kidnapping or a hit then I think we can assume that it was planned and if we want to find out who did it, it would be useful to know how long ago you planned your sporting rendezvous. Someone would have been forewarned and there must be a limited number of people who knew in the first place. If it does turn out that he met with some sort of real unfriendliness there are a few pertinent questions that will have to be asked. However we can assume that any intervention by the ungodly would not have taken place on the autoroute. Too difficult and too public. Thus we are left with an intervention after he left the motorway as before he joined it in town in Pau would have equally been rather too public.'

'Two autoroute exits are possible. One into Tarbes leaving a short stretch of country road about ten miles to get home. The other possibility is to on drive to the next exit and come off at the same junction you have just used coming from the opposite direction and home via the road that you have just used. While you weren't necessarily looking closely, I assume that you would have spotted anything untoward along that road as you went along it. This last assumption is, of course, open to question. However a regular traveller would probably take the first convenient exit not stay on the autoroute that actually will take him beyond his destination before allowing him to get off and turn back to home. No, if I had to take a guess I would examine the route between the house and Tarbes. There is only one sensible route, junction 13 into Tarbes then the D21 to Leslades. I have had a look at it and there although the countryside is quite open, a few farms here and there, there is a spot about half way along where the road goes through a small forest called the Fôret de Sarrouilles. The road takes a bit of a detour through the wood and at one stage does uphill via a very abrupt hairpin turn. Any car would have to slow down a lot to get around. Additionally there is another road that joins at the apex of the turn. If I was planning to snatch McDowell or to shoot him I would choose that spot. Very secluded, trees everywhere, multiple escapes. Target slowing almost to nothing. I'll call you when I have confirmation of the autoroute exit.'

Gentry stopped talking. Smith thanked him and cut the call. Actually he was again impressed with Gentry's ability to see the essentials of a problem and plan accordingly. This is what Gentry was best at and why over many years Smith had refused to work with anyone else. He didn't bother asking how Gentry would find out about the autoroute timing. He just knew that he could. He turned the Range Rover onto the small road that would take him onto the D5 and the little village of Laslades where he turned west towards Tarbes. The road was quite built up with small houses scattered regularly along its length. It was also quite straight and not, Smith thought, ideal for the sort of misadventure that he was increasingly believing had befallen McDowell. However after a few minutes the road did, as Gentry had described, turn left into a wood and started to run downhill into a sharp hairpin bend. As Smith slowed down to take the right-handed turn and noted that he was moving at no more than fifteen miles an hour. He was also going down hill. If McDowell had been coming up he would have been slower still. Smith also saw the small road that joined at the apex of the hairpin. On an impulse he stopped the car and pulled into the side of the road just before the corner. Immediately he knew that Gentry was right. If there was anywhere on this road that was suitable for an ambush, then it was here. He had seen only one car during the whole time he was on the road.

He took the Glock from the glove compartment, got out of the Range Rover, and looked around him. The junction had shards of windscreen glass scattered around and although most of the surrounded grass verges bore tyre marks of various descriptions, one set seem to go straight ahead as if a car coming up the hill had just driven straight on while half way round it and into a shallow ditch beside the road. Instantly a film played itself in his brain. McDowell came up the hill to the bend, slowed right down and started to take the turn. Something happened and he just drove straight on off the road into the ditch nose first. He bent down and sure enough there was bits of headlamp glass embedded in the bank.

It was almost certainly a shot, a simple enough shot straight through the oncoming windscreen coming from the wooded bank behind him. He climbed slowly up the scrubby hillside that rose quite steeply in a line directly back from the apex of the corner. The trees were by no means dense but there would be perfectly adequate cover for a gunman to wait unseen. He would have chosen exactly the same place himself. It took him less than a couple of minutes to find it.

'Bloody amateurs,' Smith though bitterly as he bent to pick up the little brass cylinder glinting dully in the scrub that covered the ground. 'They didn't even bother to clear up after themselves.'

At that moment his phone rang.

'McDowell left the autoroute at the Tarbes exit at five to four yesterday afternoon..'

Smith interrupted to finish his friend's sentence.

'..and died precisely on the corner you picked about ten minutes later.'

There was a silence over the phone until Gentry muttered quietly.

'Shit.'

Gentry's voice was not at all pleased at discovering that he had guessed right. He knew all too well what it meant.

'Quite,' said Smith, 'Shit exactly. They obviously had the thing well set up as they must have taken the car away on a trailer or maybe it was drivable. Who knows? There are a few glass fragments lying around but little else. The shooter, however, left his brass. One can only guess whether it was on purpose or not.'

'Hum. What was the round?'

Smith turned the brass casing in his fingers, examined it closely and gave it a good sniff.

'Small. Looks like a 6mm to me or, come to think of it, is touch smaller even. Maybe a .228.'

'That's a hunting calibre more than a military one. Are you sure its not a 7.62?'

Smith didn't answer. He knew considerably more about guns than Gentry who he wouldn't have trusted with an air pistol let alone a killing gun. He did note, however, that Gentry was interested in a 7.62mm cartridge. It was the calibre of a Dragunov. He continued:

'Most .228 rifles are American. If they were Americans, then hunting would provide a good cover. However either someone wanted us to find it or was simply sloppy. Hell they may have used something else and just dropped this one for us to find although it does smell as if it was fired quite recently. However I think we can assume that McDowell is dead and that raises some questions. Do some checking on the beautiful Louise for me would you? They must have known his plans and very few people did. McDowell was a careful man, if I recall correctly.'

Gentry sounded dismissive.

'Surely that's unnecessary, Peter. He's dead and it may be totally unconnected with you or even us.'

Smith felt his curiosity and his anger rising. Gentry seemed to be treating him like a fool. However he said nothing.

'OK. I'll go back to Louise and say that were are still looking for her husband who might, of course, turn up at any moment perfectly innocently.'

Gentry sounded sad.

'Don't you think that's a bit rough on the lady? She surely has a right to know.'

'Not until we know what side she's on. This all took some time to set up and, as far as I know other than McDowell and I only Martine and Louise knew the date and time of our game. The club at Pau only had my name and a guest. Martine didn't know about it until the day before. Oh, another thing. I want to know what has happened to those two CIA guys I got out of Albania all those years ago. I hope they are in happy retirement and excellent health but I want it confirmed.'

'What are you getting at, Peter.'

'Nothing as yet. I certainly don't know what McDowell may or may not have done to get himself killed. The fact that it could have been a hunting rifle may just mean that he had got up someone's nose locally. I also don't know what else he may have done while working for HMG that could have resulted in this, but I wasn't involved in any of that. But the Albania job was something that linked us and I would like to know a bit more.'

'All right. I'll do it.'

'Right, I go to see Louise and then head back home. If she is the reason all this happened then she'll know I'm lying to her and that should make her nervous and, as you now, nervous people make mistakes. I should be back home about four o'clock. Call me, please, as soon as you get the information.'

Chapter 4: Opening Moves

Scene 1: A Game of Chess

There was no regular time for their periodic games of chess. They just seemed to happen. But on this occasion, the game served as a prelude to a conversation that neither of them was particularly looking forward to.

Smith was amused to see that his old friend, playing white this time, didn't use Ruy Lopez. Normally it was his invariable opening and Smith had spent a considerable amount of time secretly working on the many possible responses to that particular opening and their variations. Lopez could actually be a basis for a very aggressive campaign but Gentry was a traditionalist whose chess was as measured and thoughtful as he was himself and he tended to use the Spanish cleric's fundamental opening as a basis for a plodding if always error-free, long drawn-out campaign. Smith played as he was expected to play; more unconventionally in an aggressive sort of way, often seeming to make it up as he went along. Actually Smith's chess, like his life, was slightly more calculated than he tended to admit although his ability to improvise, sometimes with considerable violence had both kept him alive and won him more games against Gentry that he had a right to expect; much to Gentry's annoyance.

Smith wondered if there was more than a hint of compensation for his previous indolence in Gentry's choice of the potentially more aggressive King's Gambit as his opening this time. He couldn't recall Gentry using it before. Maybe he was trying to show Smith that he was his old self again. Actually that was precisely what Smith wanted but he wanted the calm, methodical Gentry not some new souped-up version. Answering fire with fire Smith immediately countered with the equally aggressive Falkabeer, distaining the pawn offered in sacrifice and continued through the somewhat unclear position that usually follows this counter with a couple of improvisations of his own. The game developed into the sort of open running that Gentry hated and Smith rather enjoyed. Smith was also the first to break concentration, take a good size swallow of the whisky at his elbow and start the conversation that they both knew was inevitable.

The game progressed in the only way it could with Gentry, normally reliant on silent thought and tactical planning, being somewhat perturbed by the knowledge that someone might possibly be out there thinking of killing him. Equally Smith, being slightly more used to it, was progressing through the game with increasing recklessness as he saw that his opponent was powerless to stop him. It came as no surprise that Gentry resigned before the inevitable embarrassment of a defeat by a significant number of pieces. They left the little Sheraton chess table behind Gentry's battered leather sofa in his library and settled into the two matching armchairs which stood either side of the great fireplace that currently contained a tasteful display of dried Provençale flowers rather than the slightly more comfortable roaring wood fire of the winter months. Gentry didn't believe in central heating. On closer observation, Smith saw that they were flowering weeds. Gentry started uncertainly:

'Well?'

'Well what?' Smith was reluctant to let the memory of an unaccustomed rout on the chess board fade quite so quickly.

'You know what.' Gentry was brusque. Again Smith was unforgiving:

'You tell me, old friend. You seem to be the cause of all this one way or another and the fact that it has come back to haunt you after thirty years isn't my responsibility although it seems that is has become my problem. As I said, you tell me. Oh, and by the way, I do mean all of it because if I am to save your hide then I need to know it all. And I mean all.'

There was a long silence before Smith continued.

'I think, my dear old chum, the time has come to fill in the gaps in my inadequate knowledge of our old Albanian operation for I've a feeling that is where at least some of this odd business originates. This time, however, I want all of the story, including the bits that you have been keeping from me all these years.'

Gentry drew breath to make the inevitable protest, so Smith went on quickly.

'I have never questioned the fact there are many things that I don't know about you, David, and I have never been too bothered. They are not my business. Even when we worked together the same general rule applied. I relied on you to tell me what I needed to know and by and large you didn't make any significant mistakes. However, this is different. For some reason we seem both to have caught someone's attention and equally we both seem to be in some danger. It also means that there is some risk to one or two people who have recently come into my life and who might become involved at the very least as possible collateral damage and I won't allow that irrespective of our previous friendship. I don't need to tell you how important this is to me, and I no longer really care about your own personal ideas about secrecy and confidentiality. If I'm to have any chance of protecting us all I need to know all the facts not just an edited version. If you continue to hold out on me, I will just walk out on you, probably for good. And before you reply I want you to consider carefully the fact that I am completely serious.'

Both of them knew that it was a watershed moment in their relationship. Smith had never before questioned the fact that over time they had slipped gently from an occasional close working relationship into a trusting friendship. During that time, Gentry had learned what Smith thought about friendship and rather feared it. Smith, he knew, had very few friends but he was fiercely protective of those few. Smith felt very little about those who weren't part of that group. There was a particular place in Smith's opprobrium for those who had been trusted and then let him down. Not too many people seemed to have survived this particular fate. It was after a considerable pause that Gentry sighed quietly and started.

'You already know some of it, and of course, you were part of the farce that actually happened on the ground. At that time in the early seventies it was felt that were signs that Albania and some of its neighbours, Yugoslavia and Romania in particular could be seen as forming a block that would oppose Soviet power in the Balkans and act as some sort of buffer between the iron curtain states and the west. The Americans were particularly keen on this and went some way to help Albania develop its relationship with China after the breakdown in relations between China and Russia. A case of your enemy's enemy being your friend, I suppose. Although this situation didn't last very long, hardly past the end of the decade, it was rumoured that, from a military point of view, at least, there were some actual concrete results. While some Chinese SAMs were delivered to Albania, the rumoured Chinese ICBMs never, of course, actually arrived, primarily because China didn't have any in the first place.

There had been a lot of construction work for a new air force base at Lezhë-Zadrima just south of Shkodër and the Americans were curious about what was going on. The plan to poke around and have a look came from our friends at the CIA. The reason that the UK became involved was because, unlike the most of the Americans in or out of the CIA, we actually knew what was going on in Albania. In fact it came as a bit of a surprise to learn that the CIA actually have an Albanian desk at all. MI6 or the Foreign Section as it was known in the early days of the service had been running a network in Albania since 1909 and for most of that time relations between the two countries have been extremely cordial albeit somewhat below the radar as they say. Of course this faded a bit after the Second World War but nevertheless we usually knew what was going on either through our own agents in place or from Albanians who maintained an opposition to Hoxha. Someone further up the tree than me, insisted that we had enough on-going operations in Albania not to want them mucked up by our heavy-footed country cousins. Thus we were involved in vetting the plan and I am afraid I rather shredded it. It was simply dreadful. Whoever put it together was an ignoramus. They didn't even have a nuclear specialist on a job that was supposed to spot nuclear weapons. They had no local support organised and hadn't even decided where and how they wanted to land.'

Smith smiled inwardly at the picture. Having seemingly decided to come clean, Gentry showed some signs of warming reluctantly to his task. He continued:

'To cut a tedious story short, I re-wrote the plan as best I could, making perfectly pain that I thought the whole thing was a dangerous waste of time. I included McDowell as the nuclear man and you were the best babysitter I had available at the time. You know what happened, of course, as you were at the sharp end. I managed to get a message to you that two of your American colleagues were not exactly on our side, just as you were met by a Sigurimi hit squad on the beach and a number of dead Albanians and two dead Americans later you got McDowell and the remaining three live Americans back to the sub and that, as far as you know, was the end of it. I seem to remember that you also got the two bodies out which I thought was rather an achievement although I would guess you weren't given much by way of thanks.'

Smith got up and refilled their glasses. Gentry seemed to be talking at last, thank God, as Smith was looking forward hearing something he didn't know already. Gentry taking a sip of his Banff malt while waiting for to Smith to settle back into his armchair.

'What you don't know is that at the time the CIA itself didn't know it had an Albanian desk. It seems to have been some sort of clandestine operation funded out of CIA slush funds which as we know are extensive. The point of it was, apparently, to oppose the Russians by helping the Chinese in their support of Albania. They helped the transport of the SAMS in 1969 and actually paid for the small and nasty stock of chemical weapons that were delivered to Albania from China in 1972. God only knows what they thought they were up to; even their own bosses didn't know about it. But as you know, once the yanks get a bee in their bonnet and decide that they are acting on behalf of freedom, country and mom's apple pie, there is little that anyone else can do to deter them.'

'Once the dust had cleared there was the mother and father of all enquiries. I was brought in to help. I should have refused, of course. However ultimately heads rolled in a big way. There's nothing more fierce than a CIA boss with a red face, especially when the cause of his embarrassment is one of his own people. The little group was closed down, the staff kicked out of the service which I felt was a little hard given that none of them knew that they were part of an illegal group and the two guys running it was put in prison. I never did hear whether they gave them the courtesy of a trial. They were accused of working directly for the Chinese but I personally rather doubt that. However, as usual, you can rely on the CIA screwing something up and this time they failed to secure the very large amount of money that had been used to run the whole stupid business in the first place. Being resident in one of the CIA's private prisons didn't stop the men funding the attempted hit on me at Bologna. The other CIA men that we brought out are both dead although they say these were from natural causes. But they would say that wouldn't they? McDowell is now also dead but from what you saw it seems unlikely that Grantkov was involved in that. It looks, therefore that the only major players from our side of the Albanian adventure still breathing are you and I.'

Gentry had obviously finished his monologue and there was a long silence in the room. It all had the ring of truth about it. Or put another way, Smith had no reason to doubt that Gentry was telling the truth. One thing struck him.

'The rogue CIA men. You don't happen to know where they are now?'

Gentry shook his head.

'Not officially, of course, but I have strong suspicion that they are being held in that rather nasty little secret CIA prison in Bucharest that they have run for very much longer that the recent bad publicity would indicate to use when the civilised yanks want to torture people. You know the place. It's certainly easier to hide them in the middle of all those supposed terrorists who are being held without trial.'

Smith took another pull on his drink.

'I didn't work with McDowell very much. Can you think why anyone else would want to kill him or is this connected with the Albania thing? For the moment to be safe we should probably ignore some unconnected local reason. '

'No, I can't. Because of Albania he just spent the rest of his service doing technical stuff at HQ; appraising intelligence reports and the like if they included anything nuclear. To be frank, I can't remember him ever being in the field again.'

Smith tried unsuccessfully to pull the whole thing together in his mind.

'We seem to have a whole rage bag of connections, possible connections and coincidences. We have a Romanian contract killer who tried to kill you in Bologna in August 1980 and who I thought, mistakenly apparently, that I had killed a day or two later. The hit was possibly contracted by a couple of rogue CIA people who may be still be incarcerated in the capital of Romania, although there is direct no evidence of this. The same hit man surfaces some thirty years later to kill a Romanian opera singer in Venice whose singing, whilst not great, was not really bad enough to merit being shot. He may or may not have seen me at the time although my presence at the scene of Violetta's rather unconventional demise was completely coincidental. McDowell is now killed by persons unknown using an American hunting rifle but the only reason we can think of is some connection with the old Albania job. The other two participants in that operation may also be deceased, possibly from natural causes but we are note really sure. All a bit of a mess you would agree and what is really annoying is that we don't know if it adds up to anything at all.'

Gentry just nodded glumly. Smith was the one to be decisive. He was still not completely sure that Gentry was being completely candid. He had not, Smith noticed, mentioned his companion at Bologna Station although, strictly speaking, the discussion had been about Albania. It was nevertheless a worrying omission.

'Gentry, please can you get onto your jungle telegraph and find out a few things that might clarify matters somewhat. I would like to know where Grantkov is now. I would also like to know if the ex-CIA doubles are in fact still locked up safely, and whether their cash has finally been shut down after all these years or whether they're capable of issuing contracts. I want chapter and verse on the deaths of the CIA good guys. If you can also find out why the singer was killed that would be interesting. Maybe it's connected and maybe not.'

Gentry finally summoned up enough energy to offer a mild protest.

'Peter, it's highly likely that none of this concerns us.'

Smith was waspish in his reply.

'I am very surprised at you Gentry and, if I was being honest, rather disappointed. You know perfectly well why I need to know what, if anything, is going on. With you or without you I'll find this stuff out. You're not the only one to have contacts from the old days but I'll probably make a lot more waves than you would. However I will probably not be in the mood to spare your oddly maidenly blushes as I dig about.'

Smith got up followed by a slightly worried Arthur who was not at all used to hearing raised voices between these two. They both took their leave of each other and Smith turned as he and Arthur went out of the door.

'You've got twelve hours to come up with something good or I will do it myself.'

Scene 2:   Supper with Girondou

For all his bravado it was with a slightly uncomfortable feeling at the back of his neck that he struck off down towards the Rhône for a walk aimed at both satisfying the dog's perennial desire to get out as well as his own requirement for thought and to stay on the move. The present predicament, he thought with a grim humour, was at least likely to get him fit if he actually survived to enjoy that long-lost condition. Walking with Arthur always provided a good opportunity to do the sort of mental filing that was necessary from time to time. He was conscious that these walks were getting fewer and less frequent since his relationship with Martine had developed. There always seemed to be a reason to do something else or to accept someone else's offer to do the job for him. He made a mental note to change that. The dog, or rather Emile Aubanet's genuine pleasure in playing host to him was yet another rather subtle tentacle that tied him increasingly to that family. For all his latter day passion for Martine, he remains a little fretful over his loss of independence; or was it sentimentality about a preferred solitude?

His first thought was one of practical detail. If Gentry couldn't find Grantkov, how could he? Gentry's resources and network of contacts and people who owed him favours was extensive; much greater that Smith's. However the thought was dismissed quickly because he knew that Gentry would probably do it. There may be aspects to all this that Gentry was reluctant either to communicate or to confront but Smith was sure that his old friend would not let him down. He knew that if he did Grantkov was not the only person to be after him. So he turned his head to the question of what he would do when he found the Romanian.

His pondering of this particular eventuality was interrupted as he was half way across the Tranquetaille bridge onto the north shore of the River Rhône when his phone rang.

'So what have you got yourself into now, Peter?'

Smith had very few friends in the area but this was one of those few. He immediately put his thoughts on one side and replied with genuine pleasure.

'Alexei, how nice to hear from you. How are you and how is the family?'

The cultured voice of the local chief of most of the Marseille crime syndicates winged back to him across the satellite link.

'Oh, we are all fine. The girls have new boyfriends as usual, Angèle is still as beautiful as ever, I am still not in jail and we all miss seeing you from time to time. But it's actually you I'm worried about.'

'Me, old friend?'

'Yes you. We try to live a quiet life here in the South of France on the basis that if we don't make too much noise, people further north with more time on their hands than intelligence in their arses, will leave us alone. But you don't seem to be able to get out of bed without landing yourself in what, you Welshmen say, I believe, is 'ot water.'

Smith smiled at the accuracy of what the Frenchman said as well as the undercurrent of concern. Alexei Girondou had been both an unlikely friend and a valuable ally on occasions in the past and as Smith had rendered some considerable assistance to him more recently, he had become a sort of honorary godfather to his pair of ravishingly beautiful late teenage daughters as well as a friend to the family. There had been time when the man's protection had been useful. Smith tried to keep a note of levity about him as his pace slowed a little. Arthur, untroubled by the noise of his companion talking to no-one he could see, reduced his step in parallel and continued to look around him for something small and four-legged to kill.

'Ah, what is it that I am supposed to have done this time, Alexei?'

Not for the first time, Girondou's voice was framed by a deep and not particularly amused chuckle.

'I have no idea what you may or may not have done, Peter, neither do I particularly want to know unless you need to tell me, but at this particular moment I'm wondering why a slightly flinty looking Romanian tourist staying in a modest little hotel in St Remy de Provence should number amongst the personal affects stored more or less secretly in his room a photograph of you and a Dragunov sniper rifle that is almost as old as you are.'

Not for the first time Smith found himself admiring the man's sources of information. It was obvious that if you ran the largest crime syndicate south of Lyon for as many years as Girondou had you would have a pretty extensive network for keeping up-to-date with what was going on. But Smith was still impressed.

'Alexei, I won't begin to ask how you found out but I can certainly say I am grateful to you yet again. My usual method of finding out these things is proving to be a little, shall we say, troublesome at the moment.'

The reply came back sharply.

'Why? What's wrong with your friend Gentry? From what you said I didn't think that he had off days.'

'Well, it has been a slightly unwelcome discovery for me as well.'

There was a silence on the line while Girondou gave some instructions to his driver in a voice, at a speed and in an accent that combined to make the whole conversation completely indecipherable to Smith – which was, of course, the object.

'Where are you at the moment, Peter?'

Smith laughed. 'At least there is something you don't already know, Alexei. I am actually halfway across the bridge to Tranquetaille taking Arthur for a walk and having a think.'

His friend's next suggestion offered Smith a good deal less of an option than it appeared.

'It's now just after half past six. Do you know the restaurant in the Hotel Mireille in Tranquetaille?'

'Well yes, I do.'

It was a restaurant that was usually well outside Smith's budget.

'I've found out a few things about this man who I gather is registered under the name of Fenice but is actually called Grantkov, I think we need to have a chat. I will meet you for dinner there in an hour.'

'Alexei, I have my dog with me and am hardly dressed for fine dining.'

The man chuckled.

'Believe me, Peter, neither will be a problem. Until 7:30 then. Oh, I presume the name Fenice is some sort of joke?'

'Er, yes, Probably,' Smith replied.

'Good. I like a good joke. Perhaps you can explain it to me when we meet.'

The phone went dead. Smith remembered that back in 1944 towards the end of the Second World War, in order to prepare the ground for their planned invasion of the south of France to form a second front to the intended invasion in Normandy, the allies of America and Great Britain carried out a series of bombing raid across the south of France targeted ostensibly at strategic installations, especially railway works, lines and bridges. After a number of false alarms, Arles received six of these bombardments in the summer of 1944. On July 12th much of Tranquetaille was destroyed and has subsequently been rebuilt in that particularly unlovely institutional concrete style so beloved of French post-war developers. At the eastern end of the river front before the Rhône turns abruptly northwards there exists the Hotel Mireille, a building of such supreme ugliness that Smith felt it would have probably benefited from another visit from the American Air Force. However its restaurant is a hidden delight and holds very justifiably a reputation for good cooking. Smith found himself looking forward to his meal.

Having called Martine briefly to tell her about his slightly unsatisfactory conversation with Gentry, he found had three quarters of an hour or so to waste and rather guiltily he remembered that he hadn't called on old Madame Durand for some time. She had been Martine's old nurse for many years, a great friend of her later mother's and, if truth be told, the life-long guardian of a secret love for Émile. Smith had met her during the first of his unintentional adventures with the Aubanet family and now she kept an eye on him and his treatment of Martine.

Arthur's tail was wagging indecently quickly long before they got to the door. Smith had no idea how dogs did this but their memory for places that they liked was infallible. The old dog loved this old woman and she him. The face that was the colour and texture of a walnut broke into a broad smile as she opened the door to them both. Arthur was beside himself with pleasure.

She had given up her usual seat in her elegant old sitting room to take up residence at the end of the unforgiving chaise longue just so that Arthur could jump up and lie full length with his head on her lap. The low tables and other things had also been moved in order to make the general arrangement more harmonious. Smith wondered how often an entire room had been altered to accommodate the very occasional visits of a retired greyhound. Not often he thought. As soon as she had opened the door Arthur, now free of his lead, rushed straight past her, into the drawing room and onto the sofa and collapsed in a heap and waited for her to arrive.

'Peter, It is nice to see you again.'

She placed three kisses on alternate cheeks according to the local custom and led him inside.

Madame Durand was well into her nineties and fit as a flea. Having guided the infant Martine into adulthood she had later become her mother's companion and had nursed her through the long and terrible illness that finally overcame her. Given other circumstances, she might have become Émile Aubanet's mistress. She remained Martine's closest confidante and she was fiercely protective. She also understood more than most about life here in the Camargue and she was an intimidating but loving friend to Smith as well. This was the man who her beloved Martine had chosen and her support was unyielding. She was a fierce old woman and Smith had come to love her almost as much as he loved Martine. Arthur clearly had no doubts either. She arranged his whisky and hers. He was interested that she had poured for herself the same as for him - weak with ice and Perrier. She also noticed that he noticed and looked over her spectacles at him rather gravely.

'Just because I am old enough to be your mother doesn't mean I can't spot a good thing when I see one. I seem to remember that you British say that imitation is the most sincere form of flattery. Well, consider yourself flattered by a ninety-year-old.'

Smith smiled as they took their seats. Arthur replaced his head contentedly in her lap and fell instantly and contentedly asleep. She continued:

'I apologise, Peter. Welsh of course. I know how unhappy I would be if someone called me French. Now tell me what are you up to this time.'

Smith took a long pull of the weak scotch and told her. All of it. All that he knew. Details only. He left nothing out. She listened attentively and in silence. When he finished his story she replied:

'Apart from the fact that someone is trying to kill you, something that I am sure you can resolve, your problem remains the same as always, Peter. You have expectations of friends that friendship can't often deliver. People will always let you down, no matter what you hope or believe. Perhaps as you solve this particular problem, as I sure you will, it might be as well to remember that.'

'Everyone, Madame?'

She looked at him with a twinkle in her eye.

'Well not absolutely everyone. You have had the very good luck to join a group of people down here that you can trust. That is because life here is a little different to life elsewhere. In many other places friendships are formed between strangers and trust grows as their relationship grows. Trust is something that is a goal. Here in

Provence, friendships start with family, from a place where trust is built in from the beginning, generations ago. Families who have worked the Camargue for a living over many centuries understand that life is impossible without being able to rely on each other. Trust is as fundamental as the blood in our veins. Trust is not something that has to be earned here, unless, like you, you are an outsider. It just exists. That is why you, having been adopted into this community, you need never have to worry about betrayal. Only by outsiders.'

Smith was surprised to realise that he had taken this for granted too. She continued.

'I think that you can trust Alexei Girondou as well. After rescuing his wife for him last year, he too would do anything for you. I knew his father years ago and he was an honourable man too - for a crook that is. Very different from us, of course. Marseille was a foreign country to us mere farmers but the old man used to come to the Mas des Saintes from time to time to talk with Émile when he was a young man. I seem to remember that they got on rather well. How he keeps his position surrounded by all those crooks I really can't imagine but I suspect he might be able to tell you a thing or two about trust and friendship. Different things, too.'

Arthur was spark out with is head resting heavily in the old lady's lap so Smith got up and refilled both their glasses.

'Thank you, Peter. Now, enough of this present little adventure. Tell me about the more important matters.'

Smith had not been looking forward to this traditional bit of their conversations.

'Again as they say in England, if not in Wales, when are you going to make an honest woman of Martine.'

She paused and laughed at what she had just said.

'I assume that rather odd expression refers to living together rather than anything else. With your background, young man, it would be highly presumptuous to think of your being responsible for making an honest person out of anybody.'

He joined her in smiling at the thought while frantically trying to think of a way to change the subject. She understood.

'All I will say - again - is that I am not getting any younger and I want to dance at your wedding. I will have to have another word with Martine. She isn't getting any younger, also and good-looking young men like you don't come along every day.'

Now Smith burst out laughing and Arthur woke with a start.

'While I enjoy your calling me a young man it's hardly accurate. In any case I can't think that a woman who is as intelligent, beautiful and wealthy as Martine would find much difficulty in finding someone else if she wanted.'

The twinkle was still in her eye as she replied.

'Now that's where you're wrong, Peter. She has very high standards on a number of different levels and the chances of her finding someone who corresponds to what she wants and needs on as many of them as you do are not high. However I won't flatter you by going on. Just make sure you two don't take too much more time making your minds up.'

Smith drained his glass.

'Madame I must be leaving. I have a friend to meet.'

She nodded.

'Yes. I hope you enjoy your dinner with Monsieur Girondou. I would also appreciate your opinion of the restaurant in the Mireille. I have heard mixed reports about it lately and Martine tells me you are something of an expert in these things.'

She smiled as they got up because he was plainly astonished. The appointment had been made scarcely an hour before. How on earth…?

Obviously delighted at her cleverness she got up and accompanied his and a somewhat reluctant dog to her door. She reached up and he bent down and avoided the three touches to alternate cheeks. She kissed him very firmly on the lips.

'Nothing terribly mysterious, Peter. Martine called me to say you might be dropping in. But next time perhaps you could stay a little longer. Maybe when you are not just on the way somewhere else.'

Smith nodded with a slight embarrassment. She was, of course, right and they both knew it.

'Martine said you were a good kisser, young man. As usual she is right.'

With that she gently closed the door.

The hotel is located in a bit of Arles that few people ever get to - Tranquetaille the part of Arles whose main claim to fame that is was memorably described by the legendary early twentieth century and still reliable German guide writer, Fritz Baedeker, as not worth crossing the river to see. Entering the restaurant, he was startled to see that the place had had a makeover. It was some months, years even, since he had visited the place but he vaguely remembered a sort of austere, Novotel modernism. The place had gone Provençale, as, it seems, had the rest of the hotel with excessive amounts of those colours, hard yellow, orange bright greens and blues that people wrongly associate with Provence in general and the mad Van Gogh in particular. Smith presumed that the changes were intended to entice people across the river.

His host, already seated in a corner of the now rather overblown room, rose to greet him as he and a bemused Arthur were led by a distressed Head Waiter through sparsely populated restaurant. Clearly the presence of a very large greyhound in his completely artificial Provençale extravaganza was difficult for him. However the reason for his reluctant acquiescence held out a welcoming hand and shook Smith's warmly. He smiled and said in a voice that carried the length and breadth of the room:

'No, I didn't realise that they had turned it into bordello either. The food had better not have changed as well.'

The maître d'hôtel coloured and minced away.

Alexei Girondou never seemed to change. He was small, bronzed and immaculately dressed in a light beige suit and polished Gucci loafers. A white shirt and conservative tie with matching handkerchief completed the ensemble. Smith was much more informally dressed in a polo shirt and cotton trousers so Girondou immediately took off his jacket in order to try to lessen the contrast. The perfectly ironed cotton shirt only succeeded in doing the opposite. Ironing was not one of Smith's strengths. Arthur, having greeted a second old friend in the space of an hour, lay down on the thick pile carpet under the table with a loud groan. Restaurants are usually good places to be in his experience. All he had to do was wait. His host smiled across the table as a chilled coupe of champagne was put at Smith's elbow.

'Well, my friend, how many?'

'Four. Two singles and a couple.' replied Smith.

Girondou tossed his head back delightedly and laughed out loud.

'You're not losing your touch at any rate. Four it is.'

There were some twenty diners in the room and four of them were his bodyguards. He continued.

'Yes, I wouldn't normally dine with so many but we have just come from a job.'

Smith did wonder that it was going to be an expensive evening for his host, if, that is, the hotel dared to offer a bill. Girondou reached across to his discarded jacket, took a photograph out of its inside pocket and handed it to Smith. It was a clear picture of Grantkov, sitting on a café terrace in the sun sipping a Pastis and wearing a straw hat. Girondou turned a genuine but slightly concerned smile on his friend.

'Need any help?'

Ever since the phone call on the bridge Smith had been thinking how much to tell the man. He was very worried by Gentry as the man was acting so strangely. Initially Smith thought this was just down to worry about being a possible target. It is an unusual skill to remain calm and focussed when you know someone wants to kill you and has the talent and the resources to succeed. But he was beginning to wonder whether there was more it than that. Given that it was more than likely that his life at some stage would yet again be in Gentry's hands, as it had so often in the past, he felt it would be nice to think that the man was firing on all six. He had no such confidence now and he probably needed someone else. He made his mind up. The story would be told for the second time in less than an hour.

The food was still good, thank God, although the décor had been transformed into a combination of internet van Gogh and do-it-yourself shop Louis Quinze. Smith talked and Girondou listened. The courses and wines came and went while Smith talked but weren't ignored. It was simply a conversation for one. Arthur was supplied with regular titbits from both their plates from time to time and he clearly decided that under the bright orange tablecloth was a very good place to be. Very good indeed. In the end Smith told the whole story, starting with that Saturday morning thirty-odd years ago in Bologna and finishing with his recent game of chess with Gentry. He left nothing out and included enough subjectivity to make Girondou understand some of the pre-history. He finished just as they finished the meal.

Girondou broke the silence that followed the story-telling.

'I suggest we go for a digestive stroll, my friend and we must decide what to do.'

Smith immediately felt reassured by the use of the word we. Outsiders might have thought that Girondou was a peculiar man to become friendly with. He remained at the very top of the Marseille criminal fraternity and ran most of the well-known operations that one would normally associate with this. He, or rather his people, could be as violent and as nasty as necessary whenever it was necessary and regularly were. Yet because he had a brain, as good an education as was possible to get at the Institut d'Études Politiques in Paris and a highly ordered and analytical mind, he had risen to the top and now stayed there more by negotiation that violence. Other crime families occasionally challenged for power but were usually calmed by a combination of peer pressure and, when rarely necessary, extreme violence. That was, however, always the last resort. While Girondou preferred consent and collaboration he never had any hesitation at all in resorting to more traditional methods of negotiation where necessary. His relationship with his more pragmatic neighbours from Sicily was cordial and entirely mutually productive and the Mafia left him to it. He was also a charming, elegant, sophisticated man with a delightful family and tastes to match. He and Smith had been thrown together during a previous adventure and had immediately got on well. They were very similar in many ways and they both admitted that they would probably been equally successful had their roles been reversed.

Girondou nodded slightly at the couple that were dining a few yards away. They almost immediate got up and left the restaurant. The advance guard would be in place outside the door in seconds. Smith was intrigued to see that they really were a couple, a man and woman. Girondou saw Smith's look.

'Yes, she scares the shit out of me too. She prefers knives.'

'Enough said,' thought Smith, feeling a slight cold shiver.

It was still hot although the light had long gone from the day and Girondou linked his arm familiarly through Smith's as they started to walk along the river. The pale orange street lamps that sporadically spotted the river bank in a un-maintained sort of way barely lit the road way and there were many shadows. Smith was amused to think how safe he felt. His companion started the conversation knowing full well that what he was about to suggest would probably not be received well. He resolved to try in any case.

'There is, my friend, a very simple solution to this rather stupid situation. Say the word and your Hungarian will be out of everyone's life let alone just yours. Half an hour and it is finished. Just say.'

'Romanian.'

'What?'

'Romanian. The man is Romanian.'

Girondou snorted in a sharp way than made Arthur turn his head quickly and look up for a moment without actually breaking step. Girondou was not impressed.

'It was, I'm told, that fine communist Josef Stalin who once said that a difference that makes no difference, is no difference. Whoever he is this man could be a thoroughly dead Romanian in no time at all. He is out of his depth down here. He's not one of us.'

His arm tightened very slightly.

'Just say the word.'

Not for the first time did Smith feel an unusual flush of friendship with this man. He mused yet again at his strange relationship. He, a retired and less than sociable old art historian and part time spy. His companion a sophisticated, successful major criminal. He with a small house and a couple or three thousand Euros to his name. His friend a multi-millionaire with property God-know where. The man could also read his mind.

'It is because you are my friend as I am yours and we both know that that means, especially down here in Provence. I live a precarious life but I know that you will take care of my family if something happens. That is worth more than gold, my new friend. More than gold.'

Smith was curious.

'How did you find him, Alexei?'

'Oh, perhaps you could say it was by chance but in fact it was just because a well-established system worked as it was supposed to. I like to be informed about anyone odd who pops up in the area and who does not fit the usual profiles. All the hotels and many of the Bed and Breakfast places know that I like to know and they usually find it in their interest to let me know if someone appears and they get a feeling that they are not all they seem to be. You know the sort of thing; too many crew-cut yanks in the same place at once, more than the usual number of flics or other official types, members of the competition, people with deep tans in the middle of winter. You know the sort of thing. There are generally not difficult to spot and usually they turn out to be harmless.'

'Christ, you must have an army of people on your switchboard.'

Girondou laughed.

'Not really. The little ones tell the bigger ones and so on up the line and only a few report in every day. If anything seems interesting, we pop along and have a look. As I said, I like to know what is going on.'

Smith couldn't imagine the size of this network but it must be very large. As if reading his mind, Girondou continued.

'Most of them see the virtue of keeping me informed.'

'And the hazards of keeping things from you too, I presume.'

The smile remained broad but hardened a little.

'You might say so, yes.'

They walked on for a moment. It was only because he was trained to see these things that he knew the four guards that cocooning them from intruders were there. Smith smiled at the easy but efficient planning. Had they been walking anywhere but along a river bank, they would have need six and not four. The high river wall protected one flank as the stone wall went thirty feet straight down into the river.

'What gave Grantkov away?'

Girondou smiled.

'He asked for sparkling water with his Pastis and insisted on paying for it when he was served.'

It was Smith's turn to smile. Paying for your drink as soon as you get it is an old piece of tradecraft. He used it himself regularly. The last thing you need if you want to leave in a hurry is a screaming waiter thinking that you are leaving without paying and running after you making a fuss. Grantkov must have be on edge, Smith thought. In his place, he would have taken the risk and paid later or at least made sure enough change was always on the table. The water was just a cultural thing and a mistake. Grantkov had not operated down here before and he obviously had had no one to brief him.

'I still don't see how he would merit your attention.'

'To be honest it didn't but the hotel owner just didn't like the look of him. You get a bit of a feeling for your usual client in a little tourist hotel like that and the guy didn't fit. The owner went in to change the towels when the man was away in his hired car and found a bunch of tell-tales and traps. He simply just noticed a little wedge of paper between the wardrobe doors and a book resting across the top of an overnight case, exactly aligned with the sides. Not the sort of thing that your normal tourist gets up to. A call was made to me and I sent a team to have a quick look. They found the rifle in a simple locked case and the photograph of you and another man who

I presume to be Gentry in a compartment in the bottom of the man's sponge bag in the bathroom. We were lucky that the hotelier is retired foreign legion policeman and knew a little about hiding things.'

'Grantkov would have taken a lot precautions. Your visit has probably been noticed in spite of your man's care.'

Girondou shrugged.

'We found a couple of tiny paper wedges on the floor and replaced them when we left. No talcum powder around baggage clasps or any of that James Bond stuff. We're not amateurs, Peter. In any case I hardly think it matters even if he thinks you are onto him. He may be so worried that he gives the whole thing up and goes home.'

'I doubt it, Alexei, I doubt it.'

His friend quickly consulted his phone and became business-like again.

'So what is it to be my friend? Say the word and the man will be dead within a few moments. Fish food if there are any fish left in the Etang d'Estaque. I have men in St. Remy. The man may be a famed assassin but he is on my patch here.'

Smith shook his head slowly. The prospect was beguiling indeed and he, for one, didn't minimise the favour that he was being offered no matter how much it was owed to him These things were never quite as risk-free as they are portrayed in books. There was no personal profit in this for Girondou and the offer was made purely from friendship. Smith was touched.

'I don't think so, Alexei. Not yet anyhow. I need to know about Gentry. This is a man who I have trusted for years as I trust you now. I find it a little difficult to find out now that he may have been lying to me. If he did it once then he could be doing it still. I need to know and Grantkov is the way I will find out. In the short term we might take him in hand or we might have to let him run and I need to see what Gentry does.'

'And if you find out?'

'Then I will know whether he's my friend or not.'

The consequences of this knowledge were left unsaid and Girondou again tightened his grasp on Smith's arm.

'Christ, Peter. I hope you never come after me.'

'Oh ,there is no chance of that, Alexei. I can think of no reason why I should. You are not a man to let down a friend. In any case…'

'Yes?'

'I could cope with the anger of the entire criminal fraternity of southern France but taking on Angèle and the girls would be a very different kettle of fish.'

The laughter from both was genuine. Smith loved Girondou women almost as much as he loved Martine and his own daughters and they both knew it.

The gangster became business like.

'How can I help, Peter? I'm not going to stand by and watch you get your head blown off just so you can find out whether your oldest friend hasn't always been straight with you. This is a very high risk strategy indeed and although you know that perfectly well, it does no harm for me to point it out. There's another thing, too'

They walked in silence for a little before Smiths said: 'What?'

'You're are not the only person you're putting at risk. This is not the Aubanet's fight but they could take some of the flack. You never know.'

Girondou felt he had to say it but also knew that Smith wouldn't be happy to hear it. He had known this peculiar Englishman only a year or two but he had learned that he had become at the same time his best and most trusted friend and the only person he was really afraid of. The silence extended until they had walked further; a lot further. When Smith's reply came it was, inevitably, not at all what he expected.

'Pull your men off Grantkov at least to an arms distance. He is not quite as stupid as he seems although I am pretty sure that, unusually for him, he is probably acting on his own. He usual MO is to have a large team about him he may not have the experience of doing it all himself. If he has a team, then Gentry should find them. I wouldn't mind a couple of people to watch out for Martine and her father. I doubt whether they are immediately at risk and Jean-Marie is good but I don't want to be worried by all that while I am solving this particular problem.'

Girondou knew better than to revisit the territory. He had only just escaped and was still unsure whether he was, or would be unscathed. He just nodded. 'I'll give you three and Henk.'

Henk was ex-Dutch special forces and had arrived under Smith's auspices during an earlier adventure and stayed as Girondou's Head of Security. Girondou continued:

'Don't worry. Henk has imported a fellow KCT dropouts who can deputise perfectly adequately. Nice man, actually. I think that Nicole is rather sweet on him. What about you. Don't you need someone?'

Smith thought for a moment and nodded.

'I probably should have someone to watch my back for a day or two until I locate Deveraux and get him here. After that it will probably won't be necessary.'

'Deveraux? It will be nice to see him again. I am beginning to feel sorry for Mr Grantkov. He should have let sleeping dogs lie, I feel.'

'Woof,' said Smith without a trace of humour.

It was time to part. A car materialised out of nowhere and Smith saw his friend into the rear seats. Henk flashed a smile of genuine warmth across his shoulder from the driver's seat. Smith leant over the door and half into the car and addressed his friend almost in a quiet whisper.

'I have to know, Alexei. I just have to know.'

Girondou put his hand over Smiths that was wrapped around the frame of the open door.

'Yes, Peter, I understand this because I understand you. What I don't understand is what is going to happen to Gentry if he fails to, shall we say, measure up to your expectations?'

Smith made no reply but closed the door gently and stepped back from the kerbside. He watch the car pull away into the night and looked around to see that he was alone. It was only as he retraced his steps across the Tranquetaille bridge that he saw that the couple were still following about a hundred yards behind.

'The woman who likes knives,' he thought, 'intriguing.'

The game had begun.

Scene 3: Another Chance for Gentry

Gentry showed no sign of being happy about an early morning visitor; quite the contrary. He was grumpy and uncommunicative. Smith kept a silence for a long time, more than five minutes and probably nearer ten. Gentry was impressed and a little intimidated. He had been working off and on with Smith for nearly forty years and he had never seen him quite like this. Wisely he said nothing. With a long sigh, Smith started and Gentry knew better than to interrupt. The roles were reversed and it was Gentry's incompetence or perhaps lack of candour that was the reason. He therefore listened to his friend doing his job for him in an embarrassed silence. He also began to understand the reason for his chess record. Smith was more analytical that he had imagined. The boot was very definitely on the other foot now and his discomfort deepened. Smith started his resume with a sort of tired resignation. Again, Gentry thought sourly, rather unlike the usual Smith.

'It is, in the first place, necessary to separate what needs to concern us now and what is not relevant for the moment no matter how interesting it might be. Grantkov, for whatever reason after all these years, wants to kill us – or rather either of us or both. It's hard to tell at the present. There is also little purpose in speculating why. He does, and that's it. We therefore either have to persuade him not to or prevent his doing so. He seems to have arrived in Provence and it also seems unlikely that he's just on holiday as he had his rifle with him.'

Gentry looked up sharply. He was obviously wondering how Smith knew this but Smith ignored him and went on.

'The motive is irrelevant unless it bears on a potential solution but the time between events in the past and now tends to suggest that it won't. Grantkov uses the long gun and, after that unsatisfactory episode in the train compartment, I suspect he'll probably stick to that. He was never a close-up man and won't want to try anything as intimate again. This gives him a problem with you, Gentry, but not with me. We know that this house isn't overlooked except possibly from a great distance from your glass office on the roof. However if Grantkov has managed to make some ammunition powerful enough to travel more than five hundred yards, go through your armoured glass with enough energy to kill you on the other side, it would have blown up his old Dragunov in his hand before making the journey.'

Gentry wanted to nod but his pride prevented it. He was not enjoying being told how to suck eggs.

'There are no vantage points where he could find a secure firing position to overlook the rest of the house, and in any case, I presume all the windows are made of the same stuff as the office. All you have to do is not leave this house, keep your head down and Grantkov will not be able to get to you. For me the problem is different. I am very visible. My house is a complete security nightmare, surrounded by overlooking properties that are empty for half the year, tourists of all sizes and shapes coming and going from dawn to midnight, carrying a wide variety of parcels, packages and luggage of all sorts any one of which could conceal a fully assembled Dragunov let alone a broken down one. Put the damn thing in a full length Samsonite and put a couple of those dreadfully noise little castors on the bottom and no one, not even the police would bother. I can, of course, solve the problem of the vulnerability of my house by not being there. The mas is much more secure for all the obvious reasons. However there is nowhere that I can really go to ground without endangering others and in any case, one of us has to be out and about and solve this little problem once and for all.'

Smith paused, not expecting an interruption while he thought a little more. None came. He still wasn't sure about Gentry. He still seemed a little detached; displaced even. Smith felt for a missing piece, something that he hadn't known or noticed or guessed. It was an uncomfortable feeling as it was alien to their long relationship. No matter how difficult things had got in the past, and difficult would have been an understatement at times, there was always a companionship that provided a context to solve the problems. It was a bit like a marriage. It was not usually what was said, good or bad, nor was it what was not said when there was no reason to expect it. It was to do with what might have been said when it wasn't necessary or when it was necessary when nothing was said. Those were the words that made a relationship comfortable and secure. Gifts that are neither necessary nor expected are always most valuable. He continued, deciding that action was preferable to introspection and he just gave up on his monologue. He was getting nowhere. Giving Gentry a parting frown he just got up and left the house and made is way thoughtfully out into the hot Arlesian morning.

Chapter 5: Keep Your Enemies Close

Scene 1: The Enemy Identified

Grantkov sipped another Pastis. He sat out of cussedness in the same place. It had immediately crossed his mind to move hotels. All the tell-tales had been back in place when he returned to his room, but he knew. The only way that he wouldn't notice that someone had searched his room was if he hadn't been expecting it. It had been done expertly. But people like him either expected to be under surveillance or they didn't. If you didn't expect it then all the traps in the world wouldn't protect you. You didn't need to see your carefully placed little wedge of paper actually on the floor to know that it had been moved; not if you put it in position in the first place expecting it to be moved. Then you notice. Nothing has been out of place when he returned to his room but he knew. He simply knew. It was the reason he was still alive. He always knew.

However he was worried. Worried because he knew it couldn't have been Smith. Had Smith been in his room he probably wouldn't have known about it. Smith he knew was one of the best, also one of the strangest. He was probably a better field man than most. He was a better spy to use a somewhat overstressed word. He was certainly the best killer Grantkov had even known and, if he was being completely honest, that included himself. People like Smith who did it all for principles were infinitely more dangerous than those, like himself, who did it for the money. But Smith had also been an amateur. Still was, for all he knew. Never a full time spook but a man who worked when he was asked; asked by Gentry that is. Grantkov smiled slightly. It was his one advantage. His one trump card without which he would never have gone up against the strange Englishman and his new life here in the south of France. He, Grantkov, knew about Gentry. Smith didn't. Smith's intervention on that train across the Alps from Venice had been the only reason he had failed. He, like most of his employers, discounted that wretched bomb in Bologna. That was just bad luck. One of those things. But missing Gentry twice in almost as many days had been under his skin for years and he was here to put that right and someone searching his room wouldn't put him off.

So who the hell had searched his room if it wasn't Smith? It wasn't some local thief trying his luck. It is unlikely that they would have been so careful. In any case there was nothing missing. Whoever it was, the gun case had been opened. He was pretty sure of that. Maybe they had been scared away by its contents. A full-blown Russian assault rifle is hardly the sort of thing a casual thief would expect to find in a sleepy Provençale hotel bedroom. He decided not to worry about it any more. What was done was done.

He had spent the day being a tourist. He had hired a car on arrival in Marseille using one of a wide variety of identities that he had used over the years. He had booked himself into one the small hotels in St Remy de Provence and spent the day looking around doing the tourist route around the Camargue. He seldom got out of the car. He still limped slightly on both feet even after thirty years and avoided walking any great distance when he could. Another unpaid debt he thought grimly. Now it was the early evening and the heat had calmed a little. Having showered and changed, he sat in the corner of one of the many little cafés that lined the semi-circular Boulevard Victor Hugo in the town centre, looking out, as ever, watching the passers-by with more than casual interest. He had chosen St Remy because it was small and relatively anonymous. It was near enough to the Camargue and to Arles for convenience and he had been reluctant to stay in the town itself. The chance of his being seen in Arles by either of his two quarries was pretty small but out here some twenty miles away it was infinitesimal. The memory of the chance meeting in Venice was still vivid.

He took a small sip of his Pastis and tried to shake a mood of disappointed lethargy that had descended on him since his return from the hot three hour round trip through what he regarded as boring and unpleasant landscape. He was part financing this particular adventure himself and he had found that none of the smaller cars left at the rental offices at Marseille airport had air conditioning. Pre-booking was not a possibility for a man in his profession. He was reluctant to pay any more than he wanted for a bigger, suitably equipped model because he suspected that the car hire people were just lying to him to get him to pay more and he wouldn't give them the satisfaction. It was a decision he now regretted. The temperature in the Camargue had been a hundred degrees, give or take.

He reflected, somewhat morosely, that killing people was actually not very difficult. In fact it was a lot easier than people imagined. The tricky bit was not getting caught or not dropping your employers in the shit either by getting caught or leaving a trail that investigators could follow. Most people who had hired him over the years knew that. They were professionals too. They also knew that it is the preparation and the planning of the escape that take the time and carry most of the risk and that is what costs the money. The actual act of killing was relatively straightforward. Whatever the method, it had been usually been chosen because it was preferred and thus the killer would be sufficiently skilled for the actual hit itself seldom to be a great problem. For him, he didn't really care whether the target was a five hundred or a thousand yards away. He was a good marksman and he knew his weapon intimately. A more modern weapon than the old Dragunov would not have made him any more effective. He never took on a hit at much more than a thousand yards anyway. He never missed either. More than fifty jobs over thirty years had been completed always with the complete satisfaction of his employers whoever they were. Well, all but one, and that one had weighed heavily on him for the last thirty years. He knew that the particular circumstances of that one failure meant that no-one held it against him. His reputation remained high, even recently when the market had become saturated with young gung-ho men with Rambo mentalities, dripping with technology. Big, senseless children who were also cheap. Only after the inevitable failure was the false economy usually discovered. He had held to his price and let his reputation do the negotiating – except you didn't negotiate with Grantkov. Nobody did. You paid two hundred thousand dollars or hired someone worse and took the risk. He had never been without work.

But it was that one failure that had brought him to Provence. He had never, of course, forgotten about it, but he had forced the embarrassment to the back of his mind and long since learned to ignore the persistently painful memory. However it had been those two or three seconds a month or so ago that had brought it all back; the three seconds during which the momentary flush of satisfaction in another job well done as that woman's head emptied itself over the green velvet curtain turned to anger as he caught a glimpse of the man who all those years ago had shot him and thrown him off a train as it sped through the Alps.

He was now in his fifties and had no intention of retiring yet. After the Venice job he had been spirited quickly away as planned by a fast boat and was landed on the far Croatian coast an hour later. After a quick telephone call to confirm that the balance of his payment was safely in Switzerland he decided not to return to America immediately but went instead to old family home in Bucharest. He usually went to ground for a month or two after a job. The killing never bothered him particularly but he was conscious of the fact the tensions of carrying out an assassination from planning to conclusion could get to him without his actually noticing. He always imposed a couple of months off on himself after a hit. A month that was usually spent reading, walking his dogs, listening to

Bach and cooking for himself; time to himself just in case his subconscious started to remember things that his conscious didn't.

Thus it was only sometime later as he was sitting having supper in his favourite restaurant, the Rossetya on Dimitrie Bolintineanu, that he realised how upset he was. The missed hit was not the problem. Anyone would have missed when the final millisecond of the hit was knocked off line by a bloody great explosion. He had been comfortably set up and his aim had been hit by the shockwave. His bullet had apparently killed the nonentity standing beside his target although he didn't now for certain and he didn't either have the luck to have his original job done by the lethal mixture of TNT and T4 that had killed eighty five people and injured more than two hundred in and around the second call waiting room that summer morning. All that mattered, naturally but it didn't keep him awake at night. It would be nice to finish the job for his own satisfaction but that wasn't really his main concern.

No, what rankled was the man who suddenly appeared behind him in that compartment on the Venice to London Orient Express just as he was about to finish the job left hanging in Bologna a couple of days before. His Milan contacts had told him that a slightly wounded Gentry was being repatriated in a typically arrogant British manner; travelling as a tourist without close protection. He had never done a job on a train before. It was not natural long-rifle country. He would be forced to use a handgun. He hated them. Small, over-complicated, inaccurate and unreliable; he had no experience and certainly no great confidence in the weapon. He would also have to get close and his was really uncomfortable about that. He was not particularly queasy about the prospect itself. You get a very good view through the telescopic sight that was usually mounted on his rifle. No, it was the messiness, the lack of discipline that he didn't like. It was almost an aesthetic thing. He was an academic. Long range, detached, calculated. Apollonian not Dionysiac.

Having walked down the corridor he had arrived at the door to Gentry's compartment having to push past numerous people standing gazing out into country as the night flashed by. He felt uncomfortable and thoroughly uneasy. He hated the bodily contact. Improvisation was never his forte. His delight at seeing the door slightly ajar as well as his wish to get the job over with and leave as quickly as possible completely overrode his natural suspicion and he stepped into the compartment pulling the silenced Makarov from his jacket pocket as he did.

It all happened at once and with a speed he hadn't planned for. In fact, he hadn't really planned anything, so out of context was he, and he paid the price. He was half way through the door, just enough to register that Gentry wasn't there, when the compartment lights suddenly went off and he received a crushing blow to the kidneys from behind that propelled him onto the floor face downwards. He vaguely remembered losing hold of the little gun and hearing the compartment door slamming closed and a lock being turned. A very strong pair of hands picked him up and slammed him bodily backwards onto the seat. It was still completely dark and, looking across the narrow compartment, he could just make out a figure seated across on the other side of the compartment illuminated momentarily from time to time by lights flashing past at nearly one hundred miles an hour. The man was causally but smartly dressed, looked perfectly relaxed had held his own little gun aimed directly and unwaveringly between Grantkov's eyes. The man spoke.

'If you move you die.'

It was a simple opening gambit for the conversation that suddenly filled Grantkov with dread. He knew he was minutes from death; possibly seconds, at the hands of a man he had never seen in his life. It was obvious and the people in Milan hadn't told him. The British had sent a shepherd.

Suddenly his head exploded with pain as the man opposite ripped the gun across his face with extreme violence and the warm sensation of blood trickling down to his neck confirmed that his face was split from one side to the other. The man spoke again:

'Who ordered the hit on Gentry?'

Grantkov knew that nothing would save him and in a last act of defiance, said nothing. How the hell did this man know he was after Gentry not the other man. No-one, he was sure, knew that. The gun in the man's hand coughed asthmatically and the pain from his face was replaced by the agony of a shattered foot. The man repeated in the same flat voice:

'Who ordered the hit on Gentry?'

Another silence. The additional pain from the second foot made him pass out.

Later in hospital he learned that he had fallen from the train. He had had the luck to hit some thick hedging and by complete good fortune he had come to rest with only some broken ribs, two damaged feet and a lot of bruising and multiple lacerations which at least served to disguise the injuries to his face. All this was easily explained after he had been taken to a local hospital by a good Samaritan who had been walking his dog and had nearly been brained by the flying Romanian as the body rushed over his head and landed in a track-side bush. The bullet wounds in both feet to a little more explaining to the curious junior doctor in charge of the emergency department. It had taken a considerable amount of persuasion to prevent the anxious young man from calling in the police. A number of pointed but general references to the Mafia and what would happen to the doctor and his family if he did call the police managed finally to dissuade him.

Only much later he learned that the man was called Smith but his contacts had been much less than helpful when he tried to find out more. Being freelance he was on his own and he found that most people thought it was not their responsibility to supply information about the man who had tried to kill him. Over the next few years he had found bits and pieces but a clear picture never formed and other things took precedence as he had to re-create his career after his recovery. Smith and the failed hit faded into the past as new clients who, of course, fell over themselves to tell him how little it mattered as their desire to complete their own particular projects overrode the doubt that one completely understandable failure should have engendered. The pain of the whole episode, rather like the agony in his feet, had faded with time. Or rather more important things took its place.

A second Pastis was requested and delivered and he started to think things through. In Venice a few weeks ago, Smith had suddenly become visible again and the hurt had returned in a rush. It took very little effort for Grantkov to decide that now, some thirty years later, was the time to kill him and, having made some enquiries of friends who owed him more now than they had thirty years ago, he found where Smith was and that he had come out of the woodwork thanks to some sort of geriatric infatuation with a local Provençale beauty and her family. It was only after probing further through some people back at Langley, Virginia who seemed to be better disposed to him than they were to Smith, that he discovered to his joy that Gentry was living in the same place. In fact someone by a mysterious coincidence that he didn't really believe in had got in touch with him soon after he contacted Langley and volunteered to finance both hits. The offer was considerably less that his usual fee but as he would have been willing to do the job for nothing, he was happy to halve his price. The offer did make him stop and think for a little as he seemed to be getting involved in someone else's problem but that was ever thus, he thought. He had his own reasons for doing the job and if someone else wanted it done as well and would pay, then so much the better. He would have done the job for nothing if necessary. It was to be Arles in the south of France. Two birds with one stone as they say, thought Grantkov as he set himself to planning.

It seems completely facile to say that the most important thing to do if you are planning to kill someone is to know where they will be at the moment you intend to kill them. It is difficult to kill someone who isn't there. But it happens to be true and to be certain about where your target will be is much more difficult that most people might imagine. Creatures of habit, of routine, are the easiest because to find out where people are, you first have to learn where they go. You have to watch them. A person who does the same thing every day, travels to work on the same train, leaves work at the same time, opens his shop at nine o'clock every day except Monday, goes to visit her mother every Sunday morning. These are the easiest. Having established the routine you can assume what will happen in the future. Extrapolate. All you have to do then is plan what to do if the person does not follow the routine on the day you have chosen. Usually you just put it all off until the next day when the routine is resumed.

This initial watching is probably the most difficult part of any assassination plan. Watching people is dangerous. It is perfectly easy to avoid being seen by the person you are watching, especially if they don't expect to be watched. Even if they do, it is not hard to avoid detection. Literary fiction is full of accounts of heroes that can 'feel' that they are being followed or watched. Grantkov knew that this was complete rubbish. Following someone without being spotted is very easy indeed. No, the danger comes not from being spotted by your target but by others who might actually have no idea what is going on. Someone standing in the proverbial doorway watching for someone for any length of time will invariably be seen by others. It is virtually impossible to avoid. Invisibility rests not in actually not being seen but in others who might observe the watcher ascribing no importance to the sighting. There is a difference between being seen and being observed. People tend not to see what they don't regard as odd, or important, or unusual. The longer you stand in one place or the more regularly you appear somewhere at the same time then more likely it is that you will be seen and, human curiosity being what it is, you will be found out. The very routine that makes your quarry vulnerable does the same to you the watcher. Thus routines have to be established and identified very quickly.

Assumptions have to be made about the future, checked a few times and then left alone. People who avoid routine either by habit or by training present a problem of entirely different magnitude. These people are not predictable and therefore often require more observation with a corresponding increase in risk to the observer.

So far he hadn't even got to first base with either of them. Gentry's house in the middle of town wasn't overlooked nor were there any convenient cafés to spend time innocently waiting for comings and goings. He had spotted Gentry once going in through a very narrow doorway that he seemed not to unlock with a key. Whether he came out again at any time was a mystery as there was really nowhere to watch from. Gentry wasn't a creature of routine as he didn't seem to do anything that required one. It was already apparent that he would somehow have to entice his target out and make him come to meet him.

Smith presented a different but equal problem. Smith was highly visible, to him at least. He lived in a small house in a square next to the Roman Amphitheatre with a small walled garden at the back. Both sides were overlooked by other buildings some of which were holiday lets and thus empty for much of the year. Plenty of possible gun positions. But not in the summer. There were also a lot of locals living in the surrounding houses all of whom would have infallible radars for spotting strangers. Smith spent considerable time at his girlfriend's farm in the Camargue. As a result of the day's sweaty excursion Grantkov had decided that this was not a good place to work. He personally hated farmers and the countryside. Farmers have sharp eyes and insatiable curiosities. The mas he had driven around earlier this afternoon was in the middle of a huge piece of land which was flat as a pancake. No vantage places at all. The chances of his getting close enough to any of the buildings to take even a log shot without being spotted by some local with too much time on his hands were remote. The hit would have to be in Arles.

However, what made Smith a difficult was his lack of routine. He came and went seeming without taking any precautions but there was no pattern to his coming and goings. Grantkov stared into the milky interior of his Pastis and contemplated the problem. This whole adventure was getting more complicated than he wanted.

Scene 2: The Enemy Closer

In general, Smith mused as he sat uncomfortably in the small, straight-backed armchair, it was better to make a rendezvous in a place of one's own choosing. Whatever one's own terms in whatever the circumstances are, it is better to decide for oneself where to do things if at all possible. Meetings with friends or business associates, battles with massed armies of competing countries, all usually went better if they take place where you want rather than at someone else's preference. In most sports he had ever heard of, playing at home, as they say, usually gives an advantage of some sort.

Having decided that he wanted to talk to Grantkov before killing him, his would be the choice of location. Grantkov was presumably scouting a similar location for himself to dispose of Smith but he was not set on conversation. He was looking for a sniper's pitch. So in Smith's case the choice hadn't been particularly difficult. A touch unconventional, perhaps, insofar as there is a convention for this sort of thing, but not particularly difficult.

Practitioners of the many and various methods of killing someone have their own idiosyncrasies and preferences. There are ways of doing things that they have developed over time and the more they practice what they do, the more habits get ingrained. Also the further from their preferences they have to stray, out of their comfort zone, as they say, the less they like it and the less good they are likely to be at performing. Getting in close to someone with a knife is pretty personal and equivalently dangerous. Close with a hand gun is slightly less so but still personal. Hand guns, irrespective of wild claims of superhuman accuracy made by Hollywood, are in reality quite difficult things to shoot straight. Not for nothing does the classic attack stance while using a hand gun – any hand gun – now so universally known through TV cop movies, show that holding the thing in two hands is better than in one. To be as sure of a kill a good assassin needs a very short distance between gun and victim. Surprising short, in reality. Go beyond twenty five yards and the whole thing becomes chancy even for a professional. Little more than a cricket pitch. Shooting someone from the front is more emotionally charged than from the back. The emotional content reduces as the distance from the victim increases, as does the sense of personal involvement. So do accuracy and the chances of success.

An assassin who uses a rifle is probably the least personally involved of all and is often the most intellectually detached. He is a sniper of whom there are many in or retired from the armed services around the world. The mythology of the snipers had been long developing throughout twentieth century in parallel with the technology. A recent film about Russian and German snipers at the siege of Stalingrad during the Second world War became a huge hit. Killing someone from a mile away seems more romantic than just throwing a grenade at them from behind a wall.

Contrary to received wisdom on the matter it's not at all difficult to use a long gun and use it reasonably well; well enough to kill people more often than not, that is. Presupposing that you have a gun that is capable of firing the right bullet over the required distance, all you have to do is hold it steady and point it in the right direction. Simple. Both these things increase in difficulty with range but in principal the variables remain the same. Just the size of the margin for error alters. Holding the rifle steady is just a matter of making sure that when you actually fire, the rifle stays as nearly as possible in the same place as when you aimed. The best position is lying down on your stomach relatively square to the gun which rests against the shoulder with the legs straight out, feet splayed out behind, slightly angled away to the side in the opposite the firing hand. Technology here has helped as well with most modern long guns being equipped with a set of bipod legs that should hold the gun as steady as a tripod does a camera. If you have to stand or kneel then the preference is to rest the gun one something. Totally free standing positions are less accurate but even then there are ways on minimising extraneous movement.

Next comes regulating the body itself, breathing, heart rate, muscular tension, grip of both hands, so that the trigger is pulled with the minimum of collateral movement.

The last major set of variables is probably the most difficult to learn but they are mostly finite. While the distance to target is the most obvious, the path the bullet will travel – and therefore where it will actually end up - will depend on a variety of issues. Presupposing the gun that sends the bullet on its way is not shaking too much – and they all do to some extent – then the shooter has to consider such things as the aerodynamic and physical characteristics of the bullet, the nature of the explosive and the speed it will set the bullet off, the bullet's momentum and its deterioration over the chosen range, the characteristics of the spin give to it by the rifling on the gun barrel. The range has to be established, height differential between gun and target, wind direction and speed and variations in them, the atmospheric pressure and variations in air temperature over the bullet's path. If the shot is truly a long one of over 1000 yards there can be wide variations is atmospheric conditions along the way. There are others variables.

Getting all thus stuff right requires practice and lots of it. Huge amounts. The shooter will always know what to do. He just needs to make sure that he always does it. Time after time with no variations. Hours and hours of solitary practice, concentration, observation and evaluation. Thousands and thousands of round fired on solitary, secure ranges. This sort of practice takes a long time and this is where the solitude comes in. Learning to be a long range killer is thus a solitary business and it is hardly surprising that for many of these people their preference is for jobs that require the extremes of range rather than close quarter work. The more the job replicates the practice, the greater the chances of success. Given that the free market sniper is likely to be engaged in an activity that is usually regarded outside the specific and legal protection of the army or similar places where killing people is legal, much if not all of this practice would be done on his own. Hours and hours of solitude, engaged in what is mostly a thoroughly cerebral activity.

Additionally there are a number of bits of research that need to be done each time a shot is planned. The location has to be explored and a shooting position selected. The size and activities of the target and anyone who is likely to be with him or her. Timetables have to be established. Planning for a moving target or a stationary one, an open or a protected one. Planning of the all-important exit from the scene.

While some of the lower-end stuff could theoretically by given to others, much of the crucial exploration and observation would be the shooters alone. All this means that most snipers remain solitary people, used to long periods away from home if they have one, on their own with few people they know around them. They have a silent and clandestine life and often their mentalities match.

Smith assumed that Grantkov had come to Provence to kill him or Gentry or both and he would expect to see them through the standard PSO telescopic sight that he used with his Dragunov rifle. Close but only optically.

Which is why Smith was now sitting in the small armchair next to the neat single bed in Grantkov's St Remy de Provence hotel room while Grantkov was sipping is Pastis less than two hundred yards away. Three yards would be very close indeed for a man who habitually did business at more than a three hundred times that distance. The Dragunov was laid out neatly on the bed beside him, full assembled but not loaded. It had crossed Smith's mind in a uncharacteristically frivolous moment that he should use it to keep the Romanian quiet while taking to him. Grantkov would have more than the usual respect for what it could do. But it took as long for Smith to dismiss the idea as being stupid it would have taken Grantkov to realise the same thing. He had toyed with the idea of putting Grantkov's Dragunov across his knees but also rejected the idea as altogether too theatrical. In any case Grantkov's 1980s iteration of the much produced weapon was still over a yard in length and weighed about twelve pounds and therefore not exactly ideal for close quarter work. In the end he just laid it symbolically on the bed beside him and put his faith in his little Glock 30 that now rested in the palm of his right hand. That too, as Smith new, would probably not be necessary. He didn't think that the Romanian carried a hand gun and in any case Smith was very good with the Glock. He laid his phone on the bed next to it.

The bedroom was again decorated in that style that hoteliers and restaurateurs seem to think is expected of them in the south of France, bright yellows and blues, olive branches and bunches of grapes. The bed linen matched the wallpaper and furniture. Smith felt a headache coming on.

He sat perfectly still and waited, prepared, if necessary to be there for hours. It was early afternoon and the temperature outside had crept into the mid-eighties. Grantkov had left his air conditioning on low and given its age and its position under the window it made little or no difference to the room other than to raise the general noise level. He also felt perfectly relaxed. The observant manager had already seen him and undoubtedly Girondou had been told within a minute or two of his arrival in the hotel. He knew that in spite of his wish to be left alone, the Marseille gangster would have ignored him and would have people around, probably lots of them. Smith felt annoyed and comforted in equal measure.

He had placed his chair so that Grantkov had to come almost completely into the room before he saw him. The last thing that Smith wanted was for the man to duck back out into the corridor leaving a question as whether to indulge in an undignified chase that would serve only to embarrass him and amuse passers-by.

About an hour later he heard the room telephone tinkle for less than a second before falling silent again. Smith smiled at kindness, unnecessary as it was. He hadn't fallen asleep.

It was, Smith realised, little more fraught than a meeting of two old friends in some gentleman's club in London; two people who hadn't seen each-other for a long time but saw reason neither for histrionics nor even formalities. The Romanian had stepped briskly and rather carelessly into the room and then stopped, immobile, looking only at the 9mm barrel of Smith's silenced Glock that was pointing unwaveringly at the middle of his forehead as the door swung closed behind him. Smith found himself wondering if the Provencal heat had caused the somewhat incautious entrance. Normally you would be somewhat more circumspect. Smith felt a slight pang of sympathy. Perhaps the old assassin was losing his hitherto infallible touch. Then he remembered the Dragunov. His nose of his Glock dipped momentarily. Grantkov got the message and just subsided gently to the ground, back sliding down the wall, sitting cross legged with his back against the wall, hands out in front of him wrists resting on his folded knees. They both knew what was expected. It was a sort of etiquette rather like using your cutlery in the right order. If you come from the same class you know what to do. Smith felt no need to search the man. Grantkov was completely useless with a hand gun and never carried one. If he had a knife, Smith wasn't particularly bothered, at least while he was three yards away. Monosyllables rules the opening exchange.

'Grantkov.'

'Smith.'

It was an opening gambit worthy of Johannes Zukertort. Dry, uncommitted, redolent of possibilities to come but completely undemonstrative; a pair of almost automatic opening moves followed by silence. Grantkov glanced at the dark hole that was the end of the barrel of the Dragunov. From his position on the floor, his head was directly level with it as it lay on the bed and it was pointing directly at his right eye. He seemed more concerned about that than a similar if more pertinent dark hole in the end of the long silencer of Smith's Glock that was pointing in the same place. That, Smith thought, was understandable. The Romanian knew what the rifle could do.

As he had arranged the meeting, Smith felt that he should at least make a start. He favoured a direct approach and ignored any pleasantries.

'Is it me or Gentry you have come here to try to kill?'

Grantkov remained silent and watched immobile as the Glock lower slightly. This time it pointed directly between the Romanian's legs. The man shifted uncomfortably as Smith answered the unasked questions.

'The silencer is brand new and therefore this little gun will make as much noise as a sparrow's fart as it destroys what is described in more polite circles than this as your manhood. It's loaded first with two rounds of 147gram Subsonic Red Tracer that will liquidise and then boil your insides without ever coming out the other side. One between your legs and one in the stomach before you are half way through saying 'Ceausescu'. You will cook from the inside out.'

It was no surprise to see Grantkov shifting uncomfortably.

'Also if you think that the local population, the police, the hotel staff or any other Tom, Richard or Henri will be concerned about you and your demise then perhaps you might like to ask yourself why I am sitting in your bedroom rather than you in mine. A lot of my people know you're here. This is my part of the world, not yours and you wont leave Provence without my say-so - ever. Don't let the Armani suits and the new Mercedes fool you. Provence can be as primitive as your beloved Balkans when it tries. So. I will ask again – for the last time. Who have you come here to kill?'

Grantkov saw Smith's knuckle whiten very slightly as he took up the first two of the six pounds of standard trigger pressure that are required to fire the gun. It seemed to concentrate the man's mind.

'Your friend,' he grunted. 'You're just my personal bonus.'

Smith now knew for certain then that Gentry had been the target in Bologna. He didn't bother asking how the man had survived the fall from the train. He had, and that was all that really mattered. Grantkov started to squirm a little. Clearly the bits of Smith's lead that he was still carrying with him in his folded feet made his current seating position less than comfortable. Smith just shook his head slightly and the man stopped.

'Next question, my friend. Is this current little adventure of yours a private thing, an attempt to make up for the one that got away, so to speak, or are you under contract again.'

The man remained silent. Smith sighed.

'In all probability, Grantkov, this is the first time in your life you have been talked to like this, so I feel I must make some allowance for that. You have never been caught before, I suppose. So let me offer you some advice. This is a friendly chat. If the chat doesn't give me what I want, then we will progress to the next stage which usually known as an interrogation. Now there are many different sorts of interrogation, of which I have had some unfortunate experience. Never nice; often completely horrid. Whatever sort it is, they all involve pain to some degree, often of an extreme sort. Now most of the things that can be done to you will result in making you into a very noisy Romanian and this hotel room is perhaps not the ideal place when you start screaming your head off. Everybody does, of course. Don't imagine for one moment that you will be some sort of exception. I know a lot of tricks but I am sure that my local chums are much more creative than I could even be. If you don't tell me what I want to know I will probably ask them to take you to some bit of Marseille untouched by either time or tourists and play with you until you do. After that in the unlikely event that you are not already dead, they will kill you.'

Smith looked across at his immobile companion and smiled broadly.

'So what is it to be, Valery Maximovich? You talk to me without pain and enjoy the very remote possibility that you might survive if you can convince me that you are no longer a threat or I pass you to my chums in Marseille to whom you will certainly talk and equally certainly die.'

'Just in case, by the way, you are thinking of pulling a fast one: that you can rely on my good offices to let you live if you tell me what you think I want to know, I will in any case hand you over to Marseille for safe-keeping while I verify what you tell me. Your possible survival depends on your truthfulness. If you tell me porkies or I am unable to verify what you tell me then plan B goes into effect when I say so. Conveniently you will already be their guest in some little dark, damp dockside room somewhere near the Quai du Maroc.'

'So,' Smith continued adopting a much harder stare, 'Let's try again. Contract or freelance'.

Grantkov had obviously never been trained to resist interrogation so it all came rather too easily.

'You are my personal problem. Gentry is a contract.'

'A new contract on Gentry. Now?'

Grantkov just nodded.

Smith thought about it. That Grantkov was after him, after the sighting in Venice, was no great surprise. Revenge. Pretty silly, in reality, but no surprise. But a new contract for Gentry was a bit surprising. There had been plenty of opportunities in the past for this to happen and it hadn't. The disturbing possibility did exist that Gentry was moonlighting from his retirement without telling Smith and that a contract arose from that. But Smith thought this was unlikely while admitting to himself that he had no reason for thinking so. Smith felt momentarily very sad that the possibility that his old friend was keeping even more secrets from him, something that would have been unthinkable to him a few weeks ago.

'And I was added to your personal hopping list after seeing me in Venice?'

Grantkov just nodded.

'No contract?'

'No.'

'Keep going on like this Grantkov and you will be getting a reputation as a soft touch.'

The man just grunted. A thought struck Smith.

'The opera singer. What was that all about?'

Grantkov shrugged.

'It was a Romanian thing.'

Smith decided not to pursue the matter. He really wasn't very interested but some sort of explanation for Martine would have been nice. Smith changed tack.

'Who placed the Bologna contract on Gentry?'

'I have no idea,' replied Grantkov. 'It was placed through the usual cut outs. As with all my jobs, I never knew.'

Smith shook his head sadly.

'That is bullshit, and we both know it. People like you always know where your contracts come from. They may think they are anonymous but you know. It is safety for you in case they don't pay properly. In your particular case it was essential as you didn't want to take a contract on an American as you would have found your residence privileges revoked. You had to know. So who wanted Gentry dead?'

There as another long silence. Grantkov looked very sheepish; embarrassed even.

'I don't know how I can make you believe me but I really didn't know. Really. The contract came through an intermediary – probably more than one as far as I know. They paid a lot for those days and all in advance. I took the job because I knew Bologna and knew it was an easy shot. I had worked there before. I swear to you I didn't know who it was or why. All I got was a description and a time and place – and the money, of course.'

'How much?'

'Fifty thousand.'

'Dollars, pounds or what?'

'Swiss Francs.'

Smith frowned. It was rather a lot of money in those days.

'Very neutral, I'm sure.'

Smith pondered the problem. Swiss francs made it difficult to trace. It was a currency as anodyne as the country that gave rise to it. He was also disposed to believe Grantkov. The man was obviously unhappy and a great deal more scared than he pretended. If he really didn't know who hired him to kill Gentry then he was of little more use. Perhaps, Smith mused, he has more information than he thinks. Only one way to find out. Scare him more.

'Well if you have nothing else to give me, Grantkov, I might as well hand you over to my friends from Marseilles. I have no further interest in you but I certainly don't want you roaming around with long gun and a desire for revenge. You understand that, don't you?'

Grantkov remained stony-faced. He knew his life hung by a thread. Smith continued.

'You might like to consider your answer to my next question very carefully indeed, for it may, as they say in all the best movies, be your last. The question is, quite simply, have you any information about that contract in Bologna all those years ago that might save your life now?'

Grantkov sighed gently.

'Nothing, I'm afraid.'

Smith nodded. The man was as good as dead.

'Except.....'

Smith inwardly acknowledged the man's sense of the dramatic.

'Except what?'

Grantkov raised his head slowly and looked at Smith with a wry smile.

'Mine may not have been the only contract on your friend Gentry that day.'

Smith didn't succeed in disguising his surprise. It had been enough to find that Gentry was the original target but to hear that his quiet, unassuming and normally office-bound friend had two people wanting to kill him at the same time was unthinkable. A thought struck him.

'Different clients or one just trying to make sure?'

Grantkov thought for a moment, presumable trying to decide whether it was better to offer Smith anything he knew. He was actually convinced that unless something extraordinary happened he was not going to leave that pokey little Provençale bedroom alive. His luck, he felt, had finally run out.

'I tried to find out, of course, as soon as I got hold of the rumour from, shall we say, a friend in the trade. He had been approached but was already booked. He actually recommended me and got the impression that his contact was not too happy with the suggestion. My personal feeling was that it was one client trying to make doubly sure.'

Having finally got the man talking, Smith tried to keep the conversation going. It was highly unlikely that everything was true but in these circumstances one never actually knows.

'Did you get any impression while you were setting up? See anything?'

Grantkov shook his head slightly.

'Nothing at all. Maybe whoever it was probably there in the station with them. Maybe it was a handgun or a knife. Close stuff. Not my thing. Maybe the man got vapourised with the explosion. Who knows?'

'How far away were you?'

'Less than a hundred yards. High and behind.'

Smith thought about this for a moment. Then another, slightly less welcome thought struck him. If indeed there was a second hit maybe it wasn't on Gentry.

'What do you know about the man who was with Gentry at Bologna? Was the second hit on him? And, by the way, just because you have decided on a little conversation, don't think that I am believing anything you are saying. Unless you convince me, you are a very dead Romanian. I won't miss this time. I promise.'

It took the slightest of glances at the unwavering Glock to convince Grantkov that this was indeed true. The man gave a slight shrug.

'I can only tell you what I heard.

Smith sighed silently and suddenly he felt a bit bored. Bored because he really wished he was somewhere else. Anywhere else for that matter. It would be an exaggeration to say he had been here many times before and he was thus in not unfamiliar territory. Sometimes he had been on the receiving end. He had occasionally been the one squatting uncomfortably against a wall in a way that made fast movement difficult if not impossible. He had been the one a few ounces of trigger pressure away from death and he knew that all hope was still not absent. Even then he knew that a whiff of a chance might appear before that final moment and he had to be ready for it; this last chance before he died. The signs were always there. Signs that his captor would lose concentration momentarily, would suddenly doubt himself for an instant, would think of something else for a second. The sign would be in the tightness of the finger around the trigger or, more likely, in the man's face; his mouth or the corners of his eyes. Body language is at the same time an imprecise and an exact science and he owed his life to the fact that he had spent a lot of his life thinking about it. He looked straight into Grantkov's eyes and saw clearly that the Russian was thinking exactly the same thing. He knew and his smile told the Russia that he knew as well. The Russian sagged visibly. This time there would be no slip ups and Grantkov knew it - probably.

What Smith working on was keeping from the man the fact that he actually really didn't want to kill him. Had he been certain that the man was going to kill him, he would not have hesitated for a second. Grantkov would have been dead already and Girondou's people would be clearing up the mess. No, he felt that he wasn't actually the target in spite of throwing the man off the train all those years before. Some things were generally accepted as hazards of war and usually generated little long-term animosity, in spite of the injuries that Grantkov still lived with. Professional assassins couldn't afford to harbour grudges. He had been told that Gentry was still the main target. Gentry was his best and longest friend so the decision to send the Romanian on to whatever next life awaited him would have been equally easy in the normal course of events. But this time he wasn't sure. Now he wasn't completely sure about Gentry being the target. More importantly he felt uncertain for the first time in all the years they had known each other and worked together. What made him feel disappointed was that now he had to make his mind up. Either the Romanian or Gentry. Something of a difficult choice he felt.

The satellite phone on the bed beside him vibrated silently. Smith was expecting it while Grantkov was startled. He glanced across the space and saw immediately that neither Smith's eye nor the Glock had moved. There was no chance to miss.

'Yes?'

Smith called out an unnecessarily loud voice that one always uses in using a machine on 'hands free'. The phone was voice-activated. A tinny Dutch accent came through the phone.

'Henk'

'Come'

The phone went dead and it was only a few seconds before a tall, good looking Dutchman came through the door and crossed to Smith's side. Smith was pleased to see that the man was not carrying a gun. It was entirely too small a space for that. Without taking his eyes off Grantkov Smith greeted him.

'Good to see you Henk. How are you?'

'Can't complain, thank you sir. And you?'

'Never better, Henk, never better.'

'The boss asked me to pop in and see if I can help at all.'

Give the man his due, thought Smith, Grantkov had not moved a muscle. He was obviously assessing what was happening but he still knew that whatever it was, Smith's Glock was pointing exactly at the centre of stomach. It hadn't moved for some time. Neither had he. Sitting in that position had its own difficulties. The longer he sat the less able he was to move quickly. He knew it and so did Smith.

Henk had been one of Smith's additions to Girondou's personal staff during a previous little adventure. He had retired after a career in the Dutch KCT shortened by a couple of youthful errors of judgement, He seems to have taken well to a life in the south of France and after a few training sessions in odd places around the world organised by Gentry, he had turned into as good a bodyguard as one could want. He would probably never up to Deveraux's standard but close is close enough in that particular case. The man waited silently. Smith addressed his captive.

'I am afraid I need to know more, Valery Maximovich and I think you know more. This is obviously not a good place to continue this conversation so I am going to hand you over to Henk here who will take you to somewhere safe and continue to ask you for some answers to some questions. You will be quite safe from the world in his care, I can assure you and believe me, these Marseilles people know more about interrogation that you or I can possibly imagine. Don't whatever you do, underestimate them. These people were doing things to people that you and I can only dream about two thousand years ago when the Romans were here. Believe me they won't have lost their touch'

He saw a slight flicker for fear in the man's eyes. The unknown always did that and for the first time he knew that that was where he was heading. Smith addressed the Dutchman.

'Take him away, would you? You will receive instructions on your way back to Marseille.'

Henk quickly crossed over to the supine Grantkov, effortlessly lifted him up to standing position, turned him around and put in him what popular American television programmes often call 'the position', feet apart, well back, hands taking the weight against the wall. Quickly and none too gently Henk pushed the man hard against the wall, pulled the man's hands behind him and snapped a plastic cable tie around the man's wrists and marched him out of the door. Smith sat still for a moment and thought about what to do next. He knew he needed a bit of time to think things through but first some arrangements needed to be made. He reached for the satellite phone and pressed the speed dial. Girondou answered immediately as he always did. Smith was always complimented when that happened. Girondou spent much of his life up to his neck in the most complicated international deals in almost an infinite variety of criminal activities yet still answered his calls before the third ring.

'Peter, my friend, I gather that we are babysitting your Romanian for a while.'

A slight smile crossed Smiths face and he replied.

'Yes, if you would, Alexei. You know enough about this little business to know what I want out of him. I think that you will be better than I at getting that.'

A rich chuckle came across the link.

'You mean we will be less squeamish than you, I think. This is most unlike you, Peter. You're not getting old are you?'

Smith refused the bait and just sighed in a theatrical way.

'I think you know better than that, Alexei. I just don't think he is entirely at the centre of whatever all this is. Grantkov is a simple paid killer, insofar as there is such a thing. He is a good man with a long gun, careful as well. He is reliable and trustworthy but he is no Einstein. All this seems to be much too complicated for him to have anything more than a bit part. In any case I need to know what he knows about Bologna thing. I also need to check if he knows anything about McDowell. I didn't get around to asking. In any case that particular little adventure smells a little American to me.

Girondou replied evenly.

'What you mean is that you want to know whether Gentry has been lying to you over all these years and part of you is afraid that you might find out that he has been. That, as we both know, is something that you couldn't handle easily. Hence you are asking me to do some your dirty work for you.'

The empty silence over the satellite phone seemed longer than perhaps it was. Smith knew that Girondou was right, of course. The possibility of finding disloyalty in someone who he had previously regarded as his greatest friend was something that he was really afraid of. For a man who made it his business not to have too many people close to him, his friendship with Gentry was one of the rocks on which he had built his life. He was still deep in thought when he realised that the Frenchman had cut the connection.

He left Grantkov's rifle on the bed where it lay. It would be collected by Girondou's people later. The manager met him at the bottom of the stairs and handed over Arthur who had been spending the last hour being spoiled rotten by the hotel staff. He bore that unmistakable air of a greyhound full of croissant and pizza. Smith thanked the man for the variety of services that he had rendered that day and went out into the car park. He noticed that someone had moved his car into the shade without, if course, the need of keys. Smith smiled slightly at more evidence of Girondou's ubiquity in this part of the world. As he drove out of the little yard behind the hotel and turned in the vague direction of home, he felt depressed. He needed to think clearly. He also needed to talk to someone; someone who could help him make sense of what seemed to him to be an unholy mess. He pressed the speed dial on his phone and Martine answered within a couple of rings.

'Dinner tonight?'

'Lovely. Here or in town?'

'At mine, I think. I feel like cooking.'

A rich laugh came across the airwaves from someone who not only could cook extremely well herself, who lived on a farm with a father whose cook was easily the best in the area but who also owned a number of little restaurants scattered around the Camargue and its environs where the food was as startlingly good as the restaurants were anonymous.

'What you mean, my love, is that you want some time to think and then someone to discuss things with without anyone seeing us doing it. Feeding me would seem to be a thoroughly efficient way of accomplishing all that.'

Smith immediately felt defensive.

'I don't suppose, my dear, that I just wanted to cook you a meal.'

She wisely decided not to continue. She knew how this whole business was getting to him, especially after McDowell's death, and she knew that her role was to keep him from sinking too far down to find the solution. She had never actually met Gentry although she knew a lot about him. It was a separate part of Smith's life that she respected. But she knew that Smith's relationship with his friend went well beyond his just being useful from time to time. It was not something that he ever talked about but she knew.

'What time?'

'About eight thirty if that's OK. Oh. And could you ask Jean-Marie to drive you?'

The reason was obvious and she didn't ask him to explain. He was circling the wagons around his family.

'Of course. See you at half past eight.'

Scene 3: Food for Thought

It was a Wednesday and by the time he would arrive back in Arles, the smaller of the two weekly Arles street markets would be finished and cleared away. Secretly he was quite pleased as it meant that he was not forced by his conscience to do his food shopping there. Arles' markets were famous but Smith was never really sure why. The food was not really better that the big supermarket to which he was now headed. They were certainly more expensive. There were fresh meat and fish stalls but again what you actually bought was often not remarkable. Some of the fruit and vegetables, commodities for which the area around Arles is justly famous, were good but a lot of what is sold is far from that. Smith often felt that many farmers, who of course, could have found it difficult to make a living just out of Arles and some neighbouring markets, used the tourist attraction of the long Saturday market that stretched the length of the Boulevade des Lices - much further if you include the clothes and bric-a-brac – as a good way of getting rid of stuff to an impressionable public at inflated prices. The Wednesday market was smaller than the Saturday one but only a little better or cheaper. So he headed to the aptly-named Géant Casino on the large commercial park stationed between the town and the autoroute. In all events Arles was not particularly well equipped with food shops. There were two butchers, one good and the other less so. There were no good green groceries. It was a continuing irony that in a town that was surrounded by some of the best fruit and vegetable growing land in Europe it was particularly difficult to find fresh produce other than on the market. There was a newly opened farmers collective shop buried in Griffeuil, ironically one of the poorest parts of Arles, but it was stupidly expensive and one had to join some sort of group to have the privilege of buying something. Not Smith's sort of thing at all.

The meat counter was first and he saw a good looking piece of veal hiding unloved in the corner of a refrigerated display case. Political correctness had taken its time to arrive in the south of France and it was still possible to get veal that tasted of meat. The piece made up his mind for him. Rather than doing something either Provençale or, indeed French at all, and risk putting Martine is a position of having to say something nice when she knew she could do something much, much better, he decided to go Italian with a simple *scallopine al limone*. Many years ago he had visited Italy regularly and had been taught a few dishes in the kitchen ruled by the black-clad mother of his Fiesole-based chum with whom he used to stay. Most lemon sauces that you get on menus in restaurants is made in bulk and stored, necessitating the use of much flower and preservatives. They were thick, glutinous and horrible. The old woman's recipe was simplicity itself because it understood that in great *scallopine al limone* it was the meat that tasted of lemon not the sauce. The veal marinated for a while in lemon, a little olive oil, salt and pepper. Nothing more. It was then fried quickly in a hot pan with butter and trace of olive oil; a pan large enough to make the sauce at one side on the heat while keeping the meat hot but not cooking at the other. No flour in this recipe, just lemon and white wine and a touch of cream. Flour nearly always made the result thick and look revolting. A tiny sprinkle of thyme completes the dish. It was have not been the traditional restaurant way of doing it, as it requires last minute cooking - never popular with any chef. A few pan roasted potatoes and a tomato salad would fill the plate. Cheese and fresh fruit would suffice although he knew that Martine would pick up a few of Madame Leblanc's wonderful but eye-wateringly expensive pastries before arriving. The provision of pastries by guests was a French tradition of which he thoroughly approved. Now a starter. Perhaps something fishy but not too complicated. His little kitchen only had a small oven and a couple of ceramic rings, so his repertoire was limited. Again his mind was made up for him. As he approached the fish counter which, in spite of the market traders and a single fish shop below the Place Voltaire near his house that only opened for one morning a week, still kept the best and freshest fish in the town, he was brushed aside by a supermarket employee with a huge basket full of tellines, that he had tasted a day or so before in the evening after his tennis match. These tiny little clams were found only in a few places around the French coast and the Carmargue was one of them. A spaghetti with a plain sauce of tellines would be a fine starter; a Carmargue version of spaghetti al vongole. Smith loved them but almost never ate them. He had a pathological dislike of working hard for the food on his plate. He hated spending hours prising unforgiving bits of flesh from chicken and rabbit bones. He refused to eat with his fingers – just as he refused to eat standing up. His just about managed to eat moules (breaking at least one of his rules) on the basis that they were half open anyway and too delicious to decline. However he usually drew the line at ferreting about inside the tiny tellines shells with an oversize fork and he seldom found a restaurant that would do it for him. The cheese was less of a problem as the supermarket had a fine selection of Italian varieties. Wine was a matter for Monsieur Simon.

Smith had discovered la Cave Arlesienne years before but it was only since it's proprietor had stopped trying to make a living out of his own small vineyard near St Gilles to the west of Arles, sold his vines to his larger neighbour and took over the running of this little wine shop, that Smith started visiting him. His regular chat about everything from the state of the weather to the state of France and everything in between was a constant pleasure. Monsieur Simon stocked Grand Vins, of course, and a knowledgeable selection of good minor growths from the southern end of the Rhone Valley that were seldom found much further afield. He had no idea what he would stock of Italian wine but he had faith that the man would not let him down. So he parked outside the little shop at the base of the city wall that ran around the Église de la Major and his house and let Arthur out. The dog shot into the shop past a line of locals each of whom was waiting patiently with a black plastic container in hand. Arthur knew he was welcome here and a fair proportion of the queue made a fuss of him as he came in. Arthur's regular nightly perambulations with Smith in tow around the quarter were well known. The plastic containers ranged from one litre mineral water bottles to ten litre caravan-type water containers. All had originally started off life white or at least translucent. They had been turned black by continual refilling with Monsieur Simon's basic house red which was dispensed from a hidden tank behind the shop wall through a petrol pump type nozzle arrangement. At the princely sum of slightly more than one euro a litre, this was the staple drink of the neighbourhood. In spite of constant flushing out between refills the black stain accumulated.

The queue moved along slowly but no-one was in much of a hurry. It finally came to Smith's turn and he explained what he wanted. Monsieur Simon frowned momentarily and disappeared through the door at the back of the little shop. Within a few minutes he reappeared with a carrier bag full of wine. He handed it over to Smith.

'I need to look up my old paperwork to get the bill together. Perhaps tomorrow?'

He looked back past Smith at the queue that had formed behind the Englishman. It was as long as when he had come in. Simon shrugged and smiled at his customer.

'Please give Madame my best wishes.'

He glanced down at the bag in Smith's hand.

'Perhaps that might make a believer out of her. Get the frizzante into the fridge as soon as possible – but not too cold, mind you. Too cold and you will kill it. I know that is necessary with much of the dreadful *méthode champagneoise* that you get on the market these days, but believe me, this doesn't deserve that sort of fate'

By the time he got home it was late-afternoon and hot. Very hot. Arthur with one of those unaccountable attacks of perversity to which dogs and some people are occasionally prone decided that this was the moment to sleep on one of the small bits of his terrace than was exposed to the direct sun and was, as a consequence, hot enough to fry the proverbial egg. It was. Smith had tried it long ago. Smith extracted the bottle of fizz from the carrier bag. Actually there were two of them. Clearly, Monsieur Simon, having listened to Smith's intended menu, had decided that they should to drink it past the aperitif stage and extend into the first course.

The wine was Franciacorta, a very traditionally made fizzy wine from Lomardy. Bellavista Franciacorta Gran Cuvée Satèn, Riserva Vittoria Moretti 2004, to be precise. Smith had only known of it before by reputation. It was named after the owner and was released only occasionally. He put the two bottles with their distinctive little oval labels with some reverence into his fridge with a silent prayer that the old machine would not screw it up and freeze the bloody stuff. Suddenly he felt the prospective evening's meal push all the other things that were troubling him well to one side. That, after all, had been the whole point of the exercise and he suddenly knew that he didn't want to spoil the pleasure of preliminary cooking by chewing over the problem that, until his bright idea about inviting Martine to dinner, had threatened to overwhelm him. The shopping had calmed him down and the anticipation that he felt while reading the bottle labels had managed to refocus what had started to become an obsession. Perhaps there were more important things than what had happened in the past. The woman coming to dinner proved that by being one of them.

With some anticipation he drew the two remaining bottles from the bag. The first was a bottle of red. A Conterno Barolo Monfortino 2002. Smith set it on one of his kitchen shelves in the shade. It was too early to draw the cork. As a rule he avoided Barolo wines as the ones that were generally available were often aggressive and too strong for his taste. However he and Monsieur Simon had talked before about the unwelcome tendency of many modern wine makers to take the easy way out when confronted with more and more hours of sun by making stronger and stronger wines. The old wines of eleven or, at most, twelve percent strength, were getting increasingly difficult to find. He looked at the bottle with a mild curiosity.

The last treasure at the bottom of the carrier bag was smaller but a complete curiosity. A unlabelled half litre clear bottle containing an equally clear liquid. It was obviously an *eau de vie* of some kind, presumably a *grappa*, given his menu. With some hesitation he put it in the fridge. Grappa afficianos are rather like whisky ones. But he had never joined them in their passion for spirits at room temperature. He preferred his taste buds un-cauterised by the passage of raw spirit for as long as possible. He liked his *eaux de vie* slightly chilled. He was completely sure that this was not the correct way of going about things but that was not something he cared too much about. Or at all, as a matter of fact.

He was about to crumple the bag and put it into his waste bin when he saw a small scrap of paper at the bottom. It was a note from Monsieur Simon. They would be drinking as his guests this evening. Smith's smile of appreciation went well beyond the simple relief of escaping the financial consequences of this selection of fine wine. He realised that it was not only an effort to impress his evening's guest but a gesture of friendship.

First, he thought, the meat. He had managed to get the supermarket man to slice the veal so he had in effect four reasonably-sized but slim escallops. He ran a little local olive oil over them, some squeezed lemon juice and some ground pepper and laid them in a flat dish to marinade. He covered the dish with a clean tea towel and put it in the shade on the table on his terrace. Meat marinating in the cold of a fridge is little more than a gesture.

Next he parboiled the little potatoes and doused them under the cold tap. When they were cold and had stopped cooking themselves, he dried them off, sliced some of the bigger ones in half longitudinally, rolled them in a little olive oil, scatted some dried mixed herbs de province and salt over them, threw them into a baking tray and slid the whole lot into his little oven ready for cooking. Next he sliced some tomatoes and laid them into a dish, covered and onto the table next to the meat. The simple oil and vinegar dressing he put into the fridge. Cold tomato salad is completely tasteless but room temperature tomato salad with cold dressing is something altogether different. That was the main course sorted out.

Never a man to cook completely unaided, he poured himself a large glass of Monsieur Simon's much more prosaic red, the one that came through the wall in a hose, and set to work on the rest of the meal. Like all fish, it was entirely to easy to overcook and fish glue is one of the easiest of the animal glues to make. Most restaurants in his experience make glue not fish. He was determined on taking the tellines from their shells for his sauce but the tricky bit was not cooking them completely in the process because that should happen a few second before the dish is served. Having filled the sink with cold water, he took the tiny little molluscs, each little bigger than a thumbnail and gave them a violent shake in the bag, and tipped them into sieve. A few that were open but asleep woke up and closed. Some that remained open he took out and threw away. He had heated a very small amount of water in a large pan until it was boiling fiercely, then threw the tellines in and quickly jammed the lid on. He took it off the stove and shook it for twenty seconds or so. Putting the pan down he took off the lid and watched for the shells opening. Being very small they opened pretty quickly. Within a few seconds he dumped the whole lot into the sink keeping the hot water back as the basis for his sauce. A few moments later he set about the tedious task of taking the dead but not completely cooked clams out of their shells and put them in a bowl for later. They would be added almost at the last minute.

By six thirty all was under control – or so he thought. He got out his best table cloth – actually his only table cloth – and saw with some relief that it was clean and ironed. He offered a silent prayer of thanks to his next door neighbour who occasionally took pity on him and generally mucked him out and brought his laundry up to date. The cloth was old. It had belonged to his grandmother. It was heavy damask linen with a broderie anglaise border. It was square which didn't exactly fit his garden table which was rectangular but it decorated one end quite handsomely. He found that he even had matching napkins to match and felt his spirits lifting. In fact they had been getting better after leaving St Remy earlier that afternoon. The cooking therapy was clearly working. He resolved not to make the evening more serious than it needed to be. He laid the table, checked that the things that were supposed to be cold were not too cold and the things that were supposed to be at room temperature were, indeed, just that. Most of the cooking would be a last minute thing so he left well alone then settled into the old Thonet recliner that had also been inherited from his grandparents and took up his current book. In keeping with the philosophy that he had tried to encourage himself to adopt in his retirement he had started on a much delayed treat to re-read some of the books that had made the deepest impression on him, many years ago when he was a student. He was currently working his way through Thomas Mann and was currently discovering not without considerable pleasure that a virtual lifetime between his previous reading and the present had resulted in his discovering completely new books. Arthur decided that he had sunbathed enough and wandered soporifically into the house and climbed laboriously onto his sofa to resume his supine afternoon. Apart from the odd excursion to replenish his glass Smith remained absorbed in the intricacies of Hans Castorp's stay amongst the inmates of the sanatorium at Davos while basking in the comfort of a Provence afternoon until it was time to wash and change.

The door bell rang promptly at eight thirty and he opened the door. His heart lifted as it always did when he saw her. The bell was a ritual. She had her own key but never used it when he was there. It was as if perhaps she knew how much of him she and her family at the Mas des Saintes had taken over and wanted to leave him at least the appearance of some of his old independence. He had lived a solitary life for many years, even while he had been married, and she felt that there would always be part of him that hankered after that. Little things like not using the house key just told him that she understood. He stood back to one side and waited until she passed him into the house. He glanced outside to see the black Range Rover pull away, its driver waving a casual hand out of the window at him. Jean-Marie obviously had a date elsewhere. He had delivered his charge safely and for a few hours, at least, his time would be his own.

They embraced tenderly and at length without speaking, each just taking pleasure in each other's touch. Unfortunately the intended quiet dignity of the moment was completely ruined by a deliriously happy Arthur who had wakened by the sound of the approaching car long before the door bell sounded. This was a very welcome intrusion into his soporific afternoon. So he cavorted around making a series of delighted yelps totally at variance with his usual dignified behaviour that normally befitted an old, retired racing greyhound. He and Martine not only loved each other but she was connected in his doggy mind with the huge expanse of the Camargue that she and her father farmed. There he was completely free to roam and hunt at will and, having learned some potentially hazardous lessons early on, that, for instance, a little Camargue black bull calf can run through half meter deep marsh water faster than a greyhound being one of the most important of them, he and Martine's father were regular coursing companions. Rather like with many humans a way to cure a potentially arthritic ex-athlete was to cease to be one. After a while, he had calmed down enough for Smith to lead his guest by the hand through the living room and the tiny kitchen through the double doors and out into the garden. It was a tiny place barely larger than eight yards long by five wide but it was all he, as a profound non-gardener, could manage. It had a small olive tree that was finally recovering from being transported on the back of a camionette some five years before, a huge oleander in full bloom, with trunks the size of telegraph poles. The mixture of grape vine and jasmine had successfully intertwined and grown over the structure he had built to cover and shade the terrace. The little orange and lemon trees in pots continued to survive without, it should be admitted, ever really bursting enthusiastically into fruit. The whole garden was enclosed with high and very ancient walls and Martine again understood why this was such a special place to him.

She was dressed simply in a slightly up-market version of her everyday farm clothes. Starched white shirt, pressed jeans and boots. She had a fedora-style straw hat on her head and a ravishingly bright Christian Lacroix silk scarf knotted loosely around her neck. As always, her sole jewellery was a tiny gold Croix des Saintes on an almost invisible chain around her neck. She reached up and put her hands on either side of his face.

'How are you, Peter?'

She knew most of the things that were troubling him and that were the reasons behind tonight's invitation. He replied with a gentle smile as he looked at her.

'I am fine, my dear. Now, quite fine.'

Having realised that they were not about to leave the house and head into the countryside, Arthur returned to the sofa where he collapsed with a loud and slightly annoyed sigh. Smith still held her close.

'You've obviously guessed that I need to talk a few things over with you.'

She nodded but said nothing. He continued:

'I suggest that we don't ruin a hopefully beautiful evening by talking shop all the time. How about if we have a drink, then eat and maybe chat about the ungodly after we have finished?'

She smiled brightly in agreement and replied slightly archly.

'Yes, that's a good idea. By the way I have given Jean-Marie the night off.'

Although he regularly stayed with her in her *cabane* on the farm, nights spent together in his house always seems to have a slight frisson of conspiracy. He sat her at the head of the table and left to pour the frizzante. He knew that the temperature was right. It is entirely too easy to over chill white wines of all sorts and his fridge was regulated precisely but unpredictably with this in mind. In fact keeping white wine at the correct temperature was the only thing it was regulated for. Food took its chances. He poured two glasses and returned the bottle to the fridge with a teaspoon in the neck of the bottle to keep it fizzy. It was a trick his father had taught him and he had never met anyone who could explain why it worked.

However it seemed to. He sat across the corner of the table from her and raised his glass.

'We are a little Italian tonight so I thought we would stay that way with the wine. To our very good – and continued – health.'

He took a sip and looked expectantly at her. Part of the family group of business that extended past farming to some hotels and restaurants also produces some very remarkable wines. These were basically a hobby and few bottles ever reached a commercial market. They supplied the restaurants and the local people almost exclusively. However Smith knew that Martine was something of an expert and he was interested to know what she thought of the Franciacorta. He could see from her delighted expression that he had surprised her. She looked sharply at him, suspecting a trick.

'Italian? Really?'

Smith nodded. She took another slightly larger mouthful.

'This is quite simply the best fizzy Italian wine I have ever tasted. It is as good as any French champagne, even,' she said with a slight frown, 'as good as some of ours too. I assume it's from Franciacorta but I have never tasted one as good as this. What is it?'

Smith smiled with satisfaction and offered a silent prayer to Monsieur Simon.

'Wait for the refill and I'll show you the bottle.'

He leant across the table and took her hand, turned it over and kissed her palm.

'You look completely wonderful, Martine. The most beautiful woman I have ever seen. Arles' reputation for producing beautiful women continues.'

She smiled with pleasure and not a little embarrassment. Smith was not a man prone to excessive exhibitions of emotion or even feeling and it was all the more of a treat when he forgot himself. She squeezed his hand.

'You are also a beautiful man, Peter, although I am sure that is the wrong word to use to a Welshman.'

The momentary but slightly embarrassed silence was broken as she glanced down and continued:

'Almost as beautiful as this tablecloth.'

The meal was a success. He had already added a little cream to the tellines stock and reduced it gently so there was a small amount of creamy sauce simmering at well below boiling. Having cooked the spaghetti he threw the tellines into the sauce for a last minute or so to finish cooking. Then all was mixed and put into a heated bowl and taken to the table. He poured the remainder of the wine.

Martine ate in silence, giving the simple dish her full attention. She finished and took a sip of her drink.

'My love that was wonderful. You cooked the tellines perfectly. You seem to understand what so many people don't. Pasta sauces are just a way to flavour the pasta and simplicity is everything. So many cooks load the sauce with food rather than just taste. You have a simplicity in your cooking that I have noticed before and I really like it.'

Smith was completely delighted for this was a woman who knew what she was talking about. He also had no doubt at all that if it wasn't right, she would tell him. Smith had never considered himself to be a cook but he had always enjoyed cooking and doing simple things well was what he liked. He was honest enough that he lacked the knowledge to do anything more complex or exotic.

'Well, thank you. Coming from you that is a compliment that I shall treasure. Let's hope you have a similarly high opinion after the next course.'

Smith's garden terrace was immediately outside his little kitchen so it was perfectly practical for cooking things at the last minute while continuing to talk to his guest. The potatoes had roasted slowly over the last half hour with a sprig or two of tarragon and rosemary and now lay keeping warm in the oven while he stood over another attempt to make a somewhat minimalist sauce. If the scallopine di vitello had taken up the lemon flavour while marinating, all Smith wanted was a very simple white wine sauce that kept its wine taste without being too thick. He had found an half bottle of Puligny Montrachet in his fridge left and he hoped that its fairly robust flavour would survive being heated. He had done most of the sauce quickly in advance. He sautéed a little shallot in some olive oil, added the wine and reduced it. He removed the shallot and added some butter and cooked the sauce only until the butter had melted. It had been left on one side of the little hob to cook on a little as it cooled.

He gave the Barolo to Martine to open as he turned his attention to the meat. He put the sauce back on a very low heat and started to fry the veal in a little seasoned butter and oil in quite a hot frying pan. He wanted to fry the meat very quickly to stop it drying out in the middle while singing the outside very slightly. The trace of olive oil was to stop the butter burning. As he stood over the sizzling pan, watching with a certain about of suspicion, he felt a kiss on the back of his neck and a glass put into his hand. He turned and they tasted the wine together. Neither of them had often tasted an Italian wine like it. It was what wine people call full-bodied but without either being strong nor particularly powerful smelling. Smith was delighted as he knew it would be perfect for what he was trying to do with the meat.

The meat was lightly but quickly browned on each side and he just put a pan lid over it, took it off the heat and poured a little of the buttery meat juice into his little sauce of sauce, giving it a bit of a stir. He put the potatoes, tomato salad and the jug of a very simple cold dressing on the table, and served the meat and wine sauce onto plates.

As before, they ate in silence. They both thought that eating was too important to spoil with too much conversation. Any cook worth anything deserved a bit of concentration for his audience without the religious reverence that had arrived since the invention of the celebrity chef. But just as you wouldn't - or, at least, shouldn't - chat to you neighbour during a piano recital, they both thought that the same went for food.

If he was honest, Smith was quite please with the way it turned out. Obviously Martine agreed.

'Really good, Peter. You succeeded in getting the meat to carry the lemon taste rather than sauce and I can really taste to wine too. Wonderful. A great success I think.'

This was continued high praise that Smith accepted gratefully. The evening remained warm and the meal continued against a background of cicadas. Martine had indeed brought some pastries for pudding. There was some cheese and fruit to follow but Martine intervened. It was getting late and they really hadn't talked yet, at least about what concerned them most.

'Let's leave that interesting little bottle of Monsieur Simon until after Arthur's walk. It's a lovely night and maybe it will be easier to talk if we are on the move.'

It was as if she wanted to move the business part of the evening away from the recent pleasure of the meal. It took a split second for a recumbent Arthur to be waiting at he door, standing excitedly but patiently while Martine took his slip lead and collar down from the hook behind the door and threaded it over his head. A moment later she was down the steps and on her way along the side of the Amphitheatre down towards the Place Voltaire and the Port Cavalière which was the original Roman gate on the north side of the city. Smith followed slightly flustered at this sudden turn of events and momentarily delayed by having to collect his Glock from the middle drawer of the dresser and stuff it uncomfortably down the back of his trousers. The light linen jacket served as a disguise of sorts. He finally caught up with her just outside the little building where a modest entrepreneur had once charged tourists an equally modest sum to view a rather bad reconstruction of van Gogh's bedroom taken from the famous picture. As he took her hand, he looked up at the house than now contained some trendy little modern design studio that nobody wanted or even visited. She saw his glance.

'Ah, my love, we live in less innocent times.'

Smith harrumphed.

'Possibly, but not any better for all our tablet PCs and smartphones.'

She didn't argue. Faced with a conversation about the past she saw that Smith was getting into one of his grumpily nostalgic moods now. Although she would have preferred just to enjoy the walk, she knew that he wanted to talk about things. So she decided to start him off.

'Well, my dear. Where are we?'

He acknowledged her thoughtfulness with a slight squeeze of his hand.

'It's a little difficult to say, to be frank. The good news is that we have managed to detain our Romanian assassin with the long rifle. You remember him from the curtain calls at La Fenice. He is presently Girondou's guest until we can decide what to do with him.'

Smith made it sound as ordinary as deciding where to send an unwanted parcel rather than whether or not to dispatch a fellow human being to the next world. He felt Martine's shudder and held her a shade tighter. He did not, however, say anything comforting or reassuring. He noted that she didn't ask him how the Romanian had been found.

'Apart from that little nugget of progress we are no further than before. We still have Gentry being maidenly about everything and McDowell's death by person or persons unknown, as they say. Grantkov comes down here possibly on his own initiative having thirty years ago taken a pot shot at Gentry at Bologna and your favourite soprano, somewhat more successfully from his point of view, in Venice rather more recently. If Grantkov's Bologna business is connected then the only thing that links everything together rather tenuously is the Albanian adventure but I'm buggered I can see how or, for that matter, why.'

They walked on a bit further in silence. They had got down to the river and had taken the path following it downstream in the direction of the autoroute and the Roman museum. Arthur was on full alert. It was a route well populated with stray cats but he was well-enough trained to understand that while he felt the collar around his neck they were off limits. As a result the lead between the collar and Martine's hand hung in a gentle unstressed curve as he automatically matched his pace to hers. She resumed:

'Tell be about the Albania thing again. This time in as much detail as you can.'

It didn't really occur to him that he was breaking the Official Secrets Act with every word he said. He was well past all that now. He retold the story in detail and it took until they were walking in front of the museum around the tiny archaeological vestige of the curve at the end of the great Roman circus that nearly two thousand years before had been home to chariot races held in front of twenty thousand spectators.

'And Gentry hasn't come up with anything?'

Smith just shook his head in a slightly annoyed manner. She continued.

'Well it's my impression, my dear, that you might be starting at the wrong end of all this. You are taking the whole story a bit like a detective story in some sort of chronological order, looking at each piece as it occurs and trying to make sense of it all as you go along.'

'And you suggest?'

'I suggest that look at what you have now.'

'And that is?'

Smith was beginning to sound a little waspish. They turned back towards the middle of the town. She ignored his tone.

'Well, as far as I can see you have a disastrous secret spy operation to Albania from thirty years ago, a country that is hardly any distance at all through the then communist Yugoslavia from Romania. You have the possible imprisonment of the Americans who planned the operation in a secret CIA prison in where of all places? - Bucharest that happens to be the capital of Romania. You have the deaths of the surviving members of this abortive operation within the last couple of years. You have a Romanian killer who, possibly coincidentally, shot a Romanian singer in front of you as well as at your friend Gentry thirty years ago. Would it be impertinent of me to suggest that you might concentrate your attentions on one particular country?'

Smith knew that she was right, of course, but couldn't immediately bring himself to capitulate so early in proceedings. Their route by now had brought them to the bottom of the Boulevard des Lices, the main road that runs east to west through the middle of the town but served to separate the old part from the newer southern half. Without much discussion they both headed up the Boulevard as it was the most direct way home and the call of Monsieur Simon's little bottle was as strong as its presumed contents. He continued with a bit of a grumble.

'I've already asked Gentry to find out about all this but he seems reluctant to cough anything up. Personally, I don't have too many contacts any more that can help. For various good reasons the CIA doesn't like me very much. My list of suitable contacts is a short one.'

'Might I suggest that a better way than just waiting for your friend to recover from his uncharacteristically maidenly silence is to use your friend Girondou? He has both your Romanian killer and, I suspect, more ways of extracting information from him that even you might guess at, as well as a whole series of connections to the

Romanian mafia and other desirables that unfortunately now run that once beautiful country. Good Lord, he is probably on Christian name terms with most of them. If anyone knows what is going on inside this Orniss prison of yours, they will. They probably run it for the CIA.'

Smith was immediately more than a little concerned.

'And how exactly does a beautiful lady bull farmer from the Camargue know the name of this particular institution. It is slightly odd information for you to have. You probably know its address too, I suppose,' he answered slightly sarcastically.

She smiled at him.

'There, there, keep you hair on. It is at number four Mures Street, it rather was. It has probably been moved now since there was a programme about it on German television a couple of years ago. They were apparently officially closed down but it probably still exists somewhere. Magda once told me about it. Perhaps if you ever watched television you might have remembered.'

Smith silently had to admit that she was right. Apart from watching cricket and rugby on his thoroughly unofficial pirated satellite feed from the UK, he never watched the thing.

'Magda?'

'My dead soprano friend.'

'And what, prey, does she have to do with all this? '

'She said that her father worked there as a warder.'

'Worked for whom?'

'The CIA, of course.'

He mumbled angrily to himself.

'What was that, my dear' she asked brightly.

He replied with an exasperated sigh.

'I said that it looks as if I should just become a bull farmer and leave all this stuff to you.'

Martine looked completely horrified.

'Oh, no, my dearest. You don't really know one end of a bull from another and, believe me, that could be a very dangerous lacuna in your knowledge.'

He was left dumbfounded less by the fact that she knew all this stuff about Bucharest but more by the fact that this extraordinary Frenchwoman had the word lacuna in her vocabulary. By now they had arrived back at the house, fed Arthur and returned to the garden. In spite of the fact that it was now near enough midnight, it was still warm and Smith produced two small glasses and the small bottle from his fridge.

It was obviously an *eau de vie* of some sort but not the grappa that Smith had been expecting. Monsieur Simon had pulled something of a fast one. However, he saw that Martine was smiling gently at him. Clearly he was the victim of some sort of conspiracy. He put his nose over the glass and drew the air from the top of the glass deeply into his lungs. It smelt of peaches or nectarines.

'All right. I give up. What am I drinking?'

She smiled contentedly.

'Well, unless I am mistaken this was made by us but some time ago. Did Monsieur Simon know I was coming to dinner by any chance?'

'I think he guessed. I don't usually go to all this trouble for just anyone.'

'Then this is some of a nectarine eau-de-vie that we made about fifteen years ago. It was an experiment of my father's and we never sold it. I seem to remember that we only made a few hundred litres of it. How Monsieur Simon got hold of it, I have no idea. However I have a feeling that this is a hint for us to try again.'

Smith took another small sip.

'Well, I certainly think that's an excellent idea. Perhaps we should restrain ourselves and you could take a little back with you tomorrow to remind your father.'

Their contented reverie was interrupted by Smith's satellite phone. It was some time since he used an ordinary mobile and this particular gizmo and ones for Martine and a few others had come from Girondou some time ago at a time when the traditional ones proved to be all to insecure. The familiar voice of his old friend Deveraux did the round trip into space and back.

'Evening, Sir. I hope this is not too late to call'.

'Deveraux, how many times have I asked you not to call me Sir and you know that it is never too late to call me.'

'Er, yes sir, sorry sir. I mean… Oh and about the time it's just that I gathered that you are entertaining this evening.'

You could hear the smile.

'And how exactly did you come by that particular piece of information, Deveraux.'

'From Jean-Marie, Sir.'

Smith gave up and concentrated on the important stuff to be done at the Mas.

'I am glad you've arrived, Deveraux. Thanks for coming. General protection stuff for now and we will have a chat when I bring Madame Aubanet home tomorrow. In the meantime you could do worse that try to remember what you know about one Valery Maximovich Grantkov and his exploits in the murky world of assassination that you know so much better than I.'

There was a palpable pause before the man replied slightly huffily. To him it wasn't murky at all.

'Very well, Sir but I really done think there is much to worry about there. Definitely second division. However I will see what I can find out on the grapevine.'

Smith cut the connection and turned to Martine.

'Deveraux has come to help out for a few days. It would seem that he regards Grantkov as less that first rate, I think. Some sort of professional rivalry thing, probably.'

'I'll be happy to see him again. I like him. But if he's not too impressed with Grantkov, where would you rank Deveraux?

Smith approached the question as if they were comparing lawn mowers.

'Well in the current world of reliable assassins for hire, I'd say Grantkov is number twenty; fifteen possibly. I would rate Deveraux a good deal higher.'

'Higher?'

'Yes.'

'How much higher?'

'Oh I would guess at two, possibly one.'

'Ah.'

There was a silence.

'Why?'

'He is probably as good as anyone at the job but he has some addition qualities that probably distinguish him from his fellows. Deveraux is versatile. He doesn't need to stick to one particular plan or method. He has no real preference as to a weapon. He can improvise. He can be unpredictable when required. Above all he is courageous and loyal to the point of absurdity.'

Martine took another sip of her father's liquor and continued.

'Odd.'

'Odd?'

'Odd' she nodded.

'Why odd?'

'Oh because you remember the last time he came to the Mas des Saintes to help out, I had to dig a bullet out of him?'

Smith remembered as she continued.

'Well those were pretty nearly exactly the same qualities that he said he admired in you.'

'How very confusing for you.' was all that Smith could think of to say. He reached again for his phone.

'Never let it be said that I don't take advice.

Completely ignoring the lateness of the hour, he called Girondou. As usual the man answered his phone immediately in a voice that expressed a pleasure in receiving a telephone call from his friend, irrespective of the fact that it was by then long past midnight.

'Don't tell me. You want me to ask some questions about goings-on in Bucharest.'

To say that Smith was surprised was an understatement.

'How on earth?...'

Girondou's delight was evident in a deep chuckle.

'You forget my old friend that we have had your Romanian as our guest for a good few hours now and I took the opportunity to have a quick word with him. Also I also do a lot of business with friends throughout the Balkans. Your rifleman is nothing very special I think. It is surprising how just the simple knowledge of a person's family members can shape a conversation if you know the right way to set about it.'

'And how exactly?....'

'You don't want to know. Now what do you need?'

The satellite link was encrypted and within a few moments Smith had brought Girondou up to date. He didn't have to tell him in addition what he wanted. The man from Marseille replied.

'Give me until tomorrow morning, Peter. Why don't you come to lunch and we can talk?'

Smith was slightly uncertain about this as he had already planned to take Martine back to the mas in the morning but his deliberations were cut short by the man from Marseille.

'Please bring the beautiful Madame Aubanet too. It is high time I met her don't you think?'

'Er, I will have to call her and ask, Alexei.' Smith was trying to buy some time.

'OK that's fine, Peter, but perhaps it would save time if you just asked her now or have you two, unlike me, already gone to bed?'

'How the hell do you..?'

'Peter, my friend, calm down. Deveraux is not the only person who is watching your back at the moment.'

Smith felt a momentary flush of anger at the fact that others were getting more and more involved in his life. He hated that that people knew so much about him and what he was doing. He looked across at Martine and said through gritted teeth.

'We're invited to lunch tomorrow with Alexei Girondou and his family.'

She saw that Smith had not covered the mouthpiece of the phone and, ignoring his warning frown, she raised her voice slightly.

'Please tell Monsieur Girondou that we would be delighted to accept.'

Girondou's voice was full of satisfaction.

'Excellent, Angèle and I will look forward to it. I am also delighted to be able to meet the lady I have heard so much about before the big event.'

It was an elephant trap and Smith fell straight into it.

'What do you mean: the big event.'

'I mean your wedding to the beautiful lady and my acting as your best man.'

Smith was as close to speechless as makes little difference.

'And what happens, old friend, if I neither get married or if I do, I don't invite you to be my best man?'

The voice that winged its way back after the customary short pause caused by the return journey to the satellite was completely matter of fact.

'In the case of the former, I suspect that half the population of the Camargue will kill you. In the case of the latter, I will. Good night.'

He laid the now-silent telephone back onto the table and looked across at Martine. He said grudgingly:

'Lunch tomorrow then.'

'Good, she replied, 'then close up the house and follow me. We'll do the washing up tomorrow,'

She rose from the table and disappeared up the stairs in the general direction of the bedroom.

Chapter 6: Casting the Net

Scene 1: Lunch and a Plan of Sorts

The approach to Girondou's house in the hills above Sausset-les-Pins on the strip of land that bounds the great lagoon, the Étang de Berre started lot earlier that one might think. The great swathe of industry that envelopes both sides of the Étang immediately to the west of Marseille was Girondou's power base; from the ports of Fos-sur-Mer and Port St Louis via Istres and Martiques to Marignane and thence to the centre of Marseille itself. Shipping and transport, oil, gas and chemicals. These were the places that generated wealth and this was the centre of Girondou's kingdom. He controlled almost every business conceivable both illegal and legal. Most of the important people, policemen, politicians, captains of industry, bankers, traders owed their positions and their current power one way or another to Alexei Girondou as they had to his father before him. The Girondou dynasty, quite simply, had run everything for more than fifty years and the influence did not stop there. Very little happened between Montpellier in the west and the Italian border in the east, between the Mediterranean and almost Lyon to the north that did not either have or need his blessing. As a result he lived in comfort but not particularly luxuriously in a large Provençale house tucked into the hills above Sausset, looking out over the Mediterranean. The house was indeed quite large and had a swimming pool. But so did most houses along that coast. It sat centrally in a plot of land that was mostly scrubby woodland with the rise of the hill at its back for protection. Alexei Girondou, the man who ran the south of France lived comfortably but unostentatiously amongst his friends and that was his secret. His protection was the people who lived around him whose eyes and ears were infinitely better guards than fences or technology, although there were those too.

The family had been influential before the Second World War but had done very little for either side during the Vichy years and later when the Germans occupied the so-called free zone in November 1942 they contented themselves with keeping out of trouble as did most of the population. It was, however, after the successful Allied invasion in the south of France in August 1944 that the opportunity for Girondou's father and his friends to start to build a criminal empire that had just got bigger and bigger. While the attention of the world focussed on the conflict that was increasingly to do with the north of Europe, old Etienne Girondou had got to work and before the actual end of the war itself some seven months later they had taken control of almost all trade, legal or illegal in the south. It was a time when there was effectively no law, no official administration as there was nothing to administer, Summary justice was dealt in the streets against perceived collaborators and all the incipient hatreds and local intolerances surfaced. The so-called forces of law were largely self-appointed and were as outside the law as everyone else. It was a power vacuum which old Etienne and his colleagues filled quickly and efficiently. They controlled food distribution because they controlled fuel. They controlled power, transport and communication. By nineteen fifty, little happened anywhere along the south coast without Etienne Girondou having something to do with it. Sixty years later the situation remained essentially unchanged.

Smith knew that as they drove through the already open wrought iron gates at the top of a winding drive that led down hillside to the house that they had been under observation for some time. Some of the speed cameras along the side of the roads that came off the so-called Voie Rapide de la Côte Bleu to the south and the smaller Route de Sausset were actually real-time real TV surveillance and automatic number plate recognition cameras and potential difficulties were identified long before they arrived anywhere near Girondou's front gate. Unusual trucks found themselves pulled over for a brake or light check. Suspicious cars were halted for speeding or a common document check. In each case the friendly smiling gendarme was backed by colleagues sporting Heckler and Kohn sub-machine guns. Few of the delayed motorists would know that these were definitely not standard gendarme issue.

Smith drove slowly down the winding drive noting the round shapes on the ground marking the location of series of hydraulic bollards that could be activated and rise to a height of a metre in less than half a second and stop a truck dead in its tracks.

As usual, Alexei and his wife Angèle were standing in front of the house to greet their guests. To Smith's delight Girondou's two teenage daughters were there as well and it was these two who rushed forward and engulfed Smith in delighted hugs and kisses the second he got out of the car leaving his host to open a slightly bemused Martine's door and let her out. Smith was a favourite uncle figure to the two girls and the fact that they were late teenage women of very considerable beauty didn't stop them becoming thoroughly girlish when he arrived. They also both knew that he loved them almost as much as he did his own slightly older daughters back in England. By the time he had disengaged himself enough to walk with a daughter on each arm over to his hosts, the others had made their own introductions. As he approached, Angèle followed her daughters example and gave him a slightly more dignified but equally passionate hug. Smith was amongst friends and they were determined to show it to his girlfriend.

Within a few minutes they were all sitting around a rough garden table drinking a glass of fizzy. Alexei Girondou, dressed in a plain pair of cotton trousers and a pale blue open-necked shirt looked across the table at the four women and then turned to his friend.

'Peter, we are indeed fortunate men, you and I.'

Smith could do no more than just nod.

Martine was still wearing the jeans from last night but had stolen one of Smiths best old cotton shirts which, even he had to admit, looked a lot better on her that it ever had on him. Angèle Girondou was in a slightly more upmarket version of the same thing, cotton slacks and a blouse. The two girls were clones of Martine, jeans and shirts. Little or no jewellery. Flat but expensive leather pumps. As usual business was put to one side while lunch was served and the conversation in the shade under the veranda ranged across farming and business to schools, colleges and boyfriends. All the Girondoux were extremely interested in Martine and Smith was silently pleased that they were obviously very impressed almost immediately. The two girls were firmly wedged either side of Smith and he had the unaccustomed pleasure of being completely monopolised. He enquired as to their plans after school. Both were heading to university, one to study economics, the other business. Smith wondered idly how the very macho south France would in time take to being run by a couple of girls. The other three adults listened in and Martine was pleased to see that her host and hostess were observing this scene of engaged domesticity with delighted smiles on their faces. She felt reassured for Smith for deep down she knew that he needed friends like these however reluctant he might be to admit it.

Smith was slightly concerned about how the business part of the conversation would take place. Usually the girls absented themselves after the meal as did Angèle as Smith wasn't sure of the extent to which she was really involved with Girondou's business. Martine was however involved in his. Thus is was with a certain relief that as the lunch drew to a close that Girondou looked across to his daughters and said fondly but firmly.

'Skidaddle you two now. Us grown-ups have things to discuss.'

With a certain amount of very attractive pouting and wrinkling of noses the two left. Girondou had clearly decided that as Martine was such an intimate parts of Smith's life, on this occasion, at least, Angèle should perhaps be part of it all as well.

When they were alone it was Girondou who continues a previous conversation.

'It's true that after the Albanian fiasco your two rogue CIA people were imprisoned for a long time in the States but were transferred to in Orniss in 2006. All the inmates, predominantly Arab terrorist suspects being held without trial and tortured for information, were actually transferred out just before the recent German TV programme blew their secrecy out of the water but – clever move this by the CIA - were moved back as soon as the dust had settled. The theory being, I suppose, that no one would think that they would use the place again. It was actually used as a secure document storage centre by the Romanians so it is ideal really. It is heavily guarded and the locals are still reluctant to pry into a government-run facility in spite of the end of the Ceausescu regime.'

'Officially, one of the two men you are interested in, Thomas Wilson, apparently died naturally of a heart attack a year ago although there is obviously no real evidence but, the second, Grant Fredricks, was actually released recently.'

'Released?'

'Yes, apparently some soft-hearted do-gooder in the States decided that the man had suffered enough and they let him go. I suppose you could understand as the poor sod had been locked up for thirty years.'

Smith grunted. 'Not so poor, I think. Did they ever recover the money?'

'Ah, no. I don't believe so.'

'OK. Sorry to interrupt. Please go on.'

'Well the story is that Fredricks took out the contract on your friend McDowell and it was done by a bunch of Chicago guns of no great importance. Three of them. I have found out who they are and can have them taken out if you wish. They are still in France so some friends in Bordeaux can do the necessary if you wish. Fredricks has apparently vanished back to the States apparently. There is some talk of the CIA setting up a protection programme but for the life of me I can't see why as he shafted them to start with.'

Smith grunted in a dismissive and somewhat unfriendly way.

'There's a strong and not altogether safe sense of sentimentality running though our colonial cousins' veins, I fear. It comes from having little or no sense of history. They haven't got one of their own and therefore see nothing to learn their lessons from.'

His audience was surprised at the note of contempt in Smith's voice. He glanced at the two ladies and noted that neither showed much discomfort at this talk of killing. Strong people, these Provençale ladies, he thought.

'OK that's makes some sort of sense to begin with but what about Grantkov. He was involved in this thirty years ago and is still in it.'

Girondou nodded and, on cue, continued his narrative.

'As far as I can see there might be two stories here. The second is the Venice thing. The non-official story is that the singer's father who worked as a guard at the Bucharest prison was paid to ice the first of the imprisoned Americans. It wasn't a heart attack. As yet I don't know who sanctioned the hit. The daughter was killed in revenge, although I cannot for the life of me imagine why the whole thing was so public. Usually this sort of thing is meant to give a message but of what and to whom is beyond me. It does taste a little of the Balkans more than the Americas. Your presence may or may not have been coincidental. I tend to think it was. Anyway, Grantkov's story is that he is here now after you for personal reasons – the train thing, you remember. But I don't really believe that either. The second story is that Bologna was a hit on Gentry again a contract all those years ago arranged by Fredricks in revenge for his part is screwing with the Albania operation.'

Smith interrupted.

'Did Grantkov actually say that he was after Gentry at Bologna?'

'Yes. In fact he was quite indignant. He said he had already told you.'

'No he didn't. Did Grantkov actually say that Fredricks paid the contract?'

Girondou nodded. Neither of them wanted to burden the present company with talk about how that particular piece of information was extracted.

'Did you get anything about the man who was actually killed at Bologna? The man who was with Gentry.'

'No. He says he has no idea. Gentry was his target.'

'And he says he is here now after me rather than after Gentry.'

'He's actually after you both. Gentry is a paid hit and, before you ask, I really don't think he knows who he is working for. You are a personal thing.'

'Christ, Alexei, that has to be so much bullshit. Grantkov is a professional killer with a reputation to protect. Who is he going to go after? The man who he missed as part of a job or the man who threw him off a train which little episode no one had ever heard of.'

'Ah. I see what you mean.'

'Quite. I suggest that you go and sharpen your thumbscrews or whatever you are using in the bastard.'

'Tighten not sharpen, my friend. Tighten'

Smith replied grimly: 'No, meant sharpen.'

There was a silence while both men collected their thoughts. Smith was the first to sum up.

'It would seem that all or at least most of this is some sort of revenge for the Albania thing. Fredricks and his late chum wanted revenge. So they paid for an attempted hit on Gentry thirty years ago and a successful one on McDowell recently. The thirty year gap can be explained by being in prison in Bucharest, I suppose. Then Wilson gets iced in Bucharest and the warder's daughter was rather publicly killed for that. Presumably Gentry and I are still on Fredrick's list and as soon as he finds out that Grantkov is out of circulation he will find someone else to take the contract. He probably knows already.'

Girondou answered: 'Yes, that about sums it up. What do we do now?'

Smith thought for a minute before replying. In any event, it was a surprisingly forthright Martine who took up the conversation.

'This is completely stupid in my view. Revenge, or the desire for it, usually has its limits and all this is well beyond what is reasonable. Even if this man Fredricks has gone completely ga-ga after his stay in Romania, I really don't see him wasting all this time and effort, let alone, cash, in exorcising some old devils like this. There has got to be something much more current. Something is going on now that we don't know about and the only person who might know, as far as I can see, is Gentry. Giving him the same treatment that you are giving Grantkov might yield some interesting results.'

Although he found himself in agreement with his guest, it was perhaps because she was suggesting submitting Smith's oldest friend to some extreme torture that Girondou chose his words carefully.

'That is indeed a possibility, Martine. Needs must as the devil drives, as your Mr Shakespeare once said. But we have to know what we are looking for before we try to find it.'

Smith murmured: 'that's not an alternative.'

'At the moment, my friend, but only at the moment.' Girondou's eyes were very dark.

Smith said nothing but noted Martine's slight nod of agreement.

Girondou continued, attempting to move the conversation from the darkly theoretical to the less difficult and more practical.

'As far as I can see we have to do two things to put all this to bed. First is to find and kill this Fredricks person. If we don't do that he might get you. The second is to find out who the man killed at Bologna Station was otherwise your friendship with Gentry will never be the same again. I suspect that this will be more of a loss to you than you are prepared to admit. The threat from Fredricks or from whoever he hires next is pretty small. I found Grantkov for you and I will probably find his replacement when he turns up. If not, you have imported Deveraux and my people are minding your back. No-one is ever completely safe but you are as safe as possible under the circumstances.'

At least Smith was presented with something he could agree to; which was the object of Girondou's exercise.

'I want Martine and her family protected too. This mad American seems to like revenge killings by proxy.'

Girondou smiled. 'Don't worry. As a rule we don't get on with Camargue farmers very well. There much too violent for us soft townies but having met the dazzling Martine, I will not allow anything to happen to her. Angèle would never forgive me.'

The lady in question just nodded slightly.

Smith was not happy.

'That is my job, not yours.'

'No, Peter, actually it's not. Much as it might not be what you want to hear, you now are part of two families that will refuse to let you put yourself at risk. You have rendered great service both to me and to Émile Aubanet. You personally saved the lives of the two people we both value above all else and this will not be forgotten by us and the people around us no matter how much you might be embarrassed by our gratitude. Monsieur Aubanet and I may be very far apart in many ways, but in this I am sure we think alike. We both accept and honour our debts. '

Both ladies murmured approval. Girondou went on quickly.

'It is pretty obvious that there is more to all this than we know at the moment. The time scales are too long it seems to me. However unhappy this Fredricks might be, these were events more than thirty years ago. It may look like a personal vendetta and that is what it may be dressed up to resemble but I really don't believe it and I am not unacquainted with vendettas. However you might be a little pre-occupied in the near future. We all work best when we're not looking over our shoulder all the time and I will put the word out that people should continue to watch your back. In the meantime I'll also put the word out across the water to find this man Fredricks if we need to know at some stage. If he has got back into the States with a substantial amount of ex-American government money at his disposal he will be on all sorts of people's radar, some less friendlier than others. If I can say that it is a case of finders keepers that that would certainly concentrate some people's minds.'

'And what,' Smith asked not without a certain heavy sarcasm, 'what do you suggest I do while all this heavy protection is going on?'

'Talk to your friend Gentry, my friend, for whatever is going on, the answers are probably locked in his head.'

This was not a suggestion that Smith was very happy with. He was beginning to feel very unhappy indeed, as he often did when control of things were taken away from him. Collaboration was never a strong point. So-called team work even less. Another unsatisfactory meeting with Gentry was not something he relished. Smith continued his sarcasm.

'Oh yes? And how precisely do you suggest I find an entry into my old friend's head?'

Girondou laughed without much humour.

'Well, not the same way as we are getting some answers from Grantkov, for the moment. Although it might possibly be effective, I suspect even you might draw the line at that.'

Girondou paused for a moment's thought.

'Perhaps another of your games of chess? You can learn a lot from a man in a chess game.'

Smith looked dubious.

'Well, I'm not sure about that.'

Girondou interrupted brusquely.

'Not from the game but from how he plays it.'

Smith smiled because he knew the wisdom of that.

'I've often wondered why you had never asked me to play with you.'

Girondou only nodded with a slight smile. It was time to go and he and Martine made their farewells. Girondou addressed Martine.

'I am delighted that I have finally met you after some years. It would please me and my family very much of we could see a little more of you.'

She smiled at Girondou and his wife.

'Yes I'd like that too, Perhaps you could be our guests at the Mas des Saintes before too long. I am sure my father would like to meet you.'

Girondou came all over the charming Frenchman much to the amusement of his beautiful wife.

'Yes, that would be good. I seem to remember hearing that my father and yours also got together from time. It is a connection that seems to have got lost over the last few years. Perhaps that is my fault and I'd very much like to rectify that. Monsieur Aubanet was an almost mythical figure in my childhood. I would be honoured to pay him my respects.'

Martine was clearly very pleased indeed and Smith found himself wondering about the affect of a re-joining of these two hugely powerful families.

They walked towards the car and the two girls materialised from nowhere and each took one of Smith's arms and escorted him. As they got to the parked car he opened the back door and pulled out a large box of Madame Leblanc's chocolates that were as ruinously expensive as they were fattening. It was one of his traditional gifts and he always delighted in giving the Girondou ladies something that his waistline wouldn't allow but would make no difference at all to theirs. When they had got into the car a thought occurred to Smith and he wound his window down and poked his head out. Girondou bent towards him.

'Alexei. One thing. Did Grantkov tell you how he actually recognised Gentry at Bologna station. I doubt if he had seen a photograph. Gentry's life at MI6 was akin to a mole. I am pretty certain he had never been in the field before.'

Girondou looked a little puzzled.

'Actually he did or rather he muttered something about a straw hat.'

'A straw hat? What's so unusual about that.'

'It was something about the ribbon around it.'

'The ribbon?'

'Yes, the ribbon.'

'And what was so unusual about the ribbon around Gentry's straw hat?'

'Its, colour, apparently.'

'And what,' sighed Smith heavily, trying to keep his temper in the face if Girondou's teasing, 'was so special about the colour of the ribbon around Gentry's straw hat, pray?'

'It was striped.'

'Striped?'

'Yes, striped.'

'Striped how, exactly?'

'Er, orange and yellow, I believe.'

Smith suddenly went very quiet as in a moment he saw exactly what was happening and at the same time how dangerous the next days were going to be. It was the missing link in all this but he needed proof. They said their goodbyes and he turned the car, slightly more vigorously than was necessary and drove up the winding drive towards the road back to Arles and home.

Scene 2: Old School Tie and All That

They had passed through Martigues, and both Port-de -Buc and Fos-sur-Mer and were travelling up the rather desolate road to Raphèle les Arles before Martine broke the silence very gently.

'So what's special about the hat, my love.'

Smith didn't answer; not immediately at least. He was busy trying to answer the thousand and one questions that flooded his mind; questions about all the things he held most dear; loyalty to friends and country, trust, responsibility, morality - his, not anyone else's. In fact it was a long time until he reacted and when he did it was with a deep sigh; a sigh of regret as to what he might now find out and be forced to confront. Slowly he reached for his phone and pressed one of the speed-dial numbers.

'Hang on,' he said and laid the phone on his lap while he thought again. Martine simply looked on and waited. After a while he made up his mind, lifted the phone and pressed the loudspeaker button so she could hear a conversation that was going to be very brief. But it was the fact that he decided to share it with her at all that had taken the time deciding.

'All OK, Deveraux?'

The voice that came back sounded slightly miffed.

'Of course, Sir. Had a good lunch?'

Deveraux steadfastly refused to take any notice of Smith's perennial instruction to call him by his Christian name now they had both left the service and was also a little insulted about being asked whether there were any problems. Both he and Smith knew better than that, or so he thought. Deveraux made gentle reference to a good lunch as a possible explanation to Smith's unnecessary question. If anyone in the world could secure the Aubanet's farm it was Deveraux and they both knew it. Smith ignored the question but asked the one that was now clearly a key to this mess.

'Do you know whether Gentry was ever a member of MCC?'

The palpable gap over the airwaves indicated how unexpected was the question.

'Er, I have no idea, Sir. You are, though, aren't you.'

Smith's brusque reply illustrated the difficulty that he was having with this whole thing now.

'Of course, I am, you idiot. I am asking you about Gentry.'

Martine stiffened slightly at the insult. It had been her who had dug a bullet out of Deveraux's back when he had been called upon to use his unique talents during the last adventure at the Mas des Saintes. Instantly Smith saw his mistake.

'Sorry, Deveraux. I'm the idiot not you.'

A calm and understanding voice came back.

'Don't worry, Sir. I understand.'

This rather elegant repost made Smith break into a broad smile and the tension at ether end of the intergalactic conversation disappeared immediately. Deveraux continued:

'However, I can certainly find out, if you wish.'

Smith found the anger rising again.

Of course I ....'

Deveraux very sensibly cut the connection. Smith tossed the phone onto the floor of the car in exasperation. Martine knew that talk was the therapy now so she quietly collected the phone and slid her hand across the inside of Smith's right thigh and held him tightly.

'And what, pray, is the MCC and what is so important about being a member of it?'

Faced with explaining to a Frenchwoman the basic necessities of British civilisation in a few sentences, Smith immediately calmed down completely and took a deep breath - which was precisely the result that Martine had intended.

'The MCC is the Marylebone Cricket Club.'

Fighting back the strong desire to burst into inappropriate laughter, Martine could produce no more than a barely controlled: 'The what?'

Faced with the enormity of explaining one of the world's most incomprehensible games and it's fundamental importance to being British, Smith was flummoxed. All he could offer was a weak:

'It's the major sports club in London for people who are interested in, er, cricket.'

Martine who actually knew exactly what cricket was and what the MCC also was relented from her teasing. It had done the required thing and that was to brighten Smith's mood somewhat.

'And this orange and yellow colour is the club colour, I presume?'

Smith instantly knew that he had been played along but, far from being unhappy, was both amused and grateful as this miraculous Camargue woman handled him with such elegance and love.

'Yes'

'So as I know that the last thing that a proper Englishman does is wear the colours of a club or a society to which he is not entitled, the question in your mind is if Gentry was not a member of MCC, as I think you suspect, what was he doing wearing a hat bearing its colours.'

Smith opened his mouth to reply but she continued almost without a break.

'And therefore if he was not a member and therefore would not have a hat with the MCC ribbon on it how did he come to be wearing one - if, in fact, he was? The real question therefore is whether he given the hat by his companion at Bologna and if this was a signal for Grantkov was he being set up by the man who unfortunately was killed by mistake when Grantkov missed his target as the bomb went off. This might, of course, also explain Grantkov's present fit of pique. The man who was obviously connected with your Albanian affair but who was a member of MCC and, I suspect, to judge by your silence since we left Alexei's house, someone whose identity you know.'

This particular piece of perspicacity was met with another extended silence.

Scene 3: Ghosts from the Past

Having delivered Martine home, Smith drove slowly back to Arles. He had no real idea how he was going to wring the truth out of Gentry short of submitting him to the same sort of in-house hospitality presently being enjoyed by Grantkov in Marseille. Even he wasn't up to that. He parked the car in the Place and was half-way up the five steps that led from the street to his front door when he stopped almost in mid-stride. Something felt wrong and, having looked around quickly to see that he wasn't going to scare a passing tourist, he pulled the little Glock from the back of his trousers. What was wrong, as Sherlock Holmes once memorably noted, was the dog.

Gregory (Scotland Yard detective): 'Is there any other point to which you would wish to draw my attention?'

Holmes: 'To the curious incident of the dog in the night-time.'

Gregory: 'The dog did nothing in the night-time.'

Holmes: 'That was the curious incident.'

Being a sight hound meant that Arthur had spend most of his life silently pursuing what he could see. Artificial hares on a track, real live hares in the field, cats. In short, anything furry that ran. However possibly as some sort of compensation for the onset of old age, he seemed to have developed some more appropriate facilities. He could hear the approaching pizza delivery moped at a range that would have done credit to an early warning radar system defending the free world from whatever it imagined menaced it. Being a sight hound he didn't generally make much of a fuss unless it was someone he knew and liked. Nor did he bark very often. But now in retirement Arthur had added this slightly annoying ability to his repertoire. Thus it was not usual for Smith to approach his own front door without some sort of fuss being made. This time there was nothing.

He could of course find a circuitous route in through his little garden but that was surrounded by high walls or neighbours but at his age it was a foolhardy route into the house and entirely too strenuous. The chances of his doing it silently were slim. The best policy, Smith felt, was to enter the house in the normal way, gun in hand, hoping that whoever was uninvited and inside his house would be relaxed by the possible normality of it all. So he simply walked in, gun held ready. The old man sitting on the sofa with a completely contented Arthur hardly moved. He did however start the conversation.

'It would be a pity after the eighty five years on this planet, to depart it with a bullet from an ex-student, Peter.'

Smith's complete astonishment was slightly diverted by Arthur hauling himself off the sofa to give his master a half-hearted belated greeting before returning quickly to the comfort of the unexpected guest's lap. He finally found his voice.

'Christ, Sir, I could have killed you.'

The old man shook his head and relied in a voice that was as gentle as his smile.

'No. Peter. I think I educated you better than that, I think.'

Smith grimaced. The word had been well chosen. This was the man who, some forty years ago, had made him understand about art and history, about the importance of what things meant rather than what things looked like. He was the man who had grilled him unmercifully about his footnotes and sources and the qualities of his arguments whether he was writing about Roman sarcophagus sculpture, renaissance neo-Platonist iconography or modern abstraction theory. This was the only man who Smith had ever truly respected during his time at university. He was also the man who had recruited him into the service. They had not met for almost all those forty years. Smith poured them both a dilute whisky, sat down opposite his guest and waited. The old man took a long draw from the glass and smiled.

'Excellent, Peter, excellent. I am pleased to see that you still have no truck with bullshit.'

The whisky was his customary supermarket ordinary and Smith knew what his old professor meant for it was he who had taught the young student to sniff out bullshit however it was disguised. Writings about art, especially modern art, are particularly prone to it. He still waited. He didn't feel able to question this man. He would simply wait. After a while, his guest nodded in acknowledgement.

'Ah Peter, you were always my best student; at many things, I think, but I fear I have to interfere in your life a little and before we start, I apologise for that. However it may well be necessary.'

Smith remained silent. The old man would get to the point when he wanted and Smith was in no hurry. He felt rather than saw his guest gathering himself for an effort and when at last he did start it was with a slightly sad smile.

'Peter I am glad that you haven't forgotten the virtue of silence. However, first I must apologise for breaking into your home. It did occur to me to sit on the wall outside and contemplate the magnificent Arena that you have as your neighbour. But as it got hotter and I had no idea how long I was going to have to wait, I thought you might forgive my coming into the shade of your house through what I would be failing in my duty if I did not describe as some thoroughly inadequate security.'

He paused but Smith stayed silent.

'I have been persuaded out of my retirement by our late masters as they seem to think that I might succeed where they would almost certainly fail. So I come to see you with their request. It was rather a long journey for an old man like me. Rather too hot a journey as well.'

Smith finally broke his silence.

'Masters, Hugo. Which particular masters are those.?'

'Well the usual ones, I suppose.'

'Perhaps yours, not mine.'

The old professor nodded slowly.

'Yes, I suppose that's true. Even when you condescended to work for the service from time to time, you were never completely under our control, were you?

Smith took this as the compliment that obviously wasn't intended.

'Not a company man, Hugo. Perhaps that's the reason I'm still alive.'

The old man nodded his agreement.

'As usual, Peter, you are probably right.

Again the silence descended. Smith was again in no particular hurry to break it. Hugo La Salle was doing the bidding of the London service; probably some unsavoury business that they needed help with and didn't have the courage to do themselves. In spite of his contempt, Smith knew that somehow this could be a connection that would begin to tie some things together and he was in no hurry at all for it to start. Neither obviously was Arthur who had long since fallen asleep again. After a while an increasingly uncomfortable retired professor of art history went on and got to the point with commendable brevity for a man of his age.

'Basically, they want Grantkov back.'

It had been a slip. With a huge effort of will, Smith stopped himself picking up on the word 'back' although it seemed to him suddenly to offer a whole set of alternatives that he had only recently begun to consider since the affair of the hat and its ribbon had surfaced. He needed much, much more information and perhaps, as Gentry seemed currently to be struck dumb, this unexpected visitor could furnish some of it. The Hugo La Salle he had learned so much from all those years ago and against whom he had brushed up on very odd occasions since would normally not have made that mistake. Perhaps he was getting old at last. Smith shivered a little involuntarily. Sic transit Gloria mundae, he thought grimly to himself. This old man once had the sharpest mind he had ever met. He decided an obviously faked insouciance was the best way forward.

'Who?'

It was the professor's turn to remain silent. Perhaps, Smith thought, the slip was not as inadvertent as he thought. He tried another tack.

'Does Gentry know you're here?'

'I'm not sure if I can tell you that Peter.'

Smith thought it might be time to show a little metal.

'Hugo, you had better be straight with me because I am in no mood to be pissed around by anyone including you. I have Deveraux down here at the moment and unless you're careful I'll set him loose on you.'

La Salle paled visibly. He knew the history between Smith and Deveraux and knew this was no idle threat. Deveraux would do anything Smith wanted without question.

'No. Gentry doesn't know I'm here.'

'And what makes you think that I have Grantkov and isn't he dead?'

' London says you have him.'

'Then London is wrong - not for the first time, I might add.'

The old man shook his head.

'I think not on this occasion. Perhaps it wouldn't be a good idea to get on the wrong side of London at the moment. There is a dreadful new breed in the Vauxhall Cross ziggurat. Very common. All products of the state school system, you see. Not our sort of people at all, I'm afraid and capable of almost anything.'

'Then perhaps when you return you might remind then of the danger many of them run by coming too close to me; if you return, that is.'

La Salle smiled slightly.

'I did before I left. but you never know. These cocky young sods might not understand.'

'Then it's up to you to make sure they do, professor.'

Again there was a silence before Smith decided to take the conversation further.

'What the hell is London doing using a old Romanian assassin-for-hire with a chip on his shoulder.'

Hugo La Salle looked very tired and raised a limp hand as if to emphasise the fact.

'Believe me, Peter, I don't know,'

Smith was dismissive.

'That's complete bullshit, Hugo. Firstly you always know everything; at least you used to. Secondly you wouldn't have agreed to come here without being properly briefed - unless, of course, London has some hold over you that would force you to come without a proper briefing'.

Again, silence. Finally Smith asked:

'Tell me about Albania, Hugo.'

'You were there, Peter. If anyone should know, you should. Other than pissing off our American friends – always I good thing, I would have thought – you came out of that one smelling of roses as I recall.'

Smith shook his head.

'Not that, Hugo. I know what happened on the ground including very nearly getting my arse shot off. I want to know what is known in these modern times as the back-story. What was it actually all about?'

'And what makes you think that I had anything at all to do with it? As you might recall, at the time, I was a simple university teacher plying my trade at that aggressively modern university on the south coast of England where you cut your intellectual teeth and where I helped you sharpen them.'

'Because, old friend' and Smith laid a heavy sarcasm on the words, 'you were almost the only person in MI6 at the time who had an intellect as well as a brain. The whole expedition was so clearly improbable that there had to be something going on more than our brave but naïve country cousins could have planned. My guess is that you, and through you, Gentry, hijacked the stupid mission for your own nefarious purposes. As usual, I was the one who ended up in the firing line.'

Hugo La Salle still shook his head.

'No, Peter, you're wrong.'

Smith suddenly felt tired off all this. The lost calm of his solitary retirement suddenly made him resentful of this old man. He found no capacity any more for understanding or desire for it for that matter. For many of the last years he had made his way without help from those who, with various degrees of disinterest, had occasionally wanted to re-involve themselves in his life. This was yet another of those occasions and he was minded to send some pretty strong messages back to London. He repeated:

'Tell me about Albania, Hugo.'

Again his companion shook his head tiredly.

'Peter, I know nothing about all that.'

Smith found, like most truly important decisions in life, this one was remarkable easy to make.

'Hugo, old friend, old chum. Unless you tell me what I want to know, you will not leave this room alive.'

They both seemed to notice anew the Glock that had remained in Smith's hand, as steady as ever since he had sat down, pointed at his visitors head precisely line up with his right eye.

'Don't you think that is a touch excessive, Peter?'

Smith shrugged.

'Perhaps, but I really no longer care. If the new generation in London has forgotten what I can do to them, and if they decide to send you out here on a fishing expedition or possibly worse, then they vastly miscalculate how pissed off with all this I am and how prepared I am to cause them pain if it comes to that. I am also very surprised that you, who should know me as well as anyone, didn't tell them that in the first place. So when you are sent back to them in a box, perhaps they will get the message. I am better at any of this than they are with all their sophistication and electronic wizardry and if it means that they have to receive a corpse via yet another waterproof diplomatic bag to make them understand that, then so be it. I am unhappy, Hugo, very unhappy and someone will pay if necessary.'

La Salle nodded in understanding. Smith continued:

'Albania, Hugo, Albania.'

Considering he was in is mid-eighties, it would seem difficult or someone to look much older, but La Salle managed it.

'I have a feeling that you know most of it already. You were sent in to look after the team and did a pretty good job. The whole thing was rogue but what you possibly don't know is that we knew that too. Our Albanian connections were much better than anyone else's and the Americans had no idea that we knew about their clandestine little department and its rather silly plans.'

That was something that Smith had guessed long ago.

'So why did we get involved in the whole business to start with? Why not let the Americans go in, fuck it all up as is traditional when any degree of subtlety is required, and get themselves all killed. Why put us in harm's way?'

La Salle smiled.

'Ah, well, you see it was not quite that straightforward. We knew of course, that Chinese missiles were nowhere near Albania, nor would they ever be, primarily because China never really had any in the first place. Certainly some chemical weapons were delivered but this was strictly third division stuff. Mustard gas in Heinz bean cans. Little more.'

'So?'

'Well some of the, shall we say, dramatis personae, were interesting to us.'

'Who precisely?'

There was a considerable pause while the old man was clearly making up his mind about something.

'Fredericks interested us.'

'Why?'

'Because he seemed to be a double - or possibly even more.'

'Who else?'

'Grantkov.'

A little of the fog cleared for Smith. A young Grantkov had obviously not been part of his incursion team. It followed that he might have been with the Albanians. Suddenly Gentry's silence could be explained - at least a little. Smith answered.

'Grantkov was given to the Albanians by Gentry to kill the rogue Americans.'

'More or less. Unfortunately you were much too good at your job and he only managed to get one.'

'And just how many of the five were actually rogue.'

'Ah, that was a bit of a problem. At the time we were only sure of two but as it turns out now it could have been all of them.'

'What do you mean could'

'Just that dear boy. We didn't actually know for certain. In fact we are not really sure now after all these years.'

Smith both looked and felt acutely unhappy.

'So Grantkov works for us.'

'Possibly. Then certainly, but now? One never really knows these days.'

'So why does London want him back so badly now?'

'I have absolutely no idea.'

Smith was at a bit of a loss as to know where to go next. Other than being an obvious mess there seemed to be little rational.

No-one particularly seemed to be likely to benefit. Suddenly he got an idea.

'Who was control for the operation.'

Smith saw a slight glint of apprehension cross his guests face. Maybe, he thought he had finally hit on something. If La Salle pretended he didn't know then he would know he had asked the right question.

'I really can't remember. It was such a long time ago.'

Smith snorted. He didn't have to point out that La Salle had a reputation of having the most prodigious of memories. It was unlikely that his advancing years had dimmed it at all – at least it didn't seem likely to Smith. He just waited for the man not to remember but to examine the consequences of not remembering. It didn't take long.

'Er, I seem to recall that it was Miles, Miles Ripley.'

'The same Miles Ripley who is currently in line to be the next Chief in London?'

La Salle nodded.

'The same.'

'And was it by any chance Ripley who got MI6 involved in the Albanian adventure in the first place?'

'Yes.'

'And it was he therefore who got Gentry and later McDonnell and me involved in this madcap CIA scheme.'

'Yes and I am impressed by your continued accuracy in your use of English grammar, Peter. It was always one of the many things that made your essays at university a pleasure to read.'

'It smells to me,' said Smith ignoring his visitor's simple attempt at diversion, 'that our Mr. Miles…'

'Sir, now,' interrupted La Salle.

'Ripley,' continued, Smith, 'would seem to me to be doing a little quiet house cleaning before his assumption of power. The question is how dirty is the house?'

At that moment Smith satellite phone rang. It was Deveraux.

'Gentry was never a member of MCC. An old friend has just emailed me the membership list for 1980. Didn't know that you qualified as a playing member, Boss. I'm impressed.'

Smith harrumphed.

'Don't be. Is, by any chance, Miles Ripley on the list?'

There was pause while the phone at the end was put down and lifted again a few moments later.

'Yes as is, by the way, Hugo La Salle which you probably knew already but what you probably don't know that rumour in the labyrinthine halls of Vauxhall Cross has it that the old codger has crept out of retirement and may be on his way to see you. I have a feeling that it takes more than the off chance of a chat with an old student to coax that old snake out of his lair.'

'And where, precisely, did you glean this particular piece of information?'

'From a friend.'

'A friend?'

'In London?'

'No.'

'Where then?'

'Not that it matters particularly but in Warsaw.'

'Interesting news; accurate even if it is a little late.'

Instantly he could hear Deveraux's concern.

'Then there are two things you should know. The first is that La Salle always has a minder these days and secondly he wears a Kel-Tec P-32 in a dinky little ankle holster. Right leg, I think. The minder will be around somewhere. It is likely to be a pretty blond boy as that is what La Salle's goes for these days. If, as I guess, the old man is with you now and listening to this the boy will be outside somewhere. Unless you say 'no' I'll telephone Girondou and get some of his people on it immediately.'

Smith's only reply was to cut the connection. He lifted the Glock that was still in his hand and re-aimed it his guest's heart. With a slight nod of his head he gestured towards La Salle's right foot.

'Take it out very slowly using two fingers only and lay it on the table in front of you. Be very, very careful and remember that you have never been closed to dying that you are at this particular moment, Hugo.'

206

La Salle looked surprised only for a moment but then did as he was told. The gun was laid carefully on the low table in front of him.

'My word, Peter. You do have interesting telephone calls.'

'Aren't you getting a little old to be messing about with these things, Hugo? A bit of a girl's gun too. Now sit on your hands.'

La Salle was outraged.

'Really, Peter. Don't you think this is just a touch undignified for someone at my age?'

Smith was obviously unconcerned about his guest's dignity.

'I don't really care, Hugo. Perhaps you should have thought about that before you broke into my house uninvited and decided to wear a gun. Your personal comfort means very little to me at the moment. Now perhaps you'll tell me why you're here.'

'Well it is true that London wants Grantkov. You'll just have to believe me when I tell you that I don't know why. I think they also wanted to know what sort of a situation you were in down here. I do think that you should be careful at the moment. There are some odd things happening in London at the minute and, although I am here on our masters' bidding, I wanted to warn you.'

'Your master still, possibly. Not mine. I would remind you and them that they have a lot to lose by getting too close down here.'

La Salle just nodded.

'Why was McDowell killed?'

The man looked genuinely shocked.

'What? My God! Peter, I had no idea. You must believe that. When was that?'

'I'm not asking you, Hugo, whether or not you knew. I want to know why, that's all. Why take McDowell out? He was completely harmless and completely retired.'

A touch of desperation crept into the old man's voice.

'Peter, I really don't know.'

The look of remorse on La Salle's face didn't look false. He was obviously shocked by the news as Smith continued.

'Well he was shot a few days ago by some pond life from America for no reason I can fathom except that a lot of strange things have been happening lately that seem to trace back to Albania in one way or another. You seem to be working for some rather smelly people, Hugo. Not good. Not good at all. Someone should point out the error of your ways, old age or not. Perhaps that falls to me.'

They both lapsed into an uncomfortable silence. Even Arthur felt the tension and decided to get up and walk very slowly out through the open kitchen door and out into the garden. Smith's phone rang again. This time it was Girondou. Smith was impressed. It was less than five minutes since Deveraux called. Girondou must have some very close protection in place. Close as in outside his front door.

'We've got the little boy. Deveraux was right. He is a blonde. However he was not entirely supine and he got a little damaged, I'm afraid. He's a feisty little thing. I gather you've got company so if you don't reply to anything I will assume you are saying: yes. I'll have the boy brought back to Marseille and see if he knows anything interesting. I don't hold out much hope. So we may have to be a little assertive when we question him but I assume that you won't mind too much. Deveraux said he thought you sounded a bit pissed off. We have had a little more success with Grantkov and I will tell you that later when we are alone, as it were. The only other piece of news is that your chum Gentry seems to be making a lot of satellite telephone calls to London and the states. They are too well encrypted for us to listen in but he is going through a CIA network whatever that signifies. That's about it. Call when your uninvited guest leaves or if you want him taken away. If this goes on, Peter, I'm going to have to buy another hotel. Oh, by the way, and your are definitely not going to like this, but the boy had a photograph of Martine in his pocket.'

With that he rang off. The photo of Martine made him very distressed indeed and when got Smith got distressed people usually died. He forced himself to calm down. It was time to finish with the old man. He had a feeling that there was little to be gained by further conversation and he was likely to do something that he would regret if it were prolonged too much.

'Hugo, please think very carefully about being honest with me. I am getting deeply unhappy with all this. I will ask you one final time what more, if anything, you know about all this. If I find out that you have been lying to me I will certainly find you in that little thatched retirement cottage of yours in deepest rural Sussex and you will live in quiet retirement no longer.'

La Salle suddenly looked ill.

'I'm getting too old for this. All I know is that Ripley is very nervous about the Albanian thing now he is on the verge of power. He is nervous about Gentry, about Grantkov and about you in particular. I really know nothing about McDowell and am rather disgusted by that. Really, Peter, I know little more. On this occasion I really am only a messenger.'

Smith again paused to collect his thoughts and made some fast decisions.

'Right. This is the way it'll go. You will return to London and give Ripley a number of messages. You will just have to hope that, like, me, he doesn't shoot messengers. First, he will have Grantkov when I have finished with him and not before. He may or may not actually be alive when that happens. Secondly he will make sure that no harm comes to me or Gentry or anyone around me – and I mean anyone. I have Deveraux here and you know what that means. If Ripley has forgotten then you might do him a favour by reminding him. Gentry is my business not his or at least should be. I've no idea why you were sent to do this. It smells like Ripley is doing something on his own account rather than official departmental business. And that is indeed smelly. You will leave here and return to England immediately and you will be watched to ensure that you do. You will not wait for your little boy bodyguard. I have him now as well and I want to meet him personally. Unless he gives me some pretty convincing answers he will find out, like you might find out narrowly escape finding out, that there are aspects of being in touch, shall be say, with your more feminine side, that the Arab dockers of Marseille are less than familiar with. At the minute, that is what I have in mind for him.

La Salle's eyes widened in astonishment.

'Peter, he's just a friend looking after my back. Please leave him alone.'

La Salle was scared but he could still read Smith's voice.

'What does he have to tell you, Peter, that will ensure his safety.'

'In the first place, I suggest you get a better bodyguard, Hugo. Sacrifice looks for some ability, I would suggest. No, I'll keep him for a while, thank you. I want to ask him a question.'

'What?' the old man whispered.

'I want to ask him why he is carrying a photograph of Martine Aubanet with him and unless I get a satisfactory answer I will personally remove his pretty blue eyes with a very blunt spoon while he is still alive and send them back to you in a matchbox by mail. Now get out of my house before I do similar to you.'

Smith watched the man who had been such an important part of his life descend his front steps and walk uncertainly down the hill and out of sight. A moment's sympathy was soon extinguished by the thought of that photograph. Deveraux answered his phone and Smith brought him up to date. Instantly he understood.

'Don't worry, Sir. Madam and her family are in good hands. In fact she and I are just about to play some Bach for four hands.'

'Just so you keep your fingers on the keyboard, Deveraux.'

He heard a rich chuckle as the connection was cut. Apart from his profession, Deveraux was also a seriously talented pianist.

Chapter 7: Engaging the Enemy

Scene 1: Problems and Solutions

Smith picked up his phone to call Gentry but hesitated. He really had no idea what he was going to say him. The feeling that his friend continued to be less than frank with him persisted and it was this, rather than the messier bits of the business that they seemed to be involved in, that disturbed him most. When it came down to it, Smith put his trust in very few people and his faith in even fewer. Martine and Arthur, without any doubt, followed by – well he wasn't entirely sure. Girondou, perhaps, although it was too soon to be certain. Deveraux, of course. They had shared terror together and they both owed each other more than just their lives. There had been a time until recently when Gentry would have been unhesitatingly on the list but since Bologna had returned to haunt him, he was no longer sure. Perhaps Gentry would join that very short list of people who Smith had trusted and who had let him down. It was a worrying thought. Worrying, not because of who they were or exactly what usually happened subsequently. In fact there was nothing to happen subsequently. All but one were dead although not all that was directly attributable to Smith. Only those who deserved it, as one might say. The survivor was in a secure mental hospital in Bucharest. That particular coincidence had been nagging away at Smith for some time: ever since the demise of Tosca, in fact. He didn't want to add Gentry to that particular list. So it was a somewhat heavy heart that he pressed the speed dial for his old chum. A rich and amused American voice came back to him.

'Ah. At last. Mr. Smith, I presume. This is Grant Fredricks and I am delighted finally to speak to you. I've heard so much about you.'

Unsurprisingly, Smith was not interested in pleasantries. If this man had Gentry's phone, he also had Gentry.

'I'll find you Fredricks. If you know anything at all about me, you should know that.'

A delighted laugh came back at him.

'Of course, I know that, my dear fellow. That's what I am so much looking forward to.'

'Gentry?'

'Oh he's fine, of course. He'll stay alive for as long as I need him.'

'And how long will that be?'

'Oh, Mr Smith, please don't pretend to be naive with me. I need Mr Gentry alive because while he lives, you will try to rescue him. You will feel honour-bound to do so. When I am sure that you are coming, then I will probably kill him. But you won't know, of course.'

There was a pause while Fredricks waited for Smith to say something. Nothing came and a slightly petulant American continued.

'OK my dear. Play the strong silent one if you wish but the fact remains that in a while I will tell you where you can find your friend or you be terribly clever and you will find out in any case. You will come, of course, and I will kill you. All very simple and satisfactory - from my point of view, at least. You will ride in like a saviour on a white horse because that is what your highly peculiar code of conduct requires of you although you know it will be hopeless as he will be already dead - probably. You won't know, of course, for certain, that is. If you didn't come, you could never live with yourself. You see I have had a considerable time in prison to examine you, my friend and I know you as well as you know yourself. Oh, and if you think that simply doing nothing is an option then you should know that if you don't convince me that you are on your way to find me when I tell you where to come, I will kill him anyway. Your conscience might well learn to live with losing your friend as you attempt to free him in battle so-to-speak. I suspect it will be less forgiving if you did so while doing nothing. So all that remains is to say, good by, Mr Smith. Until we meet again as they say. I will telephone you within twelve hours to tell you where to come when I have arranged for your reception. I, for one, will be looking forward to it.'

Smith very gently put the phone down on the garden table as if it was a Delft figure. Normally, when some intense thinking was in order he would take Arthur for a long walk around the less salubrious parts of the town. By now, however, it was just past midday and the temperature was well into the high nineties. His much-loved Lock straw hat would be enough to protect him when he wished to impersonate Noel Coward's famous song about mad dogs and Englishmen being the only creatures to venture out in the midday sun. But taking Arthur out in such a temperature necessitated carrying water for the dog and he didn't feel like doing that. So he went slowly into the house, poured himself a very weak whisky and soda with a lot of ice and took his place under his jasmine and grape vine shaded veranda. Arthur, as ever sensing when something was amiss, got up a walked silently over Smith and stood at his side and laid his head gently on his knee. He stood completely still just looking up. Smith touched the head equally gently in thanks and whispered for the dog to return to his rug in his particular bit of shade and resume sleeping. It had been a reassuring contact and both Smith and Arthur knew when that sort of thing was necessary. It served also to remind Smith of what his particular definition of friendship was all about.

Having checked his watch just in case Fredricks was being literal, he sat motionless for almost an hour. His thoughts followed no particular lines or worked through no particular scenarios. His mind tended not to work like that. He just wandered across the problem getting a series of impressions and overviews. His late godfather had been a concert pianist and once, as a boy sitting in the great man's studio listening to him practice, he had asked how on earth could a pianist follow all those little dots printed on the page when the piece was moving so fast. The explanation was, of course, that the pianist doesn't read each dot. Scanning, experience, training and practice does it instead. General impressions are transformed into particular keys being pressed in the right way and the music emerges without really conscious act at all. This was Smith's approach to life in general as well while he may not have been a great planner like Gentry but he was a master improviser.

His immediate problem was an obvious one and he didn't underestimate the difficulty of beating a plan that might have taken years of analysis in prison to concoct. There seemed to be no obvious way he would cunningly find Gentry and get him out in a conventional sense. He didn't waste time on looking for a way in for the white charger. The obsession of his opponent had kindly make that unnecessary. No, he had to find a different route; one that used his talents for improvisation and that approach meant starting at the end – the present, in other words – and working backwards. This was the bit of the thing that Fredricks could have planned for but only up to a point. Before Smith had tried to call Gentry, Fredricks was alone in his plan and everything, inevitably would have gone to it. The variables started as soon as Smith joined the picture This was the part that Fredricks couldn't plan with complete certainty so that was where he would start.

Fredricks obviously had somewhere in mind for Smith to lose his life in a vainglorious attempt to save Gentry. It would be somewhere relatively close so that meant that Fredricks had come back to France. Smith's territory rather than his. He also knew that he would need help. There were things that needed to be done quickly and he couldn't do them on his own. He needed some intelligent muscle and some IT expertise. Girondou, of course, could be relied on but given that he would have to source the muscle in what was for him personally a foreign country, quality control, as it were, might be a problem. Also Girondou's world had different priorities when it came to physical violence and some Neanderthal diving in would be less than helpful no matter how well-intentioned it might be. Gentry, of course, would normally organise this but now Smith was on his own. Smith made up his mind. He had no choice. It had to be Girondou and he put in the call.

'Peter. What can I do for you.'

'Fredricks seems to have taken Gentry.'

There was a stunned silence.

'I thought Fredricks was dead?'

'Apparently not.'

'What can I do.'

'At the moment just some IT support please. I have just talked to Fredricks on Gentry's phone. Now I have a feeling that Fredricks is half expecting me to call him. He has a plan of some sort and that sort or arrogance that would expect me to try to negotiate in some way or at least to get in touch. If this is the case then there is a slim chance that Gentry's phone may be still switched on. You remember after Angèle was kidnapped last year we made sure that your IT man had software for locating phone GPS chips. Please could you ask him to get a location for Gentry's satellite phone and let me know as soon as possible? Obviously if they've switched the damn thing off then were buggered.'

'Is the phone one of the ones I gave you last year?'

'Er, yes, it is. Why?'

Girondou chuckled.

'Don't worry, Peter. It is just a little trick that makes watching your back a little easier. That's all. Anything else?'

Smith decided to let this most recent discovery alone, for the moment at least.

'Not at the moment, but I'm sure there will be.'

Next was a call to Martine.

'Hi there, you OK?'

'Of course. Your friend Deveraux is an extraordinary man.'

'I know that, and not just on the piano either. I'll be needing some of his other talents before too long, I think. The American Fredricks seems to have come back from the dead and has kidnapped Gentry.'

'Oh God Peter.'

He could feel that she wanted to say more but she became very business-like, very quickly.

'What can we do?'

'I'll be with you in half an hour. Could you saddle up some horses for you, me and Deveraux? I think it would be good to do some planning together. I'll bring Arthur. The temperature will be down a little by the time I arrive.'

He could feel that she wanted to say all sorts of things about being careful or not doing anything too rash but appreciated the fact that she didn't. He collected Arthur and got into his car. The first part of his plan required Deveraux to get working as quickly as possible and he needed a briefing face to face. Some orders needed it. Arthur was the only happy one. He knew what the ride in Smith's battered old Peugeot was likely to mean: a free run over the farm looking for things to kill. He was probably unaware how similar were his feelings to his master's.

Twenty minutes later he drove into the dusty courtyard in the centre of the Mas des Saintes. Martine immediately came to him and gave him a hug.

'Welcome home,' she whispered into his ear. She had an idea what he was thinking. 'Let's go to my *cabane* and talk.'

The horses were ready and the three rode off into the great marsh that was their particular bit of the Camargue. A slight breeze had sprung up and with it a covering of cloud. Immediately the temperature moderated. He was still pleased to see that both Deveraux and Martine carried large water containers hanging from their saddles. She had thought of Arthur who, like most sight hounds, would quite possible run himself into a dangerous state of exhaustion if not looked after.

There was almost no conversation as they rode. Both Martine and Deveraux knew that Smith was still thinking it out. Indeed, Smith remained deep in thought while watching his beloved hound ranging far and near over the flat countryside. When he was first let loose over the farm a years or two ago he was very uncertain about the water. Most of his life had been spent running on sand tracks or occasionally hard grass fields. He had had to learn about running through water. He hated it to start with but it hadn't taken him long to realise that he had to learn to love water or the small black bull chasing him would actually catch him. Now he was very good at finding his way through the salt water inlets that veined the fields. They stopped once to give Arthur some water but half an hour later, they were sitting in the shade in Martine's terrace that faced west over a stretch of water than was almost completely pink with flamingos. Arthur looked on casually. He knew there was no future in chasing flamingos. Things that lived on water and flew in the air were of no interest to a dog brought up on furry things that ran.

Smith remained deep in thought. There was something - a lot actually - that troubled him. Essentially it was the fact that there still seemed to be two very separate themes to the current opera. Fredricks coming out of the woodwork seemingly on a voyage of historical revenge hardly gelled with La Salle's visit which was all about current stuff. He really couldn't seen the connection. His mental review got to the phone call with Fredricks and he tried to play it back in his head as accurately as he could. It took him a couple of tries but on the third, he got it. He remembered what Fredricks had actually said and suddenly much of the story clicked into place. Not everything but all the essentials. He now knew what this whole thing was all about.

They waited, cold glasses of rosé in hand while Smith brought them up to date. Exactly on queue just as Smith finished his narrative, his phone rang. It was Girondou.

'He's in Lussan. Or at least his phone is.'

'What? The Lussan just north of Uzès?'

'Yes.'

'In the village itself or in the surrounding countryside?'

'Actually in the village itself.'

Smith was incredulous.

'Are we talking about the Lussan north of Uzès, population of less than five hundred; the one perched on the top of a hill, surrounded by a big wall and reached by virtually a single road? That Lussan?.'

A rich chuckle came over the space link.

'The very same, my friend. I couldn't believe it either. But I think, perhaps you could do with a little good news.'

'Fredericks is a idiot. You could have the whole place permanently under surveillance by half a dozen men who wouldn't have to get within a mile to do their jobs properly.'

'I think that two of your English miles would suffice. However we'll know in less than half an hour.'

Smith digested the fact that Girondou had done what he thought best and probably, in reality, it wouldn't be a problem.

'Thanks, Alexei. I'm grateful. But certainly well away please. Let me know if the phone starts moving but if it does only follow. Please don't intercept yet. There's a little more to this than we might think. Fredricks left the phone turned on on purpose. He wants me not just Gentry.'

'I understand. However, you might like to know that the phone was actually switched off which if, of course, the usual way of preventing a GPS chip from telling the world where you are.

However in this case there are more than one way to locate this particular satellite phone.'

'Oh? Well how on earth did you get a location?'

'Well I have a little gizmo made by a young chap who when he isn't high as a kite, does IT stuff for me. He made some modifications to our satellite phones so that they can be turned on remotely if required. No chimes, whistles or lights. They still look dead but we can read the GPS chip. I did this in case with our phones if we need to locate them in an emergency. You remember, my friend, that I learned this trick from you when they kidnapped Angèle last year. This is how you found her, remember? I do.'

'Hum. I'm not sure if I like that very much Alexei.'

The voice was brisk.

'Like it or not, it is a little trick that might save your life one day and now will probably save Gentry's if that is actually what you want to achieve. Oh, by the way, what do you want to do with our two current guests?'

Smith was still a little grumpy as he continued.

'Well you can lean on the pretty boy and find out who he is actually working for, although I think I know already. He may have been chosen for his looks but I suspect the choice was not La Salle's. I particularly want to know who gave him the photo of Martine and why he had it in his pocket. You can damage him if you wish. I really don't case very much. But I really don't think he's an important character in all this. It might be fun to let him go in one of the less salubrious bits of Marseille and let him find his way home from there. He might learn something himself. As for Grantkov ask him about Albania. One more thing. Can you get a list of everyone who owns or rents property in that village?'

'Nothing could be simpler. It should take no more than fifteen minutes to get a list. How shall I get it to you?'

Smith paused for a moment's thought. He turned to Martine.

'You have one of these smartphone things don't you? Could you give your email address to Alexei?'

He turned back.

'Alexei can you email the list to Martine? She has one of these new-fangled telephones that work like a cinema. She'll give you details.'

He handed his phone over and the information was passed. Girondou asked Martine:

'How is he?'

'Worryingly well. I think he has a plan and knowing him when he is in this sort of mood, I suspect it'll be unorthodox.'

Girondou replied with a certain amount of conviction.

'Please don't worry, my dear. We both have reason to be grateful to Peter when he's in this sort of mood, as you put it. I'll email that list as soon as I can.'

Smith turned to Deveraux.

'How are your contacts back in London, Derek?'

Deveraux grimaced.

'If you don't mind, Sir, I'll stick to my surname. I actually dislike my first name almost as much as you are amused by it. To answer your question, I believe they are quite good still.'

'Do you know a couple or three people who could handle a little abduction for me? They'll have to be good, of course, but also be able to do it pretty gently as there will be two to lift, both female, I think. I don't want them harmed in any way nor scared any more than they need to be. They may not even have to take the people away; just sit on them for a while. They need to plan and act within twelve hours. Can you handle that?'

Deveraux graced the problem with a few moments' thought while Martine looked on with some concern.

'Yes, Sir. I think I can. You have no objections to female kidnappers, I presume?'

Smith immediately saw the cleverness of the approach.

'Very definitely not, Deveraux. Inspired thought, I would say.'

Martine could finally stand it no longer. She waited for Smith to refill their glasses and then asked:

'Peter, will you kindly tell us what's going on?'

Smith put on his most paternally patronising voice and smiled benignly as if he was again talking to his class forty years ago.

'Now listen carefully to your uncle Peter my children. You see there are many, many things that you can fake about yourself, with hard work and practice, but grammar, English Grammar especially, will almost invariably catch you out. It was, I believe, the writer George Bernard Shaw who characterised Britain and the United States as two countries separated by a common language. You can practice all you like and perfect another countries vocabulary, their accent, even their idioms – good actors do that all the time - but sooner or later you will make a grammatical mistake and be caught out. It only takes a single slip. Even within the same country, the same problem arises. If you want to regarded as part of the upper class in England you can try to learn the codes. You will learn to sit on a sofa not a settee and it will be located in a drawing room not a lounge. At the end of your meal you will eat a pudding not a dessert or a sweet. You will know instinctively when to call a boat a ship and vice versa. But unless it is native to you, sooner or later you will slip and the whole edifice will crumble for it takes just one little mistake to undo years of good work. You will use your knife and fork in the wrong order or hold them in the wrong way, pass the port the wrong way or try to get on your horse from the wrong side. In our particular instance, our Mr Fredricks made en error of grammar – or rather failed to make one. Another variation, if you like, of the curious instance of the dog in the night. It was the mistake that he failed to make that gave him away.'

By this time his audience was beginning to think that he had taken leave of his senses; except Arthur who had long since dozed off in the late afternoon heat. Sensing that he was perhaps losing his audience, Smith continued quickly.

'I remember very clearly that Fredricks said just after he answered the phone – and I am pretty sure I remember the phrase correctly. He said: 'This is Grant Fredricks and I am delighted finally to speak to you'.'

His audience looked blank for a moment but then Deveraux smiled.

'Ah, I see. An American would have split the infinitive.'

A delighted Smith smiled back as if his favourite pupil had demonstrated more than usual intelligence.

'Well done, Deveraux, well done. Go to the top of the class.'

Turning to Martine who was not entirely convinced that she wasn't in the presence of completely mad people, he explained.

'One of the many difference between The Queen's English and American occurs in what is known as a split infinitive. The classic example is the famous Star Trek introduction where the good Captain Kirk describes the five year mission of the Star Ship Enterprise as being 'to boldly go where no man has gone before.' The proper English would have been, of course, 'to go boldly' as it is not done to separate the infinitive particle from its verb with an adverb. The split infinitive may be regarded as good and acceptable syntax in America and thus be in common use but it is thoroughly non-U in England and it is easily and unconsciously avoided by people educated to a decent level automatically. An American would have said 'I am delighted to finally speak to you'.'

Martine cottoned on immediately.

'So if you weren't talking to Fredricks, who..?'

'Ah, now that's a very good question for it would indicate that we have a new player in our nasty little game here in Provence.'

'Who?' Deveraux and Martine asked simultaneously.

'Ah. I have a fair idea but I would like to wait for Girondou's list before making a guess. However, if I am right, I am pretty sure that it makes our job easier rather than harder.'

It was nearer half an hour than a quarter but Smith was not minded to remark on it as he heard Martine's iPhone bleep as the email came in. He held up his hand like a magician in a performance.

'I would be very disappointed in the name Ripley doesn't appear on that list, Martine.'

After a few seconds of scrolling down the message, she stopped.

'Yes, it's here, Peter. How on earth did you know? There is a Ripley who owns a house in Lussan.'

Smith greeted the news with a contented smile.

'Can you use your little gizmo to confirm that the house is in the bit of the village that's one top of the hill or is it somewhere below?'

A few moments later this question was answered too. The house was indeed on the top of the hill.

'Good, that makes getting in much, much easier.'

Deveraux, more used to the operational side of things, had caught up rapidly. He asked:

'And out?'

Smith smiled gently without a trace of humour.

'Oh, I don't think that getting out will be any sort of problem at all.'

Nothing more needed saying on that particular topic. Smith fell silent for a while. To do what he had in mind he needed some reinforcements and wasn't sure quite where to get them. Normally he just slapped a request down on Gentry's desk and things happened. Now he wasn't sure. He could probably do it himself but it would need a lot of time that he didn't have and pulling in a lot of favours that he really preferred to leave out there – especially while he wasn't completely sure of whether Gentry was actually worth saving. Only part of what Fredricks / Ripley had said was true. Personally, Deveraux had his contacts but they weren't for this sort of thing. He needed to know how many people were in that house and he didn't have the luxury of too much time. Two solutions came to mind; satellite or foot soldiers with portable stuff. Satellite was possible. American. Even with his slightly uneven relationship with the CIA he could probably swing it. But the Company leaked like the proverbial sieve and he wasn't really sure who the good guys were any more. Possibly but only if there was really no alternative. The only person he could really trust who had infantry was Girondou.

His call was answered immediately but he was interrupted before he could say anything. Girondou's voice was amused and business-like as he accurately anticipated Smith's question.

'Give me two hours and I'll have the answer for you. I suggest you get yourself up to Lussan. My team is landing at the Uzès aero club as we speak. They will reconnoitre and we will meet us back at the club. It is pretty deserted although it is used from time to time and the locals are used to light aircraft coming and going at odd hours - especially mine. I suggest we met there in about a couple hours? You'll find the club on the right side of the road about ten miles north of Uzès.'

After an amused pause he continued.

'We're not all Neanderthals, you know, down here amongst the oleanders and the palm trees'

Smith thought ahead.

'I have Deveraux with me.'

The message was clear. Deveraux was one of the very best extraction men in the business and he would be in charge. It was a moot point whether he actually needed anyone else but Smith knew there was a certain amount of Provençale pride at stake.

'If this is what I think it is, I doubt whether we have more than a handful to deal with, Alexei. Not more than four or five.'

'Very well, Peter, I have sent four to do the surveillance. Two of those will be good for an operation. I'll bring two more with me now. I presume we will be waiting until the night?'

'Yes.'

Smith knew that while the operation would be slightly harder under nightfall the chances of being spotted by local tourists or curious locals were much fewer. Although he had no doubt at all about Girondou's ability to divert the attentions of the local gendarmerie, it would obviously be better not to attract their interest in the first place.

'Good. I'll bring the equipment.'

The phone went silent. Smith turned to Martine.

'My dear, Deveraux and I have a little job to do up country and we have to leave pretty soon. Can you ask Jean-Marie to bring my car and then take you and the horses back to the Mas. I think it might be better of you stay there for a while rather than with us. I'm pretty sure that everything is Ok but you never know.'

Martins nodded and said:

"Jean-Marie will be disappointed to be left out of the fun.'

Smith was not remotely sympathetic.

'His job is to take care of things here and not go gallivanting around in a dangerous escapade for which he has had very little relevant training.'

Martine called the house and within a few minutes one of the Aubanet's black Ranger Rovers pulled up in front of the *cabane* rather than Smith's battered Peugeot. She felt no annoyance at being left out of what was going to happen next. She knew that he wanted her safe and did not want the distraction of worrying about her. Smith exchanged a few words with the young man who now had charge of the security at the house, and, above all, of Martine and her father and then the two men got into the Range Rover. Smith got into the driver's seat. He was not the one who would be working tonight so he would drive. She reached up and into window and kissed him but looked across at the passenger.

'Take good care of him, Mr Deveraux, and make sure he comes back undamaged, please.'

Deveraux smiled slightly sadly.

'The first, I can promise, Madame, but the second I can only promise to try. But we'll be amongst friends tonight.'

Smith felt slightly bilious at the rather soppy exchange and showed his disapproval by flooring the acceleration and spinning all four wheels, leaving an unnecessarily large cloud of dust behind him. Deveraux slouched in his seat as Smith turned north towards Nimes and Uzès.

'So, tell me about the target, boss.'

'There's a little laptop in the glove compartment, Deveraux. You can Google the place and look at the satellite maps.'

'Yes I can', came the careful reply, 'but I would like to hear you describe it first. Whatever Google might say, the image in your head is the one that I suspect we will be working to and I want to learn that first.'

Smith paused while he remembered. He had been there a couple of times as a tourist and had once in his youth actually stayed in the little hotel in the church square in the middle of the village. He developed the picture in his mind.

'Lussan is a pretty little place. About ten miles north of Uzès, it's quite a popular tourist destination – during the day, that is. Just a place to wander around and have a picnic and look at the view. No night life to speak of unless things have really changed since I was there last. Basically it's a small, oval-shaped cluster of medieval houses built on top of a hill which rises rather like a pimple straight out of a pretty flat and relatively barren bit of scrubby countryside. It's not one of those walled, fortified places with lots of walls and towers. If I remember rightly there is only one narrow road that goes around it up to the top. That road is sort of tacked onto the side of the hill so it is itself supported with quite big walls so the place looks a bit fortified but actually it isn't. Having said that, getting in and out up the side of the hill is not particularly difficult. Unless we're up against a larger number of people that I imagine, access will not be a great problem even if we decide not to use the road. The houses are pretty well clustered together. Lots of little windows, shutters, very small gardens, mazes of little alleyways. I trust that by the time we get there Girondou's team will have a good layout as well as a couple of best ways in.'

Deveraux wasn't sure quite how to ask the next question. So taking a mental deep breath he continued:

'How well is our friend Girondou equipped for doing the recce on this, sir? Locating and counting people in a building from the outside, during daylight without being spotted and getting the answer right takes uncommon skills and some pretty specialised equipment.'

Smith smiled at the slight note of nervousness in Deveraux's voice.

'Firstly, Deveraux, never hesitate to ask an intelligent question. Secondly, never hesitate to ask a question that could save our lives. Thirdly, contrary to what you might have heard from others, you should never hesitate to ask a question to which I don't know the answer. On this particular occasion I actually don't know. However, I have a feeling that the main reason Girondou stays out of the tender arms of the French law is that he doesn't quite fit the traditional profile of your usual Marseille hoodlum. With him, everything is possible. So, for the moment, we keep the faith. In any case,' he said with a smile,' aren't burglars supposed to be good at casing the joint , as they say?'

Deveraux was not exactly amused that this small attempt at levity. His ass was on the line if anything went wrong.

'Possibly, Boss, but only possibly'

Smith's smile became a touch wintry..

'If he doesn't do it right, then it will just be you and me, not for the first time, I seem to remember.'

Deveraux also smiled briefly at the recollection. He had been the one to get Smith out of a Somalian torture cell some years ago. He came in alone and carried an unconscious and broken Smith out of the pool of vomit, excrement and blood that he had been left to die in, over his shoulder to safety. Twenty-one people died that night. These two were friends of a special sort.

'If so, it might get a bit messy if we have to deal with more than six, Boss.'

'Good.' Smith grunted in reply. 'Someone might get a message if it does. The only two I want out alive are Gentry and Ripley if he is there. If we have to leave the others as a bunch of corpses then so be it. However for the sake of keeping life as peaceful as we can for Girondou, I'd prefer to leave a completely empty house behind us.'

'Do we have equipment if we have to storm the castle alone, as it were?'

Smith's smile this time was more affectionate that wintry.

'Ah, unless I miss my guess, the car that we are driving is one of an seemingly inexhaustible collection of Aubanet Range Rovers but this time with a number of factory and non-factory mods supplied by their special vehicles people. Kevlar body panels plus suspension upgrades to carry armour and bullet-proof glass. Lots of electronics and not just the ones for avoiding speed traps. But this particular one, if I remember my original shopping list correctly, will have in the back two silenced Kriss SDPs with taking standard Glock 19 magazines, six M84 Stun grenades and six M67 Fragmentation. Two sets night vision stuff and the usual protective vests and helmets. When you do finally look at the laptop in the glove box you will also find two Glock19s with four 15 round and two 33 round magazines for each.'

All that came by way of a reply was a low whistle.

'Christ, Sir. Is this usual stuff for a Camargue bull farmer to have in the back of his Range Rover? I thought they just contented themselves with green Wellington boots, Barbour jackets and a black Labrador or two. Possibly at the very worst a pair of Holland and

Hollands 12 bore side by sides, covered in mud and worth more than four times the car. Boxes of Ely No 6s rather than clips of FMJ 9mm.'

For a moment Smith went very still then nodded and looked ineffably sad.

'Ah my old friend, I fear that was before I came into their lives. It's something for which I shall probably not be able to forgive myself.'

There was a difficult silence as Deveraux saw how close to exposing his very soul Smith had just come.

'I wouldn't like to intrude on your self-pity, Boss, but I would venture to suggest that Monsieur Aubanet and his daughter, to say nothing of many of their friends, wouldn't think like that and they would be very unhappy indeed to hear you say this.'

Smith lapsed into silence for much of the remainder of the journey. Deveraux took the computer out noting, as he did, that the two Glocks were indeed there and spent half an hour looking at Google maps. He also spent a little time on the ludicrously trendy website that was now maintained in these politically correct days by the Secret Intelligence Service. He was most interested in Ripley's profile which was short but contained a picture of the man who was to become the new Chief. Deveraux didn't know what the man looked like until then. Lussan was exactly as Smith described and although he did not, as yet, know which particular house they were holding Gentry in, none of them looked to present a particularly complicated problem. Most houses built either just to live in or to holiday in would not be much good at withstanding an assault from trained troops. All over the world locks were never any good, alarms, if installed, were often toys. People never thought anything would happen to them and thus things were never really secured at night or during their absence. A bedside lamp on a cheap timer was the best that most people ever thought of when they left their houses and they were usually astonished when the came after their couple of weeks away to find the place stripped. No wonder, he thought, that insurance was so expensive. The house that they were keeping Gentry in would be better protected but only slightly. They were not, after all, supposed to be expecting a visit.

The early evening light was beginning to dim as they arrived. The little flying club was indeed on the right side of the D979 running north from Uzès towards Lussan and was typical of many such dotted around France. Four thousand feet of runway, two decrepit buildings and two much newer small hangers that attested to the fact that private flying was alive and living in that part of the Gard. Many small aero clubs in the south of France had had new life breathed into them by the arrival of rich owners of holiday houses who liked nothing more than to fly to their holiday home in their little aerial runabouts. There were a couple of Robin DR400 single engine trainers in one corner, presumably club craft used for lessons. There were also three slightly larger machines, two single-engined, high-wing Cessnas and a slightly bigger Piper Seminole presumably belonging to a local holidaying bigwig. The place was pretty basic but nonetheless it seemed looked-after and tidy. Some oleanders had been planted around and, indeed, a few trees.

Two much more substantial machines were parked of the side of the new hangers away from the roadway. One was a Beechcraft King Air 250 and the other was its smaller sister a Baron G58. Girondou had clearly come to town. The door to the larger of the two new hangers was open and Smith drove straight in and parked next to another surprise; a very battered and down-at-heel Renault delivery van painted loudly with the banners of La Provence, the local daily newspaper. An anonymous long wheelbase Renault Espace with darkened windows also stood in the corner of the hanger. Girondou was at his door as he got out. The two men embraced and then Smith introduced his two friends to each other.

'Ah. I am delighted to meet you at last, Monsieur Deveraux. As they say, I have heard much about you.'

'And I of you, Monsieur Girondou,' came a steely reply.

The two men locked eyes for slightly more time than common courtesy usually demanded. A lot of mutual sizing-up was condensed into a couple of seconds. Smith intervened.

'Now Alexei, apart from demonstrating that you have an air force as well as an army – remind me to buy shares in Beechcraft if I have ever any cash to spare, by the way – I want to know why you are looking so pleased with yourself.'

Girondou led the two over to a group of trestle tables holding three one metre wide plasma screens and the same number of laptops one in front of each screen. Cables snaked away into the back of the Espace. A young man with the vestiges of a goatee wearing a faded Black Punumbra tee shirt and torn jeans sat at the tables, setting things up, spinning himself back and forward on a wheeled office chair that Smith notes was completely silent. Smith mused that this was probably the young man who had modified the phones. Perhaps he had misjudged his gangster friend. Behind the technician was arranged a semicircle of folding chairs. In the space between the chairs and the tables stood, somewhat uneasily, it should be said, four figures in full combat black, three men and a woman. Smith recognised the woman from his walk along the Rhône. She was the one who preferred knives. On the opposite side of the hanger near the delivery van stood another pair, also in jeans and tee shirts. Smith presumed that they were locals who had arranged the transport. Girondou took the floor and motioned Smith and Deveraux and the four troops to sit. He started with the left screen. It showed and aerial view of Lussan. The picture wasn't completely clear and it was obviously a recording of a live feed. The picture was frozen to a still for the moment.

'How the hell…?' Smith wondered.

Deveraux just sat completely still absorbing everything. It was, after all, going to be his operation. Smith's question was answered immediately.

'You're wondering about the feed. It comes from a police Augusta A109E surveillance helicopter that was, shall we say, diverted for half an hour of its valuable time protecting the citizens of France – or more precisely wasting its time catching speeding motorists on the autoroute. It was in a hover at about ten thousand feet above the village so it is unlikely that it was seen by anyone on the ground.'

Neither Smith nor Deveraux bothered to ask the obvious question. However, they were impressed. Ten thousand feet was about as high as you could go in a hover without the tail rotor stalling and the helicopter wanting to fall out of the sky. The middle screen showed a sideways infra-red image of a house with the inhabitants outlined as frozen white blobs on a black screen. The right screen was a man-made graphic. It showed on split screen a ground and first floor plan of the house with each of the people identified as a red dot. Girondou nodded and the left hand screen started into action. Immediately they saw a small white van moving along the road at the base of Lussan's hill and make its way up the side around the road until it came to stop in the small square in the middle of the village. A figure got out, opened the rear doors, took out a large bundle and took them into a shop on one side of the square. Girondou took up the commentary.

'We decided to use a newspaper delivery van. Obviously it normally does its deliveries early each morning but it has the virtue of being easily available in Uzès and is a familiar sight in the village of Lussan. It delivers every day including Sundays. The house we are interested in is on the inside of the village but not by very much and is fortunately on the route the van usually takes every day. Thus we could get very close indeed to the house. We arranged for a completely unnecessary delivery of magazines to the village shop. The only chance we were taking was that someone might come out and ask why they were there in the afternoon. Fortunately no-one did.'

The aerial image continued and the van started to move slowly through the narrow streets until it stopped abruptly right outside the target house. The driver could be seen getting out and looking at the front of the van. His hands on his hips from frustration could be seen clearly from ten thousand feet in the sky.

'A puncture.' Girondou contributed helpfully.

Simultaneously the middle and right hand screens jerked into life. The fuzzy white shapes started to move around. Smith could see two on the ground floor and three on the first. He muttered 'five?'

Deveraux just nodded. The right screen combined the data and gave a bird's eye view graphic of movement on the two floors. It didn't take long to establish that one of the blobs on the middle screen on the first floor was both lying down and not moving. They watched for about five more minutes which the blobs moved slowly around the house and then the feed was cut and the aerial shot showed that the tyre change was complete and the newspaper wagon drove slowly off. Deveraux was the first to say anything. He turned to Girondou and in a voice just loud enough for everyone to hear he said:

'My compliments, Monsieur Girondou. A first rate job. First rate. I couldn't have done better myself with five times as much notice as you and your people had.'

I was obvious that all of them were delighted to hear this, none more than Girondou himself.

'Coming from you, Monsieur Deveraux, that is praise indeed and is much appreciated.'

Deveraux turned to Smith to ask the question again, for the sake of Girondou's team.

'So, Boss, how many do you want out?'

Smith thought for a moment. It was a more difficult question that might appear at first. The extreme anger that he felt at Gentry's abduction made him just want his friend out and the rest very dead. But these were particular circumstances. Now he wanted Ripley too, if he was there, possibly even more than Gentry. Ripley was were the explanation lay. But the more people they left on site, dead, alive or simply just damaged, the greater would be the inevitable fuss when they were discovered. Girondou had gone to a lot of trouble to arrange all this. Not just the expense, but he was also risking unwelcome local publicity should the thing ever become public. Smith knew he owed his friend not to make the problem any worse than it already was. He was being done a huge favour. There was no profit in this for the man from Marseille and this was Girondou's country not his. He did a quick calculation. The big Beechcraft could take a maximum of 10, especially if they were trussed up and dumped on the floor; the Baron 4 if equally restrained. Smith presumed that Girondou had not piloted himself. Given that he and Deveraux would take Gentry home by car, that left space for 14. The van and the Espace would presumably be taken away by the two locals. Thus four troops, and one technician left space for nine. Plenty enough.

'See if you can get them all, Deveraux. I don't really want to leave anything for the locals to chatter about. Empty house, if you think its possible. However, it's your call. If things pan out differently, that's OK too.'

Deveraux nodded his agreement. He also knew that they were guests and shouldn't tramp around with muddy – or was it bloody?- feet. He looked at Girondou.

'Do you have plans and exterior photos?'

Girondou just smiled again and nodded to the technician. A new set of pictures came on the screens. Deveraux who had clearly taken command of the operational side of things motioned to the four black-clothed troops who were some distance away to come closer to the screens. It was time that the people who were going in got to know the terrain. Girondou raised an eyebrow at Smith. He had assumed, as to be perfectly honest, as Smith himself originally, that Smith would go in. He received an answering grimace from Smith as the thought entered his mind for the second time recently.

'Sic transit gloria mundi, my friend.'

Girondou was sympathetic. Obviously Deveraux had decided and if Smith was being perfectly honest with himself, he would have agreed. Although he was good, he was nowhere near as good as Deveraux. So he stood back and listened to Deveraux in completely perfect, accent-less French go through the layout and the plan with the other four. Entries and exits were looked at and the centre screen was now given over to a succession of photos of the building. There was a certain amount of conversation, suggestion were made and decisions arrived at. Everyone contributed to the discussion. It was obvious now, if it hadn't been before that Monsieur Girondou was well equipped to deal with the modern world. Smith reminded himself to ask the Frenchman where he got his people from. They looked and acted like French special forces to him - the famed Commandement des Opérations Spéciales, or COS. He became increasingly relaxed about the outcome of the operation. After about fifteen minutes the group broke up. Two went to remove the registration plates from the Range Rover and the Espace. Then all but Deveraux went across to their equipment and started the business of checking it all again. He pulled a chair out and sat facing Smith and Girondou. He glanced towards the door of the hanger that had been left open just enough to see that night time had almost fallen. His first word were to Girondou.

"My compliments again, Sir. These are good people. I'm very pleased we're on the same side'

Girondou glowed with pride. Smith smiled inwardly. Girondou was only the second person he had ever heard Deveraux call 'Sir'.

'I think that we can assume that they're not expecting an attack. They'll assume that we don't even know where they are. Even it they know about the GPS chip in the phone, they almost certainly won't know the trick about turning them on and off remotely. I have to admit that I didn't. In any case we're well still inside their deadline even if it was a real one and not just an empty threat. There is really no reason why they should expect us. This strikes me as being all a bit last minute, or at least, not very professionally planned. If they were serious they wouldn't have chosen this place. This means that doors will probably be locked and windows shuttered but no special measures. If there is an alarm, which I very much doubt, we will either cut it or just rely on getting in and out so fast that is it irrelevant. One of the local boys says that the nearest police are in Uzès anyhow. I am a little concerned that if the police come more quickly that we want, we might meet them in the road coming the other way, as it were.'

He was interrupted by Girondou.

'Don't worry about the local police.'

Deveraux grinned and continued.

'I'll drive the Rover with two and the others two will follow in the Espace. There is a single entry to the house which fortunately borders the road. It is set into a eleven foot wall that gives onto a small courtyard that has the door into the house itself and an external staircase that leads to the first floor. This stair goes directly into the room that Mr Gentry is being kept in. We'll take the imaging camera and wait until either Gentry is alone. Presumably he is either sedated or tied up and only one person with him. We'll simply open the doors with silenced charged on the hinges in the usual way. Leave one in the courtyard, go in, shoot, non-fatally of course anyone who might look like being unhelpful. Get Gentry into the Rover with me and the others loaded up in the Espace and drive quietly back. We've taken out the seats in the Espace so everyone will just be in a bit of a heap. For restraints, I don't think we need anything more sophisticated than duct tape for the mouths and plastic cable ties for the wrists. I would estimate we need fifteen minutes to get there, three minutes to check that nothing has changed and set up, a maximum of one minute in the house and another fifteen to get back here. We'll need to wait a little if Gentry isn't alone to see what happens but not long as a couple of unusual vehicles parked in the village at that time of night might attract the attention of some local insomniac. If Gentry is alone, I'll go in with the ground floor troops. If he's not then I will get him myself. Silenced hand-guns only. Madame with her little knife,' he added with a slight smile. 'I think we should wait until about two in the morning. There's no moon tonight. There might be a bit of noise when the planes take off later, but I gather than this will not be the first time that planes have come and gone in the night here.'

This time it was Girondou who grinned but said nothing.

'Finally I suggest we let the pilots come in and rest and take turns ourselves wandering about outside to keep things clear.'

Smith nodded although he was less than happy to be left out of the plan however sensible he knew it was.

'Thanks, Deveraux. Sounds good to me. One thing only. As we know, one of the people in the house might be Ripley. If it is, then I want him. He will ride back with Monsieur Girondou and be his guest until we can have a word with him.'

Smith paused as a thought struck him.

'I want him blindfolded and ear- plugged. Usual isolation routine.'

Deveraux just nodded and turned away to sort his equipment. Girondou had brought additional full sets of night combat gear.

Scene 2:   Score One for the Good Guys

Doing nothing and waiting for time to pass was something Smith had been good at years ago. But now it seemed an eternity before the group rose on Deveraux's signal, loaded up and drove off. Smith looked at his watch. Three quarters of an hour. The hanger was bare. All the equipment had been loaded onto the King Air. The paper van had been taken away having been used to ferry the stuff out to the aeroplanes. All that was left was Smith and Girondou standing alone in the dark hanger. The two pilots had returned to watch over their aircraft and a warm dark night had descended like black velvet on the little airfield. The sky was overcast and their was light from neither moon nor stars. A dim glow to the south over Uzès only. Girondou turned to his companion.

'Well, what next?'

Smith thought for a while.

'To be honest, I'm not quite sure. I am hoping that Ripley will be there and we can get something out of him but I can't say I am confident.'

'Tell me about this Ripley. He's the official owner of the house in Lussan, by the way.'

Smith nodded. It was a typically stupid mistake that the man would make. He shook is head slightly and tried to formulate a précis.

'Miles Ripley – now Sir Miles Ripley CBE – has been in the British Secret Intelligence Service or MI6 as it is more colloquially, if slightly inaccurately known, full time for almost his life. He was a Cambridge man, PPE I think, and was recruited just as many of us were while he was still 'up' as they say. He was never a field man.

He just spent his life in what is euphemistically known as liaison. Continuously being posted to embassies all over the world. Known as the SCA – Second Commercial Attaché – syndrome. Always following a safe, if unspectacular path, towards the top. He developed a good and solid career as a reliable fixer in a minor way, a greaser of paths; a smoother of ruffled feathers. He was, I remember, especially good with Yanks. Some minor bit of his family was American, I believe. I came across him once or twice while he was in planning in London and he has vaguely associated with a number of operations that I was involved in. The Albanian thing was one of them, I seem to remember. However I always insisted on dealing with Gentry directly so there was never any direct connection. He had a reputation of being quiet, good at his job and never getting up anyone's nose – good higher management material, I suppose. More a politician than a spy, at least in the old sense of that word. He seems to have risen to the top and is now in line for the top job in the SIS itself. The post is officially known as the Chief or 'C' by the way. I really can't tell you much more than that.'

Girondou glanced down at is watch and saw that they still had fifteen minutes to wait.

'What are your personal feelings about the man? He certainly seems to very involved at the moment in a very un-diplomatic sort of way. Something seems to have made him break a lifetime buried deep in the camouflage of anonymity and come out to become an amateur kidnapper.'

Smith hesitated. He had had a long life spent not saying things. His life as what others might have called, a spy, was full of stuff that either he didn't want to talk about or else had sworn not to.

'To be frank, I have no feelings about him one way or another. My general impression is that he is a limp-wristed little shit but most office boys are thought of like that. If I was being honest I really know little about him and thus I have no real opinions either way. I'm obviously annoyed that he had pinched Gentry for reasons best known to himself but as of recently, I seem to find myself less unhappy with that than perhaps I should be. However if indeed he actually is pulled in with tonight's trawl then I will probably be very savage with him less because I am that unhappy but because I am beginning to get very bored with this whole fucking business.'

Girondou was not stupid or gullible but judged that this was not the time to disagree with his friend.

'If they do bring him back, what do you want doing with him? It's not everyday day I get to play host to the next director of SIS.'

Smith's voice was granite hard.

'Oh, I think you can safely assume that that particular appointment won't happen now.'

Girondou raised an eyebrow and continued.

'Peter. Where do you go from here? You will have Gentry back after all.'

Smith thought for a moment and then set out a plan.

'Starting with the least important first, I have no interest in the hired goons. I know probably where they came from and they will have nothing to contribute. You can load them up into that big Beechcraft of yours and do what you want. A detour over the Mediterranean might do. I don't really want them telling stories if they ever they crawl back to Blighty. Recycling might be best. Gentry I want to talk to personally and pretty carefully – to start with, at least. The chances are that he'll be a bit sedated. He looked pretty stationary to me on those pictures. He'll need a bit of time to get his head together before talking. I will take him home with me and Deveraux and I'll have a chat sometime soon. If he is sedated then it might take a while to get him back to normal. Ripley, if he is there, you can take with you. I want to talk with him pretty soon too but I want you to work him over before I do. He is a desk jockey at heart and will probably be very scared by a bit of pain. I want to give him a lot and then perhaps I can get something out of him. Don't talk to him. It is important that doesn't think he has anything do bargain with. Just hurt him a great deal and don't give him the impression that there is any way he can stop it happening. Do it randomly. I want him in a blue funk. I'll call you later about lunchtime and probably come over late afternoon. By then he'll almost certainly be prepared to talk.'

'What makes you so confident. He may be made of stronger stuff than you think?'

Smith shook his head.

'I am pretty sure that he had never experienced anything like this before. Unlike Deveraux and I, he certainly won't ever have been trained for it. Also, unless Deveraux is losing is touch, we now have Ripley's wife and daughter.'

Girondou looked at Smith as if he was seeing him for the first time.

'Christ, Peter, is that necessary?'

Smith felt very old and rather tired as he looked at his companion in an exasperated sort of a way.

'Alexei. In the last few weeks, I have had an inoffensive old chum murdered on a Provencal country road. I have witnessed in Venice an innocent singer having her head atomised, I have discovered that in all probability one of the very few people I have allowed to get close to me in a long and probably completely meaningless life may have been lying to me for much for the last thirty odd years. I seem to be hunted by a bunch of geriatric bent and violent CIA people who have been released back into the wild by a limp-wristed American government agency. I have discovered that some fucking non-entity who has risen through SIS ranks to be next in line to the throne may be at the very least a double agent or a traitor if not more. I have a Romanian assassin who seems to have me in the sights of his antique Dragunov assault rifle. I could go on. Do you really want an answer to your question as to why leaning on Ripley might be necessary?'

Smith paused for a second and frowned, picked up his phone and dialled. It was answered immediately.

'Everything OK?'

Jean-Marie sounded a little put out by the question.

'Of course.'

Smith was not amused.

'Make sure it stays that way, Jean-Marie.'

Smith heard what sounded suspiciously like a French version of 'pah!' and the phone was cut. He smiled gently. The boy was learning.

'As I said, in all probability Gentry will need some recover time, as will I, I think. I'm getting too old for these all night shenanigans. I will need some sleep before doing anything significant.'

Girondou turned to Smith.

'Well I can do nothing more here, so I will load myself up so I don't delay departure. I'll brief my pilots and we will get on our way as soon as my people and our guests arrive. They will be taken straight to the planes. The Espace is borrowed from a local friend and it will be collected. I'll look forward to your call tomorrow morning, my friend.'

Smith put his hand on his companion's shoulder.

'I cannot thank you enough, Alexei. This would have been a great deal more difficult and much more dangerous without your help. I am in your debt.'

Girondou was dismissive as he placed his own hand over Smith's and patted it gently.

'Friends don't keep score, Peter. For the first time since we met I felt I could really help you and than gave me the greatest pleasure. You saved Angèle's life last year and nothing can ever repay that debt. Nothing. Ever. In any case,' he continued as his smile widened, 'Angèle and the girls would have killed me if I hadn't helped.'

As he went to turn away he hesitated for a moment.

'Oh, by the way, the boy with La Salle. You were right. He was given the job of being La Salle's minder by Ripley himself. He gave him the photograph of Martine as well.'

Smith remembered the photograph and replied with a very flat voice.

'You may hurt Ripley very considerably if you wish.'

Girondou nodded, walked out of the hanger and around the corner to his waiting aeroplane. Smith just stood in silence but it was not long before he heard the two cars approaching. Smith glanced down at his watch thirty-eight minutes start to finish. Very nice, he thought to himself. No problems. The Range Rover drove into hanger and Deveraux leant across and opened the passenger door. Smith got in, noticing a dark form lying prone across the back seat. The car was turning around before Smith got his door closed.

Scene 3: A Return Home

It was less than five minutes before they saw the two planes climb overhead into the darks sky and head south. Deveraux drove fast and smoothly and Smith waited in silence. He would get a report when Deveraux was ready. He needed to telephone Martine but that should wait until he knew what state Gentry was in and therefore what arrangements had to be made. Deveraux would tell him in time. In the meantime he closed his eyes and rested. He felt about a thousand years old; too old for this sort of stuff anyway. He began a mental review. The immediate problem, Gentry's safety, was solved. His kidnapper was also theirs and in time might shed some light on this whole thing. The American part of the story was still extremely fuzzy. He neither had the people nor the motivation properly focussed in his mind. Most importantly he still had yet to connect everything up completely although he felt a lot nearer to that than before. The thing was like a game of chess. The openings were all about manoeuvring for position. It was seldom that one player established a really advantage over the other. Once past the opening there was often a cautious development stage as positions were tested and possible strategies explored always with the possibility of retreat in mind. Only when you were sure did you launch yourself on an endgame. This was the risky bit. There was always the chance of overlooking something. This is where he and Gentry had been such a good combination. With Gentry orchestrating you could pretty well rely on getting to the endgame without the possibility of being surprised by something unpredictable happening if not completely eliminated, then certainly minimised. A one or two per cent chance at most. Then it was Smith's turn to carry forward the endgame to its conclusion with both he and Gentry confident that Smith's abilities the a fast run to the end would cope with the one or two per cent. In the past it had been a winning combination with good results mined from the most unlikely situations and only very seldom did wheels come off completely. Then they relied on Deveraux.

Institutionally speaking, Deveraux had only ever worked with Gentry and Smith. Otherwise he did his own thing. Deveraux could save things that were hopeless as when Smith finally gave up the will to live after a week in a Somali torture hospital in Buur Hakaba. Deveraux arrived alone ignoring the blood and the excrement that had pooled on the floor deeply around Smith who was manacled to an old metal bed mattress leant up against the wall, and disconnected the electrodes that had been left clamped to his testicles. Even the Somali rebels had given up trying to get anything out of their prisoner. He had lifted the barely alive Welshman onto his shoulders and carried him out of the hospital, and to the pickup in the desert. No one was left to stop him. He had killed them all on the way in. Twenty-one of them. The oil company Sea King that Deveraux had somehow borrowed flew straight to a Shell rig out in the Gulf of Aden never once flying above twenty feet except to land.

It was only after Smith had recovered as well as he could back in the UK that he had discovered that Deveraux had found the young CIA man whose macho, drunken bragging in a Mogadishu hotel bar had betrayed Smith. Deveraux had returned to Somalia a couple of days later, taken the American from the same bar, loaded him into the same helicopter, and dropped him without a parachute from a thousand feet into the American Embassy compound in Mogadishu. Message delivered.

All that and more was why, as they sped through the darkness down the road south towards Nîmes, Smith felt safe and was prepared to wait. Finally Deveraux had arranged his thoughts.

'No problems. No shots fired, not fatalities, some physical stuff but not too much and I am pretty sure, no witnesses. Bunch of amateurs. Ripley is now Girondou's guest. Gentry is sedated but I don't know how much. I think he needs at least twelve hours to wake and another good few hours to unscramble himself. I would suggest that I take care of him at the Mas while you attend to Ripley. You should know that Girondou's people were good. Very good. Fuck, do you know that they ran up the wall? Ran up it and over. I thought that shit only happened in stupid Ninja movies. The bloody wall was eleven feet high. I went in through the door and they were waiting for me as I got though with bloody great smiles on their balaclavas. Especially Elaine.'

Smith finally stirred without opening his eyes.

'Elaine?'

It took a lot to disconcert Deveraux, even slightly. But he let a slight shade of embarrassment creep into his voice. Had it not been completely dark there might even have been a slight blush to be seen.

'The lady with the knife, Boss.'

Smith couldn't suppress his smile.

'Be careful, my friend. There's more to these Provençale women than meets the eye. Believe me, I know.'

Deveraux grimaced.

'Thanks for the advice. Oh, by the way, my London team is ready and can go in whenever you want. One man and one woman.'

Smith took a moment to get the timings straight in his mind. First he telephoned Martine. He felt a little guilty that he had left it for so long but felt he needed to give her certainties. She gave no indication that it was actually nearly three o'clock in the morning.

'How did it go?'

'Fine. Fine. All OK. We are coming back with Gentry who seems in good health although a little sleepy – fast asleep actually and I am not sure how long that'll last. Can you organise a room for him and someone to sit there just in case he decides to get up before we're ready – someone who can be a bit firm with him and keep him there if required?'

'Of course. When are you back?'

'In about three quarters of an hour.'

He cut the phone and turned to Deveraux.

'You can activate your London people now. If they go in now that will probably only have to stay until mid-afternoon.'

It was indeed forty-five minutes later when they arrived at the Mas. Jean-Marie greeted them with a couple of somewhat sleepy farm hands and together they carried Gentry into the house and away to some remote but guarded guest room. Deveraux headed off to his room sent on his way with a gentle tap of thanks on the shoulder from Smith who, in turn, also headed towards his bed. After a quick shower, he slid silently into bed hoping not to disturb a sleeping Martine. As he closed his eyes as quietly as he could he found, with only temporarily mixed feelings, that she wasn't asleep at all.

Scene 4: A De-briefing of Sorts

There was a time, Smith mused, as they both ambled slowly along one of the many paths that meandered around the mas and away from it into the surrounding marsh, that time was measured by the work a man could do. In the country, at least, well away from the benefits of electric light, the day started when, like now, the light rose enough for him to see what he was supposed to do, through to the moment hours later when it became too dark any longer to see anything. He himself came from a farming family and he remembered these days that required his father to rise before dawn and return after sunset. Work and light were interdependent. Now, of course, it was different, but the land of the Camargue with its vast network of interconnections of streams, dykes, marshes and hedges; small irregular grass pastures and arable plots shared between corn, rice and cattle was less susceptible to the mechanisation that had transformed the farming day into one governed by the diesel engine and the satellite navigator. But more could be done by fewer people even here too as machines increasingly ploughed, planted, fertilised, and harvested.

However here too the ritual of breakfast still resisted this condensation of time. The Mas des Saintes still beat to the old fashioned pulse that his own father would have understood. Émile Aubanet had always risen an hour before sunrise, whatever time it was, washed and dressed and set the men to work. There were always things to be done and thus breakfast, instead on being the first thing of the day, as it tended to be in more urban places, came later, after the day was set on its way. Still early, again by urban standards, but well into the working day for a farmer. Eight o'clock.

Thus it was that he and Martine woke just as the sky was lightening, she out of habit and he because he had hardly slept at all in any case, showered and decided to walk a little before the family breakfast. Arthur of course was delighted and rushed about in front of them refreshed by a good sleep and eager to get out and kill something. Smith looked at the rapidly vanishing shape and smiled at how alike they had become for today unless things went very differently to the way he imagined they would, he too might well kill someone. Someone who didn't need much hunting. They just walked together without talking, hand in hand, like a pair of teenagers, he thought with a frisson of embarrassment.

It was an odd landscape. Odd because it was flat and almost without features and than was one of the things that he had always said he hated Norfolk in the UK where he had wasted too many years of his life. He secretly blamed the dreadful inertia of that county and the boredom it engendered for getting too involved with the Service. He was paying that price now. Had he lived somewhere where people had brains rather than acres he might not have slid so easily into its clutches. Now as they walked together in a land that was rapidly becoming home he felt only a new contentment. The night had been memorable; a haven of affection that he had felt so seldom in his life and for a second he felt almost overwhelmed by the memory of it. On impulse he stopped, drew her into his arms and kissed her.

'Thank you,' he whispered.

The only response was a tightening of the hug. They walked on, now with arms around each other. Feeling the hard metallic lump at the base of his spine, Martine asked:

'Do you ever get used to it?'

She was of course referring to the Glock that Smith wore in the small of his back.

'Not really. Which it probably just as well. It's not something I want to take for granted. I think it's important always to know its there and what it can do.'

She nodded and they walked on. She leant her head against his shoulder. For a second he felt struck with a sort of feeling of sadness as he said:

'I'm sorry you've been saddled with all this. In the normal course of events meeting a retired Englishman should not result in putting your life in danger, to say nothing of those of your friends and family.'

She gave him a squeeze.

'Don't be a goose. This is much more interesting that being a simple farmer. My father thinks so as well. It all reminds him of the games he used to play as a boy when the Germans were here.'

Smith smiled. A simple farmer was an interesting way to describe herself and her day job of managing a collection of business that ranged far from farming, wine and olive oil making, to hotels and restaurants, grain and produce trading and amounted to a group of businesses that regularly turned over a sum in excess of fifty million pounds.

'So what have you in mind for today, my dear, and how can I help?'

'I'm not completely sure. We have to deal with two people who, I suspect, are not feeling entirely at home. Gentry, when he wakes up and recovers enough to put a complete sentence together, will be lost. Something has emerged from his own secret past and is killing people and as the ultimate background man he will be worried about that. He is clinging to some sort of personal confidentiality but he sees it costing lives. I am pretty sure that McDowell's killing would have shocked him deeply. So now he will have to decide between confidentialities from the past and loyalties to those present who he will realise have risked quite a lot to ensure he remains alive and breathing. Ripley is a different kettle of fish. He is a cunning little sod and there has to be some reason for his quest for the top job other than personal ambition. I am pretty sure I can stop that now, but there is something smelly about him. There's more to his particular role in all this that meets the eye; something more than just a wish to be director. I think he's a wrong 'un. Of course, he may not be his own man and possibly hasn't been for some years. However he is another fish slightly out of water and a few hours in the company of Girondou's people will have introduced him to aspects of field work that may well come as a very unwelcome surprise.'

They strolled on in silence, enjoying each other's company and returned to the mas at eight o' clock which was the traditional time for breakfast. They found a table set in the garden in the morning sun with Émile Aubanet and Deveraux already sitting, both absorbed in the morning papers. Arthur whose memory, even in relative old age, was a sharp as ever, especially when food was concerned, quickly lay on the ground at Émile's feet confident in a regular supply of pieces of buttered baguette with apricot jam. Conversation over breakfast was relaxed and general as if there was a silent agreement that whatever the day would bring, it should at least start relatively normally. Deveraux was making all sorts of enquiries about farming in the Camargue and the raising of bulls in particular. He found a willing pair of instructors in Émile Aubanet and his daughter. They were both proud of their heritage working on the marsh that went back a good few hundreds of years and would quite happily talk all day about it. Smith equally was happy sitting quietly at the table and formulating some sort of plan for the day. Finally after breakfast came to an end and even Arthur was in a baguette-filled slumber in the shade of the table, Émile turned to Smith.

'Well, Peter, how can we help today?'

Smith felt an immediate flush of gratitude and pleasure as yet again he felt a friendship that he didn't really deserve. He started with a quick glance across to Deveraux.

'Well, I gather that Gentry is still asleep.'

Deveraux nodded.

'I would be grateful if you would just babysit him, Deveraux. I suspect he will have been pretty shocked over the last day or so - especially as he will wake in a strange environment and possibly assume that he is still a prisoner and have very little memory of what has happened to him. He may still be a prisoner of sorts but perhaps some food and a gentle walk might be in order. No real conversation, please. I'll go off first and have a chat with our Mr Ripley. I presume that the arrangements in London are in place?'

Deveraux nodded for a second time. He handed Smith a piece of paper.

'They're expecting a call. Two of them. One man one woman.'

Gentry drove out of the mas and called Girondou who answered with a cheerfulness sounding not at all like someone who had been up most of the night.

'Morning Peter. How is our friend this morning.'

'Still asleep, I think. And how did your guest spend the night?'

'Not as comfortably as Gentry, I think. My people may have taken you instructions too literally although nothing permanent apart from some difficult memories. However he is conscious and can talk even if it may be slightly painful. You were certainly right. He's is definitely not used to this sort of treatment. I doubt that you will have too much trouble with him this morning. To save you some trouble and travelling time I have him in one of our houses in Salin de Giraud on your side of the river.'

Girondou passed the address to Smith who in turn put it into his GPS.

'Just walk straight in. They're expecting you.'

Less than fifteen minutes later Smith had drawn up at a house just a few miles short of Salin. It was tucked well off the road, down a narrow lane that wound past the little church of Barcarin and the back along the riverbank. It just looked like a small farmhouse, identical in many ways to lots dotted haphazardly around. The building was slightly down at heel and it took a sharp eye to see that the electricity and telephone cables and the fittings that joined them onto the building itself were very much newer than those on other houses. The little patch of ground in front was bare and looked completely unkempt - which was, Smith assumed - exactly what was intended. God only knew, Smith thought as he walked up to the house, what Girondou used the place for normally. The door was opened unexpectedly silently as he reached it by a small, casually but neatly dressed man with a slight smile and a welcoming handshake. The house was dark and felt cool, almost cold in contrast to the outside as Smith was led down a narrow corridor. Doors to rooms on either side were closed and the windows were shuttered. Again the door at the end opened as he arrived at it. Another equally well-dressed man. Smith wondered whether these were just minders or had the men of violence had a make-over. Probably the latter, he thought. There was no mistaking the tight muscles under the suits and the hard eyes that did not join in the handshakes. The man stepped out of the room as Smith entered and closed the door behind him. There was no furniture in the dark, completely shuttered room. A bare stone floor. A single low wattage bulb hung motionless from the ceiling and in one corner was a cracked wash basin and an old enamel bucket. A single rather basic straw-seated straight-backed chair also stood empty against the wall.

Ripley made a very sorry sight indeed. Naked to the waist, he was fastened to a large and somewhat ornate wooden armchair by plastic electrical cable ties around his ankles and wrists. Smith noted that the chair was bolted to the floor. He was covered in cuts and bruises and some of the wounds were still bleeding somewhat. Three fingers on his right hand were broken and one eye was completely closed and surrounded by a vivid dark blue bruise. His hair was matted with blood and sweat and he appeared to be unconscious, his head hanging down on his chest. The trousers were still Armani but their original fashionable beige had changed to a haphazard pattern of reds and dark maroons well beyond, thought Smith, the ability of most dry cleaners to renovate them. A similar range of colours stained an old baseball bat that stood propped against the basin in the corner. Ripley didn't move as Smith entered.

Smith went up to the basin and half-filled the bucket with cold water, walked over to Ripley and hurled the water at the man. Ripley's head jerked up. Girondou's men had done their job properly. The man was just able to answer questions. Smith, by contrast, was thoroughly conversational.

'Good morning Miles. It's some time since we last met. You've been a naughty boy, obviously, but what we need to do now is to establish how naughty. I must admit you don't look any too clever. I do hope you are in considerable pain. You see this is the sort of things that can happen if you come out to play with the grown-ups. A bit different from your polished mahogany Whitehall desk and the marble halls for you gentleman's club smoking room, I think. You're in a foreign country, Miles, in more ways than one.'

Smith paused to make sure that Ripley was indeed conscious and following him. He was, so Smith continued but in a slightly less conversational tone.

'Before asking you a few questions, Miles, let me make your position absolutely clear to you as you should be under no illusions about what will happen to you should you decide not to answer. Equally, in case you decide that lying might be a good idea, let me assure you that unlike at school when you could count on getting away with telling porkies, you will be held here for as long as it takes to verify everything you say to me, irrespective of how long that might be. If you tell me the truth, then there is a slim, very slim, possibility that I will let you go. However, it is entirely possible that you will die in this room. Probable even.'

Smith took note of the look of panic in Ripley's eyes before continuing. He was being understood.

'In the meantime, I have something that might help you concentrate.'

Smith took out his satellite phone and dialled the number that Deveraux had given him. A voice he didn't recognise answered and said without formalities:

'I'll put the mother on.'

Smith hit the speaker button on the phone and put it to Ripley's ear. He watched as Ripley's remaining good eye widened in horror as a woman's hysterical voice could be heard loudly coming through the tinny loud speaker.

'Miles? Miles? Where are you? What's happening? There are people here. Who are they? Miles? Miles?'

At this point Smith cut the connection. He slowly took the chair from the wall and placed it very carefully in front of his prisoner and sat slowly down on it. Ripley was already staring at him in panic, shaking uncontrollably. Smith started.

'Now Miles let me explain a few facts of life to you - or..' He let a humourless smile cross his face. '…come to think of death might be more to the point. I intend to explain to you your predicament and what you need to do to have any chance at all of escaping it. I do hope I have your attention, my dear chap?'

Another convulsion shook Ripley which Smith decided rather generously to interpret as a 'yes'.

'As you have just heard, your charming and presumably innocent wife and daughter have a couple of uninvited guests in your charming mock Tudor mansion in leafy Virginia Water. A man and a woman. They will stay there until I say so. What they actually do to your wife and daughter while they are your guests rather depends on you and the answers you give to my questions. If you tell me what I want to know and are pretty truthful while you are at it, they might be spared the sort of treatment that you have had over the last few hours. If you don't….'

Smith let his voice fade away and looked at signs in Ripley's face that the message had got through. Judging by the panic that was spread all over the man's face, it had. Smith leant forward and somewhat unceremoniously and certainly painfully tore the duct tape from the man's mouth. Smith was pleased to see that his companion hardly flinched. He was obviously hurting much more in other places and that was precisely what he wanted.

'Now,' he said pleasantly, 'let's start, shall we?

Most of the time interrogation is relatively simple. There are times when it can be difficult and, on occasions, it can be impossible. The trick for both parties is to know what is possible and what is not before they start. Often the indicators are the same for both parties. If someone has been properly trained then withstanding interrogation is not too hard. Painful possibly, but by no means impossible. Most interrogations fail because neither side understands what they are doing or really what they want in the first place. A trained suspect can avoid giving information, at least in the form that would do damage, perfectly easily. If he or she knows what the interrogator wants or thinks he wants then it is not particularly difficult to arrange to impart information he wants to hear - after a suitable interval for pain or chemicals or whatever else is in mind. A trained prisoner is often more in charge than most interrogators know. If a child desperately wants a sweet, getting one, especially after a large amount of persuasion, tears, tantrums and general unhappiness is often sufficient an achievement. Once the sweet is finally in the mouth, the child doesn't stop to think whether it is actually the sweet he wanted in the first place or whether he might have got a better one or one that would last longer or anything. So with interrogations. Equally for the personal asking the questions. The most important place to start is knowledge of the victim. Most interrogators never bother finding out. Both sides either know what they are up against or they don't. There are only four possibilities. A trained prisoner against an untrained questioner will always win. They may not survive, of course, but that is not really the point. The converse is always true as well although the interrogator seldom dies at the hands of the prisoner. A trained prisoner against a trained interrogator usually results in the prisoner dying. If both are untrained, then the result is an unsatisfactory mess. A good interrogator knows what he is up against and knows enough not to waste his time. If someone has been prepared correctly there are few ways of getting information if they don't want to tell. Often time is as effective a weapon as violence. If someone believes that something they dislike will never end then they will often find ways of solving the problem sometimes by talking. They do however always have one option that always renders them superior to their interrogator. They can decide to die. In extremis, it is a real option and is generally not one available to the questioner. Smith had been trained and knew that he was virtually impenetrable. Somalia had proved that. But he also knew about Ripley and, not for the first time, information was what it was all about. Ripley was a deck jockey. A man who sat in comfort and sent men out to die. Discomfort to him was losing a parking place or finding that his tailor had died. Real, raw physical violence was a separate and remote place and, Smith knew, it would be effective here where clever conversation would not. For a man unused to extreme pain the experience of it would be overwhelming. He knew that had the positions been reversed the excruciating pain from the snapped fingers would have log since been forgotten or, possibly, used to focus when concentration was failing. For Ripley the fingers would be all he could think about and the prospect of that continuing would be agony beyond comprehension. Of course, it wouldn't be. There were many different and further levels of agony to which the man could be brought but they would be time-consuming. Smith didn't really have time to spare.

'Miles old chap. Let me explain the situation so you are completely au fait with your position and what is the alternative. It is all quite simple. If you don't answer my questions quickly and truthfully, you will experience much, much more of what you have already experienced and, in addition, so will your wife and daughter. No one knows you're here and no one will come through the door and rescue you. The only thing that will come though the door is more pain and, in time, your death. If you are truthful with me. Miles, there is a very, very small chance that I might let you go.'

Smith looked closely at the man's eyes. He knew that the message had been understood. Smith started.

'I have two questions. The first concerns the operation in Albania. I want to know everything you know about it. I mean everything. All the people, active and passive. I want to know who was actually working for whom. I know enough of the answers already to know whether you are being truthful. If you are not then I will hurt you wife and daughter. The second question is about Bologna 1980. Why was Gentry there and who was the guy who got killed?'

Smith got up and looked down.

'That's all, old chap. I'll leave you to think it over for a while but when I come back, I want it all. I'm afraid your life and those of your nearest and dearest do literally depend on it. You are all lost people at the moment. It's up to you whether you remain so.'

With that he turned and left the room. Ripley looked after him in astonishment. He had been expecting more pain. As Smith walked back up the dark corridor to the fresh air he heard the smartly dressed Frenchman lock the door behind him. The heat was well up and the mosquitoes were out over the edges of the sluggish river as well as over the drainage ditches and pools that criss-crossed the river bank. For some reason Smith had never been attractive to mosquitoes. He struck off at a leisurely pace to give himself a little more time to plan. If Ripley talked then he would probably just let him go. The decision whether Smith would get in the way of his appointment to the top job at SIS could wait until the current adventure was resolved. He could see pros and cons. The more difficult question was what to do if Ripley didn't come up to expectations. In spite of what many who had stumbled across him during his life might imagine, Smith was not a particularly violent man. He had been well trained and had practiced a lot. But violence was always a tool; a means to an end. He found is as distasteful as most people. However unlike most people he had absolutely no qualms about its use when he thought it was necessary. He hoped that it would prove not to be so on this occasion.

He had decided on not asking too many questions. Given his present state, it was uncertain whether Ripley would have understood too much in any case. There were, he knew all to well, only two basic methods of interrogation. In one you just let the person tell a story. In the other you ask questions. The question route was best in cases when the person being interrogated was experienced or even trained. Left alone to tell a story they could easily concoct one of partial truths and an inexperienced questioner might never actually think of let alone ask the important questions. It was also best when the subject was not in too much physical pain. The story telling route was probably the best way in this particular case. Ripley was probably only slightly trained in counter-interrogation techniques if at all. He was also hurting a lot for which equally he had probably not been trained. Letting the man ramble was almost certainly be best as he would not really know how to avoid telling the truth. He would just be focussed on trying to end it all.

Twenty minutes later he was back sitting in front of the bruised Ripley. He could see that the man was still in pain. However his head was up and he looked at Smith steadily through his one good eye.

'All right, Ripley, old chap, talk to me.'

And he did

Chapter 8:   Interventions

Scene 1:   Girondou

Not for the first time for Smith it came down to friendship or, to more precise, loyalty. The two were very far, of course, from the same thing. School and some equally disappointing experiences subsequently had cured him of any wish to find many friends at all. It always seemed to in the end. One of the main results of an English - or in his particular case, Scottish - private school education was a particular view on friendship. Between the ages of thirteen and eighteen when his parents had decided that a bunch of xenophobic and occasionally sexually uncertain male school teachers could teach him all there was to know about life and therefore passed off all further responsibility onto them, he realised that the choice was a relatively simple one; you are either one of a crowd, a team player as they so nauseatingly call it these days, or not. A simple choice.

One of the regular processes that had been the punctuation in his life was the periodic cleansing of his address book. It was a process that he had always found to be more cathartic than depressing. Liberating, usually. Those on his list that survived this periodic mucking out of a pretty murky life were indeed those to whom he gave his loyalty for that was, when push came to shove, all that he felt really mattered. Never one to enjoy the gay superficiality of the usual social intercourse, he was easily bored by cocktail parties and social events, clubs and societies of all sorts. Retirement to the south of France a few years previously had brought a welcome opportunity to so a final stripping out of the unnecessaries. It may well have been that the pleasure of what he hoped would be the final time his cleansed his Microsoft Outlook contacts list that had made him approach the project with unusual vigour but by the time he had finished, he was left with a grand total of eight people. Two were his daughters, Gentry and Deveraux, a couple of equally retired ex-colleagues with whom he had shared adventures in the past and to whom he regarded himself as owing a debt. A pair of further contacts, one in Washington and the other in Moscow. That was it. A very few more names had been added since he and Arthur had arrived to live in Arles. But the grand total was still only a few more than ten. But these were central to his life and they were people for whom Smith would do anything no matter what the cost or the danger. Old La Salle had been on the list once but had dropped off some time ago through lack of contact rather than any other reason. He trusted them and, unreasonably or not, he expected that to be reciprocated. Being lied to was definitely not part of the picture and his recent interview with Ripley had given him great pause for thought. Thus he sat in the shade of a baking hot Provençale afternoon and did just that; gave the problem some thought. As with all his most important problems, it was not a strictly analytical or even a particularly linear process. He was not mapping out a strategy; a set of instruction to be given to others, clearly, logically and precisely. This was more difficult than that. For newer friends or those that were less dear to him the solution was simple. If his trust was abused they were either cut loose or died. This time he had to figure out exactly what he felt about being let down by his oldest and dearest friend.

He and Arthur were in a favourite spot; the highest point on the Alpille mountains, a short line of high hills that starts just north of Arles at St. Gabriel and that continues roughly east to west for about forty miles. They rise only to about a thousand feet and divide richly agricultural Plan du Crau to the south from the interior. They present no great challenge to a walker as they are criss-crossed with a network of well-maintained roadways that had been installed to assist fire-fighting equipment that was sometimes called out after week-end visits from picnickers. It was excellent, if sometimes dangerously hot, dog-walking country.

The highest point is actually topped, as seems inevitable these days, with a modern concrete excrescence called the Tour de Guetl that carries TV and other microwave equipment. It was however a place from where on a rare clear day you could see well out into the Mediterranean towards North Africa to the south and to Mont Ventoux and the beginning of the Alps to the north. The tower also offers almost the only shade to be found at the summit which bears little or no vegetation other than course grasses and scrubby bushes. It was a place he went to clear his head. Having parked the car on the space on the winding road that joined Mausanne with St Remy de Provence he had started to walk and an hour or so later and after a number of stops to top up the dog, he reached the summit. Sitting in the shadow of the tower had another advantage. It was the only place for many miles in any direction from which you couldn't see the tower.

Thus he sat there, his hand resting on Arthur's head drooped over his leg and resting in his lap, just letting the problem ooze though his brain like a slowly spreading ink blot over a piece of blotting paper. Ultimately the spread would slow and stop no matter how much more ink was added to the centre and at that point he would have decided.

The pattern had actually not got that far when he suddenly felt Arthur's dog's head quiver slightly and his ears prick. He heard nothing, of course. But for all the greyhound's reputation as a dog that hunted by sight rather than smell, there was absolutely nothing wrong with his hearing, even in retirement. Given the dog's persistent refusals to give up on a chase of a cat when shouted at, it was not a sense that would fail though over-use. In fact, Smith reckoned that Arthur could hear the pizza deliveryman's moped from more than a kilometre away. Whatever the obvious evidence, he trusted the dog's instincts. He felt down his right leg and plucked the Glock from the ankle holster. There were few places to hide a gun even as small as a Glock 30 in the Provençale heat if you were only wearing cotton trousers and a shirt. Arthur got to his feet and stood close, staring intently down the track that led back down the hill, Smith's hand laying on his back. He wouldn't move until it was lifted. After another five minutes Smith heard it as well; the sound of approaching walkers who were making their way to the summit. Nothing unusual about that, of course. What was unusual was that Arthur's tail was wagging. He'd obviously recognised someone. Rather like Smith's trust, Arthur's tail wags were given rather sparingly.

As the two figures got close, Smith saw that it was Girondou and his Dutch bodyguard Henk van der Togt. While Girondou was dressed very informally like Smith, Henk sported a light cotton jacket that Smith presumed was necessitated by carrying some somewhat heavier hardware. As he approached Girondou raised his hand in a sort of greeting but really more as if to ward off Smith's anger.

'Don't say it, my friend. But some time ago I told you that I would look after your back and this requires that I know where you are. However, I suspect you don't need protection at the moment as much as you need someone to talk to.'

Smith knew that his new friend was right and said nothing as the immaculate-clothed gangster sat down in the shade as his side. Henk stationed himself slightly down the track in less hospitable conditions. Girondou did, as Smith observed, receive a certain protection from a straw hat similar but definitely not identical to Smith's. His came from Locks of St, James. Girondou had remained faithful to his Italian hat maker in Spinetta Marengo. The man from Marseille started without preamble.

'Peter, I am surrounded by many people in many different places. Many I trust. But only up to a point. With a very few exceptions, the closer they are to me and the closer they are to a position where they can hurt me, the less I trust them. You, more than most people I know, will understand that this is not recipe for cynicism or a thin and solitary life. Quite the contrary, in fact. For me it is quite possible to have good and even profound relationships with people I don't trust. I personally like many thoroughly untrustworthy people. Trust is a simple matter. Trusting someone is not some mythical, fundamental value. It is that one should never put people in a position where they will let you down, to prefer their own interests to yours, to betray you rather than do something for themselves. If someone lets me down, seriously, which is something that usual results in their extreme discomfort, it is as often as not my own fault. This almost never mitigates the sin, of course, but giving people positions or information that they are incapable of keeping to themselves is usually my responsibility. You, my friend, seem to confuse loyalty with friendship. You have given your friendship to a very small number of people and you seem to demand their loyalty as a price rather than just friendship. Additionally you make the whole thing more burdensome by expecting those few on your list of friends that they be completely honest with you. My feeling is that these are unreasonable expectations of our fellow humans. It does not indicate any deep and meaningful trust just because a man has had power of life and death over you and you over him and you have both emerged from the experience alive. All that shows is that it was, at one time or another, expedient not let each other down. Relationships of any sort as really only a comfort blanket which is more or less useful some of the time. There is nothing profound or world-shaking about friendship. It is a commodity like any other; bought and sold, traded and ignored when required. Angèle and my children I love with all my heart and would sacrifice anything to keep them safe and well. But they are not my friends. They are, of course, much more than that. I trust them completely because they have no power to harm me. Not directly at least. I have made sure that whatever contact they have with my somewhat idiosyncratic life is never enough for them to harm me. I have made sure that they were never burdened with any knowledge that might one day become too heavy. In this sense family may mean very little. You will recall François, my own brother, let me down in the biggest way possible. I had him killed, of course, but I never found his betrayal particularly surprising. The responsibility was partially mine. I had allowed him to know more than was good for him. He was ultimately consumed by greed to possess what was not his to have and what would have proved too heavy a burden. It was as simple as that.'

'I am under no illusion that I owe my position and my power to the fact that many people find it more expedient to support me that to betray me. My security and that of my family resides in keeping it like that. In a way you might say that is my sole preoccupation as my business tends to take care of itself, or I have people who take care of it. There are so many people around me that in a way they become self-policing. No matter how many might want to conspire against me, there are many more who will not join the conspiracy but will prefer to seek my favour by betraying the betrayers to me. Greed is a wonderful motivator but if everyone is equally greedy it seldom works as a motivator. I never dislike anyone. I simple accept them for what they are and make sure that the odds work in my favour. I don't even dislike the people I have killed from time to time. They are not important enough for that. In reality life itself isn't that important and it is a grave mistake to try to make it so. You, Peter, are typically northern European. You are strong, silent, looking constantly for meaning in relationships and usually failing to find them. You spend your life enjoying being miserable. By contrast, I am a southern European who enjoys a myriad of relationships and friendships, family connections and a life of easy superficiality. I don't require loyalty from people because I don't need it. All I require is that people are not disloyal. These two are actually not two sides of the same coin at all. In fact, loyalty and disloyalty are, in my opinion, almost completely disconnected. You, my friend, should learn that disappointments in life exist in inverse relations to one expectations of it. That is the way happy people live down here.'

Girondou paused to give Smith an opportunity to react to the lecture but nothing came. Smith was just staring out over the horizon with his minds seemingly as far away as his gaze; at least half way to North Africa. Undeterred by the silence, Girondou continued.

'You confuse friendship with loyalty and with trust when, in reality these are all different things. You are disappointed in your long relationship with Gentry because you think he is your friend and you suspect he has not told you things that you think you should have known. You demand openness, honesty as well as loyalty and friendship. No one can give this. Gentry now stands condemned in your mind for the sins of disloyalty and untrustworthiness and you are very uncomfortable with the fact that people who usually fail you in this way come to speedy and untimely ends. You have found this out by having beaten half to death some senior British idiot who in all probability pursuing some peripheral agenda that may well actually have little or nothing to do with you. As far as I can see in all this rather pointless story you personally have not yet been threatened in any way. One old acquaintance and ex-comrade in arms has been bumped off in circumstances that can as easily be explained by an angry and cuckolded husband as it can by international conspiracy. More easily, in fact.'

This time Smith did interrupt when Girondou pause.

'So what do you advise, Alexei?' with more than a touch of petulance in his voice that was picked up by Girondou immediately.

'Just as soon as you manage to stop sulking, you could look at this whole problem more simply and a lot less emotionally.

Separate the things like friendship and your expectations of all that from the actual picture that exists real and solid. It is obvious to me that all this past stuff, Albania, Bologna, Venice, Pau and all the ghosts that have lain undisturbed since then have recently come back to life and there has to be a reason for that: in all probability a very simple one. Things like this and the personal enmities they embody don't get resurrected after this amount of time unless someone has something to gain because risen ghosts can be difficult to control. And I would guess that it is the recent rise towards the top job of British Intelligence of your Mr Ripley who is currently bleeding rather messily all over my nice Camargue farm cottage floor that is the cause of all this. I don't know any of the details of the Albanian thing but I am pretty sure that Mr Ripley is mucking out some old stables before his final step to the top. That, at least, is what it smells like to me. Whether this is a personal thing or, probably more importantly, there is some more pernicious fact that he feels might be discovered if his past is looked at too closely, I can't tell. But it strikes me that few people in intelligence rise to the top without some nasty things buried in their past and this has not usually prevented their rise. So this in itself is not the reason. More likely, he fears your close scrutiny. He has a personal skeleton that is unknown in his own world and that would ruin him. So if you want my advice, it is that you forget this self-indulgent crap about trust and loyalty and stuff that you are currently wallowing in and find out what Ripley is hiding. Punish that not your friends. Kill these stupid Americans and avenge McDowell if it will give you satisfaction, kill Grantkov if you want to, he would be no great loss. Kill Ripley's man La Salle if necessary. Your sentimental attachment to this geriatric academic faggot is a little worrying in any case. You could even kill Ripley himself but I suspect he would be more useful if, once discovered, he was allowed to get the top job. It could be a good investment for both of us. Above all, stop beating yourself up about all this.'

Smith sat motionless. There were few people that would think of talking to him like this and he found it hard to take. He knew, however, that the Frenchman was mostly right and nodded slowly.

'Perhaps this morning might have been better spent talking to Ripley about himself rather than about Gentry and others.'

It was Girondou's turn to nod in agreement.

'Yes, I rather think you're right. So before I came here I had a word with your friend Deveraux and asked him to look in on Ripley this afternoon. He will be waiting for you in Arles when you get back later.

Smith's mood reached another, lower level of foulness as he frowned out to sea in the general direction of Libya.

'I'm not sure I like your taking over my life like this, Alexei.'

The elegant Frenchman shrugged economically.

'Actually, Peter, I can't really care if you do or you don't. My instructions come from a higher authorities. Our ladies, to be precise. They would both die for us, my friend. The problem is that unless we are very careful in the way we conduct our lives, in time they probably will. They are two of a kind. Their love for us goes beyond friendship.'

'Ah,' said Smith with a sarcasm born out of embarrassment, 'Love until death, I suppose. Very theatrical.'

Girondou nodded slowly, refusing the bait.

'Yet, Peter, that is exactly it. Love until death. But it will be theirs not ours. It is the way of Camargue women.'

Later as they linked arms and walked the back or so down the track to the place they had left their cars it was Henk who followed seventy or so yards behind, Smith noted with approval. Very occasionally he also caught a glimpse of people ahead of them on either side of the track some fifty yards back into the sparse woods. Once he briefly saw was the intimidating Elaine. It was an arrangement that made Smith feel very secure but which worried Arthur immensely as his eyesight was infinitely better than his two human companions. He kept on glancing to either side and back over his shoulder with some anxiety. But then again, Smith thought as we walked in silence with his companion, Arthur knew very little about the maximum accurate killing range of a Kriss SPD set on single shot in the hands of skilled marksmen. He was, after all, just a dog.

Chapter 9: Albania 1976

Scene 1: Memories of a Betrayal

The fire fight came from nowhere. The base had been lightly guarded and they had no difficulty in moving past a few scattered and disinterested Albanian guards. As they got closer to the bunkers that had been built into the low hills a mile or so from the runway they saw some Chinese but these were little more than armed technicians rather than proper military personnel. They all had Chinese Type 63 assault rifles slung loosely around they necks. Most were smoking casually and talking loudly. Many were using torches to find their way about. They were clearly not expecting company.

Miles Ripley, in charge of the Balkan desk, had put the American plan to Gentry as a fait-accompli and Gentry had lost no time at all in raising a raft of objections much to the annoyance of his nominal superior. Ripley was obviously not happy.

'You're just biased. You just don't like our American friends. What you and your Neanderthal colleagues need to understand is that the future is about collaboration with the Americans not just wandering off in an old school sort of way and doing things ourselves.'

Ripley was almost shouted. There was no love lost between the two in any case. Gentry had been a senior planner for many more years than Ripley had been in the service. Ripley was being fast-tracked to greatness while Gentry was quite content to be slow-tracked into obscurity. Very far from being new-school himself, Gentry regarded his new boss as being equally far from the old-school that he valued so much. He thought the man was a nasty little arriviste with no culture and even less knowledge. However, he also felt that the reasons for his objections should be put on the record that was being caught by the tape machines.

'I have absolutely no objections to the American and their plans,' he lied for the benefit of the tape, 'Quite the contrary they have resources and enthusiasm, two qualities that we have these days in only modest quantities, I regret to say. I simply don't want to jeopardise a lot of good work that has been done over the last half century. We've have been involved in Albania since the time of Ismail Qemali and have good networks of contacts there still.

'Who?'

Gentry sighed loud enough for it to be recorded.

'Perhaps you might look a little at the history of this particular country as is one of your responsibilities, Miles. A touch of historical context never does any harm, in my view.'

Ripley's face went an even deeper shade of red. His voice was heavy with sarcasm.

'Well, professor, the fact is that the operation is going ahead. I have made sure we are involved. I suggest you do what we pay you for and do some planning which is what I am told you are good at.'

He leant over Gentry's desk with a look of pure hostility.

'You seem to have friends in high places, Gentry. Had you not, you would now be planning operations in Alaska rather than Europe. So just get on and do your job.'

Ripley turned and flounced out of Gentry's tiny, book-lined office but was stopped half way through the door, turned back by Gentry's concluding words offered with an innocent smile.

'Alsaka.'

'What,' he shouted, face completely purple, 'what about Alaska?'

Gentry replied with heavy sarcasm.

'You might find, Sir, that particular bit of the world is actually owned by your American friends not us. History, Miles, history. Useful stuff, I find.'

Ripley's attempt at a theatrical exit accompanied with a loud slamming of the door was thwarted by both the pneumatic door damper and the heavy, if slightly threadbare, claret red velvet curtain hung from a rising brass rail that kept out the draughts from Gentry's little basement room.

Faced with the Americans trampling all over his prized network in Albania, Gentry was forced to get involved, no matter how reluctantly. He hated working with Americans who he actually regarded as unsubtle, selfish and totally lacking in imagination. After a considerable effort of hiding both his temper and his contempt he had finally persuaded the Americans that nothing could be seen that could possibly be associated with anything nuclear. Satellite imagery as well as local intelligence from the well-established and generally reliable local network that the British had had in place since the Second World War all confirmed that no major building works of the sort needed for rocket launchers or any sort of nuclear production had taken place. Gentry's briefing when alone with Smith was both concise and scathing.

'I'm pretty sure that all that is happening is that the Albanians have decided to house some their small and ineffective fighter fleet underground in the side of a hill. In my opinion that is a particularly stupid thing to do given that small hills can be collapsed with some ease these days. Thus at best all that can be secreted in these low hills on the western edge of the airfield are some old Chinese fighters stored in hanger tunnels drilled into the mountain. My information is that this is a squadron of Shenyang F-5s and a few geriatric Russian MIG 15s of uncertain origin. The tunnels, whose plans I have in my files incidentally, are nowhere big enough to accommodate bombers. In fact the tunnels are so narrow that planes are more likely to hit each other below ground before emerging into the daylight than they are to scramble successfully. Given that these tunnels are some two thousand yards from the actual runway, my estimate for a squadron scramble, something that fighter planes are supposed to be able to do rather quickly, is something in excess of ten minutes. The whole thing is completely daft. Bombers, which you would have thought would be the delivery mechanism of choice for anything nuclear are completely out of the question. At the present time the entire Albanian bomber force consists of one aircraft, a single Harbin H-5, again a Chinese version of the old Russian Illyushin Il-28. That particular aircraft has difficulty lifting itself let alone a payload. There is certainly nothing nuclear going on here.'

'Additionally,' Gentry went on as if totally to crush the whole idea of the operation, 'apart from the fact that the current state of Chinese nuclear technology is so basic and undeveloped that the odds on their having anything that would actually go bang are very small indeed and the chances of them being able to carry or deliver anything and make it go bang in the right place are non-existent. However it was true that a few storage facilities have been constructed in addition to the hangers and given the parlous state of Albanian air force these aren't for storing conventional bombs or munitions either.'

Smith shifted in his seat.

'I can see why the Americans might be paranoid but I don't see, old friend, why you just haven't trashed the whole plan. I am sure you could.'

Gentry looked a little embarrassed which is what he usually did when he was up to something clever.

'My locals have told me that in amidst the arrival of the first F-5s a number of pallets of something were fork-lifted very quickly into the first tunnel at night from convoy of trucks that came from a Chinese freighter docked in the local port of Durrës. Now I am interested in these little packages'

Smith thought for a moment and looked across the crowded desk.

'Ah. Chemical weapons, you think.'

Gentry, not for the first time, was impressed by the man sitting opposite him.

'Yes, although how on earth you manage to keep up with this sort of thing while teaching art and stuff, I have no idea. Yes, I am very interested in these pallets. Very interested indeed.'

There had been rumours in the intelligence community that Albania's association with China had turned to the question of chemical weapons some years before. This was an established technology thanks to all the countries that had come up against each other during the twentieth century and it was an easy development for the new communist China to follow in its attempts to make the west take notice of it. The symbolic significance of having even a small amount of these illegal weapons situated within a few hundred miles of many European capitals was not lost on any of the protagonists in the cold war.

Symbolic or not, Gentry's intervention in the plans from America at least resulted in the mission having some sort of proper intelligence significance. Initially he tried to have the whole thing cancelled on the grounds that the UK had enough resources in place already to find out everything of importance without actually having to put men on the ground. However the Americans, presumably flushed with the achievement of finding out actually where Albania was, insisted on going on. The American idea of intelligence gathering was generally to kill it first and learn something from the post-mortem. Thus Gentry had been overruled by his superiors including Ripley and had came up with a plan that looked like a fast infiltration and intelligence gathering operation but that was in reality damage limitation. He valued his Albanian network. He had spent a long time patiently building it up. In a tiny and paranoid country, it had been surprisingly good at winning intelligence from its neighbours with whom is shared mountainous and un-policeable borders. Gentry had added McDowell to the team as the 'nuclear' man but whose talents could equally extend to chemical warfare. He also persuaded the extremely reluctant Americans to accept Smith as leader. The Yanks had originally refused completely to let a Brit lead until Gentry had pointed out that none of their people actually spoke either Albanian or Gheg the dialect more likely to be found in the north where they were headed which, much to the Americans seeming surprise was the usual way they would communicate with the locals. In fact, Smith didn't either but Gentry sensibly omitted to tell them this. He wanted Smith for entirely another reason. In spite of being a thoroughly part-time spy, spending most of his life teaching Rembrandt to California blondes or selling computer solutions to unsuspecting foreigners whenever he was short of money, Smith was easily the best field operator Gentry had ever known. Most of the men and women that passed through his fingers had to be taught the tricks of the trade and were thus suitable in the varying degrees to working in the field that corresponded to their mixed abilities to learn. Smith however was a natural. The best field men have to know what to do when the elegant plans hatched over brandy and cigars in Whitehall basements fall apart in some foreign place as they often do. These were the ones that tended to live longer. In Gentry's long experience, Smith was a one-off. The more things fell apart, the clearer he seemed to think and the calmer he acted. He was also someone who could be indescribably violent if the necessity arose; so much so that opponents were usually shocked into submission rather that any other method. From the very beginning, Gentry had had great reservations about the whole operation and wanted Smith there to pick up the pieces that he knew would follow. He made the point at the end of the briefing.

'Peter, I have a bad feeling about this little show. Something doesn't feel at all right about it. Watch your back and be prepared for difficulties. I will be Control on the operation.'

Smith simply nodded and tried not to show that he too was a little concerned. Gentry almost never used his Christian name.

'Just get me a couple of hours on the range with a Type 63 assault rifle would you? I need to refresh my memory.'

Gentry stared for a long time at the door that closed silently behind the departing Smith. How typical of the man that he wanted to spend some time with the weapon that they would use to kill him if they got the chance. He didn't know too many others who would bother. What worried him more however was that he had discovered from some deep-buried friends in the CIA had absolutely no knowledge of this operation at all. He was worried because he was putting his friend at risk and had not been any too truthful about telling him.

The insertion had been easy. They flew to Italy and transferred to a submarine at the US naval base in Naples. The Albanian coast was lightly patrolled and their costal forces were about as well-equipped as their air force. They were landed at a beach a few miles north of the port of Shëngjin and a short walk over the hills to the airfield. It was a cloudy night and there was virtually no light at all.

The entrances to the bunkers were pairs of heavy steel sliding doors but they had been built deeply recessed into the hillside at different angles to each other, presumably as a precaution from them all being damaged by a single explosion. This thoroughly sensible precaution resulted, however, in making the entrances invisible from each other. Equally each door was easily approached and having observed that there was no regular circulating patrol Smith took his group silently and completely unobserved through the first three tunnels. The huge blast doors were not alarmed and each rolled back easily after the locks were disabled with a small muffled charge and McDowall and the main Americans did a quick recce inside. Each tunnel was curved with a white line painted on the floor separating the area where the fighters would park from a taxi lane along one side.

Smith smelt a rat when the first three were found completely empty. A big one. No planes nor anything else for that matter. Nothing necessarily sinister about that, of course, but there were fresh marks on the floor where pallets had recently been moved by rubber-tyred lift trucks. Whatever it was had been moved. Someone had known they were coming. It was the sort of decision he was paid for and he pulled the plug immediately and without further thought. He silently signalled a fast withdrawal. One of the Americans objected but reluctantly obeyed after Smith had whispered into their ears that in Europe at least the penalty for disobeying a commanding officer on the battlefield was summary execution. It must have been something about his tone of voice that convinced him that he wasn't joking. Perhaps it was the Browning 9mm pointed at the man's head that persuaded him.

As they made their way back over the hill and back to the pickup point on the beach, Smith signalled the submarine lying at periscope depth and he deployed the group into a defensive formation to wait for the RIB to appear to take them off. He had chosen to lie on the seaward side of a low sand dune some four yards high, thirty yards from the sea. It turned into an inspired choice for just as they settled into the dark sand, all hell broke loose. Automatic weapons fire from both sides from troops located mercifully slightly deeper inland than they were. The whole dune was raked by fire with nine millimetre bullets screaming over their heads. One of the Americans ignored Smith's instruction to lie low, decided to do the macho thing and half stood to raise his Armalite AR-18 to return fire. He took a direct hit which blew out the side of his head and was knocked backwards into the sand stone dead. Smith raised his voice and shouted at the rest of the group. There was no point is pretending they weren't there.

'If you want to die, be brave and stand up. If you don't, stay on your bellies and wait. Do not return fire.'

He lay back and listened. He was forming a picture. The night was clouded and there was precious little light. That they were caught in a crossfire was obvious. The gunfire from north and south was not particularly heavy but it was continuous. However given the low light and the fact that the armourer in London said that the Chinese had not supplied the Albanians with any night vision equipment, the Albanians were firing relatively blind - as would they be themselves, of course, if they attempted to fire back. The idiot who stood up and presented a nice silhouette was just that, an idiot. The Type 63 was derived from a standard assault rifle and was a cumbersome but accurate weapon if unreliable on full-auto mode but that was of very little use if you couldn't see what you were aiming at. Smith remembered that the man had died at a moment when there was a gap in the automatic fire. It had been a single shot. Smith reached for his radio and called up the sub captain with exaggerated courtesy.

'Captain, I would be grateful is you could get half a dozen men up on your casing and put some fairly continuous fire into the two groups of enemy north and south of us. I estimate no more than four guns in each place. Aim at their gun flashes. I need about three minutes from when your RIB hits the beach. Please keep their heads down until we're aboard. I would rather not get any punctures in your rubber boat or in one of my men.'

A single 'Okay that' came from the submarine. But the captain wasn't finished.

'I thought you would like to know that I have just received a signal for you from London from someone called Gentry. It just says 'two cuckoos'. That's all.'

Smith just said 'Thanks, out', and released the send button on his radio. He called his group together shouting over the noise of gunfire.

'The RIB will be here to collect us and the sub will give us covering fire. Under no circumstances move to the boat until I tell you and I will order you individually. Wait your turn. Until your name is called stay down. When you hear your name just run like hell and get into the RIB. Do not stop and fire at the enemy. Let the sub do that. Furzenik and Fox, you two will drag Simeoni and load him up. I don't want anyone left.'

The American captain erred on the side of caution for as the dim shape of the RIB appeared out of the gloom, all hell broke loose with a fairly constant stream of heavy machine gun AR18 fire in both directions. Smith was please to hear the heavier thumping of a couple of M219s. If all this went on for too much longer the

Albanians would need buckets rather than body bags to collect their people. Smith called the first Americans forward.

'Furzenik and Fox, go now!'

The two each took a hold of the dead man's arms and left, dragging their dead colleague behind them. Smith was almost too intent in watching their progress to notice that the last American, Anderson take his 9mm Browning quietly from its holster and take careful aim at the back of McDowell's head some fifteen feet in front of him. Smith flung himself forward and immediate put a head lock on the man while wrenching the gun from his grasp. The man fell forward under Smith's weight. McDowell turned in astonishment and was about to say something when Smith ordered him to the boat.

'Get the fuck out of here, John. Get to the boat and make sure they don't leave without me. I may just need a moment. Use your gun if you have to. If any of our team object, shoot them. Now go.'

McDowell knew better than to say anything and just started the short run down to the shore. Smith turned his attention back to the squirming Anderson down. Tightening his grip he bet close to than man's ear.

'You have five seconds to tell me what the fuck if going on. Who are you and who do you work for?'

Apart from a couple of obscenities Steve Anderson chose silence. Smith let him go and waited until he had reached half way to the short when he raised his Browning and shot the man cleanly in the back of the head. It didn't take him long to pick the man up as he himself ran down the beach and threw both on them into the waiting RIB. As he ran down he felt a sharp pain in his backside as a bullet creased him. It was nothing significant but Smith immediately though that a mission that had always had the potential to be a pain in the arse, had just achieved that in more ways than one.

His interview with the boat Captain was not an easy one.

'Firstly Captain, my thanks for the cover fire. It seems they were expecting us. I would be grateful if you could put the two live Americans under arrest until we get back to Naples.'

The Captain looked somewhat reluctant.

'Mr Smith. I would remind you that these are American citizens and this is an American submarine.'

Smith replied somewhat acidly: 'And I would remind you of your orders which quite specifically put me in command of this operation. And that means that short of endangering your submarine, I remain in charge of this operation. At least two of the four worthy American citizens, as you rather euphemistically put it, who were assigned to this mission, are traitors - cuckoos as my Control in London put it. At the moment I am not sure which they are although I have a good idea. I want them kept under lock and key until your CIA and my SIS debrief us all. That is all I'm asking.'

The Captain looked thoughtfully.

'And what about you and the other Englishman. Should you not also be locked up as well?

Smith thought of objecting but immediately saw the virtue of the idea. They were very much in a minority on an American submarine with a crew of more than one hundred.

'Captain I think that would be a very good idea indeed. Just don't put us in with the Americans. Please send a medic too. I would quite like to be able to sit down for the debriefing.'

As he left he thought he caught a slight grin on the American's face. Back in London Smith's debrief with Gentry had been as short as it was unsatisfactory. In fact, having given an account of what happened, it was Smith who asked most of the questions. Gentry was obviously acutely embarrassed.

'Don't you think you owe me some sort of explanation, Gentry?'

Gentry looked like a whipped dog as he answered with a weak smile.

'I do indeed but unfortunately I can't give you much. I got a message from someone in the CIA warning me that there were a couple of wrong 'uns in your team but it came just after you left the sub. As you know I had no direct communication with you and the only channel was via the boat captain. I had faith that you would solve the problem with your usual panache'.

'What did the Yanks actually say?

If possible, Gentry's embarrassment deepened.

'Er, actually they seem to have vanished. They were offloaded at Naples and seem to have been swallowed up never to have been seen again. Certainly a request from me to the CIA to be able to interview them was greeted with a puzzled 'Albanian operation, what Albanian operation?''

'What about your friend Ripley? What has he to say for himself.'

'Mysteriously absent, Peter, mysteriously absent.'

Smith could hardly contain himself.

'Jesus Christ, Gentry what the fuck is going on. You don't usually cock things up like this.'

Gentry just succeeded in looking even more miserable.

'I will say that something rather odd has happened. Originally, the Americans wanted to talk to you about their dead people. I gather that they were not particularly happy about the circumstances in which Mr Anderson died.'

Smith snorted.

'You can tell them that the bloody man was lining up at the back of McDowell's head so I shot him.'

Gentry frowned.

'I think that in the interests of Anglo American relations we should hide behind the fact that both your Browning and the Chinese Type 62 use 9 mm ammunition thus engendering a certain, ah, ambiguity in what might have happened. I think that our American cousins might get a bit pissed off if they knew we executed one of their number.'

'Even if he was working for the other side - whatever that is? In any case it was only the one. Simeoni was shot by one of them. However, to be frank, I don't give a tuppeny fuck what the Americans think.'

'Perhaps, Peter, perhaps. You know how unimaginative those people are over there. However they no longer seem to want to talk to you. Now that is very unusual indeed.'

Smith's closing words were uttered half over his shoulder as he left Gentry's office.

'Next time you decide to run a half-baked, unplanned dangerous and completely pointless operation in the Balkans with a bunch of gung-ho traitorous Americans leave me out please. Either that or next time I will kill them all just to be certain.'

It was an episode that both of them subsequently pushed to the back of their memories as later operations developed and Smith learned to trust Gentry again.

Chapter 10: Conversations

Scene 1: Gentry's Turn for some Questions

When he finally got back to the mas that evening it was late and he found Gentry sitting in one of the deep leather armchairs in Émile Aubanet's study looking thoroughly morose. The study was, Smith remembered, a supremely comfortable room with six floor to ceiling windows along one side giving out onto the arcaded quadrangle that surrounded the courtyard. The other three walls were lined with glass fronted bookcases each individually lit. These were interspersed with small paintings, again each lit by dim lights, each offering a bright, intense, oases of colour. The paintings were by Gauguin, van Gogh and Cezanne, all from their times in Provence. All were unpublished and unknown. All mercifully freed from the avarice of the art market and parasitical attentions of collectors. They just hung gracefully in this working space to give joy to those who took the time to look at them rather than calculate their value. The books cases too held their share of treasures from Europe's publishing history. Many were incomparably valuable but equally they were much read.

Smith came in and sat opposite his friend. Gentry was pale and obviously uncomfortable. The two sat looking at each other in silence for a long time. For Gentry, Smith was one of the people he knew best but remained an unknown quantity. Also he was afraid of him in a way that one shouldn't be with friends. For Smith, Gentry was a completely known quantity but a man who sat diminished in his estimation. As he looked at his companion, Smith remembered Girondou's words and tried to look beyond the past and instead forward into history. He had to remember that Gentry was out of his depth, floundering in a world that he knew only by proxy. Apart from the dust-filled adventure of Bologna, Smith was pretty sure that Gentry knew nothing of the duplicity and violence of the real world that the spies he controlled actually inhabited. Gentry was an intellectual; an academic. He knew nothing of the reality of betrayal, of duplicity, of doubles and triples, of ideology which was destroyed whenever it met the reality of the gun or the knife. A world where the stupidity of the people who inhabited it meant that there was often no alternative to violence. For Gentry his was a game and an intellectual one at that. In truth Smith knew that people are never that clever; never that detached. Most people were inadequate and unimaginative; given a momentary fix of power by a gun or a sight of a bound and gagged interrogation suspect leaking bodily fluids of all sorts over an unforgiving floor, they lost sight of the fact that this was not the real world; insofar as they ever understood that. In short, Gentry had never known how really unpleasant and stupid most people could be to each other.

As he looked at is friend, Smith felt a kind of sympathy; an envy, of sorts. His part-time spy craft was valued precisely because he knew about these things. For Gentry it was almost certainly a matter of ignorance being bliss. Finally it was time. Smith addressed Gentry in a low, unemotional tone. He knew that his friend was at his most vulnerable and had no mercy.

'David. If you don't already know, I think I should tell you that you owe the fact that you are sitting here alive and undamaged apart from a few disagreeable memories to the fact that a lot of people, none of whom you have ever met, have put themselves at considerable risk to save your life. They have done this because I wanted them to. These people are part of my new life, David and I now, because of you, I owe them more that I can possible repay. It is high time you were straight with me. You won't have another chance.'

Again the silence filled the room with Gentry collected his thoughts. When he started it was barely audible.

'In December 1945 two members of the right wing so-called Iron Guard of Romanian partisans who survived the war escaped to what is now known as the west. They came to the UK. They were pretty fascist in their policies and they hated almost everything that was not Romanian - Germans, Jews, you name it. Everyone, it seemed.'

'A few years later they had a son who was originally called Avram Rădescu. An unremarkable child by all accounts who progressed quietly through the English state school system, a passage made easier by his parents changing their name to a more conventional Ripley. Avram became Miles and the boy evolved into, to all intents and purposes a normal English boy, especially after the parents applied for and received British citizenship. The parents had acceptable English and quickly were picked up by the MI5 as it then was as the new communist regimes in Balkans developed. Their role was to supply information without getting directly involved in operations. Indeed at that time in the years immediately following the war, there weren't really any operations to be involved with.'

'In a way it was inevitable that the young Miles Ripley should join the service in the wake of his parents. MI5 was obsessed with Russia and the cold war was starting. Anyone who had real knowledge of the iron curtain countries was valuable and the selectors were none too choosy. Miles, of course, learned from his parents and their friends and inevitably got a slightly biased view on things. Internal controls were none to good either and although the spy scandals that have so entertained the public subsequently were common knowledge within the service, little was ever done about them. There was however a good deal of paranoia about pro-Russian Englishmen leaking secrets by the trunk-full. Miles initially followed his parents in their extreme right-wing views and policy makers saw this as being positive rather having long enough memories to be suspicious of other aspects of fascist philosophy.'

'Be that as it may, the young Ripley was absorbed into the service and started a slow rise. He spent his apprenticeship in other departments. He spent time the America and only came back into my area later at the end beginning of the seventies. I was always slightly suspicious of him. He seemed too good to be true to me but these were paranoid times so I will admit I did nothing. I was then in charge of the new Balkan Desk and it was a minor role when compared with the bigger picture. Everyone was obsessed with Russia, of course. Very soon I found out that Albania was going its own very individual way and jumping into bed with China rather Russia. In reality it was a relationship that always sounded more important than it was but from time to time it registered on the radar. More importantly some people saw Albania's flirtation with China as an important factor in combatting the all-pervasive affect of Soviet Russia and its influence over mid-Europe.'

'What no one in the service realised, including me, was that Ripley became a Maoist. God knows how or why. It was so unlikely a possibility that it never occurred to us. Certainly students were regularly burying their pimply innocent faces in copies of Mao's Little Red Book but the thought of anyone actually believing that stuff enough actually to change their allegiance was risible. What everyone forgot was that Ripley hadn't got an allegiance in the first place to speak of. He may have looked like a Brit but that was not the case under the skin. Ripley went to China on a number of occasions but his parental fascist credentials were so strong that no one really looked at that. He also had developed some serious contacts with some Americans who, like him, thought that Albania's infatuation with China was an opportunity rather than a threat.'

Gentry paused as if to allow Smith to intervene and help along a narrative that was obviously causing him considerable discomfort. Smith remained silent forcing his erstwhile friend reluctantly to continue.

'What some of us suspected was that Ripley was passing stuff to the Chinese. Low level stuff, mostly. It was all he seemed to have access to. However the general consensus was that given the state of their technology, the Chinese were in no state to take advantage of much of what Ripley gave them whatever it was. There was also a school of thought, championed by your friend La Salle that the fact that we any sort of conduit at all to our slitty-eyed friends was something that was worth preserving irrespective of whatever Ripley may have been giving them. La Salle thought that Ripley with his newly found passion for western decadence could easily be turned is the necessity arose. I must admit that I tended to agree. It was decide to leave things alone while the service turned its attention to the Russians who seemed to be, as it were, already at the gate.'

'Thus Ripley just fell out of sight. What we ignored - I ignored - was that the dreadful little man had his chums in the States who thought that Albania could be a key player in their struggle against the implacable enemy Russia. Thus when the Gjadër thing arose, the CIA were not in general unsympathetic to an operation. What they had failed to detect, rather like us, was that while they officially wanted to know what was going on in a slightly detached sort of way, their little subterranean pro-Albanian group was horrified. Fredricks and Wilson hijacked the plan and Ripley was immediately contacted as the enforcer. The rest you know.'

Gentry stopped, more in hope than expectation. However he was disappointed. Smith just said:

'Bologna.'

There was another long pause while Gentry gathered his thoughts.

'In August 1980 Ripley instructed me to accompany him to Italy to talk to some contact of his whom he wanted to recruit to our little Albanian team. I wasn't happy but although I suspected Ripley of being less than straightforward with us, I thought he was relatively harmless. What I didn't know was that he wanted me dead and out of his way as he presumably thought that my suspicions were more dangerous to him than, in fact, they were. We met the man in Bologna. He turned out to be interesting but little more that that. After the meeting Ripley and I were supposed to take the train back to Paris and thence to England. The rest you know.'

Smith thought for a moment.

'What do I know, David? Tell me.'

Again Gentry had to focus.

'Ripley and I arrived at the station and were checking the departure board and suddenly there was a goddam enormous explosion and I passed out. The next thing I knew I was in the back of a car, bleeding somewhat painfully. I ended up in Venice and you came through the trattoria door. The rest you really do know.'

'The hat, Gentry, the hat.'

'The what?'

'The hat. You were wearing a straw hat with an MCC ribbon. It wasn't yours. How come?'

'Now I come to think of it, I lost my own straw and Ripley insisted on lending me his. Why it that important?'

'That was how you were identified as the target.'

Gentry looked very, very tired.

'You know, I still have no idea why they wanted to kill me.

Smith sighed.

'I think that you have to ask yourself who rather than why. Someone took out the contract I assume because you were close to sussing Ripley. It seems an obvious reason. It might well have been Ripley himself. I assume that you were fed the cock and bull story about your companion copping the bullet instead of you after you got to Venice. I am pretty sure you never actually saw a body at all. You recall that you passed that particular piece of fiction on to me too. Given that your trip to Italy was off the record, there was no surprise that Ripley was still in there after I got you home. I, of course, was ignorant that it was Ripley in the first place. The second contract story has just been added recently to add confusion. This all comes back to Ripley. Now he is on the verge of the top job he is cleaning the stables and using his old friend Grantkov and some thoroughly disgruntled Americans to help him do it. McDowell and I are on the list and you knew it. Just as I suspect you knew it in Albania all those years ago.'

'Peter, I never found anything provable on Ripley and after a while I stopped looking. Albania got less and less important and China seemed to be getting all its secrets from America and Russia rather than us. I had other things to work on in the Balkans. If Ripley was indeed a Chinese spy then he wasn't doing anything too damaging, so we left him alone.'

While he would admit that he now had more information that he had at the beginning of their conversation, Smith still had the feeling the Gentry was not levelling with him. But curiously he found himself getting used to it. He was by no means happy, of course, but he was beginning to get a bit bored. To be fair that Gentry was possibly still a bit scrambled and resolved to take the matter up at another time when they were sitting in more familiar circumstances. Gentry lapsed into his now customary silence and Smith just quietly left the room.

Chapter 11: Burying the Dead

Scene 1: McDowell

Seat belts were forgotten as they sat in the back of the Range Rover while it sped along the autoroute east back towards the Camargue. Martine had edged towards him and now she leant against him, held steady and in some comfort by his arm around her shoulders. It was a position that seemingly few of the well-intentioned but ultimately nerd-like designers of the innumerable safety devices that these days festoon cars of all sorts, had ever imagined. Certainly their self-righteousness would overrule if they even thought about accommodating such intimacy. These solitary people obviously thought that personal safety completely transcended the necessity for company, or reassurance, or love of any sort. Presumably they ate bio-degradable, vegetarian take-aways at night alone in their safe apartments watching their sandals dry out and worrying about someone stealing their bicycles. The passenger they understood was required to exist isolated from his companions, locked in grand solitude into his ergonomically designed personal chair, protected by multiple seat belts and harnesses and airbags hidden in everything from the headrests to the ash trays which, of course, they had not yet had the courage to dispense with completely. She knew that he was troubled and, so was she. She was trying to work out how to tell him.

McDowell's funeral had gone off well - as these things tend to. Considering he was an outsider the little whitewashed church in Laslades had been almost full. Smith wondered if that was because Louise was French. Perhaps she had family in the area. Smith realised that he knew almost nothing about her. He was quite surprised to hear that they had only been married for a few years. He and McDowell had never really met socially and for some unaccountable reason he had assumed that they had been married for longer. There were certainly no children in evidence at the church. The priest had said a few words that hinted at a genuine affection for the man who had lived locally for about twenty years. Louise had asked Smith if he wanted to say anything but she was not surprised when he declined. She understood that most of the memories that these two had shared were ones that could not be spoken about publicly.

The group that came back to the house after the burial looked to Smith to be little diminished and to judge by the general noise level, the locals were determined to celebrate as much as mourn respectfully. It was an approach to death that Smith heartily approved of and he felt the spirit within him rise as that in his glass sank. He looked around constantly to see if there was anyone whose face even vaguely rang a bell. He didn't recognise anyone. It didn't really surprise him. Whoever was involved in McDowell's murder, they weren't going to turn up here. They had nothing to gain from being there. Martine circulated. There had been no shortage of men wanting to chat to this Provençale beauty.

'Well?'

It was less of a question than a gentle prod. He had lapsed into silence and she knew that the past was again weighing heavily. She addressed the back of their drivers head.

'Did you see anyone of interest, Derek?'

Deveraux smiled to himself.

'And where, exactly, would I see anyone, Madame?'

She smiled at the rear view mirror.

'At the funeral, of course, Derek. You were there, of course.'

'Madame, I was but I'm pretty sure you didn't see me.'

'No, I didn't, Derek. But I'm beginning to know how these things work.'

His eyes smiled back at her.

'The boss did, though.'

She jerked her head back from his shoulder and looked at him.

He smiled gently back at her and nodded.

'Deveraux is here to protect us, my love. You must expect him to pop up occasionally.'

She slumped slightly petulantly back into her corner of the speeding Range Rover. Deveraux continued.

'I saw nothing unusual before, during or after the funeral or the wake. Nothing at all that looked wrong. Most of the congregation looked like murderers but that was probably just because they were farmers.'

He saw Martine in his mirror open her mouth to protest but then smile as she caught his eye. There was silence that extended as the French countryside sped by on either side. Martine finally decided that it was time to add her three penneth.

'There's something you ought to know. Louise isn't French.'

Both Smith and Deveraux looked expectantly and waited.

'Oh yes. Her French is fluent. Completely fluent. But down here in the south we live with many different sorts of French, even completely different languages which people who don't know us very well group together as French. We also know many different regional accents from all over France. We are very used to them. Louise McDowell has an accent. Only a very slight one and it appears only very occasionally. But she has an accent and unless I am mistaken its Balkan. I don't know what country specifically but it's certainly Balkan.'

It was a link. Not the final one in the chain by any means but another one.

'Dev.' It was the closest Smith ever got to using his Christian name. 'Could you find out exactly how long McDowell was married and how it all happened?'

'I'll do my best, Boss. But don't you think that Gentry would be better at this?'

There was a gap before Smith replied with a slightly clenched jaw.

'I'm not entirely sure whether Gentry is entirely up to this sort of thing at the moment and, in any case, I am not sure whether what we would get the truth from him.'

The silence continued. Martine caught Deveraux's eye in the corner of the rear view mirror. He nodded imperceptibly. He had drawn the short straw, not for the first time in their relationship.

'Boss. You need Gentry on this. I can get the information but you need him. You need to get you mind straight about him.'

Smith gave a short angry shake of the head. He really didn't like this. Deveraux glanced in the mirror and got another tiny look of encouragement from Martine. Suitably buoyed or at least encouraged, he went on.

'Like it or not we need Gentry. You have your strengths, Boss, but you're not Gentry. Honest or not, we need his brain. He can connect all this stuff up. You are the best I have ever known at the stuff you used to do. But your not a planner, you're not an analyst. I bet you've never done a crossword or a jigsaw puzzle in your life - or if you have you didn't enjoy it and you probably cheated. This whole thing is a mess and you can't solve it. You need Gentry.'

Smith quietly got really angry. Martine could feel it and was surprised at the moderation of the comments that finally came from Smith.

I think, my friends, that this is something that you might like to leave to me please?'

With that he lapsed back into silence. Martine leant her head again against his shoulder and was please to feel him take her hand in his and keep in there. The high speed journey back towards Arles continued. The silence wasn't particularly oppressive. They just left him alone with his thoughts. He knew that they was wrong but he really couldn't be bothered to persuade them. His mood wasn't helped by the meaninglessness of McDowell's murder. They hadn't been close but as far as Smith could see his friend had posed no threat at all to Ripley or to anyone else. Perhaps Girondou's advice was getting to him after all.

Chapter 12: Conversation with Ruy Lopez

Scene 1: Gentry

The little chess table was, as usual, set up between them behind Gentry's battered leather sofa, pieces set out and neatly aligned in readiness for their usual game. They sat in their usual Sheraton Shield Back armchairs. Each player had his particular form of whisky near his right hand; Gentry had his unadulterated Banff malt, Smith his well-diluted and iced supermarket scotch; both glasses on plain silver coasters to protect Thomas's best inlay work. They never used the customary choice of pawns concealed in the hands to decide who played white. They were happy with their habitual chairs and simply had come to an arrangement to alternate the lead. Theoretically this time was Smith to play white. However the game remained un-started because this was not the reason for the meeting. Smith could feel his friend's uncertainty, fear even. He had long since decided on his approach. For once he would have to trust his friend.

'David.'

The use of his Christian name brought Gentry into focus suddenly. It was a rare event.

'I am going to assume that if there were gaps in what you tell me it is because some mumbo jumbo that theoretically binds us both to the Official Secrets Act prevents you from telling me and not because there is something you have done that you want to hide from me'.

Apart from the point that was obvious to both of them; that there was absolutely no reason for making any such assumption, Smith left unsaid the consequences of that as he continued. Gentry had the grace to look a little relieved.

'I really don't want to know if that is true or not, by the way. To make it easier for you, I'll just tell you what I think the story is. There are a lot of gaps but I'd like to think I've got a lot of it. I don't want you to fill in the blanks - yet, at least - but I do want you to say if I say anything that I have got wrong. OK?'

Gentry just nodded slightly aware that he was being let off lightly - for the moment, at least. Smith took a deep breath and started.

'As far as I can see this whole thing is about Miles Ripley. From a very early stage, sometime probably back in the nineteen seventies he became a communist spy. Nothing odd about that, of course. Britain has a long and honourable tradition of producing such people, some of them very good: the Cambridge four, or five or six whatever number it finally became, the atom spies, Klaus Fuchs being the most famous. Many others I'm sure. What makes Ripley special or rather different is that he became a Maoist rather than a Marxist and therefore when deciding on becoming a full-time traitor he chose for China as his master - or is it mistress? - rather than Russia. It was an unfashionable passion and somewhat rare and much the more secure for all that. I suspect that his brief was more economics and industrial stuff than military. China got all the military information they could cope with from mother Russia at the time. He ended up in your Balkan bit of SIS and you were suspicious from the beginning. I have no idea why you caught on so quickly. Maybe it was because he didn't know the correct variations of Petrov's defence or the Queen's Pawn opening. Maybe he didn't know his Margaux '53 from his Petrus '57. Maybe he liked Chop Suey too much. God knows. But the whole idea of spying for China was so preposterous that no one took you or him seriously. Nothing really happened then until the Albanian operation where you discovered that there was a fetid little group of yanks who were so paranoid about the Russians that they had formed a CIA within the

CIA to run operations to support Albania as that was probably the nearest they ever got to real Chinese. Very secret and very well funded. You ran the operations side of the Balkan desk so it was inevitable that you got involved. We both know what happened then.'

Smith paused and took a long contemplative draw of his scotch.

'The operation went as we know it did. A complete fuck-up in which I was forced to do some things that forever blotted my copy-book with the Yanks and left me out in the cold. You scuttled back into your dark hole in London and carried on planning the downfall of communism and all it represented or something. You used me again from time-to-time on some other operations around the world but I had made it perfectly plain that I wanted to be a part-timer and you seem to respect that. The rogue Albanian unit living in the bowels of Langley was closed down and the naughty Americans were gathered up and the bosses put in the secret CIA prison in Romania and forgotten about.'

'Fast forward to Bologna six years later you survive either a hit or a terrorist explosion or both by luck or good judgement on one of your very few forays out into the real world. You were accompanied by someone who I am beginning to assume was Ripley and, by the grace of God and some miscellaneous terrorists, you survived in spite of being targeted by Grantkov who had been specially imported for the job. Actually betrayed is a better word and Ripley's generous offer of his straw hat was the identifier. However you put about that your anonymous companion didn't make it, beyond the moment when you actually knew the truth. If it really was Ripley then he obviously did survive. It Ripley actually was killed and the present bearer of the name is a ringer then I will really lose patience with this whole thing, dispose of Grantkov and the new

Ripley, both currently in my possession, put out a contract on all the remaining Americans and just head back to my retirement with a sigh of relief.'

He looked over the untouched chess table at his companion.

'It was Ripley wasn't it?'

Gentry simply nodded. Smith continued his narrative.

'I am told to get you home and I choose the Venice to London express and had a difficult encounter with the Romanian hit man who for some accountable knew what train we were on. God knows how but I am beginning to suspect your friend with the MCC hat. I assumed I had killed Grantkov as I shot him twice and chucked him off the speeding train. As it turns out I was mistaken but, hey ho, we can't all be right all the time.'

'Forward again to the present. Martine and I witness a very public execution by a resurrected Grantkov of a Romanian singer who had the misfortune to be related to the prison warder who presumably iced Wilson. I don't know who organised this hit. It was either Hendricks or Ripley but it hardly matters. I assume this was a warning to someone. Unfortunately, Grantkov sees me which seems to stir up nasty memories and sends him hot foot down to Provence with a two-fold mission; to complete the job he botched in Bologna and do something personal to me. Cash from Fredericks for at least one of those two hits. I organise a real tennis game with McDowell who, lo and behold, has somehow acquired Balkan wife - possibly even a Romanian one.'

He paused and asked the question.

'Romanian?'

Again a silent nod from Gentry. Smith sighed.

'Presumably Louise was some sort of imported minder and when events arrived at the present, someone - Ripley or Fredricks - decided he was again dangerous. Our tennis game provided the opportunity and the information was passed by McDowell's loving wife.'

'McDowell gets hit by some American goons presumably working for the recently released Fredericks and this is when it turns into amateur hour. Ripley hires some pretty mediocre muscle to kidnap you and imprison you in his own holiday home for Chrissake and tries to con me into riding in to rescue you and offer myself up as a rather complicated suicide candidate. I hope you don't mind my saying so but this potential new director of SIS is something of a dork. We rescue you and you're returned home where after you assume the sort of pained reticence of a sixteen year of girl who has just lost her virginity.'

'So the current state of play is that I have Grantkov cooling his heels in some damp Marseille cellar. I have Ripley ditto in a marginally less uncomfortable Camargue farmhouse and you sitting here being disappointing and limp in equal measure. Hendricks is presumably in the States fulminating against the world and counting the considerable funds that Uncle Sam unaccountably omitted to remove from him. I now have to decide what to do with the four of you.'

Smith paused again primarily to give Gentry the chance to notice that his whisky needed replenishing. Gentry seemed not to notice and Smith got up and did it himself, not without a slight frown of displeasure. If his chum was forgetting the common courtesies, then he really was in a poor old way. Suitable reinforced, Smith sat down again and started the coda to what had become a monologue.

'Like most things in life, my old chum, I think all this is pretty simple. If I got some of the details wrong, then I don't think it really matters. This is all a matter of Ripley trying to clean up his past in preparation for getting the coveted top job and his own glittering future in the corridors of power. He was and remains a traitor to Great Britain having spent much if not all of the last forty year spying for China of all places. Clearly new his bosses wouldn't be happy if they found out. I assume this is much more to do with industrial and commercial espionage rather than military secrets. China has always had a very limited passion for that sort of stuff. No, commercial information, especially in the IT field where China increasingly is the supplier of choice to the Western world. It must also be for money. I really can't think that Ripley, with his taste for good living, would remain a committed Maoist for forty years, even if he had once been as a student clutching a pint of beer and a little red book in some Oxford pub. You spent much of your life trying and failing to nail him and he knows it. Now he is near the top he is susceptible to rumour rather than needing actual proof and you have gradually become dangerous to him. Thus he sets Grantkov on you. Grantkov sets Grantkov on me. I assume that you used McDowell for other jobs which also made him a risk and Ripley sets his American chum to that little problem.'

Now, Smith felt, was the time to get his friend reacting if not actually involved. Part of the next phase of his plan needed Gentry.

'How am I doing, Gentry?'

Finally a thin smile crossed Gentry's face.

'By and large, Peter you have got most of it. All the important bits. Certainly. What next? You seem to be holding all the people if not all the cards. You don't seem to need me very much.'

Much to his enormous sadness, Smith found himself in agreement. But he kept this agreement to himself. This whole story had taught him some valuable lessons. However he needed Gentry for one part of the end game.

'Obviously we can't let Ripley get the Directorship. After what he had done and what we know that would be grotesque. However, I wonder if you might like to enlist one of your chums in the Service and turn him. He won't need much persuading given that we have enough evidence to put him in prison for the rest of his life. Perhaps he might like to reverse, as they say in ballroom dancing circles. Given the penetration of China into our economy and our IT infrastructure, it might be useful to add to our defences. Obviously you and I can't do this but your probably know someone who can. If he get a little reluctant just remind him of his family and some recent visitors to the rather grand family house. You shouldn't have too much trouble, I would have thought.'

Gentry nodded in agreement without, of course, knowing precisely what he was agreeing with.

'Yes, I think something along those lines might be arranged. What are you going to do about Grantkov?'

Smith sighed.

'Well, as long as I can fix Hendricks, he won't come after you as he isn't paid. As long as I can persuade him to let bygones be bygones and stop bothering me, then I hope he should cease to be a problem. If he doesn't agree or can't convince me that he means what he says, then he won't leave Marseille alive.'

Gentry was still too silent for Smith's taste. Smith finished his whisky and stood up. He looked down at his friend.

'I am relying on you to fix Ripley, David. If for some reason you don't I shall be very unhappy indeed. You do understand that don't you?'

Gentry nodded.

'Yes, Peter, I do understand.'

'Good.'

Smith turned and left again without a further word.

Chapter: 13 Finale

Scene 1:   An Old Man's Secrets

Mercifully it was a fine night. Overcast but not actually raining. One of those nights that often accompanies a last September Indian summer day. Maybe some rain early the next morning but not much. It was, more importantly, very dark in the little lay-by in the small country lane. Smith's hired car was black and was a little overhung by the drooping branches of the surrounding hedges. He was sitting slouched down in the back seat pressed into the corner. Deveraux was beside him slumped below the window sill level and completely, but silently, asleep. The car thus looked empty to any observer, casual or not. It is surprising how people would conclude there was nobody in the car if they saw the front two seats obviously empty. Odd but true. Surveillance is usually better kept from the back seats especially if there is little chance of needing a quick departure. He was a mile or so from the eponymous opera house which, thank God, wasn't functioning that night. Surveillance is much more difficult when you are continually being passed by hordes of dinner-jacketed hooray Henrys and their excessively dressed mates dragging picnic hampers in their huge four-wheel drives to one of those nauseatingly upper-middle class events during the 'season' for which England is so well-known. Ascot, Henley, Badminton came to mind all-too-easily. No, this particular evening the rich little village of Glynde near Lewes in Sussex was quiet and empty. Across the lane about fifty yards away down the lane was a little gate set in a napped flint-faced garden wall and that was the object of his patient attention. Deveraux had set up some preliminary surveillance the previous week and had found out that the boy usually went out at about nine o'clock for an evening drink in the village pub, presumably as an antidote to standing as some sort of body guard come sexual gratification for his eighty-year-old charge. The rather smart village had some time ago been adopted by the wealthier end of the Brighton gay set and many of them occupied the pub every evening, much to the disgruntlement of the locals.

Smith glanced at his watch, a late nineteen fifties Heuer chronograph from the time before the fine Swiss maker had ever heard of Saudi Arabia and decided to play TAG with it. Before also the time when the moronic health police decreed that having microscopic amounts of radium paint on the face was likely to make your testicles or, at the very least, your wrist drip off. Smith had worn his beautiful old watch, a present from his father for passing his school exams at 15, every day, all his life. The watch had never lost more than a second a year and Smith still had both his wrist and balls is full working order or so far as he could judge. Neither seemed too limp. It was also the reason he could tell the time without flooding the inside of the car with light that would almost certainly given his position away to whoever might be looking.

Sure enough it was few minutes past nine when the boy came through he gate. Smith nudged his companion into consciousness and smiled slightly as he saw the light beige leather trousers, pale blue linen shirt and a cashmere sweater equally in the palest blue knotted loosely by the arms around the shoulders. He didn't have to see the polished moccasins loafers to know they were there. The boy had obviously recovered from his adventure in the South of France. Smith settled to wait another ten minutes. Maybe the boy had forgotten his condoms. One never knew about these things.

In truth he hadn't really decided what to do. He would, as they say, play it by ear. He had come prepared for a number of solutions and he would just pick the one that he felt was most appropriate at the time of choosing but his planning had got little further than that.. He knew he had to do something and it was his job to do it. The other bits of the endgame had all gone well. Ripley had 'decided' not to accept the top job citing obligations to his family and the totally mythical long-term illness of his wife that had recently been diagnosed. Smith silently gave Gentry an appreciative grimace. A nice touch, that. He seemed to be willing to co-operate on other matters, as well. Maybe the old boy was getting back into harness after all. Grantkov had been released into the wild, damaged again, but this time seemingly convinced that to continue to pursue Gentry was pointless as there would soon be no-one left to pay for the hit or Smith as that path was certainly fatal. In any case Smith could very easily have had him removed from the picture permanently and Grantkov understood that. Even amongst assassins there is a sort of code of conduct. Perhaps the arrangement was reinforced by the fact that it was Deveraux who delivered the messages to the Romanian. Even Hendricks was no longer a problem. Girondou had asked his American colleagues to look into there whereabouts of the man and had been reliably informed that Hendricks had suffered the consequences of trying to put some of his money to work in the Detroit-based drug distribution business. The locals got to him before Girondou had had the time to ask the favour. The hit team from Tarbes was disposed of by Girondou before they left France.

    Smith somewhat reluctantly got out of the car and closed the door silently. He walked soundlessly the short distance down the lane and let himself through the gate. Deveraux had told him that that it wasn't alarmed. Smith knew that both lines, the telephone and the alarm to the picture-book pink thatched cottage, had been cut. Deveraux had also offered Smith to have the mobile phone cell that covered the house cut but that might have encouraged unhappy gays in the pub to leave early as they were unable to be in contact with their later evenings entertainments. Smith would just have to make sure that the old man didn't use his mobile. None of the widow shutters was closed and he saw that La Salle was alone, seated in a chair beside a fireplace, reading. He let himself in through the front door which wasn't even locked. He had his silenced Glock in his hand as he entered the sitting room. No point in taking chances even if the man was in his eighties. His greeting carried no colour.

'Hello Hugo.'

At his age La Salle was not given to rapid reactions but he still looked completely startled and simple froze. Smith crossed quickly to the seat on the other side of the fireplace and quickly examined it. He indicated briefly with his Glock.

'I would be grateful if you would get up slowly and sit in the other chair, Hugo.'

Both of them knew why this was necessary. If La Salle had anything hidden near him it would be near his usual seat. Once he had changed seats, Smith sat in his host's.

'Well Hugo. What you suggest we do now?'

La Salle said nothing and waited. Smith continued conscious of the fact that the boy might come back soon and it would be a pity to have to shoot him in the very unlikely event that Deveraux failed to intercept him. No. That was unthinkable.

'As far as I can see, Hugo, you're responsible for most, if not all, of this mess. You recruited me forty odd years ago in the time-honoured way at University just down the road from here and if you tried to turn me, I can't remember. You recruited Ripley at Oxford when you went there and succeeded in turning him. God knows how many others. In fact that's one of the things I want to find out this evening. Actually that's really the only thing I want to find out this evening. You have been a traitor all your life and now is the time to end it.'

La Salle sighed.

'Peter my dear chap. I am well past eighty. Even if Her Majesties Government had enough proof to make a case against me, which I severely doubt, they wouldn't want the publicity. Even if they had evidence and could stand the public contempt a guilty verdict wouldn't put me in jail. I'm too old. We're not at war so there's no capital punishment. Your revenge is somewhat limited, don't you think. So why don't you just wander off into the night where you came from and leave me alone.'

Smith sat silently for a while, the gun held loosely on his thigh, still pointing at the old man who by now had a slight smile on his face.

'That's uncharacteristically impolite of you, Hugo. However, first things first. I want a list of all the others you recruited.'

It was La Salle's turn to smile in a superior sort of way that Smith remembered from his art history seminars years ago. The man had been an arrogant bastard even then. But back then he had reason to be.

'If you think I have records, old chap, then you are much, much mistaken. You will get nothing from me no matter what you do to me.'

'Actually, Hugo, I know you have records. You are an academic. Your medium is the written word and you are very good at using it. You are, or perhaps were, before little boys became your priority, a scholar whose life was notes, footnotes and bibliographies. You aren't comfortable unless you have things in writing. No, somewhere in this house you have records if for no reason other than as an insurance policy. Something to sell if you were even caught. No, you have records here and accessible. This evening, Hugo, you have at last been caught. Perhaps it is time to use your bargaining card before it's too late.'

'Peter, my dear, you may be a considerable fellow, but your are not Her Majesties Government. I'll keep my powder dry, if I may, until your boss comes a calling. Then I might talk a little with him. But not to you, I think.'

Smith's mobile buzzed. It was Deveraux who had picked up the boy making an early return. Smith steeled himself for the next, rather difficult, bit of this conversation.

'Actually. Hugo. I don't really have a boss as such. I'm surprised you assume I have. But whatever you think you've got to bargain with, I want to see it. Now, Hugo.'

There was a shake of the head.

'I don't think so, Peter. I'll wait if you don't mind.'

'Hugo, perhaps it might be a good idea if I explained a few things to you. Things that might be a surprise. Essentially you are on your own. Ripley is stuck a few feet short of the top job. Hendricks is dead, Grantkov is tamed and out of the picture. Gentry is….well the jury is out at the moment but I don't think it would be wise to rely on him too much. As for keeping something to ensure your survival when they catch up with you, I would give some thought to surviving this conversation first. Your current boy friend, or perhaps he supposed to be a body guard of some sort, is currently trussed up like a chicken in Deveraux's boot. You have no phone lines which mean that whatever surveillance you may or may not have rigged up in here is going nowhere for the moment. Deveraux has a scanner that will tell me if anything more modern is trying to get to you. If I don't get what I want, Hugo, it is a racing certainty that you have less than one hour to live. There will be no point in trying to bargain with the powers that be for your freedom or for any immunity from prosecution because you will be dead and probably buried. You have no friends in Whitehall any more, Hugo. You are just an embarrassment to be hushed up and ignored. Too many people have reputations and positions to be lost by siding with you. The deal is this and there is no negotiation. Give me your files or I will just kill you and find them for myself. You must remember that you are not talking with a very civilised man. There is no due process here in spite of hiding down here in civilised leafy Sussex. You have been a traitor to Her Majesty all your working life, Hugo. You will not have your day in the Old Bailey, even in a closed court. I want those files and I will have them with or without your help. This is a small cottage and Deveraux and I have all night to look for them.'

Perhaps it was old age, but La Salle seemed momentarily unmoved by the prospect of dying, so strong was his reluctance to being told what to so by an ex-student.

'What on earth makes you think I would be stupid enough to keep information like that here in my home?'

'Because, Hugo, I know you. I've known you for a long time and you are a child of your time. You are an old fashioned academic and have all the impossible snobbery that goes with that. Yours is the adopted world of the intellectual. You get off on footnotes and references, on libraries and bibliographies, on the esteem of your colleagues. Your world is paper. Yours was the generation that used the great hand-pasted catalogues in the British Museum reading room. You like paper because that is what real intellectuals use. Knowledge is notes and books. You wouldn't hide files in a hole in the ground or on the Internet. You probably don't know what the Internet is. You wouldn't know a personal organiser, an iPad or a smartphone from that non-existent hole in the ground. I'm told that you have hardly stirred from here for the last ten years. You like paper files and that I am willing to bet is what you have. Maybe you have a safe or maybe they are just somewhere here in the house in plain view. After all, Hugo, until now you had no idea that anyone suspected you. Thus I offer you the choice. Give me the files, your records of who else you recruited, records that you hoped might save your skin if push ever came to shove because, believe me, it just has.'

There was a silence while La Salle gave the whole thing some thought. Smith was alert. The man may have been in is mid eighties but there was nothing wrong with his mind. Smith really didn't want to call Deveraux in quite yet. He had a slight feeling that he knew what they would find in the house and for the moment the fewer people who knew the details the better. La Salle made to get up but was stopped by a slight movement of Smith's Glock. He looked exasperatedly at his captor.

'How the hell am I supposed to get the stuff out of my safe if I can't get up?'

'Just put both hands in your jacket pockets and keep them there until I tell you.'

'I need my stick', La Salle was getting really grumpy.

'No you don't, Hugo. You may have forgotten but you didn't use on the other day in Arles. Now get up and walk slowly to wherever you have hidden the files. Do not take you hands out of your pockets. Please don't try to be silly. I have in mind to kill you but I would rather be at a moment of my choosing rather than yours. It might be less painful for you that way too. Trust me.'

La Salle snorted and walked slowly and perfectly steadily out of the sitting room, down a short corridor lined with some very classy English watercolours and turned into what proved to be a gentleman's study. Smith became conversational.

'I hope you've made a will, Hugo. It wouldn't be right to let some of those Cromes and Cotmans to fall into the wrongs hands.

There's a pretty little Stannard there that I wouldn't mind myself. However as I am probably going to kill you this evening, perhaps I might not be the grateful recipient.'

La Salle did no more than issue an annoyed 'Harrumpf' and stopped before a nice little oil. Smith squinted more closely without ever letting the silenced Glock waver.

'Ah ha. You really are a traditionalist, Hugo. A safe behind a hinged picture. Wonderful. And, if I am not mistaken, a nice little…..'

Smith paused while he looked closer at a small glowing little landscape.

'Jesus, Hugo, that's a little Stubbs. I've never seen it before.'

La Salle was nothing if not sarcastic.

'I'm glad to see that all this derring-do and killing hasn't dulled your eye for a good painting. It is indeed a Stubbs and unpublished as you so accurately identified.'

Smith's mind flashed to another collection of unpublished painting that nestled in the Mas des Saintes before returning to business.

'Open the safe, please, Hugo.'

'Aren't you afraid that it's alarmed, dear chap. Perhaps if I open it, the local plod will descend with, as they say, blues and twos all ago and apprehend you.'

Smith smiled.

'It's not alarmed. I know that because when we tested the telephone lines coming from this cottage, neither of them was an alarm. Additionally there is no hi-tec stuff attached as Deveraux would have found that last week when he started watching you. You don't have a simple external alarm as the local gentry would get really pissed off if you started making noises in the middle of the night. This is the sort of village where they would prefer you to be robbed in dignified silence rather than make a brutish jangling to disturb their slumbers. No, Hugo, no alarm. Oh, and I case I have missed anything, any noise at all and I will shoot you. Silently, of course. Any other helpful thoughts before you open the thing?'

La Salle just took one hand slowly from his jacket pocket and pulled back the hinged Stubbs. Behind as a simple combination locked safe door, less that a foot square. He glanced over his shoulder at Smith, who just nodded.

A moment later the little door swung open.

'OK, Hugo, just step and sit down in that little chair'

He motioned to a single straight-backed chair that stood facing a large and rather elegant partners desk that took up slightly much of the little study. Within a few seconds he had emptied the safe and spread the contents on Le Salle's desk and sat down in the master's chair. He started to go through the stuff. Sure enough in a collection of other things was a small stack of thin files, some fifteen in all held together with a large elastic band. Smith recognised most of the names on the covers, one in particular. He opened it and read enough of the contents to know that it was accurate - or at least he knew that most of the facts in it were up to date. He felt a deep depression descend on him. La Salle must have detected it because he became anxious, almost pleading.

'It's the stuff, Peter. No fakes, nothing made up. The real thing.'

Smith nodded sadly.

'Yes, Hugo, I'm afraid I believe you. Copies?'

The old man shook his head and looked anxious.

'So what next?'

Smith finished thumbing though the remainder of the safe contents. There was little of interest. Finally he replaced the rubber band around the files and looked steadily at his old professor.

'Hugo. I should really not be sure what to do with you. You are and have been a traitor to Great Britain for the best part of the last sixty years. Communist, Maoist, Marxist, it makes little or no difference. You have recruited spies who have worked against the Crown and, in my book, the penalty for that must be death. I have no idea how many people have died because your activities but it is probably a goodly number. In my personal opinion you are a man of no value and deserves to be crush underfoot like a cockroach. Normally I would have no hesitation is doing that myself. I don't need the authority of someone in London to keep me at peace with my own conscience. I know what I am and what I believe in and I am content with myself. I sleep at night and putting a bullet in your head now would make no difference at all to that. I am neither a murderer nor an assassin but I can perfectly easily be either or both. Given what you have done, to kill you now would be my idea of justice and, when all said and done, mine is the only opinion that matters, to me at least. It's the only opinion I have to live with and, as I said, I am content with that.'

He paused and looked across the man who clearly now knew that his time had come. La Salle sat absolutely still and seemed to be empty. There was little to be won by killing this man, Smith thought. It was too easy. Perhaps he would have liked to make the man suffer. But that too was pretty pointless. Suffering is only useful if you were alive to remember suffering. He made up his mind and looked again at his old teacher and friend. He tapped the bound group of files.

'This is what will happen, Hugo. I will deliver this stuff to those particularly unpleasant attack dogs in one of the bits of SIS that don't live in luxury at Vauxhall cross. They can mop up these people. I will add a file that I have assembled on you to the pile. Given that we will drive straight to London, which is about an hour away, I reckon you have about three to four hours before they come trampling over your pretty flowerbeds to get you. You can try to escape, of course, but given that you don't have a car, your phone lines are cut and your boyfriend will be deposited by the roadside half an hour north of here, I don't think you'll get too far. You will be caught by the Service you have betrayed. They will probably not be kind to you.'

Smith continued to hold the Glock steady and felt down with his left hand into his jacket pocket. He drew out a small glass bottle. As he held it in front of him on the desk it rattled slightly. It was actually a bottle within a bottle. La Salle looked on as if mesmerised. Smith took the thing back in his left hand and slowly used his thumb and forefinger to unscrew the black plastic top. Once it was free he let the smaller glass vial slide out onto the leather top of the elegant desk. It rolled slightly and then stopped. No fingerprints. The tiny amount of colourless liquid within it settled. He returned the outer bottle to his pocket and continued the conversation.

'The alternative, Hugo, is for you to pour yourself a large glass of your favourite scotch, put in your favourite music and settle into your favourite armchair. You can either wait for the great unwashed from London and start doing some unspeakable and very private things to you or you can add the contents of this little bottle to your scotch and drink it. I'm told it's completely tasteless. You had better be sitting because it all happens rather fast, I gather. From a strictly personal point of view, Hugo, I can only hope that it is not as completely painless as people say. The thought of you in pain at last would comfort me somehow.'

Hugo La Salle looked at Smith with despair in his eyes.

'You said that if I gave you those files, you'd let me live.'

Smith looked straight into the man's eyes and remembered McDowell.

'I lied,' he said.

With that he gathered up the files and left.

Scene 2:   Changes in Perception

The chessboard was again was set out and the game in progress. Smith played white and this time completely surprised Gentry with a Stonewall attack but flew off at a tangent after the sixth move. Gentry, of course, was perfectly capable of defending but was overwhelmed by the ferocity of Smith's attack. Smith was very angry and his chess showed it. No sooner had Gentry thought about his next move, Smith just attacked. It was like one-sided speed chess and Gentry had never encountered anything like it. It wasn't his sort of thing at all. He had never seen violence on a chess board like it. Needless to say he was defeated many moves before the end and he just wanted to get it over with. He resigned before he noted that Smith had not taken a single sip of his whisky. He laid his king gently on its side and lifted his eyes questioningly to meet those of his friend across the board.

It was a while before Smith put his hand inside his jacket and took out a bunch of papers, folded longitudinally so it would fit.

'I removed this from the ones from La Salle's safe before putting the rest through SIS's letter box. I thought you might like to read it. I don't believe there's a copy.'

With that he got up from his chair, turned and, for the second time in as many days, left without saying more.

Manufactured by Amazon.ca
Acheson, AB